From the archives of the Comptrollerate-General for Scrutiny and Survey

TREASON'S
TIDE

Robert Wilton has held a variety of posts in the
British Ministry of Defence, Foreign Office
and Cabinet Office. He was advisor to the Prime
Minister of Kosovo in the lead-up to the country's
independence, and has now returned there as a senior
international official. He divides his time between
Kosovo and Cornwall.

From the archives of the Comptrollerate-General for Scrutiny and Survey

TREASON'S TIDE

arranged by

ROBERT WILTON

CORVUS

Previously published in hardback in Great Britain in 2011 as
The Emperor's Gold by Corvus, an imprint of Atlantic Books Ltd.

First published in paperback in Great Britain in 2013 by Corvus,
an imprint of Atlantic Books Ltd.

10 9 8 7 6 5 4 3 2 1

A CIP catalogue record for this book is available
from the British Library.

Paperback ISBN: 978 1 84887 801 3
E-book ISBN: 978 0 85789 436 6

Printed in Italy by 🦅 Grafica veneta S.p.A.

Corvus
An imprint of Atlantic Books Ltd
Ormond House
26–27 Boswell Street
London
WC1N 3JZ

www.corvus-books.co.uk

for Elizabeth
for everything
for ever

From the archives of the Comptrollerate-General for Scrutiny and Survey

TREASON'S TIDE

Introduction

Buried treasure is rare in historical research; I stumbled over the roots of this story by chance. During one stint of my career in the UK Ministry of Defence, I worked in the Old War Office Building, a striking, if not quite successful, piece of Edwardian grandeur on London's Whitehall. A colleague piqued my curiosity by telling me that, if I visited the MoD library in Scotland Yard (the capital's police took the name with them when they left 120 years ago, and now alas the library has gone too), I could find out who had occupied my impressively panelled office back when we had an Empire and Europe was collapsing into the First World War.

I was disappointed to read that I was not treading in the footsteps of some famous field marshal, but was instead the direct descendant of something called the Comptrollerate-General for Scrutiny and Survey. It didn't even sound military. I soon forgot this dull bit of bureaucracy, whose members had, I imagined, spent the First World War shuffling papers and counting buttons while better men charged to their deaths in the charnel houses of the Somme and Passchendaele.

Then, eighteen months ago, I was trying to pull together a short story involving Christopher Marlowe, the sixteenth-century poet and playwright whose death in a bar-room brawl has long been assumed to be the result of his dabbling in the murky world of Elizabethan political intrigue. Among his activities in the days before his death was one brief interview – though it may dramatically have altered the course of his last hours – with a court official entitled... the Comptroller-General of Scrutiny and Survey.

Intrigued by this connection across the centuries, I went back to the War Office records. There, after a great deal of burrowing and thanks to two MoD librarians whose patience no number of lunchtime beers could ever repay, I found the remarkable archive on which this book draws.

The activities of the Comptrollerate-General for Scrutiny and Survey do not exist in regular records. The further one digs, the more it emerges as a very peculiar institution indeed. That we know anything about it is thanks to the extraordinary man who was its chief during the later part of the First World War. Colonel Valentine Knox was a classic product of that generation, perhaps the last in which it was possible to have a brilliant military career while being certifiably eccentric. After a spat with him in the Boer War, the young Winston Churchill had tried hard to destroy Knox's career, but later, once the future prime minister had spent time in the trenches in 1915–16, he described him as 'one man I would unthinkingly follow into hell itself, on the calculation that Satan would most likely have evacuated the premises, Knox having made them too hot for him.' Knox was captured twice and escaped twice, active in every arm of the forces including the fledgling Royal Flying Corps, and was wounded with staggering frequency, the last time when he was blown up in Palestine single-handedly attacking an armoured car while on horseback. By the time he was made Comptroller-General – minus an eye and with a German bullet lodged permanently against his spine; some even credited him with a wooden leg – he was one of the most highly decorated, and least popular, men in the British army.

Knox had to fight hard to bolster the reputation of his ancient organization in the face of the new espionage departments that would later be known as Military Intelligence (5) and Military Intelligence (6). The best way to do this, he decided, was to bring together and quietly publicize whatever information he could find about the history of the Comptrollerate-General. Since Knox's disappearance after the war – some ninety years ago – his archive has been collecting dust in the basements of the War Office and then the Ministry of Defence.

Introduction

To have it in one's fingers it is a thrilling flirtation with the past, from flowing Elizabethan parchment to florid Edwardian typescript, torn, scorched (like the three small pages catalogued as SS M/827T, which feature in this book) and in one case actually bloodstained. From this frustratingly sparse set of documents springs an astonishing institution: a secret department of the Crown, altering its shape and affiliation and even name over the years, bringing together soldiers, diplomats, entrepreneurs, misfits, fortune-hunters and not a few outright frauds, and active in every significant war and international crisis in British history for at least four centuries – always discreetly, usually unofficially, and often at the most precarious moments of national security.

I was keen to tell the story of this extraordinary organization, unknown to the general reader and underrated by professional historians even when they'd heard of it. However, a history of its centuries of existence will take much further research (I'm not even sure yet whether the Comptrollerate-General for Scrutiny and Survey is not, in some guise, still operating within the British armed forces or wider government machinery). The records of its individual operations are too fragmentary, and frankly too dry, to make books in themselves. But popular history writing today focuses more on human stories than it used to. Accordingly, *The Emperor's Gold*, the first coherent product of my research, presents one of the organization's operations as a piece of dramatic narrative rather than dry analysis. As well as being a bewildering tale of intrigue, it restores the significance of overlooked episodes such as the London riots of 6 August 1805, and throws new and remarkable light on the naval movements of that autumn, when Britain was within hours of invasion and defeat.

The strategic framework of events for this account is common knowledge. The detail is drawn directly from Knox's archive of the Comptrollerate-General for Scrutiny and Survey, along with other relevant sources currently available (specific documents are referenced with the SS prefix, or equivalent; references are not given here for the many other documents that have contributed colour and background, including the notes and correspondence of Sir Keith Kinnaird). The exact play of dialogue and emotion is of course my conjecture, consistent with the data and tending, I hope, to illuminate rather than distort what happened. If my fictionalization of these incidental elements inspires the reader to their own investigation of the facts, then so much the better.

R.J.W., February 2010

THE SEA

A shipwreck is a roaring machine of destruction.

The schooner's bow was wedged in a cleft of rocks now, thrown up by a muscular shove of the sea; her spine was broken, and the clawing of the waves around the carcase was pulling her apart. Giant breakers threw bursts of destruction back and forth over upper decks long stripped of men and cargo. Before she had been sleek, a creation shaped for speed. Now, held up at an angle, twisted and collapsing, she was ugly and unnatural. The quarterdeck smoothed by the tread of captains was submerged, planks a jagged edge in the shark's mouth of the sea. The figurehead that had cut through the oceans reared up stupidly and askew, punched and taunted by the waves. The great beams that had eased the schooner's glide through the water now heaved and broke under its pressure. The hidden collapse of a deck or the extinction of a pocket of air created an irresistible suction on the surface, a sudden explosion of spray. Each sweep of water cleared more detail from the decks; each surge of the sea wrenched at the violated structure. A charge of breakers rushed the stern; another vast twist, and a mast snapped. It toppled tired and silent, dragging down the yardarm and a mane of rigging before disappearing in the froth. Roaring out of the furnace in swoops and punches, the wind plunged down to snatch ropes from cleats and tear sails from their yards, to dance and snap away in the bilious sky. Out in the darkness of the sea, casks and spars bobbed and disappeared. Somewhere, a last living body lost its air and flailed, sluggish, to nothing. Just the skeleton of the schooner was left now, to be swallowed piece by piece by the foam.

It happened only in black and white, and a sick flickering of grey and green that shifted between them under the helpless moon.

This little destruction of man's conceit, the tiny human tragedies swilling around the drowned decks, was only a detail. The storm was born in the unknown distance of the ocean, in the disordered stomach of the elements. Out from a thousand miles of midnight the water charged the land, heaving up in crests and spouts that wrestled and fell, lurching open in whirlpools that sucked back the waves around them, the sea eating itself with grey tongues. There are few havens on this extreme stretch of the English coast; unnamed miles of slate cliff mark the land's front line with the water. Off their base lurk molars of rock, maddening the currents and dooming generations of men. Still the pistons of the sea drove it on, to hurl itself at the land at last, to climb the cliffs and detonate in clouds of spray. Then it fell back, the surf scrabbling around the cliff-foot for a hold, its fingers finding every cleft, milk spattering on the rock. An eternity of reinforcements galloped behind, rank after ominous rank in the abysmal, screaming night. Within the din of the storm, the crunching of the sea's jaws on the wreck, the collapse of timbers, there was no human sound at all.

Far up on the cliff, Jessel watched the savagery wide-eyed. He'd seen it before; there was a kind of thrill at nature's terrible power. But even he felt human for a moment and, hunched in a sodden cloak with frozen limbs and drenched hair and eyes flinching against the driving rain, lost high above the roaring shambles of the sea, to feel human was to feel very small.

Down in the little fishing village, where the storm wind whined and whooped through the roof slates and threw blasts of spray down the narrow streets, Parson Trewint looked out into the darkness of the bay, leaning into the gusts with his arm thrown up against the violence of wind and water. As clergyman, he muttered a prayer to an indifferent God to bring his parishioners through the maelstrom. As local Magistrate, he frowned at the thought of tomorrow's damage, of the disputes over fallen chimneys and scattered lobster baskets, of the scuffling over debris deposited on the beach once the storm had blown itself out and the sea receded. And as a man, widowed, exiled and forgotten in this mean extremity of the world, he wondered about the terrifying and lonely deaths of the men on the schooner, far out along the cliffs and surrounded by brutal, vengeful nature in fullest flood. Now, surely, they were all gone, just so much driftwood and grit in the retching of the sea. The Parson let his arm fall, stared out into the storm, then turned and hurried home through the slippery alleys.

But miraculously, out of the fatal desert of the sea, out of the inhuman carnage of the dying ship, out of the clutch of the waves, there came a man, an unconscious, bloodied man found on the rocks, white and still. Some freak of providence had thrown and wedged him there, some carelessness of the sea had let him go undrowned. Two children saw him in the dawn, approached warily, and began to peck at his clothes for trinkets while the gulls waited overhead. But the sea had left nothing except rags on him and, as they scrabbled, the dead face flickered and gave a shallow cough, and they scrambled away over the rocks.

Parson Trewint carried the body in himself with his servant, a cloth over the face and the sea mist still hanging cold in the streets. Word had come from London, by the usual means, for just such a man. So to those few who saw or heard of the body from the sea, Parson Trewint put out that he was dead after all. He sent word back, locked himself in his house on the edge of the village, and tended the ghostly figure alone. On the second day there came a message, and on the second night a coach and two horses, to a certain oak a short way up the valley. Long after midnight, the Parson and the coachman carried the unconscious body along the hedges to the oak, and grappled it into the coach. The coachman bowed to the Parson, jumped up onto the box, and whipped the horses away into the night.

Not a word had been exchanged. The Parson listened for a moment to the eerie rhythm of hooves and wheels, invisible and growing fainter, brushing at the mud and leaves on his cloak. Then he turned away and began the awkward tramp down to the village.

A day later word came back to the Parson, by the usual means, that the man had died, died for a third and final time, somewhere on the journey. And his existence – and the name he might once have had, and the life he might once have had – passed first into memory, and then into nothingness, while the waves still beat on the fragments of the ship on the cliffs, and ground the rocks themselves to dust.

On the western edge of the mainland of Europe, the soldiers were awake and polishing long before the sun had risen out of Asia to join them. A full two hours before dawn, the first shouts of the veteran Sergeants had started to soar across the acres of the encampments and challenge the cockerels. Quickly the Corporals were up and shouting too, hurrying through the tents with practised curses and shoves of scabbard or boot. Soon the buzz of the army began to rise, a swarming of metal on metal and skin on leather and the hum of expectant voices. Black leather was burnished to a mirror's gleam, white uniforms brushed to an impossible purity in the sea of mud, plumes dusted and moustaches trimmed and buttons fastened and buckles clasped and horses combed and cannon hitched and swords sharpened. In the streets of Boulogne, while the civilians drowsed and wondered vaguely at this distant military bustling, only the occasional chatter of hurrying boots disturbed the silence, as here and there an officer hurried to camp in the half-light, sword not properly buckled and a couple of coins left behind on a pillow.

It was the same all along the coast. It was the same at Étaples, destroyed more than once by the English over the centuries and now home to a whole army corps. It was the same at pre-historic Wimereux. The same at Ambleteuse, where the Romans and the Saxons had embarked for their invasions, and where the estuary had now been re-routed in preparation for yet another. In all of these places, ships were gathering in widened and deepened harbours, against brand-new breakwaters, and on the beaches men were exercising, as numerous and certain as the waves. This was the greatest army in the world, one hundred thousand strong, and this was to be one of its greatest days.

By dawn, the first of the regiments were ready on parade. As the minutes and then the hours passed, the numbers and the colours multiplied. A forest of a thousand muskets sprouted from every blue-and-white fusilier battalion. Next to them came the bearskins and moustaches of the grenadiers, and then the dark blue uniform of the light infantry, and the yellow plumes of the voltigeurs. Then cavalry, the skittering horses of the arrogant hussars; the solid green wall of light cavalry uniforms, and the brass-and-iron helmets of the heavy; the glorious red and green and gold of the horse chasseurs of the Guard. Finally, striding towards the front came the long blue coats and high bearskins of the grenadiers of the Old Guard, the proudest infantry regiment in the army, and by extension the finest on earth. Six feet tall, and a veteran, a man had to be to join the grenadiers. The Old Guard looked down on Europe.

Steadily, inexorably, the parts of the machine meshed together. One after another, the regiments advanced, wheeled, came to a halt, adjusted and settled, one after another across the vast coastal plain until its greens and browns disappeared under the sea of white and blue and red and the gleaming metal ready to throw back the rays of the sun. A tenth of a million individual spirits disappeared, the flat accents of the industrial north and the twang of the southern mountains, all of the morning's cursing and complaining and chattering and bragging, every ache of head or heart or groin or foot, each spark of imagination or homesickness, all dissolved in the discipline of the organism.

The organism waited: first cold, then stiff, then increasingly hot and stiff. Waited without caring, because they knew they were the best in the world and because today was a celebration of the fact. Waited without caring, because they knew they had been brought to that peak of professionalism, and brought to this narrow strait of sea, for a glorious purpose. Waited without caring, because he was coming.

In the distance, on the Paris road, rose a cloud of dust and the faint sound of cheering. Once detected, the tumult swept rapidly closer to the perfect horde laid out on the plain. Ears strained under bearskins to pick out the cheering, and eyes flicked furtively sideways in the rigid faces as they glimpsed the dust.

At the junction on the edge of the city where the Paris road turned and began to drop down to the harbour, a rare flash of official humour had added a new signpost. The wooden finger pointed straight out over the city towards the sea. It read simply: 'To England'.

⌐━ ⌐

'Tom Roscarrock.'

Dimly, heavily, still fighting up through the waves.

'Your name is Tom Roscarrock.'

Great fat mounds of water shouldering him down into the darkness.

'You are Tom Roscarrock.'

Far, far above him: moonlight on the water, a flickering promise of heaven, but he was so cold now, so deeply and permanently cold.

'Listen to me: you are Tom Roscarrock.'

His own arms wallowing uselessly around him in the dark heavy sea, head straining and aching.

'Tom—'

Then the huge smack of a beam thrown against his head by the waves, a fat jolt of dumbness that staggered his mind. 'No!'

'Yes. You are Tom Roscarrock, and you are a dead man.'

⌐━ ⌐

In the autumn of 1769, a second son was born to a minor member of the gentry of the island of Corsica, a backward wasteland of boulders and bandits that its French masters viewed with a mix of superiority and distaste. A year earlier, the boy wouldn't even have been French, but Louis XV had just acquired the island, so French he was. He went to religious school in France and then military academy, where his fellow students laughed at his accent and his spelling. He was thought likely to make a good sailor, and considered applying to the British Royal Navy, but went on instead to an unremarkable career as an artillery officer in the royal army of France.

Then the country collapsed in revolution and Napoleon, son of Carlo Buonaparte, returned to Corsica to fight for liberation from Paris. But allegiances were mobile and opaque in those unsteady times, even on the rocks of Corsica: Napoleon got himself promoted to Captain in the French army, despite having led a riot against it as a Corsican Lieutenant-Colonel; he broke with his nationalist friends, had to escape back to France, published some revolutionary writing, made influential acquaintances. Then, when the port of Toulon revolted against the Revolution, it took the eye of the young artillery scholar to spot the critical piece of ground that dominated the city and turned the battle. From the Cairo hill, with the cannon soot thickening the blood of those who had fought for the summit, the military legend of Napoleon was launched.

Now the Corsican gunner was an emperor, emerging through the slaughter of the Revolution to the greatest power, and the greatest triumph, that any Frenchman – perhaps any man in the history of the world – had ever known. He'd transformed the chaos into disciplined victory. He'd transformed social disintegration into a national pride never before seen. Now, on the Boulogne plain, the dust cloud coughed out a figure in white, and the trumpeters of all the regiments of this undefeated army barked their acclaim.

He rode like a soldier in the exhilaration of triumph, not trotting sedately to a review but charging across the plain impatient for new glory. Two thousand drummers began the insistent musket chatter of the call to arms as their Emperor raced to the sea. Three hundred picked horsemen galloped with him, his personal escort, the elite of France. They rode as bodyguard, but in truth their greatest claim to honour was being deemed worthy to follow most closely the little man who had transfixed Europe.

The plain erupted in smoke as the cannon roared their respect into the sky, each one belching out its powder and staggering back on its wheels under the recoil, a hundred plumes of smoke and fire that billowed out towards the sea, one after the other in perfect synchronization. The plain rang with the frantic pealing of all Boulogne's church bells. At last the Emperor's party reached the centre of the parade, a new tumult of dust swarming up as three hundred horses stuttered to a halt and turned in the heart of the human amphitheatre, and with one final explosion of sound the whole army came to the salute in front of their living god.

From the edge of some barren, primaeval dream came sound, waves washing and crashing in the darkness, and then somehow sharpening into the harsher noise of human voices.

'Welcome back, Mr Roscarrock.'

The other voices were muffled, distant – outside.

'I thought we might have lost you after all. You're a stubborn body, aren't you?'

This voice was sharper, nearer, needling him in the pinched, dull accents of a Lowland Scot.

'Come along, Mr Roscarrock. Are you with us now?'

The voices outside were shouting – shouting something, what? – and then roaring a mob's approval.

'Come along now.'

His eyes flicked open suddenly, large and brown and staring up at the source of the words. Standing over him, appraising him, was a tall man in his fifties. Dark eyes were set hard into the gnarled old face like slate on the sand, and they widened in interest at the new sign of life beneath them.

'There you are, Mr Roscarrock.'

His eyes closed in a heavy frown, and his head sank deeper on the pillow. 'I'm not – you keep saying that, but my name's not Roscarrock.' The hoarse assertion came out doubtful, a headache in his drowned mind.

'What you think you remember is irrelevant now. Now you are Tom Roscarrock.'

Into the silence came a single clear shout from outside – 'Blood!' – and the mob roared its agreement.

Feebly: 'What's going on out there?'

The old Scot shook his head dismissively. 'Food riot. Three mangy labourers and a cow. They do these things better in town.'

As if in protest at his scoffing, the crowd outside roared again at something.

'I'm not—'

'No!' The angular figure whipped round, grabbed a chair, pulled it forwards and folded itself down until their faces were only two feet apart. 'We cannot have this conversation more than once. You have so much to learn, and so little time. The first, the most important, thing is this: everything you think you know... has gone. It does not exist.' The bony shoulders relaxed, but the voice dropped lower and still more earnest. 'You died in a shipwreck, young man. We have seen to that. As that dead man, you have no future; you must forget the past as well. For now, there is only Tom Roscarrock.'

Not since Julius Caesar had brought his legions to this same beach, and pointed them across the English Channel to the same promise of glory, had the world seen an army like this of Napoleon. Born in the ferocious defence of revolutionary France, hardened in the campaigns into Holland and Switzerland and Italy, again and again into the patchwork of German states, and across the sea into Syria and Egypt, it was fired with a certainty and a unity that the world had not known before: these men weren't fighting for pay, or for some distant king who despised them; they were fighting for the idea of a nation – their nation.

The army was more than Frenchmen too. In its forays across Europe and into Africa, the army of France had gathered troops from half a dozen lands, Germans, Georgians and Greeks, and bright fierce Mamelukes from Egypt with turbans and evil scimitars. Now Napoleon had brought these exotic importations to the opposite end of the Continent, from the endless summer of the Mediterranean to the dour grey straits leading north. He distilled the experience and variety of all these men into a new army with a new name and a new idea: this was the Army of the Ocean Coasts, and it was created with one intent.

Today the Emperor had come to celebrate his creation. For this spectacular occasion he had devised a spectacular symbol: a new medal, a new brotherhood – the Légion d'Honneur – and two thousand men would receive it from the hands of the Emperor himself. Two thousand pairs of boots stepped forwards across that long day, some with capes and swords sweeping beside them, most tramping up the wooden stair with mud on their soles and a heavy musket at their side. Each one of these men, from the Marshals of France to the trembling foot soldiers, felt the pressure of the Emperor's hand on his chest as the Légion was presented. Some – and it was more usually the grizzled Sergeant of the Guard than his young officer – heard private words from the great man, saw his dark eyes looking up into theirs, felt his arm on their shoulder, an affectionate pull of his fingers at their ear. 'I've seen you, eh Sergeant?' 'We've come a way from Marengo, have we not, old friend?' 'Honour France with this, my son.' Strong hard men with grey moustaches and often-wiped bayonets climbed down from the podium with tears pricking their weathered cheeks.

This was not the launch of the invasion; this was merely a morning's parade – but one of a scale and a grandeur never before witnessed.

The people of Boulogne and its surrounding villages and farms turned out in their thousands to watch. The rich – dark-coated merchants and their crisp white wives – sat in carriages looking down onto the plain. The poor deserted their fields and milled around in wonder at the spectacle. The city's shop owners, the innkeepers, the tailors and seamstresses, the speculators, the gamblers, the con men, the card sharps, the thieves and the washerwomen and the whores, all who prospered in the shadow of the army, came to give thanks. History had washed back and forwards over Boulogne with the Channel tides, and the city had known occupation and destruction from all sides, and every kind of language spoken in its streets and towers. But this new Emperor and his voracious army and their colourful triumph and noisy glory meant prosperity, no doubting it. Boulogne knew a good thing when it saw it.

Every attempted movement sent spasms of pain across the muscles of his torso. Even shifting his eyes made his temples burn. He lay still under the sheet and the musty blanket, trying to feel and count his limbs between shallow breaths. His eyes probed cautiously around their bloodshot confinement.

The shouting from outside penetrated most clearly from a single window high in one wall of the room. The room was bare – whitewashed, but a very long time ago. The room was unfurnished except for his bed, one table, and one chair. The room's shape and the quality of the noise from outside suggested an attic. The only light came from a lantern. To the little window again: it was dark outside.

His whole body was exhausted, every muscle stupid and spent. His brain was heavy and slow, and a faint nausea lurked in his gut.

The gaunt Scotsman was still talking.

'These are strange and unholy times, Mr Roscarrock. Desperate times. And desperate times need desperate men. That's where you come in.'

Outside, the single raised voice was building to an indistinct climax, and he nodded towards the sound.

'I don't mean these hotheads, with their penny-pamphlet liberties and their little groups of hungry followers. There's deeper work than that for you. We'll talk again.' He stood up. 'For now, just know that your world, your existence, has shrunk to this room and this strange man who stands before you talking madnesses. This is all that you are, Mr Roscarrock, and all that you will be.'

The voice outside peaked in a single high call, and was met with cheering. Riding the noise, it began a rapid call and response, and with each question the mob bellowed a 'No!' with ever greater volume and excitement, until all the voices merged in one climactic roar of animal intent.

The Scotsman turned his face towards the window, and cocked his head at the sounds of protest as if able to gauge their character and threat. Then he looked back to the bed.

'I have strange and unholy work for you, desperate work.' He smiled the same thin smile. 'But first: get some sleep. You're in no state to listen or to talk, certainly not to work. And work you must.'

Painfully, from the bed: 'I can't walk.'

'You've twenty-four hours to recover.'

'Twenty—'

'The protest's breaking up. Things'll quieten now, and you'll not be disturbed. But they're gathering again tomorrow, and it's not safe for you to be in one place for long.'

'Why—'

'I'll return at the same hour tomorrow. By then you must be rested and ready to move.' He gestured to a mound under a cloth on the table. 'There's food enough for you, and water. Eat. Sleep. Build your strength now, mind.' He turned away, and then back, and when he did one half of the leathered face twisted up. 'I'm afraid I must lock you in for those twenty-four hours, Mr Roscarrock.' The face hardened to stifle the protest from the bed, an attempt to rise that ended in a hiss of pain. 'Not so much that you'd get out, but that others might find their way in.' There was a thin smile now that didn't touch the eyes. 'Treat it as a period of experiment, by all means, Mr Roscarrock. You'll be well enough to move soon, I'm sure, and no doubt you could find a way to draw attention to yourself or even break out of here.' He stepped in towards the bed and his thin arm reached out slowly, followed by the fevered eyes from the pillow. The bony fingers extended, and gripped a shoulder through the sheet sharply enough to bring a gasp of discomfort. 'But the chances are better than evens that you'll die for it. And if you die, be sure that many others may die as well.' The little eyes were fierce, glaring down at the pale bewildered face beneath them. 'Rest, you hear, Roscarrock? You'll need to.'

Then he was gone, with quick and silent movement and the delicate click of the lock behind him. Outside, the shouting was dispersing into chattering, occasional harsh laughter, and movement away. From the bed, an arm rose in an instinctive animal desire to communicate, then fell again as the agony of the wrecked muscles flamed across shoulder, back and chest. There was a mute gasp of pain, and the eyes flickered, and soon there was unconsciousness again.

❧

Two millennia before, the fields of northern France had rumbled and rung with Roman leather and metal on Roman feet and arms. As the beaches grew busier with timber and axe, and small craft were knocked together and started to come and go from Boulogne with reports of the sea or cargoes of fish and apples from along the coast, the Romans built a lighthouse on the cliff above the town. Its flickering through the fog was the last glimmer of civilization over the shoulders of the legionaries setting out across the unfamiliar element for the barbarian island that marked the edge of the world.

Now the tower had become its own memorial, one grey wall on a shaped mound, the rest of the stones borrowed over the centuries for roads and walls and houses. But this was still a place for a man to look across the strait and wonder, and some of the stones had found their way into the foundations of a new tower.

After the elation of the day, the homage of the army that was his greatest achievement, the noise and the colour and the sheer power that was in his hand as it had been in no other man's before, the Corsican rode up towards the clifftop in silence. Always, on his flank, was the sea. Before he would have seen it as a mere factor on a battlefield, would have gauged its potential for benefit or challenge as if it were a forest or a marsh or an approaching column of cavalry. Now it was an obstacle, a measureless wall, watching him as much as he watched it. And as the land rose, the sails of the English blockading squadron became visible.

He dropped from his horse, dismissed his bodyguard and attendants without glancing at them, and stalked into his eyrie alone. Most of the structure was a single chamber, built high around a conference table, walled with maps of the sea and the English coast in every possible perspective and scale. Today the Emperor strode past them unseeing. In a corner of the room was a telescope on a tripod, as tall as its owner and focused permanently on his enemy.

He put his head down to the eyepiece, and the image of the English coast filled his sight as it so constantly and restlessly filled his mind.

There was a cough behind him. The Emperor kept his head down over the telescope, and there was no further interruption to the silence.

'I used to love the sea, Fouché,' he said eventually, still bowed over the image of the English Channel.

He stood straight suddenly, with a great hiss of in-taken breath. Through the window, the water was still there, and he continued to watch it. 'I'm an islander. I grew up in boats. For a time, I wanted to be a sailor.' He shook his head, almost a shiver. 'Now, it opposes me. It mocks me.'

He turned to face his silent listener. 'Show me one face of a hill and I will describe to you its other; I will tell you everything about its soil and its rock and what a column of men or a squadron of horses may do on it. Show me a hill, with a forest on my other flank and a league of firm ground between them, and I will create a masterpiece. But this!' – he gestured two or three times with an angry thumb over his shoulder, voice more shrill and echoing off the ceiling – 'this... this great grey parade ground, wind and rain and nowhere for a man to stand steady, this is an element for gamblers, or for witches; not for a general.' He gave another theatrical shiver.

The man in front of him was tall and thin, pale yellow hair scraped over white skull. Throughout the Emperor's performance he remained still, face impassive, eyes unblinking. Now his Master was staring up into those eyes with something like resentment, and prodding him three times in the chest.

'And you, my Fouché, the most feared, the most ruthless man in all France, you are supposed to be... easing me of this burden.'

Fouché spoke slowly, steadily, carefully. 'I understand Your Excellency's concerns, even though I have none of your grasp of grand strategy. But England is weak. Her army is a rabble. Her people are starving and restive. Her oppressed Irish subjects are on the edge of revolt. And the heart of her society is weakened by intellectuals who are more attracted by our own ideals of liberty and fraternity than they are by their corrupt and decaying monarchy.'

Bonaparte had begun to scowl halfway through this recital, and now he brushed away its conclusion with an impatient hand and strode away round the conference table.

'You and your idealism, Fouché! What advantage is this fraternity?' He reached the telescope, shoulders hunched and fingers rattling along the tabletop in exasperation. 'You slaughtered a thousand protesters with cannon, Fouché, but did you ever sink a single British ship?' He turned his head back. 'Where is this weakness? Can I see it? How is it of use to me? The English fleet is still out there, bottling my ships up in harbour. I am forced to sit here, the countryside infested with General Metz and his Royalist sympathizers. A few fat philosophers and some starving Irish peasants – is that all you have for me?'

Fouché took a step forwards, his voice still rationed. 'Excellency, you know the power and reach of my Secretariat.' Bonaparte scowled again. 'Excellency, you look at a stretch of terrain and you plan your battle accordingly.' The scowl died, the dark eyes watching. 'For me, England's decayed society is my battlefield. I look at its divisions and its frailties and its sins, just as you look at a river or forest or marsh when planning your victory. I have the agents in place to stir unrest in any corner that I choose. I can turn London inside out. I will exploit England's own vulnerabilities and I will paralyze her. Excellency, by the time the English realize what is happening to them, I will see you dining in Windsor Castle.'

Bonaparte gazed at Fouché for several moments, warily. Then he bent again to the eyepiece. The blank, bright face of the English cliffs leapt into his vision. Was it his fancy, or could he make out the figures of his enemies on the green crests?

On the evening of the 12th of July, with the moonlit clouds sitting watchful on the hills to the west, Joseph McNamara came for his third and final protest meeting in the town of Tiverton. Again he stood up on a cart outside the Magistrate's house, and again he gathered around him a hundred disgruntled local people. Interspersed among the locals were a number of McNamara's associates, men with zeal in their hearts and weapons in their pockets. The Magistrate was known to be away in London for the month, his house here on the edge of the town tended only by disinterested servants. It was an ideal location to preach a little sedition, to prompt some limited destruction of property without risking the kind of excess that could send a man to the gallows, and perhaps to provoke the authorities into some anti-democratic repression of these innocent peasants, standing dumbly in the mud and the flickering torchlight with their empty bellies and incoherent anger.

Government spies would report that McNamara pursued his usual rhetorical course: a passionate, pseudo-legalistic blending of complaints against the Government, the rich, the King, the brutal magistracy, the unrepresentative Parliament, and the impossibly high price of bread for an honest man with a family to feed.

He was ten minutes in, enjoying a favoured diversion on the monstrousness of the fat Admirals directing the current, unnecessary war against the liberty-loving French using flour to powder their wigs while poor men could be using it for bread, when the Scotsman slipped through the shadows on the other side of the house and made his way up to the attic.

When he went in, locking the door behind him, the figure on the bed was still, with closed eyes. The lantern burnt dim on the table, leaving black patches on the hollows of the face. The Scotsman watched for a moment with narrowed eyes. Then he walked softly around the room, as if not wishing to disturb the sleeping man. He lit a candle, scanned the table, sauntered to the window, returned to the door. At every step he glanced over to the silent form on the bed.

After a minute he approached, pulled the chair away against the wall, and sat down.

'Not bad, Mr Roscarrock,' he said softly. The eyes were alive with something like pleasure. 'Really not bad at all.'

There was no response from the bed.

'I'll have to ask you to cease your pretence of sleep now, for we've business to talk. I've no intention of coming near enough to let you at my throat with the Magistrate's breadknife. In any case, a young, fit man like you – you can kill me whenever you choose.'

Slowly, the brown eyes opened and gazed warily at the older man. An arm appeared from under the sheet, then the hand, and finally the yellow glint of a blade.

'Dressed too, I see,' the older man said as the figure on the bed threw off the covers and sat back against the wall. 'I've some boots for you once you're ready to—' He stopped as he caught sight of a wrapped bundle under the bed. 'Good, Roscarrock. You've saved some food to travel as well, haven't you? I hope the Magistrate doesn't miss his pillowcase. And you've used the knife to prise out the nails from the window frame and to loosen the lock; you gave yourself two ways out, however it went between me and your blade.' The dark eyes ran over the man on the bed, and then the floorboards. 'The dust's well disturbed hereabouts; I'd say you've been exercising your body as well. How do you feel? Are you ready?'

'As you say: I can kill you whenever I choose.'

'Feel free, Mr Roscarrock.' The face cracked into a yellow grin.

The figure on the bed stretched himself into a straighter sitting position, and weighed the haft of the knife. 'I'd say we're about equal now: I don't know what's happening, and right now you can't do anything about what's happening.'

'I'm not such an old cripple as that, but for the sake of discussion I'll agree with you.'

'I want answers.'

'For the most part, I've only questions. But you may try me.'

There was silence from the bed, then a darkening frown, and the old Scot smiled. 'Isn't that the way of it? You find yourself in a position of power and don't know how to use it.'

'All right. Who are you?'

'I am Sir Keith Kinnaird.'

Again, wary silence from the bed. 'As simple as that? How do I know that's the truth?'

'You don't. As it happens, it is true, but I admire your instincts.'

'And what are you?'

'I am a senior official in the Comptrollerate-General for Scrutiny and Survey.'

'I've never heard of it.'

'No, you haven't. We're not in the news-sheets, Mr Roscarrock.' The gnarled face leant forwards and the lips pulled back into the grin. 'An organization that does not exist, for a man who does not exist. Aye, you'll fit in fine.'

'What is this... Comptrollerate-General?'

Sir Keith Kinnaird sat back in the chair. 'The Comptrollerate-General for Scrutiny and Survey is whatever it wants to be. Don't ask me when it started, because no one knows anymore. It is centuries old, at the least. And don't ask me what it does, because that's forever changing.' The face darkened. 'It may indeed have changed without my knowing of it. Roscarrock, we've been ruled by Saxons, Danes, Normans, Welshmen, Germans, and even' – he flashed his teeth again – 'some noble and misunderstood Scots. But for a thousand years, wherever the ruler came from, this country has enjoyed a coherence, an essential stability, and – barring the odd upset – a constant system of government.' He waved a dismissive hand. 'Ministers, governments, even kings come and go; the Comptrollerate-General will endure.'

A wary shake of a head still lost in the waves. 'I don't... where are we?'

'In the Magistrate's house in Tiverton – in the County of Devonshire.'

A nod to the noise outside the window. 'And did you mean for us to be in the middle of a riot?'

A smile. 'The empty house suits their purposes and ours. As long as they don't burn the place down, we'll be fine, and Mr McNamara will distract attention nicely.'

'You're very – wait... distract whose attention?'

The Scotsman nodded. 'That's the sort of question you should be asking, Mr Roscarrock.'

'And it's the sort of question you should be answering, Sir Keith bloody Kinnaird, if you'd rather I didn't cut your throat and disappear.'

'Young man, your course is set once you leave this room, whether or not you leave me dead behind you. Like it or not, you are involved with the Comptrollerate-General. I've gone to great lengths to protect this meeting, to give you the best chance, but...' He watched the face on the bed absorbing this, and a mean smile flicked across his own. 'Not the England you recognize, lad?'

'So what am I doing in this? And why—'

'A man with a past is a man whose loyalties are known, a man whose vulnerabilities are known. Too often, a man with a past is a man whose future is known.' The Scot leant forwards. 'For a man to be a success in this trade, Roscarrock – even just to survive – he must be infinitely flexible. Do you know anything about China?'

A scowl from the bed. 'What? No. I never sailed beyond Spain.'

'A very wise and patient people, and great philosophers accordingly. In this trade, Roscarrock, a man must sometimes use the force of his character to achieve results, but very rarely his identity. Show your identity and you are immediately restricted: slower, and clumsier. You must learn to move through this world without tripping over your own self. Follow its currents. Use them. Surely you understand that metaphor.' He caught the expression from the bed. 'It would be too much to expect you to be a philosopher as well. Be like the sails of your ship, Roscarrock: use the wind to take you where you want to go, even though you cannot change or control the wind. You will be a mystery, and occasionally perhaps a surprise. That may be of use.'

'This is all madness.'

'Yes, young man.' Kinnaird said it as if it was obvious, and stood up impatient. 'It is, and if you were capable of seeing out of your smelly hold of old fish and smuggled trinkets, you'd know it. A few tens of miles across the shortest and shallowest of sea channels, all human society has been turned upside down. Out of that blood and chaos has emerged a tyrant who is determined to steal all of Europe and inflict his country's anarchy. He has swallowed all who stood in his way, and now he will swallow us. On the beaches of France, Roscarrock, just a few hours in one of your schooners, is the largest and most effective army that Europe has seen since the fall of Rome. All it needs is a fair wind and a moment's inattention by the Royal Navy. And Britain? We're like a... like a one-legged chicken cornered by a fox. Have no illusions, Roscarrock. If Bonaparte steps across the Channel, he will eat this country in hours. We have no strategy to offer against him, we have no idea to bring together our people, we have no army worth the name. The few militia that we do possess aren't even capable of dealing with the food rioters, let alone the Irish rebels who will rise again and overwhelm us as soon as Bonaparte attacks from the other direction. We are pouring all of our money into futile attempts to buy distractions on the Continent, and we might as well be tipping it into the sea at Dover.'

He sat again. 'This is indeed madness. And while it endures, while the navy holds Napoleon off, while we try to build an army, and another European alliance, all we can hope to do is find the tiniest cracks in the Emperor's France – the Royalist sympathizers, the passed-over officials – and explore them, and exploit them, and weaken Napoleon. Weaken him if only a fraction; weaken him if only for an hour.'

He hissed out a sigh. 'That, to answer your question, is why you are here.'

'But why me?'

'Three reasons. You're born to the sea, and that may be useful. You speak French. And—'

'What use is that?'

'We're at war with the French, Mr Roscarrock – or hadn't the news reached Cornwall yet?'

'You don't need to speak a man's language to kill him.'

'We can't kill thirty million Frenchmen, Roscarrock, and even if we could, we'd only find ourselves surrounded by Germans. No, we can't destroy France, but we need a different France. And for that, we need to find the Frenchmen who are different. Remember that, Roscarrock: the lasting security of this nation, the peace of all Europe, can only be found in France. So yes, we might have to talk to one or two of them.' He leant forwards. 'English stability, French instability: that's the key.'

'You said there was a third reason.'

'Aye, I did.' But Kinnaird paused before going further, looking into the large brown eyes in front of him. 'You're a lost soul, Roscarrock, a wandering soul, even before my agents spread the word of your death. Orphaned by your unknown parents; orphaned by the old priest who died while you were still a boy picking pockets and getting drunk on ale and water. Now orphaned by the sea. No one knows you now. You are no one.'

'You seem to know a hell of a lot about me.'

'I didn't pick you out with a turn of a card and a hopeful smile.'

'I thought—'

'Orphans have their uses, Roscarrock. You're a loner. You're hungry. You're resourceful. You can sail; you can ride; and you can fight.' He smiled narrowly at the frown in front of him. 'You'd be amazed what a man can know if he keeps contact with the right people, and if they keep contact with other people. Magistrates, Roscarrock, and priests, maybe a publican or two: the backbone of this country, and its eyes and ears as well. From all I've learnt, I happen to judge that there's enough romance in you to care about what happens to this country, but I can't prove that. What matters is that you're insubordinate, independent and determined. And you're mine.' From an inside pocket he pulled out a worn piece of paper, and his glance ran down it. 'As I say, no one else knows you now. There is no one else. Your acquaintances died on that ship, and few tears were shed for them.' He waved the paper towards the bed. 'This was your life, Roscarrock, and now it's fathoms deep, all of it' – he glanced again – 'from Ezekiel Adams to Thomas Yeo, and Captain Simon Hillyard, your smuggling rogue of a friend.'

There was movement from the bed for the first time. Long legs swung round to the floor, and a tall, fit body unpacked itself to its full height. Still without speaking, he stepped forwards, and then held out the knife until it touched the folds of the Scotsman's neck. 'If you know me, old man,' he said quietly, 'you'll know that you're speaking of the one truly good man I've ever known, and even if it damned me, I'd cut your throat just to take his name back from your lips.'

Kinnaird took in the dark certainty of the face. Then he said quietly, 'Like I said, you're a stubborn, argumentative sort of body.'

The brown eyes looked down at him. 'Stubborn enough to refuse you, certainly.' The knife hung watchful at a hip.

Sir Keith Kinnaird suddenly looked rather sad. 'There's no such thing as refusal, young man. You can choose whether to co-operate, but without me you're a dead man. You have no other life, but what I offer you.'

'I could kill you, and—'

'Then you'd be a dead murderer. Do it by all means, and save some surgeon or Irishman the trouble. But don't think it will change your destiny. You're a dead man, Roscarrock. Only I can make you live.'

Glass shattered somewhere below them, and both men flinched. Kinnaird scowled at his own nerviness and turned back. 'Even Mr McNamara runs out of words in the end. We'd best be moving. A roasted hero is no use to me.'

'I have no idea what you want of me.'

'The nation is in the balance. The destiny of Europe may be settled within weeks. A man of your unique qualities may do much. Go to London. Present yourself to Admiral Lord Hugo Bellamy; I'll tell you how as we walk. Follow his orders. He has the fate of Britain in his hands, and will know where best to deploy you. And never forget to be an independent, stubborn, wandering soul.'

'That's it? After all these elaborate precautions?'

'That's it.' Kinnaird leant forwards. 'Pray these elaborate precautions never become truly necessary.'

He waited for the other to put on his boots, then threw him a coat and a short knife. 'You can leave the Magistrate's cutlery here; I thought you'd prefer a sailor's blade.' The black eyes scanned the room for any remaining sign that one particular man had been here, then he blew out the lantern and they left.

This time he left the door unlocked. Tom Roscarrock was loose.

Outside, the raised voice of McNamara soared on, hectoring and growling. Kinnaird continued to talk insistently as they made their way down. Once lower in the house, they could hear the underswell of the crowd, caught up in the oratory and murmuring and grumbling and calling their agreement.

'Wouldn't you rather there weren't so many people?'

Kinnaird's yellow grin: 'There speaks the sailor. You sail off into that ocean of yours and pretend to disappear. In your wooden boat with all its canvas and shouting men don't you think you stand out a little, surrounded by nothing but water? If a man wants not to be noticed, where better to do it than among a lot of other men?'

The other shook his head doubtfully, and followed through the gloomy silence of the first floor. In an open doorway, he could see the spectres of furniture covered in dust sheets, pale and flickering in the light of the moon and the crowd's torches. He was in an unknown part of the land, with a hostile mob outside and only a lunatic for company, and his dead man's boots trod hollow on the floorboards.

'If we're lucky,' Kinnaird went on as they reached the top of the stairs, 'the dragoons will get bored and start a fight with the mob. A handy riot would do us nicely.'

Again a shake of the head in the silence behind him.

The foot of the stairs gave onto a corridor, lit only by a high window and the moon outside. Odd shapes loomed out of the gloom as they stalked forwards – a chair – a clock, unwound and dead.

'Wait!' Kinnaird felt a strong hand on his arm.

He stopped. 'More questions, Mr Roscarrock?'

'Just one: if the crowd are still talking' – he waved a hand towards the rattle of unhappy voices from the front of the building – 'then who broke—'

'Who broke the window?' Kinnaird nodded in understanding. 'Really very good, Roscarrock.'

A shadow appeared on the wall at the end of the passage. Then it darkened and filled to the shape of a man – a man with a distinctive uniform helmet and the shimmer of a sword in the gloom. The sword was unsheathed. The passage was twenty paces long, and the shadowed figure began to stride those twenty paces towards them.

He came silently, only a rustling cloak and the implacable pace of heavy boots on the boards.

Kinnaird gave it one try: 'We're glad to see you here. Consider yourself under my authority, and—' But he knew it was irrelevance, and as the dark figure bore down on them, now only ten paces and still the boots drumming forwards, Kinnaird reached into his coat and dragged something out. A squat pistol barrel flashed dull in the moonlight, but it was too slow and the vast shadow had seen the movement and now there were only five paces between them, and the shadow ducked sideways and accelerated and as the pistol flashed and cracked into the empty darkness the boot steps became thunder and the man was on them. The sword flashed high against the window and swooped down; Kinnaird gasped between a scream and a curse and fell clutching his arm, the useless pistol dropped to the floor, and now the shadow was a swooping vulture of death, six feet of trained killer with sword arm raised to strike once more and bulk carrying him unstoppably onwards.

He stopped. The sabre was halfway down in a gauntleted arm and the body was still hurtling forwards when the sea-knife drove straight into its heart, and two bodies crashed together to the boards.

The house was silent again.

Kinnaird wrestled himself to his feet and dragged the assassin's bulk off the man underneath it. He helped the other up, then ripped the sash from the corpse and began to bind his own bloodied arm.

'What in hell is happening?'

Kinnaird stopped his tight-lipped activity for a second and looked up. 'He was trying to kill us, Mr Roscarrock. Get used to it.'

'But that uniform: he was a—'

'A dragoon. This'll give McNamara a problem or two. Yes, Mr Roscarrock. A serving member of His Majesty's cavalry. And you just killed him.' Kinnaird's vague form moved closer, and the skeletal face leered into the moonlight. 'Desperate times, desperate men.' Then he turned and walked softly away down the corridor.

At the end, he turned back. 'There will come a time when you can be you again – a moment perhaps when you must be you again. And you'll know when. But not yet, eh Roscarrock?'

Then he disappeared into the darkness.

———

Bonaparte listened for five minutes to the recitation of Fouché's scheming, sometimes looking over his shoulder to examine the dead face more intently, otherwise bent to the telescope. Finally, in the middle of another steady sentence, he yawned. Fouché finished the point and stopped.

'All right, my friend,' the Emperor said wearily. Then with reassurance, looking up at him: 'All right.'

'Your Excellency is content?' Fouché began, and knew immediately that it was a misstep.

'Content?' In a second the Emperor was in front of him again, hand pulling at the buttons of his waistcoat. 'No, Fouché, I'm not content!' He pulled away towards the window, and Fouché had to move with him until the hand absent-mindedly released the waistcoat. 'London is irrelevant! If I could put myself and a regiment of chasseurs on the beach at Dover I would control England in a week, with or without your agents. But between me and Dover is that small stretch of water out there, and that small stretch of water is infested with the Royal Navy. Whatever else is wrong with English society, even if their army ceased to exist tomorrow and every Irishman marched on London, it wouldn't matter because we'd still be here on the wrong side of the sea and the English navy would still be in the way.' He glanced to the window, staring balefully out at the sea, then turned back. 'I don't need your agents, Fouché, to tell me that the English navy is the finest in the world, while half of my sailors can't take a bath without drowning.'

Through the window, the English sails were on the horizon again, haunting him.

'How many months have I waited here?' he asked quietly. 'I have the finest army on earth down on the beach there, and it's going rotten with idleness and syphilis because my Admirals can't give me the English Channel!'

Fouché stepped closer behind his Master. 'As Your Excellency will remember, we are almost in a position where that factor can be resolved.'

Napoleon looked up and over his shoulder. 'I've heard too many fantasies, Fouché. I have been betrayed by too many optimists. You truly believe that these arrangements of yours can neutralize the Royal Navy?'

Still the voice was flat and cold. 'I calculate it, Excellency. I know it.'

The Emperor watched him, then straightened the wrenched waistcoat for him. He turned back to the sea. 'It's very simple, Fouché. If you give me the English Channel for twenty-four hours, Britain and her Empire are finished.'

ENGLAND

21st July 1805

Tom Roscarrock entered London in the dazed silence of an early Sunday morning, before the bells had begun to shatter the mist and drag sleepers from Saturday night to brief piety. He had been a full week on the road. He'd come by roundabout ways, with feigned moves and odd digressions, and he'd come by diverse means, sometimes on horseback, many miles on foot, and once for a day's stretch on a barge down the Thames. In Bristol he'd knocked out a vagrant sailor who'd been following him; in Wootton the Parson had stared across the tavern at him for a full hour before Roscarrock slipped quietly into the night; he used back windows and the hour before dawn for his departures.

The vastness of London staggered him, but he eased into its anonymity with a kind of satisfaction. He walked the streets for four hours just to get used to their rhythm and bustle; the tempest of coaches and horses and squelching, cursing pedestrians revived the lightness of foot needed for a heaving deck in the unruly April Channel. Each glimpse of the crowd came at him like the murmur of a restive crew; the intentness at first bewildered and then amused him.

He leant in a particular doorway on Whitehall for an exact hour, measured by the chimes of a church bell. An interval as long again, and then he spent an hour in the shove and din of a Soho tavern. Kinnaird had been pedantic in describing the routine, and he used a precise phrase given to him by the Scotsman when, another hour later, a man with a new coat and old broken shoes sat down next to him in a Fleet Street coffee house. The man – too young for the coat and the snatched coffee – said nothing more significant in return than a time and a different coffee house; then he slipped out into the street, looking for drier patches of ground on which to walk. At the time and the place, another unremarkable face – though had he remarked it in the tavern? – and five words in the doorway: 'Seldon House. Eight. Servants' door.' The machine was comfortable in its efficiency, and it made him uneasy.

He sauntered along the alley at the side of Seldon House and past its servants' door some half an hour before eight, matching pace with the footmen who had delivered their Masters to the front door and now idled around to the back quarters of the townhouse to find something to drink. Fifteen minutes before eight, he ambled back down the alley from the other direction and slipped into the darkened arch of a building opposite the door. He was nineteen again, stalking the streets of Falmouth, brittle and alert while the press gangs were at work.

By the time the bells of the city confirmed the hour with each other, the servants' door of Seldon House was deserted. The front of the building was stone, but this side was brown brick, irregular windows gleaming into the darkness. The alley – mud and stench and the weird sense of coming from a different and less civilized century than the fine streets it joined – was silent. As the last of the bells faded, Roscarrock tried to readjust his ears to the sensitivity his eyes had achieved.

From his left came the dull tread of a horse, and the rattle of its bridle, and then its rasps of breath. He followed the percussion of hooves and bridle and the intermittent breaths as they neared, shifted his weight from one leg to the other, wondered again what he was waiting for.

There was something wrong with the muddy pace of the hooves, some irregularity. He frowned, wondered at the effect of the arch on his hearing, and suddenly the irregular pace was a separate movement from the right, a pair of boots coming towards him.

A moment later and he saw the boots, and a coat made grey in the gloom, and a battered hat. They slowed, five yards away in the middle of the alley, paced forwards cautiously, a hand reaching into a pocket. Then the horse filled his vision, a sudden black flank and cloaked rider slumped on top blocking out the lights of the house, and still plodding and rattling and rasping. The shadow jolted past, uncovering the lights of the house as it went.

The boots, coat and hat were standing two yards away, staring straight towards him in the darkened arch, and from under the hat there came a faint chuckle.

The hand was still at the pocket, and the man stepped towards the arch. Impulsively he scratched the back of his neck with his free hand. Then he said softly, 'How long have you been in there?'

Roscarrack kept silent. The darkness was still on his side.

'You have the darkness, I have the pistol.'

'I also have a better sense of timing, and perhaps a pistol of my own.'

A shake of the head. 'We'd have seen it before now.'

Roscarrock saw a scratch of a neck from hours previously. 'You were in the coffee house this afternoon.'

'I was thirsty. I'll let go the pistol if you step out of the darkness.'

'After you.'

Two hands spread in exaggerated openness, and Roscarrock took half a step out of his shadows. The grey face under the hat nodded, then said simply, 'Jessel.'

'Roscarrock.'

The grey face considered this for a moment, then nodded again. 'We had word of you.' He turned and stepped to the back door of the house. Roscarrock moved after him. Jessel knocked twice, pulled the hat off and swept a hand through long fair hair. Under the lamp at the door his face flickered and shone. It was a mobile face, pale blue eyes and strong, sharp nose, and it snapped round and seemed to sniff at Roscarrock as if some extra trace of light or scent might be gleaned.

'Why are we here?'

'Meet the chief.' Jessel released the 'f' with reluctance, and nodded at the house.

The door groaned open, pulled with difficulty by a maid: short, plain, out of breath and resentful at being relegated to the back of the house.

There was an instant of silence, and Roscarrock said, 'Hell of a disguise.'

Jessel chuckled again and handed a card to her. The door closed.

It opened again a few minutes later, and they were in and shown to a small ante-hall, flagstones and whitewash.

They waited in silence. Jessel idled around the room, picking up and examining odd items – a tankard, a book, a hat – as if considering whether they were worth stealing. Aware of Roscarrock's scrutiny, Jessel eventually turned to look at him.

'No questions, Roscarrock?'

'Would you answer them?'

The smile jumped back to Jessel's face. 'Probably not. Might pass the time, though.'

His taciturnity had always been Simon Hillyard's joke about him, through the long, companionable nights on the schooner. The meander of conversation, the certainties, the freedom, nagged at him now like a headache.

The door latch snapped up with a crack that startled them both. His back to the door as it opened, Jessel grinned, swapped the grin for gravity with the same speed, and turned. He bowed his head slightly, and murmured, 'My Lord.'

Roscarrock's eyes widened at the man who ducked under the lintel and then stood with raised jaw and cold eyes, irritated as if they had walked in on him. Good nutrition and senior rank never reached the far south-west of England, and even to the most worldly of Cornish sailors a man fully six and a half feet high, in the full and glistening uniform of an admiral of the Royal Navy, was striking in that plain room, a peacock in the heather, a lion at an alehouse table.

The large head barked out a curt 'Jessel' of acknowledgement, but the gaze was on Roscarrock.

'This is Roscarrock, My Lord.' Then, muttered: 'Admiral Lord Hugo Bellamy, Roscarrock.'

Admiral Lord Hugo Bellamy gave the impression that he wasn't sure why he was here, let alone why he should be interested in the silent man opposite him – as if his mind was forced at the same time to consider a great many men in a great many whitewashed rooms. 'So – ? Oh' – and the eyes widened like some huge shark spotting prey – 'you're one of Kinnaird's dredgings!' Now the heavy head dropped down and up Roscarrock's full height more critically. 'What stone did he find you under, then? A prison or a parsonage? Not another deserter from the university or the regiment, I hope; I've too many of those. The soldiers are incapable of intellectual reasoning, and the clerks do too damned much of it.' The large eyes were bloodshot, and they narrowed slightly as they read Roscarrock's face. 'That crazed old Scotsman will have had his reasons, no doubt.'

It wasn't exactly admiral's uniform – Bellamy had taken the coat and ceremonial features of his naval costume and adapted them around fashionable evening dress. Every aspect of Lord Hugo Bellamy seemed outsized and held together under pressure, and the heavy features on top of the great trunk of a body, the strain with which the coat held in the chest, made the cold, thin voice more surprising. The words were measured out. The hands too were a surprise, pale and fine, and Roscarrock had the unlikely fancy that the Admiral was some kind of musician.

Bellamy gave no suggestion of wishing to spend more time in the wrong part of the house than was absolutely necessary. 'Let me tell you how desperate we are, Roscarrock.' He spoke brisk and flat. 'The nation is physically and emotionally on the brink of collapse. At any moment an Irish rebellion or a wave of popular protest at prices and politics could destabilize the country, and our Government is simply incapable of adequate response. Every week, the Comptrollerate-General uncovers new plots against the Cabinet or the King, any one of which would lead to anarchy. Parliament feels it, and the bankers feel it, and London is tottering. I sit in the highest councils of the state, Roscarrock, and it is not an impressive experience. We're doomed, and they know it. A few miles away, watching I imagine in considerable amusement, Bonaparte is camped on the beaches of France with the greatest army since Caesar's.' The big shoulders lifted and rolled; this recitation of the challenges facing him was an act of physical exercise for the man.

'Most of all, we are desperate because we depend on men like you: misfits, scoundrels and deceivers. I should take pride in leading the one organization on which our leaders rely, but I cannot because I know what that means about the rest of them. The Home Office network of intelligence and control is little more than the Magistrates – mediocrities increasingly hysterical and isolated among their restive populace. Our army, or that part of it not rotting in India, is small, corrupt and ill-disciplined. In any crisis, I expect the majority of the ranks to join the rioters. Our navy is stretched from the Indies to Egypt, and nowhere capable of a decisive action: the men are tired, bored and riven with scurvy; the ships are falling apart. Unless the Royalist resistance in France comes off the fence imminently, the Admiralty's one faint hope is that they might have the opportunity to hamper Napoleon slightly when he decides to push his armada across the Channel, but even that will depend on a freak chance of wind and leadership. Is this penetrating?'

Kinnaird's words: English stability and French instability were the key. Roscarrock said softly: 'You're not at sea yourself, Admiral.'

Bellamy's eyes merely widened, while Jessel's ballooned in a suddenly pale face. The Admiral frowned, but it was calculation rather than anger, and then a faint hard smile appeared on the face. 'Your insubordination may be useful, Roscarrock, but only if it can escape your ignorance. I – you are some kind of sailor, perhaps?'

'Only a little.' He'd spent too long with Kinnaird: natural reserve had become unvarying caution.

Bellamy hadn't listened. 'I am no kind of sailor whatever, Roscarrock, and I hope that your pride in the sordid traditions of our navy will overcome the shock. I cannot swim, I cannot sail, and I could not

distinguish between a poop deck and a dose of the pox. When some of
the most important men in the Kingdom chose to name me chief of the
organization with the single best hope of preserving national stability
and countering the threat from France – perhaps they did so on mere
whim, Roscarrock, perhaps they knew one or two things that you do not
– they saw fit to promote me admiral. The title is an irrelevance. There
are technical men capable of manoeuvring ships at sea and throwing them
against the French, and I wish them well of it. For myself, I will pass the
time here in London trying to co-ordinate our national defence against
Napoleon – if you, Roscarrock, with your expert knowledge of Admiralty
strategy will permit me.'

The sarcasm was delivered heavy and humourless, and the Admiral
had no interest in a reaction. The great head leant forwards, eyes
staring into Roscarrock's from inches away. 'I am obliged to imagine
that shrivelled old Druid Kinnaird has chosen you with his unique eye
for the unusually capable. You will oblige me by directing your wits
against Napoleon, and not against the vagaries of British Government
administration. Jessel!'

Jessel stepped forwards. The point had been made, and the Admiral
wasted no more time on it. 'Obviously now that Mr Roscarrock is with
us Napoleon will sue for peace more or less immediately. Just in case
he doesn't, I don't suppose you've made any progress in finding me my
Irishman, my tailor, or my fleet?'

Jessel shook his head with a grunt. 'Beating every bush, My Lord.
Beating every bush.'

The Admiral was still watching Roscarrock. 'Take your time, Jessel.
There's really no rush.'

A hand appeared on Lord Hugo Bellamy's shoulder, a delicate creep of
colour across the dull cloth. In the bland room, in the stolid masculinity
of the conversation, the sudden frail beauty of the flesh and the glint of
jewellery on the fingers was fresh air. Bellamy half-turned his head, the
fingers flickered and withdrew, and Roscarrock followed the movement

down the ungloved forearm to a lithe elbow and then up to a naked shoulder, and so on to an exposed throat, a strong jaw, a pair of parted red lips, a fine straight nose and a pair of blue eyes that were watching him in amusement.

'Who is this, Lord Hugo?' The voice affected lightness, but the eyes held strong and unblinking on Tom Roscarrock.

Bellamy's own glance flicked irritably back to Roscarrock. 'No one, Lady Virginia.'

The eyes hadn't moved. 'Mm. That's a pity. Such a waste of a handsome face.' The poised head, blonde waves pulled up artfully, addressed Bellamy's ear. 'One of these days, Lord Hugo, you must try to bring a someone.' Then she was gone.

Lord Hugo Bellamy scowled at his two employees.

'Your survival in this world is defined by your utility, Roscarrock. I encourage you to be productive. Now be off.'

Roscarrock ignored him, still watching the space left by the woman's exposed neck and upper back. He switched his attention to Bellamy for a moment, nodded once, and turned away.

Gabriel Chance watched his fingers moving over the page, bobbing up and back with perfect regularity and rhythm, threading the words into the paper. Chance was proud of his writing. Proud that he could write, proud of the fine strong letters. 'My beloved Flora': 'beloved' had three flowing upstrokes, framing the tidy little loops stitched into the page – a fine word to write. 'Flora' began with a strong downstroke, the extended and gently curving foot pulled towards the heart. The fingers holding the pen were strong. That's why Chance wrote well: learning, patience, and strong fingers.

This is why Gabriel Chance hated to write: his fingers were the needles he never seemed to use anymore. Soon there would be a machine for writing too, and it too would hiss and rattle in his waking dreams, so that even his head had become a choked and smoking manufacture, so that even his head was no longer free.

He would liberate himself of this oppression. The words of a tailor would unleash a second flood and wipe England clean of the darkness.

When he focused again the page, the beautiful letters, were crumpled in the strong fingers.

———

Sir Peter Pilsom, His Majesty's Justice of the Peace and Magistrate for Tiverton in the County of Devonshire, was an impatient man at the best of times. At ten tired minutes after midnight, after five days on the road, after an unnecessary overnight stay in a lice-infested inn because the imbecile coachman had taken a bridge too hastily and cracked a wheel, after his idle and possibly larcenous servants had fallen into some further misunderstanding by which the house had not been dried and warmed for his return, it was not the best of times. Sir Peter stood shivering in the mud outside his gate, rubbing life into his seat-sore backside with concentrated fervour and glaring at the man waiting anxiously near him. Then, as light began to flicker in the house ahead, he started to stamp towards his front door.

Ahead, from somewhere inside the building, the maid stabbed the gloom with a single, biting shriek.

———

MONSIEUR THE MINISTER OF POLICE MEETS WITH THE MINISTER FOR THE NAVY, PARIS, THE 21ST DAY OF JULY, 1805

M. Fouché: I trust you have kept your visit a secret.

M. Decrès: Even your spies could not tell you I have come.

M. Fouché: The Emperor is impatient. He demands his invasion.

M. Decrès: The Emperor understands less of the sea than I do of the moon. But of course I am at his service.

M. Fouché: Our naval movements are now so closely related to wider national security activities that you and I must meet regularly to co-ordinate.

M. Decrès: Do I understand that the Ministry of Police will be directing the Ministry of the Navy? Haven't you enough to do hunting General Metz?

M. Fouché: The Ministry of the Navy will have its full responsibilities. We are all subject to the direction of the Emperor.

M. Decrès: I am sure that you will be prompt in relaying the Emperor's directions to me.

M. Fouché: The navy has proved incapable of giving the Emperor and his army the support required. I am arranging measures to increase the effect of the navy.

M. Decrès: Naval measures?

M. Fouché: No. But the navy must now be guided by more than the winds.

M. Decrès: Does the Emperor understand that without the winds the navy cannot be guided, however brilliant the other measures?

M. Fouché: Kindly remind me of the dispositions and intentions of the fleets.

M. Decrès: Admiral Ganteaume is closely blockaded in the port of Brest. Admiral Allemand has a small force in Rochefort. Admiral Villeneuve is in the West Indies distracting the English and rendezvousing with a small fleet of Spanish ships. When Villeneuve returns he will be joined by Allemand and hopefully Ganteaume, and the combined fleet will be large enough to provide all possible support that the Emperor could wish. Together perhaps fifty ships.

M. Fouché: If Ganteaume and Allemand can get out of port.

M. Decrès: I am confident that your additional measures, whatever they are, will solve all difficulties.

M. Fouché: The Emperor will be gratified by your confidence.

M. Decrès: Do I understand that these arrangements are to your satisfaction?

M. Fouché: They are entirely to the Emperor's satisfaction, and should be continued unchanged.

Afterwards, M. Fouché very open about the Minister for the Navy: he received his promotion for an embarrassing defeat; I do not mind him being a sailor, but I mind him being a bad one; I do not mind him being a nobleman, but I mind him being an imbecile. Still, even the navy cannot fail or interfere with what we have in train. The Emperor's invasion barges will sail unhindered.

[SS F/109/76]

＊～＊

Richard Jessel leant closer to Roscarrock as they trudged through the night streets. 'The prudent man should not let his mind wander,' he said slyly.

Roscarrock glanced at him. 'You want me to be a monk as well as a martyr?'

Jessel grinned. 'Just saying don't raise your hopes higher than your degree. Virginia Strong's not for the likes of us.'

'I don't know. Seems just the sort for me.' He smiled back at the man beside him. 'Who is she?'

＊～＊

EXTRACT FROM THE DIARY OF SIR JOSEPH PLUMMER

Twenty-first of July, Seldon: the usual admixture of great men, average minds and foolish chatter. The Paris salons of the last generation were to our London houses as the tragedies of Aeschylus to a Southwark alehouse bawdy. Men who think themselves intellectually as vast as Voltaire, and as committed as Marat, prattle like boys of schoolroom mischiefs. Fancying themselves dangerous, their women babble of radical ideas they do not understand, and dream of revolutions in nothing but dress and marital scruples. Sir George Wheen, who would die rather than see his stockings dirtied, talks of the benefit of war on a nation's character. My Lady Pelham, who has I should imagine never clapped eyes on a single representative of 'the people', wonders with affected gravity at the virility of the revolutionary class. I am paraded before these painted philosophers like a performing bear, a freak show of radical thought to be prodded and marvelled at while their gilded world continues untarnished.

Lord Hugo Bellamy there. A stolid creature, paddling like the rest in the shallow waters of theory. But I fear him, for his foolish face frames a watchful eye, and his words never meander forth without that his mind has first considered the fruits of his watchfulness. Sometimes too some shrewd caution or insight in those words slips out, betraying a calculation at odds with his manner. Perhaps he is just one more of these timid dabblers, with greater control of his tongue than most. Somehow there is more to him. I have known Admirals who were royal tyrants and Admirals who were democratic radicals, but never an Admiral who was not in some way a politician. I wonder at Lord Hugo's politics.

Also Lady Virginia Strong. She is an extraordinary creature: the natural beauty of a Helen, the charms and carriage of a

Cleopatra, and a mind perhaps sharper and clearer than any Englishwoman living, and most of the men. But again I fear a complete elasticity of principle. Her ideas are wholly the servants of her interests. She could summarize Sophocles in perfect Greek, if she thought it would secure her an audience with the King; she would with utter intellectual coherence preach social revolution, if her whimsy settled on the seduction of the stable boy. Strong she may be; her other two appellations I sincerely doubt.

The hope of a true revolution in this country is not to be found in these people. And yet their chatter as much as their neck-cloths and hair-arrangements helps to set a fashion that others may follow more crudely. Their flirtations with radical ideas could yet lead to the impregnation of some stronger seed of upheaval in the belly of the people, a truly revolutionary offspring that would condemn its gross parents to their rightful obsolescence.

[SS M/1092/1]

22nd July 1805

It was a sky for brutality, bland and sickly white and thick with humidity to come. It squatted over the parade ground, and already sweat was tickling the necks of the soldiers. They stood rigid in three blocks of three ranks, forming three sides of a square. The faces in the front ranks were blank reflections of the indifferent sky, careful to avoid further provocation. Faces in the second rank showed more life, flicking wary glances at the centre of the square. In the third rank they were active and angry, distilling to mutterings from the sides of clamped lips that went prudently unheard by the Sergeants.

The fourth side of the square was formed by the long whitewashed glare of the officers' accommodation, and the six men fresh from their breakfast who sat on horseback in front of it. The horses shifted uneasily, tails flicking and feet shuffling in the dust. Three of the officers glared into the square with contrived stone disdain; one had fixed a stare into the distance; two glanced around the ranks of men uneasily.

In the whole complex of Colchester barracks, only one man was not in uniform, and not at attention. In the centre of the square, Private William Watkins stood tilted forward against a crude wooden triangle, arms outstretched and lashed above him, naked except for dirty white breeches.

Indifferent to discipline, a fly abandoned its exploration of the puffy leather of an officer's boot and darted into the square, conducting two inspection tours of the triangle and then settling successively on Private Watkins's head, shoulder, and finally back. The naked shoulder blades twitched involuntarily.

In the hands of an unsympathetic Sergeant, a single stroke of a leather whip across naked flesh will create an instant scald, immediately bright pink and subsequently swollen as the body tries to repair itself. Subsequent strokes across the same area will quickly break the skin, and blood will seep thick and dark from fine cuts along the length of the stroke. By ten strokes, the individual cuts will have been torn into a patchwork of larger open wounds. By twenty strokes, a human back will be a permanently damaged piece of lean meat, the nervous system reacting in increasing confusion to such wide and deep damage, and the body will be trying to drug the brain into unconsciousness. Soldiers know little of human physiology, but every man had seen a flogging and a few had felt them and watched with tears of remembered humiliation.

The fly shuffled, jumped, and resettled, and again the shoulder blades twitched.

❧

It was tiresome to have to move so soon after finding a comfortable lodging, but Fannion knew that he could risk no more than another night or two in the shopkeeper's attic. The aftershocks of the onslaught by the Magistrates on their shops and slums were still rippling through the Irish community hereabouts, and his landlord's wearying state of nerviness and faint hostility would shortly have him moving on even if the possibility of the soldiers didn't. He knew the man's type: more concerned by property than principle. Neither poor enough nor rich enough to be carefree: just enough money to have to worry about it. Liverpool seemed full of Irishmen like this, and there'd been not a few in Dublin as well.

The wife was something else, though. She was turning comfortable and complacent – Fannion wondered why there were no children – but there was still a freedom in her movements and a liveliness in her eyes that made him guess at a country upbringing. She'd come to Dublin and sold her beauty to a decent man, because a decent man offered a stability and prosperity that her mother couldn't have dreamt of. But there was a wildness in her still, and the heavy respectability of the cities only kept it smouldering. She hadn't minded the arrival of the tall, dark poet from Cork. Fannion allowed himself a pleasurable daydream – and then a terse reminder that to a cautious respectable Irish shopkeeper the one thing more disagreeable than a rebel in the attic was a rebel in the attic with his wife.

There'd been an intelligence to the soldiers' sweep that he hadn't expected. The rudeness of the men, the clumsy tactics in the houses they searched and the people they'd picked out, this had been no surprise. But there was something in the direction of the men, and something in the questions they'd been told to ask, that suggested there were bright men as well as bullies at work in England's magistracy.

There was something else, too. This worried trawling of its own back streets for ill-defined sins spoke of an uneasy Empire. If Liverpool's Magistrates were confident of their stability and their soldiery, they wouldn't be letting the militia loose to harass beggars and housewives. England was brittle: dried out and tottering, and she would burn more easily when a match was lit.

A burning courthouse warmed the heart as well as the hands, but he had to restrain himself. He would have little difficulty in stirring up trouble as he travelled – a bit of political theory here, a little economic outrage there – Lord, what couldn't he do among the Irish labourers in Liverpool docks? Perhaps he'd cause a couple of incidents after all, just to keep his hand in and the English off balance. But Irish freedom wouldn't come from a few burning toll gates in Lancashire. A complete and permanent shock to the British Empire could only come from Napoleon, leaving English society to collapse under its own rottenness and the Irish free to seize their opportunity. That took co-ordination, with the French and with those who secretly wished them well. Come to England, that had been the invitation; our mutual interests would be advanced by an outrage in London, and you are the man to contrive it. Wasn't he just?

He had to focus on the destination. And for that, he had to be careful about lapsed Irishmen like the shopkeeper. The man would do nothing to bring discredit on himself in the Irish community, which was large in the city and brought him most of his money, however much he liked to think otherwise. But he would do anything to avoid trouble, and when first introduced in the churchyard Fannion had seen immediately that the wide eyes viewed the poet-rebel as trouble personified. So he'd been gracious, polite and restrained, silent on politics and only quietly optimistic that this hospitality to a fellow countryman would no doubt be well-regarded by the community. Even so, there was a calculation and a caution in the shopkeeper's eyes, and Fannion knew it wouldn't take much for the man to decide that his interests were better served by an anonymous note to the Magistrate, and shortly afterwards, at a discreet distance from the house, Fannion would find himself surrounded by muskets.

Sometimes he found himself loathing the Irish. They were a lot better in theory than they turned out in practice, scratching away wretched, diseased lives among the peat, or earning a pound and dreaming of being English. The shopkeeper had come from Dublin five years before, with a good coat and a hard-filled purse and a restless wife. Fannion could see them on the boat, cautious and compact, the tradesman masking his apprehension with piety and the wife not sure whether to look forward to the great smoke of the English port or back to the green hills from which she'd escaped. The tradesman had had patience, and prudence, and industry, and all the other virtues that had been used to distract and delude his people for so long, and he'd prospered in the English town with its English values. He'd worked himself into a solid and profitable reputation in the Irish community in Liverpool, and used it to buy the furnishings of English respectability.

Fannion stretched himself out on the blanket. After the weeks of barns and stairwells and ten-to-a-room labourers' squats, an attic to himself was splendid privilege, and a blanket and mattress luxury. The roof didn't seem to leak much, either. The shopkeeper had invested here; he was spending to stay. Fannion stopped himself and tried to examine dispassionately the mixture of resentment and scorn that had risen in his throat. Resentment was not healthy; no, he should be spurning these trivial comforts and plotting their destruction, and he could not afford to yearn for them, not with his lifestyle. But a blanket and a mattress and the hidden, west of Ireland wildness of a shopkeeper's wife, now...

There was something like pity, too, for the small tidy tradesman who'd come across the Irish Sea to find stability and respectability. For when the violence started he would find that the best timbers only burnt better, and that his neighbours and their Magistrates would attack his Irishness long before they defended his civility.

The Minister of Police was always out of his office on business in the late mornings, and it was the natural time for the Minister's servant to step out into the filth of the Paris streets and run such errands and make such purchases as the Minister's frugal domestic habits required. It was likewise natural that at the end of his round of the markets and merchants, the Minister's servant should step into the inn at the sign of the Sun to refresh himself. The more curious observer would find nothing surprising in a servant visiting such an undistinguished establishment. The more curious observer might wonder slyly whether the servant took purely nutritional relief in the place. The more curious observer would have no interest in the servant's conversation with the landlord, two uninspired men at the dead hour of the day, and would have no idea of what really passed between them.

Joseph found that he rather liked Minister Fouché, and he felt uneasy about it. A man of consistency, and even temper, and polite manners. A most terrible and brutal person, he had been told, who had done unspeakable horrors to thousands of citizens in Lyons and other towns. But to the man who swept his rooms, the man who poured his wine, the man who shaved his naked proffered throat at a disciplined hour every morning, the Minister was unfailingly correct. To Joseph's simple calculation, both men knew that the Revolution was supposed to have promised a world without servants, and both knew that any civilized man – certainly one with the Minister's responsibilities – needed a servant. So they had come to an unspoken understanding about their relationship.

His regular visits to the inn were natural, but Joseph walked them naked and sweating. This was the itching icy nightmare: the certainty that every eye in every street was staring at him; the certainty that at the end of the nauseating, tortured steps that took him unavoidably to the sign of the Sun, its dirty yellow beam advertising his shame, he would step into the inn and find the Minister staring up at him; he knew that his journey was leading him towards death, and not the noble public death of the martyrs like his poor Master, but something lonely and painful and cheap; he knew that the Minister's civility was coldness, and that his coldness was a lethal indifference to the distinction between life and death.

Taking down his recollection of the Minister's conversations, the landlord was ponderous and pedantic. He had to be – it was essential – the young Master had said so. But the seconds thumped past as soldiers' boots marching to the door, the minutes opening out in front of Joseph like a screaming mob.

He wished that Lady Sybille could see him now. He'd always been so uncomfortable around the family, so clumsy and out of place, but only now he realized how safe it had been. Now he was on his own – his own decisions, his own risks. The inexplicable Revolution had liberated him to an utter loneliness.

He hurried back towards the Marais district. He was desperate to leave the inn behind him, and the Minister expected no variation in the timing of his midday refreshment.

Half an hour reflecting the sour, flat stare of the river had been no kind of substitute for the sharp clarity of the sea, and the attempt only made Roscarrock aware, for the first time in more than a week, of how much he missed his element.

It had been the disappearance of his former life, more than the Scotsman's veiled threats, that had sent him to London. His ship was blasted on the Cornish rocks, the few companions of his life lost to the sea, and for now that world only offered beggary and cheap drunkenness. Without a ship, he was nothing.

There was no way backwards, and the only positive way forwards was through the Scotsman's madness to London, and hopefully through London to something else. One day at a time; one meal at a time.

The Scotsman's words he remembered as fragments of a dream, hallucinations that suddenly leapt back at him from the apparent normality of the city. Secret societies and French invasions: sour mouthfuls that he'd swallowed in his delirium and that now lurched in his uneasy gut. Then this Admiral, with his grim fatalism and desperate hopes.

They seemed like nothing to him, these fantasies of politics; but he must live the life in which he found himself. One day at a time; one meal at a time.

For now, that meant bread and cheese and milk in a room off The Strand, waiting for Jessel. But the man who entered and recognized him was not Jessel.

A thin man, strands of black hair trickling down over his skull like spilt ink, a glance at Roscarrock, and a look of such shock as to stagger its recipient.

Roscarrock's thoughts, storm-tossed in this furtive room in this furtive life: he didn't know the man; surely he didn't know the man; but the man recognized him, that was startlingly clear, so did he know the man? What was wrong, in this twisted fugitive life, with knowing a man or being known?

What was wrong was screamed from the expression in front of him: utter surprise, a grasp at self-restraint, a glance around the room, and then satisfied resolution. The ink seemed to trickle further down the forehead, and the face beneath it settled into something like hunger as he looked at Roscarrock.

Roscarrock wondered then at his own face – who was this man? Had he seen him somewhere on the road? Somewhere in a previous past? – and he realized that he was half out of his chair in instinctive animal reaction to that first stunned stare of recognition from the doorway.

With the suggestion of a smile, the thin man stepped backwards and out through the door. Roscarrock followed.

Why am I following? Who am I following? But the ideas were lost in the waves of adrenalin and anger. Out of the door, left, nothing, right, a back in a brown jacket and the man turning and standing, still, gazing at him. The rest of the movement and noise of the world shrank and faded around them: two men gazing at each other; and the thin man smiled.

I have not seen this man! The face was neutral, the face glanced at the people moving around them to and from the shop, and then it settled into that grim smile. *Have I seen this man?*

Silently, the man turned away and disappeared down an alley beside the shop.

Hot, frustrated, Roscarrock followed.

The alley was short, and it was empty. No brown back. No doorway. A small dusty yard opening up at its end; odd lengths of wood stacked or lying; rubbish.

I am following this man because he knows me, and I want to know how. Forwards into the alley. *I am following this man because he knows me, and there are no men who know me anymore.*

The yard looming, empty; the scattered wood.

There is no possibility here that is not dangerous.

A short beam of wood swung across the alley end like a gybeing boom, and half a second later and half an inch higher it would have crushed his throat. An explosion of noise as it smashed into the corner of the building, somehow dulling the scream of pain that roared through Roscarrock's shoulder. His height, his hesitation, had saved his life, but now he ducked and pushed himself forwards into the yard.

Safety was behind him, safety was the tight defensible confine of the alley and the busy, normal street beyond. Instinctively Roscarrock was back against the side of the yard, up fast, half-standing, feet braced, hands finding a solid surface and ready to propel him any how. A shadow in front of him, a looming body – how many slippery dockside alleys? How many sweating heaving decks? – and Roscarrock launched himself forwards into the body. They went down hard together, the thin man crying out as back and head rattled the scattered planks, then rolling, scrabbling, a knee in Roscarrock's chest and fingers clawing for his eyes then clambering up and off from him. Roscarrock rolled away, came up to the crouch, found his man, and now his man had a knife.

Too many clumsy bitter sailors; too many harbour pimps. Moving swiftly in the dust, Roscarrock's fingers found a stout length of wood.

A knife is a close-quarters weapon; a ready, crouching man is a hard target for it. *First he needs me off balance; first he'll try to kick my head off* – and Roscarrock swung the timber in a swift arc that caught the swooping ankle and sent the thin man hopping back. Now up, up, a hand at each end of the makeshift club to block, but still the other man's off balance, so swing again at the knife hand, fast and vicious and a scream and the knife clattered across the yard. Forwards – hard – two hands on the timber again and feet pumping against the deck and drive the timber into the bastard's throat.

The thin man lying sprawled back in the dirt, turning red, Roscarrock over him, the pain in his left shoulder burning now as he pushed down with both hands, hard edge of timber cutting into the scrawny throat. A gristly choking, the face purpling, eyes squeezing larger and pleading, the lank strands of hair spilling into the dust.

Who are you? What do you want of me? What am I doing? I need answers!

Roscarrock clenched his shoulders, the timber plunged a last brutal inch, and the goggling rosy face died with a hiss.

A scratch of boots in the dust behind. 'I'm sorry I'm late.'

Roscarrock spun round. It was Jessel, the Government agent, now looking down at him with something between interest and amusement.

'He was trying—' *Was he, really, trying to kill me?* 'I didn't—' *Didn't I know him? Didn't I want to kill him?*

Jessel had stepped forwards. With the toe of a boot he lifted the length of wood off the crushed throat, and then he examined the face with bored distaste.

'On the whole,' he said, 'I should think they'll say that you did.'

He stooped, Roscarrock crouching back stiff against the yard wall with his blood still fierce in his head, and rummaged deftly through the pockets of the brown coat.

'Calling himself Tyler.' He straightened the dead man's coat, and glanced at Roscarrock. 'But not anymore. Come on.' He led them a different way out of the yard.

Somewhere under Whitehall, Roscarrock was introduced to a room and a man. The room was metal-lined, both to protect it from fire and to ensure that if necessary its contents would burn very quickly. It did not officially exist. The man was called Morrison Cope, Clerk to the Admiralty, and all reports were sent to him. Mr Morrison Cope did not exist either.

Nothing about this world is real. No more real than the stranger who'd known me; no more real than his bloodshot dying eyes.

———— ◦ ————

PROCEEDINGS OF THE ADMIRALTY BOARD,
FIRST LORD, ADMIRAL LORD BARHAM, PRESIDING,
THE 22ND DAY OF JULY 1805

[PROCEEDINGS OF THE ADMIRALTY BOARD, VOLUME XXIV]

'You were seen at Seldon House last night, I think, Bellamy.' Lord Barham, a sharp seventy-nine in an age when most men were dead at sixty.

'Your Lordship has informants better even than my own.'

'Seldon, was it, Bellamy? Hedging our bets are we? Keeping in with the radicals so they don't cut your throat when the great day comes?'

'Perhaps, George, they think they're keeping in with me.'

The First Lord, with Lord G. Garlies, Admiral J. Gambier, Admiral Lord H. Bellamy and Sir E. Nepean being present, the Board convened at eleven of the clock.

Adm. Gambier described the general movements of our fleets: Adm. Lord Keith blockading off the Netherlands; Adm. Cornwallis patrolling the entrance to the English Channel; Adm. Cotton blockading Brest; Rear-Adm. Orde blockading off Cadiz.

'Blockade and blockade and blockade. All the Frenchies safely trapped in harbour. Very prettily done, and not a single British sailor has killed a Frenchman or eaten a proper meal these three months. This cannot endure for eternity, Gambier.'

'We must trust to our superior seamanship, My Lord. It has endured successfully until now.'

'The frogs can fail and fail again, and our men continue sick and hungry sailing back and forth on blockade duty. If we fail but once, we will be damned by history as the men who gave London to Napoleon. God's sake, gentlemen, this Board has absolute control of all that is left of Britain's defence. We can't just sit on our fundaments wondering at the weather-glass. What of Calder?'

'Little yet, My Lord. We have had no further sighting of the French fleet of Admiral Villeneuve since the *Curious* reported it, and we must hope Admiral Calder finds it. He has now been reinforced, My Lord, and we look for an engagement at any moment.'

'Fleets, Bellamy?'

'Rear-Admiral Calder will likely be outnumbered four to three or five to three, My Lord.'

'Satisfactory odds, My Lord.'

'If he takes them, Gambier. If he misses, the enemy fleet is loose in the Channel.'

Adm. Gambier described the orders lately given to Vice-Adm. R. Calder, and reported Vice-Adm. H. Nelson returning from the West Indies.

'Have we no word of Nelson?'

'Not lately, My Lord.'

'Ten weeks that man has been amusing himself in the Indies, and for nothing. We persuade ourselves that our solitary hope is to keep the French bottled up in their ports so that their invasion barges cannot sail, and then we allow their senior Admiral to escape into the open sea. Nelson wastes a month in the Mediterranean, then scurries off to the Indies in pursuit. We keep promoting that man because he's supposed to be a fighter. But rather than bringing a decisive action, he's been led astray like a first-year lad in a Portsmouth tavern dance. He's now missed Villeneuve again, giving the frog free run of the Atlantic and the chance to slip up the Channel and deliver Napoleon to our doorstep.'

Their Lordships re-approved the existing orders to the fleets on blockade and to Vice-Admirals R. Calder and H. Nelson. Their Lordships a pproved regular expenditures to the pay account, to the shipyard account, to repair and maintenance of Admiralty property, and to Scrutiny and Survey.

There being no further formal business, the Secretaries withdrew.

'No doubt, gentlemen, after all that good news, we may expect something special from Lord Hugo. Where's your mystery fleet, Bellamy?'

'I regret, My Lord, that we still do not know. It remains the firm indication from our agents in France that there is some new and additional naval force outside the regular formations. Its base is unknown; its command is unknown. The combined resources of France and Spain are more than enough to have supplied the necessary boats and men, stiffened by officers of quality from other fleets and those old officers not murdered by the Revolution.'

'And the implications of this fleet?'

'Our latest report from France – from somewhere close to Fouché, Napoleon's Minister of Police – shows him confident that they have a way to neutralize the obstacle presented by our navy. He does not give details, but we must speculate that he refers to this fleet. I would defer to my sea-going colleagues on the implications, My Lord. But if it's loose, this fleet could appear at any moment to challenge one of our blockading squadrons, or to support the invasion itself.'

'Bellamy, you begin to depress me. What are you doing about this?'

'We continue to scour France for information, My Lord. But you will understand that they are the most testing conditions in which to operate.'

'I don't doubt it. Have you the resources to buy the information, and to disrupt where you can?'

'Your allocations to Scrutiny and Survey are carefully deployed, My Lord. The same vessels that we use incognito to transport agents to France also deliver much-needed gold to the Royalists active between Paris and the coast. My requisitions will continue to be made formally to you.'

'Anything else?'

'There was concern that Admiral Villeneuve might attempt to land troops in Ireland, but we have had no word on that.'

'You've had no word? How do you propose I find out, Bellamy? When some Catholic assassin knocks at my door? A French landing in Ireland would be a disaster. Nepean? You governed there.'

'My Lord. When they tried their landing in '96 we were only saved by a storm. Otherwise we'd have lost Ireland quickly and completely, no doubt of it. Every French naval movement is greeted with excitement in Ireland. A rowing-boat of Frenchmen would be taken as liberation.'

'Liberation? God save us from Ireland: it is an infernal place and an intolerable burden. If I could give it up without it filling with Frenchies, I would do so this afternoon. To conclude: we have not yet heard whether the French have invaded Ireland, and can only hope that they have not. We have not yet heard of a mob marching on London, and we can only hope that they do not. We have not yet heard whether Robert Calder has intercepted Admiral Villeneuve, and can only hope that he does or else they'll be sailing up the Thames within the week. Most of all we can only hope that we find this new French fleet, or else the game's up and we all start learning the "Marseillaise". Hope, gentlemen, is all we have, yes?'

In five hours Roscarrock was introduced to five people in five parts of London. At no point was his name asked, nor – with one exception – did he learn the name of any of those he met.

In a field behind a dairy in Islington he was pointed to a bay horse by a small man with an earring and a face scarred and tanned like a walnut, who watched him make two circuits of the field at trot and canter. As he walked the horse back, Roscarrock saw the man murmuring to Jessel, but the visit was otherwise without words.

'Untutored, but you sit easily, apparently,' Jessel said as they walked back to their own horses in the dairy yard.

'Which means what?'

'It means you'll do, for most work. Nothing fancy, but you'll do.'

In a windowless yard south of Fleet Street, Roscarrock was put in front of another stranger, a man of perhaps fifty, who wore breeches and an open shirt that showed the muscles of someone much younger, and a pinned sleeve in place of a left arm. The man stared at Roscarrock's face for a moment, then looked carefully down and up the six feet of him. Then he turned away and picked up two swords, one of which he threw to Roscarrock.

'Now come at me.'

'I beg your pardon?'

'Attack me, man! Come on.'

Roscarrock swung casually towards the one-armed man, who parried the stroke with a vicious flick of his blade and a scowl of impatience, both of which stung. Roscarrock started at him with new concentration, his opponent initially withdrawing a pace and then gradually pushing him back with light movements and skilful blows. They fenced for two minutes, Roscarrock spurred by the skill and by irritation that the man was so clearly gauging him at the same time as fighting. Eventually the man contrived another sharp parry that by timing alone sent Roscarrock's sword arm wide and left him off balance and open, and barked a bored 'Enough'.

He punched Roscarrock lightly on the shoulder with his sword hilt. 'All right, lad. Well done.' Then, to Jessel, watching in amusement from the doorway: 'Give him an axe or a pitchfork, nothing finer. But he's fit, and he's got a body quick enough to match his intelligence. He tried to follow on with his shoulder and his elbow once or twice, and they don't teach that in the schools. A fighter, not a fencer. He'll do.'

They headed east along the river, the shouts of the boatmen and the gulls rising from the undergrowth of masts and oars.

'Jessel, Lord Hugo mentioned an Irishman, a tailor and a fleet.'

Jessel was silent for a moment. Roscarrock took in the madness of boats, masts and sails, the woven shouting of birds and men, the mixed stench.

'The Irishman is called James Fannion. That's the name we have, anyway. He was responsible for every kind of evil in Ireland – inciting unrest against the Government, stirring up arson, attacks on individual officials and priests. He was involved in the rebellion of '98, but he was too clever to get caught and hanged. He's certainly a man of violence – Dublin knows at least three murders committed by him – and he brings hatred and unrest like a rat with a plague.' They crossed through the rattle of carriages and headed down towards the river. 'Unfortunately, our people in Ireland lost track of him. He made himself unpopular even among his own kind, and he escaped from Dublin three weeks ago. All we know is this: firstly, wherever he goes he will carry the possibility – say the likelihood – of violence; if he could co-ordinate with radicals in England he could cause chaos, and if he could get to France, which God forbid, we'll have war from two sides, because the Irish will rebel sooner than take a piss in the morning and Napoleon will exploit the confusion.'

'And second?'

'He's here. Somewhere in England.'

In a private room in a coffee house by the old bridge, Roscarrock found himself opposite a heavy man who sniffed down his wine-blasted nose at Roscarrock's inferiority of dress and breeding, and then addressed him in simple French. Roscarrock replied with the same. The large man winced at his accent, and continued with increasingly sophisticated sentences until Roscarrock dried up. The man said, 'No Spanish, I suppose? No Italian?' Roscarrock shook his head. The man started to gabble at him regardless, and smiled through apparent pain as his pupil floundered for meaning.

Roscarrock was given a drink, and the stranger relaxed his bulk back against his chair and rolled his head around towards Jessel. 'He's no linguist, of course, but he'll muddle through with that peasant French of his. He'll do. The mind's quick enough, believe me.' Back to Roscarrock, examining rather than addressing him: 'Such a pity. I do wish they'd either educate people or leave them on the farm to do something useful.'

Walking north away from the river. 'The tailor, the one Lord Hugo mentioned?'

'The tailor is the kind of man Fannion, the Irishman, would like to link up with. We first got word from Manchester of a radical preacher – not a religious man, but a self-proclaimed philosopher who was spreading anti-Government ideas and addressing groups of workers and encouraging violence – burning machines and the new factories, that sort of thing. A failed tailor. Hardly unique, but Manchester reckoned he was something a bit different. All we had were fragments, but he was heading for London and he'd a particular purpose in mind, that's all we knew. Then they lost him.'

'Name?'

Jessel shook his head. 'A tailor from the north country, a travelling man who causes unrest wherever he goes. We need to find these men, Tom. Can't have the country collapsing with Napoleon knocking at the door.'

In a first-floor drawing room in Holborn, Roscarrock met the lawyer's widow. When the middle-aged woman first walked noiselessly into the room, and Jessel nodded meaningfully towards her, Roscarrock was about to order a drink. Instead she sat down beside him and laid out several sheets of paper, covered with lists and tables of minute and beautiful lettering. She then delivered a five-minute lecture, apparently without drawing breath, on codes, ciphers and secret writing. It was black magic to Roscarrock, but he'd spent enough time around charts and the intricacies of navigation not to be uncomfortable with the detail or the logic. After a further ten minutes talking and testing him through a series of examples, the matron patted Roscarrock on the back of the hand, and nodded primly to Jessel, before floating away to another part of the house as inconspicuously as she had come.

As a servant closed the door behind them, Roscarrock said wearily, 'I'll do?'

'You'll do.'

Roscarrock grunted, and they began to walk south again towards the river. 'And Lord Hugo's fleet?'

Jessel turned to him. 'There I can tell you even less. Not my regular concern. The Admiral hopes that our English networks might turn something up, but it's a damned faint hope. Two or three sketchy reports from France: somewhere, Napoleon has a whole fleet – we've no idea how many ships – five, ten, twenty – and we simply have no clue where it is. In the right place, at the right time, it would turn the war in a day.'

The fifth stranger was in the cellar of an apparently empty house next to St Bartholomew's Hospital. Jessel had a key for the door, and led the way along corridors and down stairs of whitewashed plaster and dark wood, everything clean but barren, before using a second key to let them into the cellar room.

'Music teacher? Dancing master?' Roscarrock was saying as he followed him in, and Jessel nodded to the centre of the room and stepped forwards.

The fifth stranger was lying on two wooden trestles, completely covered by a thick calico sheet, dead. Roscarrock knew he was dead, but Jessel pulled back the cloth just to prove the point, and they looked down at the grey, stupid face. As the skin had paled, so the hair seemed to have darkened, and the black eyebrows were pulled together in a faint frown. Death had come as a puzzle to this man, and so it would remain to him for eternity. The ultimate vulnerability made the face seem particularly young.

'To answer your question,' Jessel said quietly but with brutality, 'he's you. And me. He's a fieldsman for the Comptrollerate-General for Scrutiny and Survey. And that's almost certainly what killed him.'

Roscarrock looked up from the waxy mask below him. 'You make your point very effectively, but I'd already gathered the work wasn't conventional.'

'Good to know you don't collapse in a faint, stagger to the door, or babble to go back to wherever Kinnaird found you.'

'I'll do.'

Jessel nodded dully, and looked down at the corpse. 'His name was Simon Conway. One of us, like I said. Good fellow. Been at it a bit too long, started seeing a Frenchman in every tree. But a good fellow. Found under a pile of straw in a barn in St Alban's, stabbed from behind.'

'What killed him?'

'He didn't exactly have time to send a report.'

'I mean: what was he investigating?'

'We're trying to identify the regular stopping-points for radicals and insurrectionists on their way to London. What or whom he was investigating I don't know. We all trot on a pretty long rein.' Jessel looked down again, and patted the dark dead head softly.

On the stairs, door locked behind them, 'So, one of these days you'll be bringing some youngster to come and look at me down here.'

Jessel kept tramping up the stairs. 'Oh, I don't know. If it all goes terribly well for you, it might be me on the boards down there instead.' At the top he stopped, and said with a kind of relish, 'Comptrollerate-General's not a place for long-term planners.'

Out on the street, two deep breaths of real air. 'Jessel: if I had fainted, run for it, said it had all been a terrible mistake?'

Jessel walked a few steps before stopping, and turning with a grim smile. 'Like they said: you're quick enough. Few of us come into this with much of a choice. But once you're in, to know even the little you know is to know too much.' He started to walk again. 'If the Essex marshes aren't convenient, there's always the Thames mud at low tide.'

Roscarrock nodded balefully, and followed. 'Right. Thanks. I'd better start enjoying myself, hadn't I?'

Jessel clapped him on the back and they continued to walk westward through the London streets, ignorance and innocence bustling earnest around them.

Sir Peter Pilsom, the Tiverton Magistrate, had shown no desire to delay his sleep further, regardless of the presence on the premises of a murdered dragoon. But the coachman was sent back into the night, to inform the local Colonel of Militia that there was a dead soldier in the house of Sir Peter and that Sir Peter did not want it. The Colonel was himself jealous of his sleep, but thought it better to seem to act promptly on a matter involving the Magistrate. The Magistrate acknowledged, amidst a flow of slurred obscenity that had the servant retreating from the room before it was half-finished, that it would be better to respond hospitably to the arrival of the Colonel of Militia; one never knew when one might need them, after all.

So it had been a pair of sleep-deprived and extremely irritable men who convened before cock-crow in the Magistrate's hall to agree that there was indeed a dragoon lying ice blue and obscene on the flagstones. The Colonel, in as much of a uniform as would give the impression of professionalism and respect, felt instinctively that any fault or suspicion must logically settle around the Magistrate, but apologized in any case for the inconvenience. Sir Peter, slope-shouldered and shuffling in his dressing gown, felt that in some obscure way the military were careless in allowing their soldiers to be left around thus, and there was a kind of inefficiency in losing much-needed men at a time of heightened unease. He offered the Colonel a cart to have the body taken away the sooner, and the two men returned to their respective beds, heavy-eyed and grey-jowled and mumbling at the shortcomings of the other.

Whether he'd dallied with a woman, or a man, or some criminal proceeding, it was clear to the Magistrate and the soldier that the dragoon was the one essentially at fault in the vexatious episode. But by the time the Colonel took possession of the body later in the day, he accepted that there was a murderer to be hunted.

❦

'How is Roscarrock?'

'Quiet, quick, and sharp, My Lord. Sir Keith picks well.'

'That I have never doubted. And who is he, Jessel?'

'Hard to say yet, My Lord. He's mentioned no family. He has the patience and watchfulness of a professional soldier, and the robustness of a farmer.'

'Find out. I'd trust one of Kinnaird's discoveries to be a good operative, but who knows for what side? This organization is a swamp of shadows and chancers. At every remove from myself I find greater ambiguity. Not a trivial point, Jessel. We need to know how useful he is, or how dangerous.'

'My Lord.'

'How useful *and* how dangerous, perhaps.'

'Quite so, My Lord.'

'Roscarrock: where's that name from, for a start?'

— ∞ —

The sun never rose on the morning of the 22nd of July 1805; not in the eastern Atlantic, where winds from the Americas threw vast waves against the Spanish coast and harassed ships trying to manage the unwieldy passage between the Mediterranean and the North Sea. On the morning of the 22nd, the darkness of night dispersed to nothing better than a dense grey fog that hung like a heavy cold on fifteen British warships and their Captains. Vice-Admiral Robert Calder had woken to find himself the focus of the strategic ambitions and fears of all Europe, and unable to see beyond his own bowsprit.

Now Calder stared balefully into the fog from his quarterdeck, the ship's Captain uneasy beside him. 'I suppose we must trust that the Admiralty have judged the business right, sir.'

'I do not find myself able to share your confidence, Cumming. At their direction I have abandoned the blockade of two French fleets to pursue this illusion of an engagement, and already those ships may have escaped into the Channel. Someone in London fancies a glorious triumph for breakfast, and I must risk a disaster to try to deliver it.'

Faintly, through the fog, came dim shouts of command from the nearest ship; intermittently, a twist of the fog would show a shadow in the gloom, a sail or a stern or a trick of the dark.

'We have to stop Villeneuve returning to the Channel, sir. If we don't—'

'I intend to, Captain. But Villeneuve might be sailing under my stern as I stand here and I'd never know it, and meanwhile in my absence from Rochefort I may give the French navy the run of the Channel, and Napoleon free passage to Dover.'

'The fog seems to be lifting over there, sir.'

'The glass seems to be falling. Do all your men idle in that fashion,

Cumming, or is that a special detachment of loafers?'

'What do we know of Villeneuve's fleet, sir?'

'Perhaps twenty ship of the line to our fifteen, and a handful of frigates to our two.' The Admiral sniffed. 'Sporting odds, Cumming, and I'll take them, except we can't – there!' The arm shot out, and Captain Cumming's telescope snapped up and out to follow it. 'Starboard quarter. Topsail in the fog. Quickly, man, what do you see?'

The combined French and Spanish fleet of Admiral Pierre de Villeneuve, returning to Europe from the West Indies with tired and hungry men and Admiral Nelson far behind, was sighted at eleven in the morning of the 22nd of July. Cumming's HMS *Prince of Wales* barked out two speculative cannon shots before the fog covered the enemy fleet again.

For six gloomy and tedious hours, Calder manoeuvred his fleet after the French, the ships tacking and advancing with painful lethargy in the indifferent wind. The fleets slipped gradually south and west, pulling further away from the English Channel and the waiting French army and the vital blockades. A flirt of the fog would give the two Admirals glimpses of each other, and as quickly veil the temptation. A hurrying of the wind would suddenly offer the possibility of attack, and then drop to nothing in the slow Atlantic swell.

Sometime after five in the afternoon, Captain Hyde in HMS *Hero* found himself with the wind behind his stern and the French and Spanish line of ships over his bow and ordered the *Hero*'s guns run out ready for action, in a voice cracked with tiredness and thirst.

'There's another one. He lived when he should have died.'

A raised eyebrow. 'A problem?'

'We don't know yet.'

A frown. 'Well, whose side is he on?'

71

'We don't know yet. But more importantly, he doesn't know himself.'
A thin smile. 'What to do, then?'
'For now, we leave him in play. We have hopes. He could be useful.'
A narrowing of the eyes. 'And if and when he stops being useful?'
'He dies. What's one more dead foot soldier in the war of Empires?'
A grunt.

23rd July 1805

The wind gusted suddenly, and a ripple of excitement hissed through the long grass that stretched to the horizon and down to the water's edge. Out in the estuary, the rowing boat bobbed and the silence of the Kent morning cracked in a shrill male voice.

'Oh, for the love of God! Cannot you people keep this boat still for one second?'

The American accent was still strange to the two men at the oars, but they were well used to the tone. They shared a silent glance of irritation, and felt the boat stabilizing itself naturally.

'Must I tell ya again what we're dealing with here? You wan' us all destroyed? You want them picking pieces of ya outta the trees?'

The wind eased again on the Elmley Marshes. The grass shook, and subsided.

Out on the water, the American continued working in silence. He'd been leaning over the side of the boat for half an hour now, and the thin mattress under him had ceased to offer much benefit to his aching chest and shoulders.

To the north, the water opened out into the Medway basin and the marsh grasses curved away towards the fort at Sheerness. The main channel of the estuary, protected from the sea by the Isle of Sheppey, was a constant bustle of shipping of every class, from men-of-war to jolly boats stuffed with dry biscuit, all the noise and activity of a great fleet headquarters of a great maritime empire.

There had been sailors here since the dawn of man; there had been mutiny here within recent memory.

Sheltered by a barren spit of land, screened by trees and bushes and the emptiness of the marshes, the American worked out of sight of the bustle. No ship or building could observe or be observed. On the nearest shore, two Marine sentries slouched against their muskets.

Across the whole sweep of marsh and water and cold sky, only the American's hands were moving. Under the gentle stroke of the tide, they were very cold.

A sudden wordless cry, and two pairs of eyebrows in the boat rose in weary expectation.

'That's it. We're set. Let's move, you men!'

The lugubrious shifting of the boat and the clunking of oars in rowlocks sent a shower of gulls up from the water, and their cries merged with the cawing voice below them.

'Move, will ya? There's twenty pounds of powder there!'

The rowing boat slid away towards the shore, moving steady with the practised skill of the oarsmen. The American, perched edgy in the bow, peered constantly over them towards the dwindling apparatus he had just left.

A scrape of keel on stones, the clambering out, and silence again across the Kent shorescape. The sentries had stiffened professionally as the American landed, and now gradually slouched again. The gulls settled back onto the water.

And then the water erupted into an instant tree of foam fully fifty feet high, and a heartbeat later a thunderclap blasted the sky. It rolled over the grassland, resonated weird around the inlets of the estuary, and the monstrous cloud of spray splattered down.

On shore, the men wiped the mist from their faces. Only the American stood still, eyes busily absorbing every detail of the explosion.

Across the estuary there was imperceptible movement against a shadowed tree trunk. Another set of eyes was eating the scene intently, helped by a small collapsible telescope. In the gloom of shadow and undergrowth, a dappled face shifted slightly, and the eye of the telescope moved from the explosion to the men on shore, and particularly to the American, who had been working in France and now was not.

Back on the near side of the water, sitting inconspicuous against a tree on the bank and a little distance away from the soldiers, there was another silent watcher. His eyes had been sweeping slowly back and forth over the estuary for an hour, only occasionally allowing themselves the distraction of looking at the American in his little boat. The eyes caught a flash from across the water, snapped towards it, narrowed and focused. A large head came forwards, as if a few inches more proximity could clarify what was happening in the waterside bushes three hundred yards away.

The head rigid, the eyes fixed and unblinking – and another flash from across the water. That was the second hint of surveillance in three days. A secret observer of Mr Fulton's experiments had to be assumed. A message would go to London, to Mr Morrison Cope at the Admiralty, by evening.

And in the fields beyond, as the last of the white plume of water dropped below the treeline and the echoes of thunder faded, two Kent farmworkers stared at each other, and looked back towards where the greenery shielded the estuary from their sight, and wondered.

———— ✦ ————

My dear Gabriel,

I had your letter from Sheffield, and keep it by me. I hope that my letters reach you like you said they will.

I am well here. Purvis is still a brute but Jenny Purvis is kind and she is glad to have me stay and they are being good to me. I would I was in our little home but I know that is not possible. There is a little sewing and so I help. The corn is high now and it will be a good year, thanks be to Him. Last night old Dunn died and Mrs Tunny is sick. There was trouble at Tunny's over him letting go two of his men on account of the prices and blood was shed and now it is for the Magistrates. You said that the beast of the state lives on the blood of the people and so maybe there will be more blood.

I am glad you found the poor metalworkers in Sheffield pure of heart and fit men to bring God's better world and I am glad that you were well treated. I hope you have met the like in other places since. Gabriel, I do not know and I do not think I would understand what it is you go to do. But you were so full of light and set in your mind when you left and I hope your will and faith sustain you still. I beg Him constantly that he will have a care for you and more than you do yourself. For it is always your way to put your words ahead of your own good. I am sure that all you say of what is wrong with our world is true, but sometimes I am fearful that it is not wise. I hope He knows you do His work and shelters you and shines His light on you.

Mostly I hope your certainty makes you happier. And it is this sustains me thinking of you. I miss you sore.

Your devoted wife,
Flora Chance

[SS M/1108/1]

What to write, anyway? Chance looked down at his waiting fingers, fluttering futile at him like a downed bird.

He felt his ideas resonating in his head, a song heard from another room, felt their force burning in his chest. When he spoke, the energy and the music flowed out of him in a miraculous torrent that he could neither explain nor control. But he never remembered what he had said. If he tried to find a word, to capture an idea, it twisted and slipped away through his fingers.

Flora was worried. Flora thought he was unwise. Flora could not understand; his blessing was to be the one wise man in the age.

His fingers flickering; his tailor's fingers waving goodbye to him.

Strong fingers: the aborted letter crumpled inside them.

❦

ABINGDON IN THE COUNTY OF BERKSHIRE,
MAGISTRATE SIR THOMAS TOLLMAN,
VISITED THE 23RD DAY OF JULY 1805.

Nil. List appended

[SS J/593/56]

A fat complacent man, sighing boredom and disdain at the two Government men. They had not been offered bed, food or even drink after a day on the road.

'God's sake, man, it's all very well for you down in London, with the Life Guards and the watch and the whole damned Cabinet to escort you to the privy should you so choose. I'm the solitary outpost of Government and civilization here, and I've nothing between me and the mob but the front gate, and I don't get money enough to look after that properly.'

'Must be very worrying for you.'

'Don't trouble yourself on my account. The gout'll kill me before one of these peasants ever summons up the wit.'

'Are you aware of any specific and serious sedition?'

'I can give you a gaol full of specifics, none of 'em serious. Behind your city walls you may think of sedition as something occasional and shocking, but out here it's everyday stuff, normal conversation. Every milkmaid and beggar's a rebel when the mood takes 'em, and I can't say I blame them. You've got your routine list here, and you can save me the trouble of sending it. The same situation as last month, the same crimes and quite a few of the same names. All of them a night or two in the cells for damning the King or toasting France, none of them worth your while.'

'You don't think the threat's serious?'

The bulk struggled forwards from the depths of the upholstery, bloodshot eyes staring up at the two visitors. 'Serious? Young man, the country's a tinderbox. These yokels are bored, poor, hungry – and desperate. A clear voice to rouse them tomorrow, and they'd burn this house down on the way to the inn. A flag to follow, and they'd march on London. But don't think the answer's in your damned lists.'

<hr />

Shrewsbury; the house of a lawyer – a widower. An honoured guest, with a letter of introduction from a mutual friend; a Welsh name, but an accent that sounded – to those familiar with it – Lowland Scots.

Sir Keith Kinnaird alone in the guest room after supper, sorting papers and thoughts, destroying the former in the grate and trying to conjure the latter from the smoke.

Gough the artist had disappeared, and with him the contents of his 'sketch book'. It was possible that he had taken himself further into some distant part of the Kingdom on the trail of a crucial investigative lead or of the perfectly picturesque ruined abbey. It was more likely that he was lying dead in a sewer.

If Gough was dead, then Gough had been discovered and investigated and tracked. If Gough had been tracked, then it must be assumed that they were even closer to himself than he had feared. There would be others like the Tiverton dragoon hunting him.

And perhaps hunting Roscarrock.

Garrod, Alleyn, Christiansen and Roscarrock. The Engineer, the Lawyer, the Schoolmaster and the Sailor. Between them, in their characters and talents, they spanned the activities of the organization.

Four dead men against the Comptrollerate-General.

24th July 1805

FIELD REPORT, RECEIVED THE 24TH DAY OF JULY 1805.
(MILITARY DIRECT)

*In barracks on the 22nd of July, a group of soldiers from the West Suffolk
Militia numbering at least ten began by complaining at routine discipline
and so fell to seditious talk. The Colonel a bastard and a tyrant, the other
officers fools and sons of whores, the military system corrupt and vicious.
The punishment handed out to one Watkins, an idler rightly flogged for
serial indiscipline, was represented as arbitrary and cruel. Tubb, Corporal,
wished he could see all the officers roped for flogging. Foley, Private soldier,
a known troublemaker, said the barbarous treatment given to Watkins
and others was the natural product of a false society. That only when
those currently in authority were hanged, every man of them, could a fair
society be created with cheap bread and votes for all men etc. The war an
unnecessary sacrifice of poor men for rich men's profit. The King a diseased
and deranged foreign tyrant. There was no dissent, and much agreement,
expressed at these vile attitudes.*

*The source of this information is of course a soldier himself, but one who
knows his loyalty and his duty. He is, through fear of retribution, adamant that
no action should be taken as a result of his information. But clearly something
will have to be done to stifle the spread of such sentiment, a gross departure
from the decent disciplines of military life, almost certainly amounting to clear
sedition, and trifling close to outright treason.*

[SS AA/6018]

THE STORY OF JAMES PACE/PAICE AND THE INSTRUCTION OF THE WORKING MAN

Aylesbury in the County of Buckinghamshire,
the sign of the King's Head, landlord Peter Pulleyn,
visited the 24th day of July 1805.

[SS T/2108/50]

The King's Head is a frown of dark timbers on Aylesbury's market square. When Jessel and Roscarrock trotted through the dew-cleaned morning into its courtyard, it was in the fourth century of its hospitality. The outside had been recently painted, and the inside too showed prosperity and care. Landlord Pulleyn, stocky and soft-spoken, was hospitable even early in the day.

'The King's roads are a weary place for the traveller,' Jessel said quietly.

The landlord's eyes flicked once around the empty room. 'But the King's roads are safe and free,' he replied. 'God save the King.'

'God save the King.'

The landlord nodded slightly, offered them drinks. They spoke of the weather, which had been mixed. They spoke of farming, which was healthy as far as the weather went, but not the prices. Before entering, Jessel had consulted one of a thin roll of pages that he carried in his coat, and knew something of the Pulleyn family; the Pulleyn family were coming up well. They spoke of trade; trade was fair, so long as the coaches kept coming through. Sometimes the local men had money to drink, sometimes not so much.

'Any trouble?'

'Nothing that beer doesn't cause, and nothing that beer can't cure.'

Roscarrock saw Jessel's restraint, watched him working to match his rhythms to the conversation. He pushed his mind back into the world of winds and tides and endless patience. The threats to English stability were growing and gathering, but they didn't know how they would come and how they might be discovered. For now there was just nervy routine, waiting for some gust of information, an ebbing of conversation that would bring revelation. He wondered at the cavalryman lying dead in a house in Tiverton, a knife wound to his heart.

'What do they talk about these days, the labourers, the apprentices?'

A smile found a well-worn place on the landlord's face. 'Same as they have for five hundred years.'

'Politics?'

A shrug. 'Some. And no, they're not happy about it. But nothing to worry you gentlemen in London. If the King's Ministers could make beer and women a little more free, that would deal with most of it. There's enough work at the moment, and enough food, and we haven't had any bad rounds of sickness lately.'

The landlord paused, and straightened a mug unnecessarily. Jessel, about to speak, saw it and stopped himself and took another mouthful of beer instead.

'You gentlemen come across any James Pace?'

Mild curiosity in the shrugs. No, the gentlemen hadn't.

'Might be up your street. I can't say. Said he'd been a schoolmaster. Got a face for books, if you know what I mean. A few Monday nights now he's been in my back room with some of the young men. I asked one of them what they was up to. The youngster said he was educating himself. I said I hoped that didn't mean politics. He said no, he was improving his mind with this Pace. He said it was the instruction of the working man. That was the exact phrase, sir, and I heard one of the others use it as well.'

'But you don't know what they talk about.'

'Not really. Sometimes seems to be he's just helping them with their letters, sometimes it sounds like things are a bit livelier.'

They took a description, dates, and said they'd look into it. Jessel paid for their drinks generously.

GREAT ATLANTIC BATTLE

ADMIRAL CALDER DEFIES LARGER FLEET

TWO SPANISH PRIZES TAKEN

We learn in letters lately received from Vice-Admiral Robert Calder of a recent engagement in the Atlantic hard by Cape Finisterre, in which fifteen of our ships fought a long and bitter action against twenty French and Spanish hulls. Admiral Calder, in HMS *Prince of Wales*, ninety-eight guns, Capt. W. Cumming commanding, writes of a protracted and difficult chase through heavy fog, and great skill and heroism from the British crews in the face of a determined and more numerous enemy. It is not to be doubted that our fleet carried the day, and the *San Rafael*, eighty guns, and *Firme*, seventy-four guns, are now in our hands, and other French and Spanish vessels severely damaged. HMS *Windsor Castle*, Capt. C. Boyles, ninety-eight guns, and HMS *Malta*, Capt. E. Buller, eighty guns, received heavy treatment in the course of their endeavours, but Admiral Calder saw them escorted to safety.

The fleets came within sight of each other before noon, but it was not until five of the afternoon that action was joined, Admiral

Calder directing the attack despite the greater numbers of the foe. Heavy exchange of fire continued until eight or nine in the evening, when darkness prevented further action. On the following morning, the French and Spanish ships withdrew to Spain, Admiral Villeneuve declining the chance to come once again to close quarters despite a favourable wind. As well as the loss of two ships of the line to our fleet, and the most severe damage and loss of life in the rest of his ships, Admiral Villeneuve also suffered a great many men taken prisoner. Our losses were much lighter, only forty-one of our gallant sailors losing their lives in the combat.

The withdrawal of the enemy fleet to the south and east must be assumed to have prevented for the moment their forming a combination with other French detachments and covering an attempt on our shores. It is to be regretted nonetheless that greater damage was not inflicted on this, the largest enemy fleet. Vice-Admiral Nelson is not yet returned from the Indies, and Napoleon continues to command many more ships of the line in French and Spanish ports than we can oppose against him, and any successful combination between them must bring severe peril to our shores.

[THE LONDON EVENING POST, 24TH JULY 1805]

———◆———

PROCEEDINGS OF THE ADMIRALTY BOARD,
FIRST LORD, ADMIRAL LORD BARHAM, PRESIDING,
THE 24TH DAY OF JULY 1805

[PROCEEDINGS OF THE ADMIRALTY BOARD, VOLUME XXIV]

'You've seen the news-sheets, of course, My Lord.'

'Where else would I discover the activities of my own navy?'

'The action off Finisterre may have soothed the public mood a little.'

'They'll be panicking again by noon.'

The First Lord, Admiral J. Gambier, Admiral Lord H. Bellamy and Sir E. Nepean being present, the Board convened at eleven of the clock.

Adm. Gambier described the general movements of our fleets: Adm. Lord Keith blockading off the Netherlands; Adm. Cornwallis patrolling the entrance to the English Channel; Adm. Cotton blockading Brest; Rear-Adm. Orde blockading off Cadiz.

Adm. Gambier read the despatch from Adm. R. Calder, at sea.

'My Lord, I have the honour to rep—'

'Spare us, would you, Gambier? Gentlemen, is there any dissenting opinion to the view that Calder flunked it?'

'Two—'

'Your loyalty is noted, Gambier, but we are obliged to face the facts. For the first time this year – in a number of years – we had the chance of decisive action against a significant portion of Napoleon's navy. Two rotten dago ships pinched and two of ours saved ain't going to stop an invasion, not by a distance.'

Their Lordships approved formal thanks to Adm. Calder, and urgent messages to Adm. H. Nelson.

'Other business. The wretched American, Fulton, is still at us to try his torpedo mines.'

'I'm cautious, My Lord.'

'I'm downright leery, Gambier! But the damned fellow hooked Stanhope when Stanhope was in Holland, and now he has Pitt himself itching to see him blow things up.'

'His true loyalty is to the old colonies, My Lord. Then he was in France, as you know. He trialled a secret underwater ship for the French. They employed him for some years, and I cannot say that they do not employ him still. His commitment to this country extends no further than his hand in our purses.'

'All very well, Bellamy, but that's an even stronger reason why we need to clasp him to ourselves now so he don't go back again, I suppose.'

'We have him under protection, of course, My Lord. If the French cannot have him, they may try to ensure that no one can.'

'We're stuck with the fellow, gentlemen, for now. I wouldn't trust him with the spoons, let alone all the powder he asks. But we must let him play with his explosions, and see if he doesn't do himself a mischief. If he starts drifting back to France we may have to end his wanderings permanently.'

Their Lordships approved the payment of expenses to Mr Robert Fulton. Their Lordships approved regular expenditures to the pay account, to the shipyard account, to repair and maintenance of Admiralty property, and to Scrutiny and Survey.

There being no further formal business, the Secretaries withdrew.

'What now, Bellamy?'

'My Lord, from Admiral Calder's report, Villeneuve was withdrawing towards Spain. Knowing the man, he will take refuge there for the moment and repair and restock his ships after his months in the Atlantic and this engagement. But Napoleon will have him out again as soon as he can. I fear we are no further forwards. Meanwhile, My Lord, we have unconfirmed news that Admiral Allemand has escaped Rochefort and is loose at sea.'

'How many?'

'Four ship of the line, and lesser vessels.'

'Damnit. Four more we've lost trace of? And no word of your missing French fleet?'

'None. We are seeking every possible source of information in Paris.'

'Hugo, can't you manage a distraction of some kind? Make Napoleon look elsewhere?'

'The Royalists in France won't rise again, George, not after last time. That horse is blown. The one man who could inspire real unrest is an old Royalist General – Metz. He'd stir them. But no one's even sure he's alive anymore; if he is, he's in hiding, and we can't contact him. In any case, the money he'd need to attract and sustain enough followers would be astronomical. The gold that this Board prudently votes to Scrutiny and Survey will keep the Royalist networks alive in France. If we use it shrewdly, we can spread a little dissent. But no amount of gold can buy a victory at sea.'

'You are no consolation, Bellamy. Gentlemen, our own ships are more scattered than before; the French fleets are all returned to Europe, and there are now two that we cannot easily locate. We chased a fleet to the Indies and it comes back hardly scratched, and we're still waiting for Nelson to catch up. The danger of invasion is at least as great as before. Damn Calder!'

———— ◆ ————

CONVERSATIONS OF ADMIRAL P. C. J. B. S. DE VILLENEUVE,
RECORDED 1ST DAY OF DECEMBER 1805

Poor Calder. You English can afford to be careless with your heroes, perhaps. As Voltaire said of that Admiral you shot, whenever it was. I suppose that if you have a Collingwood and you have a Nelson, you may treat your Calders pretty casual, isn't it so? He was a little cautious, I grant you. But then, who would not have been, with the fog on that wretched day, and your English Channel open behind him? Me, I would have done as Calder did. He bought you days, and days at this time were priceless, is that not so?

[SS G/1130/10]

FIELD REPORT, TAKEN THE 24TH DAY OF JULY 1805.

4PK. Credit –. Names and violent intent (details attached)

[SS X/27/91]

Jessel and Roscarrock reached Hackney with the falling sun, sore and silent on their sluggish horses. Hackney had an inn, the Dolphin, and the Dolphin had a comfortable corner by the fire, and the two men looked hungrily at the large mugs of beer that loomed over them in the landlord's fists and then settled on the table.

The landlord turned away, and as they instinctively followed the movement they discovered that a pale man had been standing close behind him and was now scanning them with quick, careful eyes. The eyes snapped back to Jessel, and nodded impatiently towards Roscarrock.

'This is Mr... Grey, Phil,' Jessel said in answer. 'Professional acquaintance.'

'He don't look like a Mr Grey.' Again, to Roscarrock: 'You don't look like a Mr Grey.'

'You don't look like someone who needs to know,' Roscarrock said politely.

That got a yellow grin in the white face, but still Phil floated, looking another question. Jessel lifted his left hand off the table for a moment, revealing a stack of four coins.

Another grin, and now Phil sat, pulling a stool against the wall so that he could watch movement in the room but have his face shadowed by the mantelpiece. 'That's the stuff, Mr Albert. Not sure that's enough though, is it?'

'I haven't heard enough, Phil. Landlord!'

Another drink arrived, and Phil held it two-handed in front of his mouth, taking it regularly with measured cat-sips.

'You hear of a tailor, Phil?'

'I heard of—'

'Radical man, traveller.'

The eyes were grey and constantly mobile. A check of the two faces watching him. 'I'm pretty sure I have.'

'And I'm pretty sure you haven't. I'll tell you when I want something made up, Phil. Now isn't when.'

'All right. I'll keep an eye. Travelling tailor, eh?'

Jessel nodded. 'Reformer. Man with a mission. Perhaps coming your way. Might try to talk to some of your friends.'

'I don't got no friends, Mr Albert, you know that. No friends, Mr Grey, that's me.' He offered the fact with quiet professional pride.

'I find that very hard to believe,' Roscarrock said, and Phil scanned his neutral face. 'Mr Albert said I'd learn from you about the reforming men hereabout.'

Phil's mouth shaped for another bit of patter, but his patrolling eyes found something in Roscarrock's glance and he shifted suddenly into an unfamiliar earnestness. The chancer had disappeared, and he was the methodical sipper of beer again.

'To them, I'm a carpenter from south of London, see? Only I lost my trade. There's a little group of us meets now. Craftsmen, like me. Some young men, some family men. New man's become more frequent, Mr

Albert; Penny, Peter Penny.' Jessel absorbed the name. 'We drinks a little, and we talks a little. Political discussion, only none of us really knows enough to talk proper politics, so it's just Napoleon this and prices that. We are generally for political reform and negotiated peace. That Ted Wass, Mr Albert, he says he wants to march on Whitehall and force the Cabinet to sign for new rights. The smith, he says he's got some pikes stored, and Wass says maybe they could get some muskets off militiamen they know or get the militiamen with them. But Fenner, the weaver, this is all a bit strong for him. He says he wants a grand agreement of all groups like ours and he doesn't want no violence.'

'How many Wasses, how many Fenners?' Roscarrock asked.

A nod at the question; a sip. 'Mostly Fenners. Family men. Family men enough to care, but too much to be desperate.'

He shifted the beer mug to the side of his mouth, and his glance held on Jessel. 'Want I should stir 'em up a bit, Mr Albert? See what they're really made of?' There was a flash of the chancer again. 'Done some lovely burnings in the old days, Mr Grey. Reformers' houses, that sort of thing. Times change, eh?'

Jessel ran a hand through his blond hair, then shook his head decisively. 'Doesn't seem you'd make much of them, Phil. But watch them, you hear? Especially your friend with the pikes.'

Glancing at the room, he pushed the four coins across the table. Phil's beer mug dropped in his hands and he watched the coins carefully. Another four joined them. He looked up.

'Honest, Mr Albert, I need more. Not so much the risks, though they is as always considerable, but family stuff.'

Jessel's pale eyes gazed into him. Then he pulled a further two coins out. They watched Phil walk silently from the inn, head down. 'Even the Government spies are starving,' Jessel muttered.

25th July 1805

It was four in the morning, it was cold, the mist had turned to drizzle, and the wind was blowing onto the French coast. For the First Lieutenant of HMS *Amethyst*, bucking in the grey swell just a mile from that coast, everything was conspiring to ensure his maximum discomfort. Independence of command, even for the length of a watch during months of miserable blockade duty, was the proving ground of the young officer, the opportunity to show competence and perhaps excellence. It was also the opportunity to put the whole package onto a French reef. Captains thrown from their cots into the sea and then captured by the French did not produce favourable reports on the First Lieutenants who had allowed it to happen.

For the thousandth time on this god-awful watch he checked the sails, frowning up into the drizzle with arm held over stinging forehead, and then the coast, cold telescope eye chilling his own.

'Ketch on the port bow, sir!' The shout came frail through the wind and the drizzle. 'Making for the French coast!'

'What flag?' he called back into the grey morning.

'No flag, sir!'

'None?' Most of the blockading squadron was held well out to sea, close enough to bring the French to action should they attempt to break out but far enough to limit the strain on the seamanship of exhausted crews. Only individual ships like the *Amethyst* were left to hug the coast, watching and hoping for the first sign of a French attempt to break the drenched stalemate, and trying not to run aground.

'He's just run one up, sir. Don't recognize it, sir.'

'Well check it, man!' An unknown ship sneaking into the coast in the small hours of the morning meant smuggling. Smuggling was supposed to be bad for the British economy in some way, but it didn't feel like a way that would justify rousing the cold and grumpy frigate to action before dawn.

A Midshipman was beside him now with an open ledger, thin and weathered. The signal book was properly for officers only, and the freezing sixteen-year-old held it with reverence in his white fists. 'It's one of ours, sir, but I've never seen it before. It means Admiralty business.' The pale open face looked up at the First Lieutenant. 'What does that mean, sir?'

The First Lieutenant was following the heaving and plunging of the ketch as she battered her way towards the grey outline of France. 'It means you don't want to know, Mr Ellis. It means forget you saw it.' The boy looked over at the ship and back at the First Lieutenant with heightened awe. 'Don't worry, Mr Ellis. Probably someone in the Admiralty fancied a French tart for a change. Let it go.'

The Midshipman smiled gravely at the adult joke, then hurried away to pass the order to maintain course.

The First Lieutenant raised his telescope. *Not hardly*, he thought. An unflagged ship sneaking into the coast in the small hours of the morning under an Admiralty flag – which had now vanished, he noted – meant intelligence work. It meant some poor sod splashing ashore with a sack of gold and a prayer and not much else, hoping like hell that whatever recognition signal they'd glimpsed from the shore came from a Royalist, and not from a Royalist with a sentry's musket in his ear.

There was a solitary figure in the bow of the ketch, cloaked and hooded and watching the approaching coast. *Well might they*, the First Lieutenant thought from an HMS *Amethyst* that in this cold and lonely dawn suddenly seemed a more comfortable place in which to pass a morning and a war. In the course of the months on blockade he'd seen a few such ships pass in the shadowed hours between day and night, discussed them casually and quietly with the Captain when they were alone. A world with none of the distinctions of uniform and discipline, none of the clarity of combat. A world where death was nasty and alone and forgotten. A world where life depended on a ketch making another pinpoint and unseen landing on the grim French coast, and on the loyalty of a chain of people who were already betraying a whole country and could hardly be expected to care much for one foreign spy.

A momentary change in the wind pulled the hood back from the figure in the ketch, and the First Lieutenant glimpsed the head beneath for the instant before the hood was snatched up again. The hair was longer and fuller than... Good God!

———

ROYSTON IN THE COUNTIES OF CAMBRIDGESHIRE
AND HERTFORDSHIRE,
MAGISTRATE SIR MATTHEW CRIPPS,
VISITED THE 25TH DAY OF JULY 1805.

Nil

[SS J/1144/17]

'I'm glad to see you, gentlemen. Glad.'

A frail, earnest young man, barely out of his twenties. A son brought early into his inheritance, Roscarrock decided, presumably by disease. Genteel poverty, described in the rotting windows, the cracked glasses, and the solitary servant who fulfilled all functions in the house. Drinks, the offer of food, lodging, thrust at them along with the pale face of their host, perched on the edge of his plain oak chair.

'Nothing unusual, Sir Matthew, just a passing—'

'I've despatched the routine list on the petty sessions to you. I – I hope there's been no difficulty with the mail coach.'

'I'm sure—'

'Frankly, gentlemen, I'm worried.' The young pale face intense, the voice straining towards the businesslike. 'These people... these people are desperate. Their homes are – are terrible places. And the food they eat, well – there's nothing, there are people who are starving, actually starving.'

Roscarrock watched with something like pity. This young man had had to grow up fast, into a world he'd never dreamt of, only yards from his door.

'Some of them who come up before me for seditious comments are just drunks, or malcontents. But with some, there's... there's a hatred... or, or a despair that's even worse. We had bad trouble five weeks ago, with Jenkins, one of the bigger farmers. A travelling pamphleteer, one of these... I don't know – perhaps a man of ideals or just a troublemaker – anyway, over a few evenings in the inn he stirred up some of Jenkins's men, and then the men started making demands, and refusing to work, and there were... threats, quiet threats. Jenkins had to whip one man, and he chased the troublemaker out of the area himself, and then some of his animals started being harmed.' Sir Matthew shook his head rapidly, a little bird's movement. 'There's no structure any—'

'I don't think you sent us the name of the pamphleteer, Sir Matthew.'

'We never found it. You got what description we could manage.'

Polite thanks and goodbyes. 'Gentlemen,' Sir Matthew said fraily on the threshold, 'Gentlemen, I hope what I'm doing is useful.' Polite thanks. 'It would mean so much if my work was being... recognized – in London. One wants to – to get on, you know.'

Outside, Jessel shook his head.

'I don't want to sound rude about my new employer,' Roscarrock said, 'but... these people: are they the extent of it?'

'Disappointed?' Jessel closed the gate behind them, and squatted down against a young oak. Behind him was the London road that so haunted Sir Matthew Cripps, and beyond it the fields sloped up towards a line of woodland on the crest. Jessel scratched the back of his neck against the tree with great concentration, then settled back on his haunches.

'People like that one – magistrates, parsons – they're what you might call the foot soldiers. They're everywhere, we don't have to pay them particularly, it's part of their job in any case to keep an eye on people. They give us a lot of the background information – those lists, say. Nothing fancy, but it all builds up, and just occasionally you get a diamond. Mostly it gives us the records to check against. That schoolmaster the other Magistrate told us about, for example: Pace.'

'The education of the working man?'

'Him. I checked, and we've come across him before – Magistrate's records, you see? He's turned up in a few other places, had a night or two in gaol when the inspiration got a bit carried away.'

'But we're not worried about him.'

The angles of Jessel's face wrinkled up. 'He doesn't smell like a problem. When Napoleon makes him king of liberated England, you can tell me I'm wrong. But he's all ideas and no action. A schoolmaster, like my father.' He flicked a glance of concern at the unfamiliar confidence. 'A schoolmaster who got sick and couldn't be a schoolmaster anymore. He does more begging than sedition.'

Roscarrock had found an oak of his own, and settled down against bark and grass. 'Sympathy for your father?'

Jessel shook his head in slow and emphatic relish. 'I hated him. No man ever had a fouler son. But no, the real troublemakers don't hold open meetings in public bars on main roads. And we won't find them by talking to innocent innkeepers and panicked magistrates.'

'Who, then?'

'Most likely one of Kinnaird's specials, nothing less.'

—◆—

The difference between a hunted fugitive and a corpse in a gibbet is a good pair of ears, and James Fannion had survived long enough to trust his ears before his brain. There'd be time enough for thinking in the grave.

As he stretched on the mattress in the attic, willing the passage of another empty morning, his ears heard knocking at the door far below. It was too trivial for his brain even to process, but the sound alone had him on his feet.

His brain started to recall where the shopkeeper and his wife would be, and strayed into trying to remember the location of the shop and whether lonely, unpassioned Rachel had said she was going to the market today. His ears heard the voices down in the hall, and that took him through the door of the attic room to the top of the stairs.

Voices. One voice; loud, unconversational. Orders.

Then boots in the house, several pairs. Soldiers.

Brain still back in the attic, Fannion was down the steep ladder-staircase three at a time, hands burning on the timber rails and feet dancing and stumbling and resounding through the house. The difference between a hunted fugitive and a corpse in a gibbet is an eye for an exit, and Fannion's exit depended on him getting down to the middle floor of the house before the militia got up to it. Somewhere his brain was wondering about silence, and concealment, while his feet kicked him forwards off the boards and sent him swerving and bumping to the top of the main stairs. Shouts from below, and down he plunged, grabbing at the banister post and swinging himself round to the second half of the flight. Down faster than he could control, staggering forwards into a table, the table rocking and settling, pushing it aside and hurling himself along the passage, pictures clattering from the wall as he lurched past. There was red movement suddenly in his eyes, a uniform hurrying up from the floor below, a staggered, stupid face and a slow fumbling at the musket, and as the soldier reached the landing Fannion threw himself into him; shoulder and arm sent the man back against the wall and collapsing down the stairs, there was a flash and a crack of noise as the musket went off as he fell, and Fannion was still driving himself down the corridor like an elephant on fire. Behind him shouts and boots, always shouts and boots, as long as he could remember it had been shouts and boots, and he threw his whole weight against the door ahead and erupted into the bedroom, head and arms and knees ringing with bruises. One leap took him onto the bed, another took him off it against the window; he threw up the sash, kicked one leg through into the air, ducked his head under and out into the sudden glare of daylight, then grabbed the sill and swung himself down. There was an instant of lurching doubt in his gut, and he let go.

The flat roof below was a drop of three feet – he knew it, he'd checked it – and he felt nothing in his feet and legs as he landed, staggered, and scrambled towards the low parapet. There was supposed to be a pipe – he'd seen a pipe – there it was – and again he swung over the edge; feet scraped for purchase between pipe and wall, hands flapped for a hold at the top. The alley was only four or five feet below him, and he was down in a second of rust-raw hands and feet slipping on the rough stone. On his feet again, back slumped against the wall, gasping for breath and heart hammering: left or right? Move! Down the alley, pressed against the wall for an extra second of invisibility from the men following him onto the roof, reining his legs into a walk and his gasping into regular breathing. Look for the crowd; disappear.

'Stop there!'

For a stupid second he thought the voice came from the pursuit behind him, and not from the soldier who'd just stepped into the end of the alley with musket held out towards him. An older man – not a new recruit – a worn red face and heavy sideburns and enough gravity to give a frail edge of confidence to his apprehension.

'Quickly, man! Come with me! We've got him!' Fannion was throwing out words in desperation; he had to close the distance to that musket, had to get inside the barrel and the bayonet.

'But – but you was off the roof! I heard you!'

'Of course I was! God's sake, man, come on!' Hurrying past the hesitant soldier, left arm brushing the musket vertical and reaching to catch the man encouragingly on the shoulder, to turn him, and right hand into pocket.

'But – wait—' and Fannion grabbed the soldier by the collar and drove his knife up into the chest.

He held there for an instant, two men and a musket in an uncomfortable embrace, feeling the man's blood hot on his hand, the man's groin against his taut thigh. 'There we go. That's it, mate,' he said softly. The big white eyes were shocked, and strangely young again, and then they died.

Fannion eased the body to the ground, remembered the pursuit, looked back up the alley and heard the sound of voices on the low roof, saw bayonets and the edges of uniforms moving to the parapet. How many sentries had they posted? He wiped his shaking hand on the dead man's shirt, stood, and hurried on.

Twenty soldierless seconds later he was in the main street, and into the crowd. He matched pace and direction with the person nearest him, tried to lift his head so as not to seem hunted, tried not to catch eyes so as not to draw attention to however he looked.

Damn the fucking English. Damn the fucking English and their fucking tame Irish slaves. Damn the whole fucking world of shouts and boots and dead men. Now he'd see them burn.

The smell changed. The current of people's movement had changed too. Fannion looked around him. He was in a marketplace, and stood still for a moment among the swirling shoppers to find his bearings.

Christ's sake, it was her! That bunched red hair high off the neck, the full breasts he'd watched over the table for a week, Rachel was here, a conventional shopkeeper's wife doing her conventional shopping. His brain urged anonymity and movement. There'd be soldiers flooding into the square in a second; they could have it surrounded by now.

Blood in his cheeks, Fannion took three strides to the dairy stall, put one hand on her shoulder and another around the curve of her jaw and kissed her full on the lips before she could react.

'When you want to join the rebellion again,' he said softly, 'you come and find me.' Then he turned and weaved his way back into the mob.

———

The audience of leaves whispered around them. Still settled against his tree trunk, Jessel took a lump of bread from his pocket and began to chew at it with slow attention, moving it to the side of his mouth to emphasize a word. 'When the American colonies finally went their own way – and there are some pretty hair-raising stories about what this organization was up to – but when it was all lost in '83, some people high up in Government found it easy to blame the Comptrollerate-General. Maybe if people had paid more attention in the sixties it might have been different, but who knows? Same with the Paris Revolution: some people found it convenient to say the Comptrollerate-General should have done more – though what we could have known, or what anyone could have done if we had known it, probably don't signify. Rough time for the organization, anyway.' He stretched his legs out, and crossed them. 'Then, couple of years back, just before I got involved, seems there was a very strange time indeed. A bad time, a time no one talks about, a time no one – even Lord Hugo, who's quite new – really knows about.'

'How is that possible?'

'We're not like a bank or a regiment, Tom. The Comptrollerate-General for Scrutiny and Survey doesn't have statutes and official meetings and membership lists and rules and procedures. To the population, we do not exist. A very few people in the Admiralty and the Government know of the organization and what it does. Some officials have heard of it, but we let them assume what they want to assume about a department with a dull name like ours. Half the people who do work for us – those Magistrates, say – will never hear the name of Scrutiny and Survey. Ships carry our messages and our agents and our gold, and do not realize it. Even me or you, we'll never know more than a handful of other people who know.

The Comptrollerate-General is a chain of relationships, a constant series of conversations, a few memories.'

Roscarrock nodded. 'Good security. Something goes wrong, the effect is smaller.'

'Exactly. A couple of years back, something did go wrong. Chiefs changed over quickly – a talk of corruption – maybe worse. Connections broke down at the top, the chain fell apart lower down. Bits of the organization must have just... drifted away. Contact stopped, time passed, and eventually the Comptrollerate-General was just a couple of conversations you'd once had with a stranger from London, if you even knew that at the time.' He nodded in thought. 'Good security, like you say. But chaos at just the wrong time. When the war resumed in '03, a few in the Government recognized it was time to get a grip. Lord Hugo was one: clear head, clean hands, at the right time. Anyway, the way he tells it, taking over was like finding the house had been burgled in the night. Barely anything left. The one thing still standing, the one thing functioning, the one thing holding Scrutiny and Survey together, was a puritanical Scotsman.'

'Kinnaird.'

'Kinnaird. And sometimes Lord Hugo makes it sound like Kinnaird was the mangy rat in the corner of the burgled house eating the last of the cheese.'

'Who is Kinnaird?'

'Who knows? You've met him – what – once?' Roscarrock shrugged non-committally. 'You know more than most of us. He's part-businessman, part-politician. He's no idealist, but he's supposed to be ruthless. Important thing is – and Lord Hugo'll say this, even though he thinks Kinnaird's a maniac – he's a one hundred per cent pure gold genius at intelligence work. For a time he was pretty much running the Comptrollerate-General, and if there's anything that's working today, the chances are he set it up. Half the procedures were devised by him. The fleet of little ships that run errands into France for us – most of them smugglers and cut-throats – that was his idea. And then there's his network.'

'His?'

'Doesn't feel like it's ours. A small network of agents across Britain, identified and developed by him. Not fieldsmen like us, but men who observe; men who explore; men who reflect; men who will stay silent until you find them and ask them for their insight. He reaches into France, as well. I know even less about that, but the whispers make it a legend. The network *de la fleur*.'

'The flower?'

Jessel shrugged. 'People recruited by Kinnaird or under his direction, overlapping with the Royalist underground led by an old general called Metz. He's a legend, too – or perhaps a myth. Metz's influence reaches across northern France, they say; sympathizers everywhere. All sounds a bit optimistic to me, but it's not my area. Anyway: that's Kinnaird's network.'

'And why aren't we talking to them now?'

Jessel pulled his legs up to his body, and leant forwards. 'Because we don't know who they are, not more than a few.'

'You don't know? Lord Hugo – he must know.'

'No lists, Tom, no regimental muster on the common. We know some because they're open in the reports they send. Some report anonymously. Some don't report directly and we've little chance of finding them. And here's the thing' – he grinned wildly – 'Kinnaird's not telling.'

'He's that secretive?'

A shrug. 'You've met him, and if he picked you you must be closer to his thinking than most of the rest of us. He's secretive, he's... obsessive, he treats his plots and his arrangements like a new religion.'

Roscarrock shook his head. 'The Admiral must love this. Can't he—'

'Order Kinnaird to co-operate?'

'I suppose not.'

'They rarely meet, and they're not exactly similar people. Kinnaird disappears for days, then pops up with a bit of insight, then wanders off again. If Lord Hugo had anything else to build his organization on, he'd have pushed the old man into the river long ago, just to be free of the irritation.'

'So what's Sir Keith doing now?'

'Who knows? Probably the same as us, and he'll come and give us the answer when the mood takes him. But until he's got something useful, he'll say nothing. He won't be sharing the names of any of his agents, and those we know about are reluctant to talk to anyone except him.'

Jessel picked up a pebble, tossed it once in his hand, then took it between thumb and forefinger and threw it slowly and precisely at Roscarrock's boot. 'And that, Roscarrock, is why Lord Hugo Bellamy is so interested in you.'

The whole affair was an irritation that he could ill afford, but the Colonel of Militia in Tiverton accepted grudgingly that he couldn't simply throw the murdered dragoon into a grave pit and forget about him, tempting though that was. A Lieutenant was given the order to make the necessary enquiries of the nearby regiments, and the clear impression that the Colonel wished nothing more to do with the matter. The Colonel dismissed the young officer, made a sudden scowl of annoyance into his empty office as he wondered again why it wasn't the Magistrate who was making an investigation of this kind, and tried to think of lunch.

He was allowed three days of peace, the Lieutenant having absorbed the point that his Colonel did not see the business as a priority. But the young man had become interested in his mission, and willing to overcome the Colonel's irritation when he brought it back to him. No one claimed the dragoon. No one knew him. He was not a local man nor from a unit stationed locally. He had no kind of identification in his pockets. No explanation could be found for how he came to be in the Magistrate's house, and how he came to be stabbed to death there.

The Colonel, with a pleasing rush of clarity, realized that he could now at last get rid of the problem. He wrote a short description of the affair and ordered it sent to London – they could hunt the murderer if they chose – to be followed more slowly by the coffin of the dead man.

26th July 1805

The mist swelled fat and heavy out of the English Channel, and bumped dully against the ancient Dorset cliffs. None of the inhabitants of the village of Burton Bradstock, a few thatched cottages hiding behind the cliffs, had cause to scramble down to the beach so early. But once they did so – once the mist had rolled back from the long shingle sweep of the Chesil Beach – they would find that the night sea had cast up a new offering. From a distance it looked like a piece of driftwood; then perhaps a low rock; nearer still, and the first beachcomber would wonder at some unknown sea creature floundering stupidly in the shallows.

Close to, this scrap of rubbish from the sea was unmistakeably a man – a man long drowned, skin white, clothes saturated and rank. The tide nudged and rummaged at the corpse, washing the hem of a coat, strands of hair and a forgotten hand back and forth with gentle indifference. Rings had been pulled from fingers before the body entered the water, and the fine shirt that would have drawn attention on a deck now floated sour and sogging. The gulls circled overhead, bossy shrieks disguising their wariness of the puffy plaster face.

Another of the Comptrollerate-General's ships – that informal collection of irregular vessels devised by Sir Keith Kinnaird – would need a new captain.

MONSIEUR THE MINISTER OF POLICE MEETS WITH GABIN,
INSPECTOR OF POLICE,
THE 26TH DAY OF JULY 1805

M. Fouché: I am not in the habit of dealing directly with Inspectors.

M. Gabin: I am honoured, Minister.

M. Fouché: I have formed an assessment of you from what I have read and what I have heard. Your actions are swift, effective, and without scruple. Your reputation is impressive.

M. Gabin: The Minister is too kind.

M. Fouché: I have neither time nor inclination for receiving or giving flattery. The Revolution and the rise of the Emperor have brought a world where a man rises on his merits. I welcome that. A man also falls on his merits.

M. Gabin: I understand.

M. Fouché: As of this moment, you work directly to me, and report directly to me. If you have any doubt or question about that arrangement, speak now.

M. Gabin: None, Minister.

M. Fouché: Just as your work will be outside the normal arrangements, so will any reward for success and any punishment for failure.

M. Gabin: I understand, Minister.

M. Fouché: Be useful to me, and you make your career in a morning. Fail me, and you return to your Brittany pigsty. Betray a word of this or any future conversation and you will be at the bottom of the Seine within the hour.

M. Gabin: A man who understands loyalty respects a chief who understands loyalty.

M. Fouché: We understand each other. The Emperor desires England. It is his dearest wish, and it is therefore the duty of every Frenchman to advance it. It is obstructed by two things, the only solid parts of the whole rotten apparatus of British Government: the Comptrollerate-General for Scrutiny and Survey, and the Royal Navy. I have a scheme that will neutralize both. You will be my sole agent in executing the French portion of that coup, and you will thereby assist me to deliver England to the Emperor. You will have absolute authority to use the forces of the police in my name, and you will be able to command the assistance of the military on the same basis. This letter, and my personal seal, will open all doors in France.

M. Gabin: The Minister honours me with the task. I offer my life to it.

M. Fouché: Let us hope that is not necessary. Within weeks, London will be paralyzed by a violent outrage; shortly afterwards, the Royal Navy will be removed from the Emperor's path. The collapse of the Comptrollerate-General for Scrutiny and Survey will be part of this.

M. Gabin: I have not heard of this Comptrollerate-General.

M. Fouché: Of course not. With the exception of a few men working for me, any Frenchman who knows it is by definition a traitor. This organization is responsible for all that is truly secret in England, and all that is truly dangerous in France. It is filled by officers of unusual ability, and led by a man of remarkable vision and shrewdness. Our first step in defeating it will be not underestimating it. While my plan is brought to completion, by myself in concert with our friends in England and Ireland, you have one immediate task. It is of the utmost secrecy and importance.

M. Gabin: I trust the Minister not to need a repetition of my commitment.

M. Fouché: Quite so. It has come to my attention, with no
possibility of doubt, that there is a spy in the
immediate vicinity of the Minister for the Navy – or
perhaps even myself. You may take this as an example
of the reach of the Comptrollerate-General for
Scrutiny and Survey. I expect to know more very soon.
Even if it should be Minister Decrès himself, you will
begin now to find this person, to discover everything
they know, and to deliver them to me for punishment.

[SS F/109/77]

The records show that Henry Forster, of Lewes in the County of Sussex,
entered Corpus Christi College, in Oxford University, in 1795. The
records show solid academic achievement, at a time when the majority
of his fellow students used that ancient institution as an architecturally
striking drinking club and made no pretence at scholarship whatsoever.
Henry Forster was reading for the Church, and the records show that he
graduated as a Doctor of Divinity in 1799.

The records do not show Henry Forster's frustration at the prevailing
attitudes of his fellows. They do not show his growing interest in natural
philosophy. They do not show – although some indiscreet individuals could
tell the story – a highly unfortunate dispute with the Bishop of Oxford over
certain points of theology and science. The records do not show doubt, and
disappointment, and drifting ambition, and crises of faith uncovered in the
bottom of a tankard and the glimpse of a woman's shoulder across a sweating
tavern.

Other records show the death of Henry Forster's father, and the
inheritance by Henry's elder brother of the family property in Lewes. They
do not show Henry's previous estrangement from his father, nor the long-
standing mutual indifference of the brothers.

Further records show Henry Forster's assumption of the role of vicar in the parish of All Saints, Oakham, in the County of Rutland, in 1800. Those records do not show, nor need they, how disappointing an appointment this might have seemed to those who had held such hopes of the promising young scholar when he went up to the university five years before.

Henry Forster's name does appear on another record, not publicly available. It is dated October 1802. It gives Henry Forster's name – unusually, since shortly afterwards names began to be replaced with cipher marks in this series of records – his position and his background.

HENRY FORSTER, VICAR OF ALL SAINTS, OAKHAM IN THE COUNTY OF RUTLAND.

Family alienation; professional disappointment; philosophical doubt. Self-knowledge. Credit ++. KK

[SS K/A/50]

No record, not even that long-buried page, can show the autumn night in 1802, the rattle at the door biting sharp through the gusting wind, the gaunt older man on the threshold, the offer of hospitality, the conversation at first polite, then more intelligent and intellectual, the mutual probing and the earnest disputes. No record can capture an exchange that continued through a whole night, and the relationship that developed.

OAKHAM IN THE COUNTY OF RUTLAND, VICAR THE REVD HENRY FORSTER, VISITED THE 26TH DAY OF JULY 1805.

A regular gathering of thinking men. Possible knowledge of tailor. More to follow

[SS K/50/43]

The daylight caught the Vicar's spectacles, and Roscarrock was examined by two shimmering white discs. They were level with his own eyes, and flashed into his face as the two men stood silent in the doorway each waiting for the other to speak. Then the beams dropped to scrutinize his clothes, and the dark eyes behind them were momentarily visible.

The Vicar frowned in happy curiosity, and his mouth half-opened as if he was trying a taste on his tongue. Decided, he said with satisfaction, 'You're from Kinnaird.'

Not how it was supposed to begin. 'I'm – The King's roads are a weary place for the traveller.'

'Come in! Yes, they must be. Have you come directly from—' The Reverend Forster was leading the way in, then turned back to where Roscarrock still stood on the threshold. 'I'm sorry. Mischievous of me. I'm supposed to say something in return there, aren't I? Sir Keith is such a brute about these procedures, and one of my little pleasures in life is not playing his game.'

Roscarrock smiled and stepped onto the flagstones of the hall. 'I'm sure who you are, Reverend. Are you sure who I am?'

The Vicar grinned at him, clapped him on the shoulder and closed the front door. 'There's a type. A certain... quality of silence.' He led the way into a parlour, established Roscarrock in a chair after proper introductions, and went to get drinks. Roscarrock looked around at the oak and leather furniture, the books, the handsome chess set, the few pieces of silver. It was more a man's space than it was a clergyman's. Nothing explicitly religious, and certainly nothing feminine. He hadn't gathered before whether the Vicar was married, but knew now.

'Wine for you, water for me. I assume this is a business visit.' The Vicar sat opposite him.

'If it becomes social, I'm sure you know someone to manage the necessary conversion.'

The Vicar chuckled politely, and pulled off his spectacles. He was younger than Roscarrock had first guessed – about his own age, and with the colour and vitality of an outdoor life. 'I say,' he began with sudden earnestness, 'Sir Keith's in health, is he?' He seemed momentarily more nervous.

'So far as I know.'

'He wouldn't tell you if he wasn't.' Forster had relaxed again. 'Probably wouldn't tell himself. His body will decide that it's a secret his brain need not know about. Have you seen him recently?'

'A week or two back.'

'And no doubt he's off on his travels, somewhere between Manchester and the moon, and hasn't told anyone where he's going. Tell me' – he leant forwards – 'did he... choose you himself?'

Roscarrock hesitated. 'Yes – like you.'

'Good. That's good. It's months since I've actually had a visit from him. I write the occasional report, of course, but it's nice to get a visit. You don't play chess, I suppose?'

'I only know sailor's rules, and bits of bone and cloth for pieces.'

'Sailor's rules? Now that would be something.' He cocked his head sideways. 'That explains the... the watchfulness about you. Have you somewhere to stay?'

'My colleague is trying to get us a room at the inn.'

'I'm sure I can find you a stable hereabouts if not.'

Roscarrock smiled. He was relaxing into the Vicar's chatter, and that even more than the memory of the crude games of chess they had played brought poor drowned Simon Hillyard to his mind.

He sat deliberately more upright.

Reverend Forster folded his hands in his lap. 'You're probably wanting to ask me if I've uncovered any conspiracies lately.'

'Have you?'

'No.'

'That's out the way, then.' He sat back. 'You must get an unusual insight. As Vicar you talk to everyone – listen to everyone – as no one else can.'

'That's why the Government uses us as it does. You're presumably worried that my parishioners will be marching on London shortly to murder the Cabinet.'

'I'd rather they didn't.'

'Why not?'

'You're taking a lax approach to the Commandments, aren't you?'

The Vicar was leaning forwards again, his face more lively. 'I mean: have you, personally, taken an active decision to join the side you have? Have you reviewed the arguments and decided that the Cabinet should be saved?'

'Of course not. Very well – good question. I suppose' – Roscarrock swept a hand through the dark mat of hair – 'for me it's like a ship. The Captain may be a bastard, and the rules can seem foolish, but if there isn't a captain and his orders aren't followed, there's chaos.'

'Better tyranny than anarchy?'

'Better servants than drowned men. Tell me, Reverend: does this line of questioning come from a university education, or from time among your flock?'

'Also a good question. The former. Spending time among my flock gives me every sympathy for the poor wretches. But my curiosity about the natural order is an intellectual one. Aren't you curious?'

'The faces would move me long before the ideas did. I've seen a whole village trying to survive poverty and near-starvation and the knowledge of its own hopelessness. I've lived that once myself, and I see the same faces in villages everywhere. I don't blame a one of them for wanting to cut off the King's head, out of pure impotence. I just don't think it would help.'

'No. The French have proved that to my satisfaction. You must have some more wine.'

When he came back with two drinks, the Vicar was distracted in thought. He handed Roscarrock his drink, sat back in his chair and screwed his eyes closed. 'I think... that it must be a natural predisposition of a government to think in purely governmental terms.' He opened his eyes again with the air of one expecting to have conjured something magical, but found only Tom Roscarrock watching him patiently. 'The Government has no imagination beyond its own limited vocabulary. The only consequence it can imagine, out of the terrible variety of our national distress, is an attack on elements of government.'

'Self-preservation.'

'That's Kinnaird the businessman talking. Lack of imagination is what it is. It sends men like you to ask men like me whether anyone's threatened to kill the King in the last week. It waits fearfully for a crude attack on itself. It uses paid agents to incite conspiracies that would never naturally form, in order to prove that the world works as it wrongly believes. The Home Office thinks it's being very clever, drawing potential conspirators into the open to be able to crush them, but it's only reinforcing its own delusions. The Government creates a game that no one else wants to play, writes the rules, cheats at them, and declares itself the winner. This is the pedantry and wilfulness of a child.'

'Reverend, I enjoy what I understand of your argument. I come from a place where rebellion's bred into us – it's something in the air, like the salt. There've been times in the last couple of years when London ceased to have any control there at all. You may find it funny, but I've grown up happy never to have anything to do with the Government. And I don't claim to have followed all its laws. But government isn't something you can choose to play with or not. It may not be efficient or fair, but it's how the world is built and how it's managed and how it's defended. Chess would be just pointless manoeuvring, without a king.'

'Why not an emperor?'

'Now you're just changing labels. And changing them violently, which helps no one.'

Reverend Forster was waving his empty glass to emphasize what was coming; Roscarrock wondered if he'd switched to wine after all. 'It is crude and ignorant government thinking to imagine that everyone is in one of two states – in a conspiracy to overthrow the Government, or not.

Kinnaird would tell you that. Unintelligent. As if I was to stand in my pulpit and divide the congregation into sheep and goats. I don't claim always to like or sympathize with them, but I try to understand them.'

'And that's why I'm here.'

◆━◆

It had been Joseph's happy discovery that one of the doors sealed up by the Minister to create his more closed, windowless study enabled him to listen to a conversation inside without the disastrous possibility of the door suddenly being opened. Now he pulled away from the panels with blood in his cheeks and bile in his mouth. The Minister knew. Of course he knew. There was no one more likely to be the spy than his own servant, his Joseph. The Minister was considering the possibility of a spy in the other Minister's house merely for completeness. In a matter of seconds the two men would come out of the closed room and they would come for him. The Inspector, the man of famous ruthlessness, the man with the face of a pig and the open, enchanting eyes of a virgin. The Minister, the man of fatal logic, to whom the guilty person would be delivered for punishment.

He must run. If he could get out of the house, he could run. He could get to a horse; he could get to the river. He might be able to outdistance the Inspector racing behind him, at least for a while. He could run and he could find somewhere to hide. Even in the little garden, there might be a bush, or a hole, somewhere to hide, like at Doudeville. Run!

But to run he must run past the door to the Minister's office. Even a single outstretched arm of the Inspector, such a solid man he seemed, would be enough to block the passage. Through the sealed door he could hear – nothing. They had stopped talking. Were they now listening to him? His hammering heart, his shaking hand, could these be heard? Of course not, surely. *'That's silly, isn't it, Joseph?' Oh, Lady Sybille, I wish you had not gone and that none of this had happened. Why can't we be back there then? Why am I lost and tied in this now?*

Clear footsteps from inside the office – footsteps across the floor – and now the soft rush of the oiled door opening, the Inspector and the Minister coming for poor Joseph. Could he hide in the recess of his listening place? If he pushed himself against it might he somehow not be seen? *That's silly, isn't it, Joseph?* Here was the solid body of the Inspector in the passage, here was the Minister following him.

They turned away. 'A signal will come from London when all is ready,' the Minister was saying. 'Within a fortnight, I anticipate. Then the fleets will converge.' He was shepherding the Inspector towards the back door of the house and away. What deception was this?

He still couldn't run. The Minister and the Inspector were in the way. Perhaps he could run out the front once the Minister had turned for the back, but the Minister would hear the running, and he surely couldn't run into that street with so many people staring at him. He was shuffling, weaving, edging forwards, his fingers following the wall and seeking its certainty. Beside him was the open door of the study, the open trap, the place where a man would be delivered to the Minister for punishment.

'You always panic so, Joseph. Always with the longer words.' *'I'm so sorry, Lady Sybille, but there's just too much to try to take in.'* On the desk there were two leather folders. The open door, the open trap, the room of no light where a man was delivered to die.

'Just start at the beginning; just one little piece at a time.' Thank you, Lady Sybille.

Joseph was six paces into the room of no light, six bewildering paces, when his spirit broke and he grabbed one of the leather folders and ran.

◆

The Reverend Forster had switched to wine. He loosened his neckcloth, rolled his shoulders and stretched his legs out, before settling again. Roscarrock warmed to the young man in him, wanted to see him unleashed on a beast of a horse for a morning's hunt, or grinning into a gale.

'So, Mr Roscarrock. When Cobb, my servant, damns me and the King and God and all his angels because his new baby has just died, is that sedition? When he tells his friend in the inn how much I have to eat, and after their second drink they say how handy it would be if they could take just some of my bread and meat, is that sedition? They're contemplating a hangable crime now, yes? The day after, it's Sunday, and that man looks up at me in the pulpit and when I preach obedience to God and the King he looks at his shrivelled wife and fly-covered children and says quietly to the man in the next row that it'd be better if the King were dead and God minded his own business and some of the royal silks and church silver got shared around, is that sedition? If a woman comes to me and confesses some of those thoughts, and I tell her that God understands and that her anger is natural, is that sedition? One night, a local weaver turned up at my gate with a mug of beer in his gut and a nasty-looking knife in his hand. He wasn't used to either, but the collapse in prices meant he could no longer live in the home in which he'd been born, his world was collapsing, and since I was the nearest thing to authority he'd come to kidnap me or kill me. One of the two; neither of us was sure. If the King had been passing he'd have done the same to him, or the First Lord of the Admiralty, or the Archbishop of Canterbury or the man who weighs the fish at Stamford market. Violent sedition. I listened to him, let him cry in the corner, gave him a glass of wine and he wandered off into the night.'

'You'll get no argument from me on the realities of life.'

'There are one or two useful new men in these parts, Roscarrock. Prudent, industrious, successful. They're insulted that they're not allowed to vote. They want change to the political system. They're the ones who give money to the travelling radical man for his boots and his bed, because he's pushing what they want and maybe he has the words to stir up enough of a movement to get it. Active support for sedition.'

Roscarrock watched patiently.

'Once every month, Roscarrock, I ride over to Grantham, where I and a group of like-minded men – parsons, a couple of doctors – talk sedition.

Not an evening's drunken dreaming in the inn, but clever men seriously analyzing the merits of a different order on earth. Not just changing this or that minister, or even king, but utterly changing the structure of society. Perhaps one of us has heard some radical ideas from an itinerant preacher. Perhaps another has read something new from France. We share those ideas, evaluate them. Sir Joseph Plummer, you've heard of him? Brilliant man – what I would call a truly honest mind. The purest heart, and he believes firmly in complete social revolution. "Liberty is not a gift or a prize; it burns within us and we must choose to give it air." Brilliant. He was the guest of one of us, and we benefited from his discourse.'

He grinned. 'Rather an equivocal position, wouldn't you say? Picked associate of the Government's most brilliant intelligencer, and I'm with a group of like-minded fellows and we're describing an upheaval with more clarity than any of your radicals and malcontents could dream of. Now, let me reassure you and Sir Keith: there is not a single chance in a million that any one of us would pick up a pitchfork or pull a pistol on the Prime Minister. We are products and beneficiaries of the established order. But it is our habit when we see a fault to look for its remedy. And when we find an idea, we explore it to its full.'

Outside, the last of the light was disappearing into the woods. The place, the conversation, felt weirdly isolated.

'Reverend, we both know that Sir Keith's... friendship with you is partly sympathy of mind and partly the fact that you have good connections with... people of interest.'

'People of interest? For heaven's sake, Roscarrock, there's no "we" and "they"! Or if there is, I am definitely and completely one of the "they", and the whole population of this country is with me. The only "we" is Tom Roscarrock and His Majesty King George, God save you both. I and my acquaintances with our occasional suppers, we're like poor Cobb, and Mitchell the weaver. We have our resentments – at God, at the injustice of the world. And, like the itinerant radical men, the end-of-the-world prophets and the London philosophers, we have our inspirations.'

'Reverend, I've no interest in what's in men's souls. That's your work. But you know as well as I do that among the thousands of men who'll talk violence into their beer there are a few men of true intent and true malice. When the Irish rebelled half a dozen years back, there were clever, designing political men at their head, and they put weapons into the hands of peasants, encouraged them to bloody murder and led them to their deaths. The same thing in England; I've seen it half a dozen times in the south-west alone.'

The Vicar's words flowed fierce, weeks of stagnation and unfulfilment unleashed on a willing listener. 'You're the connoisseur of the realities of life, Tom. Here are two: unhappy men, and dangerous men. The second can't exist without the first. And if the first exists, the second is inevitable.' He grabbed at a decanter from the table and splashed wine into each of their glasses. 'Now, the great meeting. Two months ago, near Stamford. Three or four thousand people – who on earth knows? – terrified Magistrates, aggressive dragoons, a warm night, hot words. One man died of wounds from a skirmish with the soldiers, a few people – one lad from this village – have wounds that will cripple them permanently – merely an average evening's entertainment. This' – he took a large mouthful of wine – 'this is what the Cabinet see when they have their nightmares of rebellion. Burning torches, burning words, and soon they're burning hayricks and from there it's a short step to burning London. But actually there was no rebellion. The ricks remain unburnt, I and my fellow authority figures remain unhanged. After the soldiers and the angrier element had expressed their frustrations on each other, everyone went home. The Magistrates had a fit of sense and only imprisoned three or four of the leading figures.'

'So?'

Forster pulled the spectacles from his face and gazed at his guest. 'All those fiery seditious words, Roscarrock: it's just resentment and inspiration.'

'You're saying there's an excuse.'

'I'm saying there are no lines to be drawn. In determining sedition, the Government is far more capricious than the most extreme Paris revolutionary. In our world, God and the King and the Cabinet have set themselves up as the sole authorities. When someone's angry, who else do they turn against?' He stopped, breathless, and Roscarrock had the sense that he'd seen the Reverend enjoy a vigorous day's hunting after all. 'I'm... frustrating you. I'm sorry.' He replaced the spectacles on his face, winding the supports around his ears with precision.

'Reverend, I've no argument with most of what you say. But you're talking us into chaos. Intellectually you might reach purity, but you imply anarchy. I'd rather be irrational but stable here, than intellectually immaculate in a political hell like Paris.'

'And innocents must suffer in your search for stability?'

'I don't care about the drunken dreams of labourers and you know I don't. That's why I'm talking to you and not the Magistrate. I care about those few men – and they are only a few, but they exist – who carry determined violence in their minds and chaos in their knapsacks. Because they're as fatal for your flock as the pox.'

The Vicar nodded, sadly. 'You're right, of course. But, regardless, innocents will suffer.'

'Reverend, in education and experience I'm closer to your farm labourer than I am to you. I understand how a man can feel anger and humiliation enough to want to throw a stone at the Magistrate's house or to kill the King. But I don't think they should be allowed to do it. Your religion gives man a hierarchy, tells him to do what he's told.'

The Vicar beamed. 'My rel— Isn't it yours too?'

Roscarrock shrugged. 'Sailor's rules.'

A knowing smile. 'I see. My religion, as it works today, was no doubt the creation of governments, and is the servant of governments just as much as if every priest in the Christian world was passing reports to someone like you. But my religion also offers us the image of a better world – the possibility of freer, truer men – a heaven on earth.' The words became quicker and more fluent, and Roscarrock wondered at the solitary evening sermons the Vicar had spoken to himself, knowing that he would never be able to preach them. 'Tom, I crave stability and security as much as you, as much as anyone, and I accept my place in this creaking old society of ours comfortably and gratefully. But I betray the mind that the creator gave me – I betray his divine offer of the perfectibility of man – if I close my eyes to the horrors that exist around me – in the houses of my neighbours.'

He leant forwards, fists clenched in front of his swaying body as if to close with Roscarrock for another bare-knuckle round. 'Do you know the terrible injuries a man can get just working too long on a farm? Do you know what infection does to a broken leg or a back that's been flogged a hundred times? Have you seen a young girl unable to open her eyes for the smallpox blisters? Have you seen infants and pigs sharing the same filth? Have you seen a child starving to death because his mother doesn't have milk enough in her own wasted body, Roscarrock? Did you ever look into the dead eyes of that father?'

Roscarrock's face had changed somehow, and the clergyman broke off. 'I've seen all those things, Priest. Don't preach to me about the working man, because I've been the working man. And don't try to touch my Christian compassion for the humble family, because it doesn't mean anything to a man who never had a family. I never had the luxury of a father's love, hate or indifference, and I never felt the influence of your God all that much. God is an inspiring fellow when he's at the university, but once he settles down to his daily work he can be a miserable bastard.' He hissed out one harsh breath. 'I believe there's a better world out there, Reverend. And honest men, working steadily and patiently, will get there. They don't need Irish rebels and French philosophers with short-cuts, because they're all just tricksters offering alternative ways to die.'

He held his hands flat and steady, and lowered them evenly onto the oak arms of the chair. 'I can't say I've much affection for your God, Reverend, or for his methods. Same holds for the Government. But changing gods or changing governments won't feed the hungry. If God and the Government will interfere with me as little as possible, I'll trust myself to muddle through.'

The Vicar was watching him with a mixture of sympathy and wariness. 'Has it struck you, Mr Roscarrock,' he said sombrely, 'that you may be in the wrong job?'

Tom Roscarrock laughed, half a dozen grim chuckles. He shook his head. 'I don't know, Reverend. Who better than a man of doubts, to try to represent God to a hungry parish? Who better than a rebel to explain sedition to the Government?'

'A man of doubts.' The Vicar tried the taste of it in his mouth. 'Roscarrock, I'm not going to give you lists of names. Sir Keith never expects that, and it is not why I have these conversations. I believe men have a right to their resentments and their inspirations, and every now and then there comes from among them a true prophet. But I will think on men whose resentment and whose inspiration might leave them particularly susceptible to men of malice.'

'You have anyone in mind?'

'I seem to remember a description – just in conversation recently – an itinerant... a tailor, I think. I'll ask some questions, and I will contact you in the usual way. Ask me no more.'

'Thank you.' He said it simply and earnestly.

'And Roscarrock, if you're in London, and Sir Keith is still loose in the landscape somewhere, you would do worse than talk to a man called Rokeby Harris.'

Roscarrock said the name of Rokeby Harris himself to be sure of it, waited for elaboration that did not come, and repeated his thanks. Then, on a whim: 'Reverend – your reports – just remind me: when did you send the most recent?'

'Perhaps... a month ago? Six weeks?'

'Fine.' Roscarrock stood, stretched his neck. 'As you'll have realized, I've not been around that long.' He wandered idly to the window, picked up a candlestick from the sill, examined the base, and replaced it.

'I wrote to Sir Keith at the usual address. The usual precautions.' As

Roscarrock sat down again, the Vicar was watching him, thoughtfully. 'And what message have you just passed to your colleague?'

Roscarrock smiled. 'Not to come and join us.'

'Ah. That's good.' The Vicar grinned at the implied confidence, then as suddenly turned serious. 'You realize, of course, Roscarrock, that they're using you to get to me.'

Roscarrock nodded silently.

'They know I'm not as comfortable talking to someone who doesn't have Sir Keith's explicit confidence, which very few men do. I've spoken more freely with you than I would with your colleague, for example.'

'Yes.'

'But you'll tell him what I've said.'

'Yes.'

'Because this organization is the closest thing to stability you can find. Your way of avoiding chaos.'

'Yes. Only there's no stability in it.' Roscarrock took one slow breath, and released it. 'I am... at sea, adrift in ways even you can't imagine, Reverend. But I'm a sailor. I'm used to having no steady place to stand.'

The Vicar nodded, then said emptily, 'I'm no sailor.'

'No.' Roscarrock watched the blank face. 'It's damnable, isn't it, Reverend?'

Another nod, sad and slow. Then, with sudden inspiration: 'It is actually damnable – it's a purgatory of rootlessness, of disloyalty, of...' – he focused sharply on Roscarrock – 'of loss of faith.'

Roscarrock nodded quiet understanding. Then he glanced at the sideboard, and smiled. 'So, Reverend, am I teaching you sailor's rules, or are you teaching me real chess?'

⌐◦~

It was the natural time for the Minister's servant to step out into the filth of the Paris streets and run such errands and make such purchases as the

Minister's frugal domestic habits required. It was likewise natural that the Minister's servant should step into the inn at the sign of the Sun to refresh himself. But Joseph's journey to the inn was feverish and most unnatural. Subject to the dominant emotion in his head, fear of what strode behind or embarrassment at the bemused glances of those in front, he walked or ran or staggered at an uncomfortable trot through the mud. He hurried oddly, the leather wallet clasped to his chest. He hurried with wide, frightened eyes and frequent, desperate checking over his shoulder. Each corner, the possibility of momentary invisibility to anyone behind, taunted him with its distance through treacle steps. Each corner he celebrated, leaning back for a second against the new bulwark and regathering himself, setting off with self-conscious, measured steps before the urgency in his chest hastened him into a trot again. But in the streets of Paris, swarming with men mad with poverty and hunger or mad with blood and ideas or mad with the loss of everything, there was no one to see and remember one more lunatic fugitive.

Joseph fell into the inn at the sign of the Sun with a clatter, and slammed the door behind him, pushing his limited weight against it. The inn's solitary customer, a heavy market trader, looked up at the noise and gave Joseph an uninterested and unimpressed examination. From the counter the landlord was staring at Joseph with undisguised surprise and anger, and this restrained his panic. He swallowed and walked to the table nearest the counter. After a moment the landlord carried over a mug of beer, placed it heavily on the table, and hissed, 'Get hold of yourself. Don't say a bloody word. Drink.' Then he ambled back to the counter.

Three long minutes later the trader left. Joseph's eyes were still locked to the tabletop, not even following the man's departure. The landlord walked to the door, spent a long time examining the street, then shut out the day.

Joseph didn't look up until the landlord sat down opposite him, account book at the ready.

'What the hell's wrong with you?'

'I'm finished. They know about me. They're after me.'

'They're what? And you came here? Oh, bloody—' The alarm in the normally placid man sent new shudders through Joseph's fragile grip on himself. 'They're actually after you?'

'I – I don't know. The Minister knows there's a spy somewhere. I didn't – I couldn't – I had to get out.'

'Well, he knows who it is now, doesn't he? And you came here. Bloody hell.'

'I had to get the report out. Where else could I come? I was always taught—'

The landlord leant slowly forwards. 'Bloody anywhere else is where.' Then his words began to tumble out: 'And you ran through town like that. Did they see you go? Were you followed?' Joseph shrank back, pitiful, and this seemed to resolidify the landlord. 'All right. All right then, you miserable sod. Let's have it all, then, good and precise, just like we were taught.'

He made Joseph go through the Minister's conversation with more than usual pedantry. But he wouldn't let his eyes shift to the door.

———

The parade ground at Colchester on the 26th of July, and another member of the West Suffolk Militia strapped half-naked to a wooden frame in the middle of the square theatre of restive faces. The muttering was in the front ranks now, and still the Sergeants made little effort to challenge it. The officers' nonchalance was forced, their eyes moving hurriedly around the arena.

This time the Colonel addressed the troops, his horse stuttering backwards and forwards under him as he pulled at it. 'This is a country at war!' he yelled towards the blocks of men. 'Our task is to defend it against invaders and traitors, and you have all sworn an oath to fight for your King. With the survival of our nation in peril, there can be no greater crime than a failure of duty, and a betrayal of trust.' He hesitated, trying to pick the words. 'It is well-known that some voices in this company – idle voices, drunk voices – have tried to lead impressionable minds down the fatal path of questioning the natural authority in this army and in this land. I will not tolerate any sympathy for vile doctrines and practices learnt of the French, and I will not tolerate any disruption of the proper respects and responsibilities of military command.'

Lashed to the frame, Corporal Tubb willed his body to succumb to the alcoholic stupor offered by friendly hands in the minutes before he'd been dragged out. The warmth of the morning was already touching his shoulders and back, taunting him with his own capacity to feel.

'This man was given authority over his fellows. With authority comes responsibility. He has betrayed that responsibility, and he has betrayed the men who follow him, by spreading ideas contrary to proper military discipline and the laws of this country. Gentlemen, I will have you understand that this regiment must be built on absolute respect for discipline. There is no greater crime than the betrayal of that discipline by a man picked to enforce it, and I have no hesitation in ordering the most severe punishment. This man will be flogged to the uttermost. He will be stripped of his rank. He and his platoon, who misguidedly sympathized with his foul words, will have their rations halved and their pay stopped for two weeks. You will learn respect, gentlemen.'

Even a typical flogging could cripple a man for life, and Corporal Tubb's punishment was more than typical. He was unconscious long before the last stroke from the Sergeant's exhausted arm scorched across his ruined back, slumped in the ropes, and as they were untied he collapsed in the dust, a broken toy. Around the warming square the stench of vomit lurched in nasty gusts, hardened men unable to swallow nature as they stared at the sacrifice offered for their education.

Tubb had stood on parade for the last time, at any rank, and he was not the only one. When the roll was called the next morning, two silences echoed around the square from his platoon. Within an hour, the body of a soldier was found in a ditch just outside the barracks. The shallow stagnant water had darkened and soiled his coat and, through the reeds, dragonflies patrolled over his battered face, gagged mouth, and flaming bruised neck.

27th July 1805

When Jessel walked in, the Admiral was focused on something he was writing, but his left hand thrust a paper towards the door while his right continued to scratch evenly across the page. 'You've read this?'

Jessel had spent the day on the road, and wanted to escape to a tavern or a bed soon. He took the single sheet and scanned the top. *Field report, received the 27th day of July 1805 (Military direct)*. He nodded. 'Just now, My Lord.'

'An object lesson in outstandingly stupid intelligence work.'

'Pretty unwise, My Lord.'

'Is the army staffed entirely with buffoons? One tries to respect them but... if we're ever left with them between us and Napoleon – and if they were let loose in Dublin! – God preserve us. The poor man had begged them not to act on his information, but they went ahead because their absurd pride couldn't have anything else, and now they've lost a solid intelligence source and probably the morale of the regiment with him.'

Jessel replaced the paper on the Admiral's desk. 'There's even a chance the avengers hanged the wrong man.'

Bellamy considered this for a moment, and his lips soured in distaste. 'One desperate denial like another. His Majesty's enemies are dangerous enough; it's a pity that his protectors are so remarkably foolish. Watch this, Jessel.'

'My Lord.'

'And take a wash. Roscarrock too. You're mixing with the quality tonight.'

———— ⁓ ————

The barking snapped sudden and clear from the direction of the Tarn, and the instinct of Seth Colson's twenty years in the Cumbrian hills turned his attention immediately towards it; the same instinct told him almost as immediately that it was not his dog. Wind-scoured eyes scanned the ground in front of him, and sure enough his Jess wasn't quite thirty yards off in the opposite direction.

Not his dog; not his business.

But the bark called again from the Tarn hollow off to his right, and Jess's ears were up, and Seth Colson wondered what dog, following what man, would be up on this same storm-seared slope of the highest peak of what they said was the highest range in the whole of England. A misstep in the white wilderness of winter up here was fatal, and a summer mist like this morning's could be just as treacherous.

He saw the dog and the dog saw him at the same moment, as he came over the slight rise that enclosed Red Tarn. Another bark, doubtful. The dog advanced a few steps towards him, then retreated as quickly to a bundle of rags that glared from the rocks and furze.

The rags were clothes, bleached by sun and wind, and they fluttered like mourners' veils over the memory of a man. The skeleton had been picked almost clean by the scavengers, the skull lolled back over a stone and stared up at the shepherd, and the bones had crept and hidden themselves among the pale brittle branches of the furze.

———— ⁓ ————

Gabriel Chance found conversation elusive, unsettling. When others spoke, he seemed to hear between their words. When he spoke, he watched the confusion frowning back at him, felt the wariness rising. When Flora didn't understand him, it made him hurt and angry. With others, he felt foolish and alone.

But if people let him talk, if they had faith in him and he in the power of his words, they seemed to relax in the words, to understand and then to feel.

Chance's days were plain. He slept a little. Some evenings he talked – to apprentices, out-of-work men, Quakers, craftworkers, families entranced by his face glowing in the lamplight after supper. Mostly he walked: Manchester, and then Nottingham, and Peterborough; among metalworkers in Sheffield and free-thinkers in Leicester.

When he walked, the crisp, gleaming duck-egg sky sang to him, a bright treble choir that lifted his face, his whole body, up by the ears. His spirit hummed to the rhythm of tidy villages against hillsides, swam in the dark earth and sheer, shining greenness of the world.

On the 27th he saw smoke again, the smear of dirt across the crystal lens of the sky.

He had to look at it: had to touch the hot iron, had to test the sharpness of the needle, the black agony of mechanical mill or pit piercing the brittle beauty of God's tapestry, smoke bleeding across the sky through his fingers. The sun was behind him as he stepped cautiously up the slope, and the tree trunks were warm as his hands brushed over them.

The chimneys rose up to meet him as he crested the slope. Two squat, bulbous brick obscenities, a pair of lungs belching out the corruption from somewhere deep inside the earth. Near them, fed by this eternal fever, was the wheel, its perpetual hiss and demonic, soul-sold energy audible under the clumsier clanging of the beast.

The beast stood over the wheel, and its unceasing awkward momentum stupefied Chance. Up and down the beam swayed, see-sawing up and down, with the same ominous beat, up and down, chained to the darkness by its connecting rods, up and down forever. An irregularity, an uncertainty, would have suggested some human spirit in the machine. Up and down, up and down, up and down, with steady implacable hatred for the variable wondering souls of men. *My arms do not swing like that*, Gabriel Chance thought as he hid behind leaves, *not if tortured to pull at those levers for eternity. My legs do not stride so even or so strong. My heart will not beat so steady or for so long.*

Somewhere within Roscarrock burnt a faint memory of a more innocent man, who had grown up in a society that knew little other than hardship but was able to move through that world freely and on his abilities. Those certainties and freedoms, and the innocence, had been washed away by the Atlantic. As he walked up the polished steps, Jessel chatting suavely beside him as a pair of footmen bowed to them, the challenges of the evening ahead and the unreality in which he swam crystallized in the simple realization that, for all his past freedom and experience, he had never walked through a doorway as grand as this.

They were shown up a fine stone staircase inside, and Lord Hugo Bellamy was near the top of it. Jessel steered them in his direction, and caught the Admiral's eye. Bellamy murmured a name that Roscarrock neither recognized nor quite caught, but Jessel responded to it and greeted the Admiral respectfully, before presenting Roscarrock as Mr Thomas Grey. The Admiral greeted Mr Grey with a polite disdain that seemed to Roscarrock the only real thing he'd experienced all day, and they stepped aside from the main movement of people.

The Admiral scanned the new Roscarrock critically, and grunted.

'Very well. What professional or manufacturing interest could you talk about for two minutes?'

The odd question jolted him. 'Ships.'

'Good. You're a shipbuilder – rather, you own a shipbuilding enterprise. Try not to give the impression you've ever got your hands dirty or wet. You could never pass for a gentleman, Roscarrock, but anyone seems to be able to get rich these days.'

'I'll bear that in mind, My Lord.'

'You'll forget it, Mr Grey,' Bellamy said with what passed for levity. 'I have other plans for you. Thus far you have lurked at the viler end of radicalism in this country. This evening you'll see the other. Some of the most wealthy and illustrious in London, who through misguided conviction, foolishness, or sheer boredom, dabble in radicalism. Among them some of the French exile community, who may have found Paris too hot but haven't forgotten the philosophical dreams that set it ablaze. Whatever the chatter of your friends in the taverns, a real threat to this country will need money and a link to Paris. Both are to be found here.'

He half-turned and nodded formally to a new arrival at the top of the stairs. 'Our hostess is the widow of a French intellectual; she came here when the Paris mob were concentrating more on equality than liberty or fraternity, and has got comfortable. She hankers for the salons, and time by time holds evenings like this. No one here would dream of doing anything revolutionary themselves, but the brains, and the backing – and the beneficiaries – of any threat to the Government will be found here. Some are just clever men and good conversationalists. Others are truly dangerous. Our hostess has invited the cream – radical politicians, reforming manufacturers, intellectual clergymen from across England.'

'A vicar of Grantham?'

'I haven't the faintest idea. Why?'

Jessel got the point. 'A broad-minded acquaintance of one of Sir Keith Kinnaird's broad-minded contacts, My Lord – Forster, in Oakham. There was a Grantham vicar on our list, but we don't think he's left his parish.'

The Admiral considered the point a second, and Roscarrock for longer. 'You may be useful yet, Roscarrock. It goes without saying that anyone here could be an agent of Napoleon's police, and I imagine that at least one or two certainly are.' Another polite greeting over Roscarrock's shoulder. 'I am known in these circles as an idle dabbler, a man of limited intellect and some unimportant sinecure in the Admiralty, who fancies himself interested in reform. That reputation took me to Seldon House, and it will keep me here for the duration of one glass of wine. Serious politics is beyond me, and serious talk too dangerous. As the wine flows tonight, and the tongues loosen, and the more serious players arrive, I shall find myself out of my depth and leave. You will stay. You will babble whatever half-baked ideologies you have learnt in the slums, you will listen to these people, and you will learn this world. I know what everyone here will say, but I'd like to know where they heard it and whom they're saying it to.'

Roscarrock nodded slowly, and turned away with Jessel.

'Mr Grey.'

Roscarrock stopped. 'My Lord?'

'How do you find us? Learnt anything useful yet?'

'Nothing you couldn't have got from the beggar on the corner. I frankly don't understand why you need me.'

'Let me judge that.'

'I'm listening to gossip and having conversations that you or Kinnaird or any well-behaved schoolboy could have.'

Bellamy stared bleakly at him. 'As ever your insights on my business astound me, Roscarrock. I have the faint hope that you may be in harmony with some of Kinnaird's rarer fruit. Each man brings something unique to a conversation, and takes something unique from it.'

'You either overestimate me or underestimate Sir Keith, Admiral.'

'You may trust in my estimation, Roscarrock.' The heavy head considered him for a moment. 'I have my routine meeting with Sir Keith and some of our associates tomorrow, and you need not trouble yourself about my handling of it. Immerse yourself as I have directed, and let us see what you dredge up.' He looked beyond them to the staircase. 'Get on with it, then. Resist the urge to pocket the cutlery.'

Jessel and Roscarrock stood together on the edge of the reception room, scanning the arena of gold and glass and glittering costume. Jessel smoothed back his hair and seemed to breathe deeply at the luxury. 'Come on then, Shipbuilder,' he said with quiet energy.

Roscarrock glanced at him as he straightened a smart blue coat and fingered its shining buttons. 'What are you supposed to be?'

Jessel savoured his own inventiveness. 'Richard Houghton is a gentleman of the middling sort, with the faint memory of class but no trace of money, forced to work at something in banking. I am estranged from my family, who cannot come to terms with the practical implications of their own penury.' He gazed into the gold mouldings on the ceiling for inspiration. 'I have recently been forced to shift lodgings, owing to dark suspicions on the part of my landlady following her niece's unexpected pregnancy.'

'You're actually enjoying yourself.'

'Well, it's better than being a Government servant slogging from tavern to tavern on fools' errands, isn't it?' He grinned, and leant in. 'I used to be an actor, Tom. I lost the taste for poverty, but never for performance.' They turned to face the room. 'Why, aren't you enjoying yourself?'

I no longer know who I am, myself. How could I possibly enjoy myself?

'I am a hard-headed man of business, interested only in ships and profits. I despise the hypocrisy and empty show of things like this.'

'That's the spirit.'

The French widow with the taste for dangerous talk lived well. St James's Square was one of the three or four most desirable locations in London, its dukes indifferent to its former prime ministers, and she was renting a house on its best side. Over the bobbing sea of heads, sash windows fully two men high showed the last of the summer light falling over the square. In the rattling chaos of vehicles, the elegant carriages of fashionable dabblers jostled with the coaches of practical men of business and industry and the horses of radical politicians and Government agents.

These men and women, the gleaming and the grey, tapped up the marble staircase and out past Roscarrock and Jessel into the drawing room that took up the whole polished width of the house. Squeals of exaggerated acknowledgement set off the underlying murmur of earnest conversation, and a rich soup of perfumes saturated the air.

'Recognize anyone?'

Jessel scanned the room. 'A few names. No one – oh, there's one to be careful of – older man in the corner, brown coat, looks like Father Time picking his next victim – that's Sir Joseph Plummer.'

'Heard of him. Thinker; writer.'

'The great theorist of social revolution and the better world to come.'

'Not one of ours, then.'

Jessel grinned. 'Even Kinnaird's not that clever.'

They stepped into the arena.

The 27th July

Monsieur,

I am now returned from Scotland, but will go north of that border again. The successful explosion at the coal mine of Hurlet, by the town of Paisley, caused damage that has still not been made good, and convinced me that the more robust attitude of the Scottish miners to danger - or the greater callousness of the owners - allows much opportunity for our enterprise.

I am observing again the pit of O'aclose, in the County of Durham. The intervention in April in this place did only slight material damage, but I am convinced that my knowledge of the place will make a greater destruction possible at the second attempt.

I must report that I suspect a man to be following me. He is not of the local Magistrates, nor a secret employee of the

*colliery owners, because I know that type
and I know the individuals who fulfil those
functions in this district. I must suspect this
man is an agent of that secret organization
of which you spoke so warily. I will remain
prudent while pursuing our aims.*

[SS MF/SH/16/7 (THE SUTHERLAND HOUSE TROVE)

DECIPHERED BY J.J., DECEMBER 1805]

Roscarrock made for the group around Plummer; at least he had a name to start with. No introduction was needed; Plummer was lecturing rather than conversing, and he was able to attach himself to the group unobtrusively.

'I'm afraid, gentlemen, you'll get no martyr's insouciance from me. I've been to prison twice, and I cannot pretend it is anything other than a vile and dehumanizing experience. And I was as comfortable as it is possible to be, compared to some of the wretches with whom I shared the place.'

Someone asked a question, but Plummer was continuing regardless. 'My confinement is significant only as a signal. It demonstrates that this Government, and this system of government, will inevitably fall. Not because their attitude will provoke any great revenge, but because their attitude reflects an utter absence of imagination. This regime will be defeated not because it resists the pressure for reform, but because it does not understand it.'

Sir Joseph Plummer was a man of average height in average clothes. But there was an ancient gauntness in his face that fascinated, a wild, knotted texture that was less human, more that of some desiccated tree. His bony body, supporting the clothes badly, made him seem taller in the same way that the roughened face made him seem older. He was somehow not quite of his time, and it made his words prophetic. 'These Ministers, they think of radical reform as if it were a regiment of Bonaparte's army, to be defeated as clearly and brutally as possible.' He shook his head. 'Radical reform is the grass growing from the natural soil of this land; it is the word on the tongue of the body of Britain. Reform is the natural emanation of all that we are, and it is unstoppable. The Ministers pretend that they are leading the majority against an upstart faction; instead it is they who are the minority, a handful of men trying to hold back the tide. The only choice we have is the role that we are to play: agent of progress, blind reactionary, or' – predator's eyes scanned the group – 'gilded spectators.'

It was no kind of conversation, and not even a debate. The old man was speaking as he would to a whole room of people, but engaging with none of them. Generally he locked his face and speech onto one member of his audience whom Roscarrock couldn't see. But now the fierce gaze and a single stick of a finger, held close to the chest with miserly control, were sweeping around the group. Roscarrock realized that eye and finger had settled on him, and a high crackle of a voice stabbed at him. 'You, sir, for example, what brings you?'

Roscarrock looked straight back at the old man. 'When there is such good talk, a prudent man is here to listen.'

Plummer looked Roscarrock up and down once, and the wild old eyes pushed a fraction forwards. 'Practical man? Business?'

'Manufacture.'

'Iron?'

'Ships.'

The eyes widened a fraction, and relaxed. 'Men such as you, sir, must decide. You will be the steam engines of the new world, but if you refuse to move with that world, you will be caught in the machinery and destroyed. No doubt, sir, you could make a little fortune building ships for this whore of a war, but she will destroy you as well in time.'

'Then, Sir Joseph, I am fortunate to have you as engineer.'

There was nothing to be gained from Plummer in his public mode. Roscarrock drifted on through the crowd, trying to classify by dress and speech, trying to catch the thrust of conversations as he passed. Two noble financiers, English and French, speaking their shared language of gold and class, indifferent to the ignorants who could not. A pretty young Frenchwoman, long limbs making a rare success of the latest dress, trying to find something attractive in the face or conversation of a London pamphleteer. A radical journalist asking earnest questions of a reforming mill owner from Wales. Two younger men conferring furtively behind a barricade of meats and pies. Roscarrock glanced at them a second time – their earnestness, their energy. Not plotters, certainly; not politicians, either, but enthusiasts of politics, and as radical and fervent as the wine could make them.

A small, neat man, every aspect of dress and voice meticulous, down to the quiet care with which his French accent tried to grapple the barbarous English vowels. 'I understand, sir, that we might have something in common. I hear that you are in ships.' The sibilants emerged so luxuriously that for a second Roscarrock didn't recognize the word. 'I too.'

The 'I too', rather than 'me too', was jarringly foreign, and then Roscarrock reflected that there was considerably more chance of the Frenchman being right than him. 'Indeed,' he said with polite warmth, and introduced himself.

Monsieur Maréchal was a merchant. Roscarrock explained that his own business was in building ships rather than running them; he regretted having agreed to that version of the lie – he'd have found it easier to bluff on sea-borne trade than he was going to on the shipbuilding industry.

'May I ask where you build?'

'Of course. In the south-west, principally.'

'Ah, but of course. Such excellent natural harbours.' A little smile. 'I am always amused at the differences in manners on such occasions. A Frenchman – and certainly an Italian – would have answered me with the size of his fortune and the names of his greatest ships. An Englishman preserves the veil of discretion over such gross details, and in so doing allows me to infer the scope of his enterprise.'

'I fear we use a reputation for discretion to justify rudeness.'

Monsieur Maréchal was shocked at the suggestion. In an essentially rude age, discretion stood out the more clearly. They discussed the health of the shipbuilding industry, the attitudes of the craftsmen. Mr Grey asked about trade. Monsieur Maréchal demonstrated his own talent for discretion; obviously it was not legally possible to trade with France, but if a man had contacts, and intermediaries, and prudence... He was hoping to expand into the Baltic. His enforced stay in London had brought him to appreciate the virtues of the colder-blooded northern Europeans. Enforced stay? Monsieur Maréchal shrugged delicately. Alas, Napoleon Bonaparte was not a businessman.

'And you, Monsieur Grey, do you come here to talk of ships, or' – the shrug – 'perhaps a little politics?'

Roscarrock alarmed himself by producing a shrug in unconscious mimicry of the Frenchman. 'Napoleon may not be a businessman, Monsieur, but he is driving politics in the most interesting direction.'

To which Maréchal gave a discreet, unvoiced 'Ah'.

They might have gone on shrugging at each other for the rest of the evening, but mercifully a third man interrupted. Simple practical clothes expensively made, bearing and approach unavoidably English. Thomas Tuff was an insurance broker from Manchester. He had an interest in the details of southern England's shipyards that tested Roscarrock's inspiration to the limit, and an enthusiasm for the technicalities of modern developments in shipbuilding that was bewildering. Roscarrock was considerably more comfortable when they moved onto the winds in the Solent, but bored of the conversation and unable to think of a single useful question to ask about insurance. He politely steered Thomas Tuff's interest towards trends in European trade with the major British ports, and then pretended to spot an old acquaintance just over Maréchal's shoulder and left them to it.

A man with dark curls was watching with unease as a pretty woman in the bluest and most fashionable of dresses addressed a group on his behalf. 'The attempt to bar Sir Francis from Parliament is simply wrong. It is the greatest indictment of our constitution. We must all, I'm sure, do all we can to bring pressure to bear to have him reinstated.'

'The support of Lady Charlotte is worth a petition of millions.' Sir Francis was clearly happier talking for himself. 'But the stupidities of the system merely draw attention to its obsolescence.'

Lady Charlotte Pelham was not done. 'We must do something. You, sir' – she was gazing at Roscarrock as if he might be bringing news of Napoleon's joyous arrival at Greenwich – 'can you help us?' Roscarrock's hesitation was clearly a disappointment. 'Do you know Sir Francis Burdett? I am honoured to introduce you.' Roscarrock introduced himself, and said that it was his honour both to meet Sir Francis and to do so in the presence of Lady Charlotte. Burdett accepted the introduction politely, and Lady Charlotte continued to chatter earnestly over the discomfort of the men.

The evening was a revelation to Roscarrock – ideas that would have got a London apprentice flogged were thrown around like toys by the aristocrats. But he would learn nothing new from these little public performances. He drifted on around the room. Two radical barristers: 'What was it Whitbread said? Conditions of the British working class are worse than for the slaves going to the Americas.' A journalist scoffing at the King's sickness, ineptness and German-ness; another journalist replying that a healthy shrewd Englishman would not redeem the institution of kingship, which was itself an offence. A French voice: 'Metz? The old General is a fantasy – an illusion. The idea that one ancient Royalist hero could inspire France against the Emperor is absurd.' A parson – two parsons – talking of natural philosophy. From somewhere off Roscarrock's shoulder the phrase 'the purifying effect of a single act of great violence'. Impossible to tell who had said the words. They might have come from a Frenchman who was standing there, but he was alone.

They swapped names. The ease with which Roscarrock was distributing a name he knew to be a fiction, and the ease with which he accepted names that might as well have been, was dusting the evening with new unreality. Monsieur Delacroix was a writer recently arrived from Paris, and apparently free to travel back and forth. He was interested in what Roscarrock could tell him of the condition of the poor, the state of the harvest, and the health of industry. He was surely too obvious to be an agent of Napoleon's police. But then Roscarrock was making up his answers in any case.

He asked similar questions of the Frenchman, trying to suggest a vaguely maritime or manufacturing interest while doing what he could to gather how and how often Delacroix travelled. Polite interest in Delacroix's writing.

On reflection, wasn't it obvious that, once a man was moving between London and Paris, it was irrelevant whether you labelled him a police agent or not? What was it the Reverend Forster had said? There were no lines to be drawn.

Another man joined them: perhaps thirty years old, the big, clear eyes of a child dragged down by a heavy jaw. This, said the Frenchman, was Mr Hodge. Presumably Mr Grey had had the opportunity to hear him speak. Unfortunately not – the tiresome pressures of business. But Mr Henry Hodge was the most highly regarded of political speakers; Mr Grey should abandon business completely if he had the chance to hear such rhetoric.

Mr Hodge was pleasantly untroubled by Mr Grey's ignorance. He gulped a large mouthful of wine, brushed a crumb from a bulky shirt front, and explained that he tended to speak in rather out of the way places. No doubt Mr Grey would understand that advertising his activities could bring the wrong sort of attention. The three of them laughed pleasantly. Roscarrock watched the solid young man: if he was a radical orator, he ran significant risks; but Hodge seemed to have less caution, less conspiratorial reserve, than most of the others in the shimmering drawing room. Obviously delighted to see Mr Grey sometime – but no doubt a conversation would do as well – man of Mr Grey's experience would hardly be surprised by much that he could say – but it might do Mr Grey good to see the passion of the crowd.

It might indeed, but Lady Charlotte Pelham had other plans. Here was Mr Grey at last; she'd been looking for him; he must meet Mr Harris – Mr Rokeby Harris; she was sure they would have much in common.

Roscarrock thanked Lady Charlotte politely, and watched her a moment longer. Her effect was foolish, but the attractive face was honest and earnest. Reform might only be a fashion to her, but she took her fashions seriously. Her social mediation, meanwhile, this constant chivvying of stolid men, had more chance of bringing together the critical elements of a revolution than any number of public meetings. She gazed back at Roscarrock with simple interest, fingered the pearls that rolled down towards her discreetly swelling cleavage, and smiled uneasily.

But the eyes couldn't stay still for long, and she caught sight of another section of the room that needed inspiration, and was gone. Across the room Roscarrock could see Jessel locked in earnest conversation with the two journalists who'd been discussing the King. He turned back to the other man, Harris. 'I suppose there's a chance that we might actually find something in common.'

Harris smiled, a careful, measured action between trimmed side-whiskers. 'I think we owe it to Lady Charlotte to try.' The voice was dry and discreet, with the swallowed, rumbling vowels of the north country. 'Ships, I gather.'

Roscarrock nodded. 'And you?'

Rokeby Harris's face was tired, a face eroded by time and experience; but the eyes were clear and earnest. 'I'm retired, Mr Grey. I invest a little. Advise.' The face, the simple quality of the clothes, the quiet measured speech, spoke honesty. Somehow it made Roscarrock wary, and a part of him winced in sadness at his own cynicism.

'And before...' At last his brain caught up. 'Wait – Rokeby Harris?' The Reverend Henry Forster's contact. The faintest of frowns flickered among the lines of the old face. 'A friend of mine said I should look out for you – that you were a man worth talking to.'

As soon as he said it, he knew it was the wrong tack. Harris just stood waiting, watching him. Everything about Henry Forster and Rokeby Harris meant restraint, and he had shown none. Harris would have no trust in such a crass approach.

'But . . .'

'But,' Harris said quietly, 'in that case it would sound as though all three of us had been wanting in a little discretion.'

'Indeed,' Roscarrock said. 'Perhaps I was mistaken.' He excused himself and moved away.

The news of the unexplained killing of the dragoon in Tiverton reached London with no fanfare. Another dusty and exhausted man clattered down Whitehall and into the cobbled courtyard of army headquarters in the Horse Guards building, slipped down from a sweating horse and walked stiffly to the adjutant's office. Another satchel was opened, another sheaf of paper thrown into a tray, and the rider let go one deep breath at a job completed before creeping back into the evening with conflicting thoughts of bed and beer in his head.

A quick glance at the tops of the sheets of paper, and the Lieutenant on duty picked out a couple for more urgent attention. The report from Tiverton stayed in the tray.

An hour and a glass of wine later, the Lieutenant began to work through the pile. Some reports were placed in new trays; those where the paper could be re-used dropped into a basket beside him; the unneeded but sensitive he screwed up and threw, with great concentration, towards the collection of paper balls in and around the fireplace.

This time, the report from Tiverton got a frown, and the word 'priority' scribbled across the top of it in rough pencil. It went into one tray separate from the others, and began its slow tour through five different offices in the building.

Two hands reaching for an ice at the same moment, and an elegant lace wrist gesturing airily to Roscarrock to go first.

'Thank you. Mr...?'

'De Boeldieu.' The brown-haired man – was he wearing face powder? – misinterpreted Roscarrock's look and repeated the name.

'Yes. Then thank you, Monsieur. Grey – Thomas Grey.'

'It must be so tiresome for you English. You get yourself in a nice tidy war with France, but still your London is full of Frenchmen.' There was boredom in the voice, but interest in the face.

'I'm surprised a refugee from France would find the conversation pleasant in this company.'

Another languid wave of the hand, matching the tone of the voice. 'Oh, a man will put up with much bad conversation if there is good wine. Besides, Mr Grey, you must not think that all the Frenchmen in London are revengeful and hunted Royalists.'

'Don't you find it tiresome that London is full of Englishmen?'

The Frenchman laughed – a deep laugh, in the throat, and its honesty and lack of restraint seemed out of place with the affected voice. 'I care little one way or the other, for the Revolution or the Royalists. But France of today is too... hard, too military a place for me. There is better French food, better French language, better French civilization to be found in London. I can amuse myself with the ideas of reform without the discomforts of revolution.'

The opinion was too carefully neutral. 'Don't you worry that London too will soon be a French military place?'

De Boeldieu stopped his glass halfway to his lips and touched Roscarrock on the arm. 'Oh, as to that, Mr Grey, London is a place of the business and of the fashion, not a place of the politics. It will remain a place of the business and of the fashion regardless of whether Napoleon or King George is on the coins and the buttons.'

'That could be a violent change.'

'I think not. The war is good for the business, but the violence is bad for the business. Your men of business would not allow violence to interrupt their affairs.'

Sir Joseph Plummer was drifting near. Roscarrock deliberately avoided looking at him, not wanting him drawn in. He smiled politely at the Frenchman. 'You don't think that Napoleon might have a stronger opinion?'

De Boeldieu seemed genuinely surprised at the idea. 'Mr Grey, the very last thing Napoleon will do is antagonize your men of business.'

'You have an optimistic view of him.'

'Mr Grey, Napoleon does not want England for your damp climate, or your peculiar manners, or your indifferent wine. He wants to neutralize and thus acquire your Empire.' De Boeldieu was enjoying himself. 'And this Empire, it is not built on the climate, or the manners, or the wine. It is built on trade, on the wealth of London. Napoleon is a most clever man, and he will not threaten the thing he covets most, I can assure you. Your men of business will enjoy the benefits of the war and refuse to accept the violence, and Napoleon will oblige them.'

'Benefits?'

The Frenchman's face opened wide in emphasis. 'Of course! You, Mr Grey, what is your business?' The brown eyes were suddenly watchful.

'Ships.'

'There! Has there been a greater age for shipbuilding? Could there be a better time to be a shipbuilding man?'

Roscarrock was intrigued by the conversation but wary of its fluency. The Frenchman was plausible, but indifferent to his own words. The combination of superficial glibness and underlying scrutiny was unsettling. It was the mirror of his own.

'And aren't you worried, Monsieur, that you will find yourself trapped between the interests of Napoleon and these cynical men of business? You say you're indifferent. But you're still a Frenchman who fled Napoleon's France.'

The airiness returned to the lace cuff. 'I did not flee. I travelled from Napoleon's France because my pleasures may temporarily be pursued here. I may return if it pleases me.' He touched Roscarrock's arm again. 'It's kind of you to worry about me, Mr Grey. But I am harmless, and do not intend to put myself in the way of trouble.'

'I wish you luck.'

'But you, Mr Grey, you put yourself in the way of trouble, with this interest in reform?'

'Trouble no. Progress yes, I hope.'

'Ah, you must defer to a Frenchman on the link between those two. Do you meet these truly radical men sometimes?'

Roscarrock was fighting to remember who he was supposed to be. 'I – yes – I can say in this company that I have met some.'

'And how do you meet them? I confess myself fascinated by the idea. Where does one meet?'

'The right inns at the right time. In the right company.'

'So interesting.' Again the fingers reached intimately for Roscarrock's sleeve. 'We must talk a little more reform, Mr Grey. I have much to learn from you.'

'I—' Already uneasy in the conversation, Roscarrock suddenly felt his other arm delicately touched as well, himself now bizarrely gripped between the Frenchman and Lady Charlotte Pelham.

'Philippe, are you keeping Mr – ah – to yourself?'

'Grey, Madam. I'm afraid I was keeping Monsieur Philippe.'

'Philippe is such a disappointment to us, Mr Grey. What can one do with a Frenchman who is neither a Royalist icon nor a radical activist?'

'With your permission, I'll leave you to try to convert him one way or the other.' A short distance away, Rokeby Harris was alone, and Roscarrock stepped to one of the great windows near him.

He took a breath. 'Do you play chess, Mr Harris?'

The old, neat head turned slowly. It was closest Rokeby Harris would come to betraying surprise. A reluctant smile shadowed the mouth.

'Occasionally. Do you, sir?'

'I'm just learning.'

The smile had faded into the lines of age. 'It takes a lifetime.'

'The first step is to find the right person to learn from.'

Harris nodded slightly. 'Mr Grey, isn't it?' The ghost of a businesslike smile on the contained face. 'A name for anonymity.'

'A Frenchman has just told me that Napoleon wants to protect British business.'

'I'd be wary of such a man, Mr Grey. He's either a liar or a fool.'

Roscarrock nodded. 'I assumed he was the former, but not on this point.'

'Mm. Napoleon covets our financial dominance, Grey, and our money, but not our selves; a man of business will hang as well as a soldier. The men of business may find Napoleon's rule rather restrictive. Why do you think so many French financiers are practising their English in drawing rooms like this one?' He paused. Roscarrock waited. 'But your friend is right. Good business will outlast a bad war. Fifty years ago we were in another war with the French, and Lloyds of London had French ships insured with them. Boulton and Watt sent their first steam engine to France. Good business. The biggest investors of today have interests across Europe. They're hedging their bets, and why shouldn't they? Would you bet on Britain?'

'Is this a bad war?'

The head turned slowly towards him again. 'As a shipbuilding man, Grey, you don't need me to advise you on business conditions. Our reforming friends here will accuse us of profiteering. But each panic about the Irish, or the French, or the angry labourers, sends the men of money into hysteria. How many invasions have we had or nearly had in the last century? 1708. The fifteen and the forty-five. Ninety-eight. More. And every time, there's panic in the City and a run on the bank. Money is fleeing England, Grey, and it's probably wise to do so.'

Harris looked out of the window into the darkened square, and Roscarrock watched his eyes moving. 'The Government is obsessed with radicalism, as if this were a simple battle between an army of radical men and an army of absolute reactionaries.' He shook his head at the night. 'Real change won't come in some military crisis, but in a quiet shifting of self-interest. Real change will come when enough people of the middling sort find that they prefer something closer to the ideas of reform. The Government's attitude to treason is similarly crude.'

'That's understandable. Treason is a man selling his country.'

'But it's almost certainly not, Mr Grey. It's a man deciding that his idea of that country is better served by accommodation with Napoleon. Even more dangerous, and perhaps more likely, it's a man working out how to come to terms with Napoleon's inevitable victory, and limit its effects on him.'

Throughout the exchange Harris had given no indication of his own feelings at all, and Roscarrock was suddenly tired of the shadows and the sour cynicism of all the philosophical talk. He stepped silently back into the whirl at the centre of the room, leaving Harris to the night.

'Napoleon is like one of the new factories, Lady Charlotte. A brutal means of achieving progress. Personally, I do not believe that Napoleon cares a jot for the ideals that he inherited from the Revolution. But he is a necessary means of creating a world where they have a hope of flourishing.'

'And Britain, Sir Joseph? Are we then a rival enterprise?'

'I fear you do not quite follow, Lady Charlotte. We... we are a surly mob of machine-breakers, anxious to preserve our mediaeval traditions.'

'Of course we are!' she said quickly. 'That's very good, Sir Joseph.'

Roscarrock at the entrance to the salon, regathering his energy and his sanity. *I am not of these people. I do not understand them. But how can I now complain at their affectations and little deceits?*

The sea seeming very far away, and then a series of peculiar images flashed in front of his face, or seemed with hindsight to have flashed, their order as capricious as the episodes of his new life: an earnest male face – a hand holding a glass of wine – Jessel glancing towards the man – the glistening blue coat of a waiter interrupting Roscarrock's view – the man looking more closely at the wine – some intensity in the face of the man's companion – Jessel again – a clumsy movement from the companion and the man jerking backwards as the wine splashed towards his coat – Jessel – Jessel staring at the scene – Jessel's predatory face spinning towards Roscarrock, but no, not at Roscarrock, past him.

Roscarrock's glance followed, to the waiter walking down the stairs. Back to Jessel – Jessel's face fiercer still – eyes burning ferociously at him now with words he could not say, and nodding heavily towards the descending back of the waiter, and instinctively, mechanically, Roscarrock started to move towards the stairs.

What has just happened? The images began to flicker and arrange themselves.

The top of the stairs, and starting down, then the waiter on an instinct glanced over his shoulder and saw Roscarrock and saw something set in his face and began to hurry. Roscarrock matched his pace, then had to hold himself back as he remembered the place, saw the man trot the few steps to the door and push through, hurried after him, and on a sudden inspiration clapped his hand over his mouth as if about to vomit. He clattered through the door, eyes searching for the distinctive sheen of the waiter's coat, momentarily bewildered in the busy mingling of men and carriages and the glitter of the lamps, and then catching it, a flash of blue in the patches of evening. Now the man was running, and Roscarrock set off after him.

I am chasing a man I do not know, for a reason I do not know. The simplicities of life on the boat, of honest, calculating Simon, of their crew, of their suddenly harmless-seeming illegalities, were in vivid contrast to this madness. But actually they were not, because again this was a deceit of his mind, because the impressions and images of his past only came later as he tried to process the chaos.

The full length of one side of the square, weaving through strolling figures and horses and the sudden blank wall of a carriage, always the flash of blue in the distance, and then not. Hunting for the flash again, a bright eye through the mask of evening, there must be... and yes, there was a side street and there was the coat, jogging into the gloom. Roscarrock's feet braced firm on the unsteady deck and took off fast on their new bearing, away from the bustle and the light.

But now the blue shimmer had gone with them, and the three alleys into which Roscarrock peered reflected back at him only darkness.

Jessel caught his eye as soon as he reached the top of the stairs again, and without holding the glance Roscarrock gave the slightest shake of his head. A few minutes later he contrived to be offered a drink from a tray at the same time as Jessel.

A nod across the room. 'Mind telling me who that is, then?'

Jessel spoke into his glass. 'The one who lost his wine is an American engineer, who you should forget about immediately. Until someone decides we have to kill him, we're trying to protect his life. The companion who knocked the wine is one of ours, and that's what he was doing.' Jessel turned away beside him. 'Picked up anything else?'

'A growing conviction that I chose to grow up at far too rough and demanding an end of society, and imminent indigestion. That Boeldieu person seems very interested in the practical details of English radicalism, unlike all these other salon idealists.'

'De Boeldieu? The fop? Lord, if he's Napoleon's man in London we shouldn't have too much of a problem.'

'Perhaps, but how many of these other ladies and gentlemen would be interested in whether and how actually to meet radical men?'

'Perhaps he's just taken a fancy to you. It is a very flattering coat.'

'I didn't get very far with Rokeby Harris, maybe because I'm not sure which direction I'm supposed to be going.'

'Harris? Your friend Forster put you onto him?' Roscarrock tried to read Jessel's tone. 'So he's one of Kinnaird's, is he?'

'I assume so. Surprised?'

Jessel shrugged. 'I knew we had him on the roll, but from the stuff I've seen he's breadcrumbs. Bit of business gossip. Keep at them, Tom.'

The polite swirl, the dance of conversation and intersecting groups, moved on.

'You must have a great many men under you, Mr Grey.' The words themselves seemed to give Lady Charlotte Pelham physical pleasure. 'What then is your feeling for the rights of man?'

'In my experience men think of food for their children long before they think of their rights.'

Someone said that this was a terribly primitive approach, and Roscarrock resisted the urge to punch him. Lady Charlotte's fingers were on his arm. 'But how very real,' she said. 'Don't you think that a wonderfully real position, Sir Joseph?'

Roscarrock hadn't noticed Plummer to one side, but he couldn't avoid him now. The old radical's eyes were fixed on him. 'I find it increasingly hard to know what's real and what's not, Lady Charlotte,' he said, without shifting that gaze or blinking once.

Yet again the costumes danced around him, and as Roscarrock moved to the side of the room to look for new and promising conversations, Rokeby Harris suddenly appeared in front of him.

'Young man, will you take a piece of good advice from a man who's old enough to care more for security than decorum?'

'I'd take good advice from Napoleon himself.'

The flat, practical voice continued steady and soft. 'You're intelligent, Mr Whoever, but you're ignorant. That makes you dangerous to others and dangerous to yourself.' A thin, grave smile. 'Here endeth the lesson.'

Then Roscarrock was accosted by a young actress who wished him to try another ice with her, and Harris faded into the crowd.

Across a table, the thick curls of Burdett the reforming politician leant in to catch the hurrying words of his companion, the orator Hodge. Burdett's eyes flicked up as Roscarrock's shadow fell across the table, he glanced back at Hodge, and then hastily excused himself with a hand on the shoulder and a regretful smile.

'I'm afraid I've scared off your prey, Mr Hodge.'

Hodge's cheeriness was unaffected. 'You mistake, Mr Grey. He's not worried about talking to you; he's worried about being seen talking to me too much. I should despise these early-evening radicals. But Burdett is a good and clever man, and he and I each have our little parts to play in what must be. Lovely wife too, rich as... as the wife of Croesus. Such a comfort to a man, I have no doubt.'

'Yours must be a harder road, Mr Hodge. Travelling from town to town; food and bed as best you can; no heiress to fund your oratory.'

Hodge was brisk and open. 'If that's a polite offer, Mr Grey, I'll not say no. Will you take a piece of chicken?' He held up a silver tray and helped himself to a piece at the same time as Roscarrock did. 'Thank you for not being shocked at my forwardness. That's the comfort of you practical men. Not a gasp nor a frown nor a fit of the vapours when a man engages with the world as he must. I'm afraid that you and your kind get the wrong end of my words every now and then – all that gold makes you too gleaming a target to pass up – but I urge you to believe me when I emphasize my understanding, Mr Grey, and my respect.' His shining gaze had dropped from Roscarrock to the table halfway through the last sentence, and he was casting around for something else to eat. 'Will you be anywhere near Bury St Edmunds, Mr Grey?'

Roscarrock hesitated. 'If I can.'

Hodge picked up a plum. 'That's good. I shall have an eye for you, and send you an invitation if I can.'

The need for inconspicuousness forced another question to pass unasked. A shoulder pressed forwards against Roscarrock's, and he found the grey beak of Sir Joseph Plummer close beside him, apparently deep in contemplation of the plate of chicken. The old face looked up, and stared forbiddingly at Hodge.

Roscarrock took in a slow and silent breath, and politely held up the meat for the old man's closer consideration. Hodge withdrew.

Plummer ignored the chicken. 'It's not saying much, but your comment to Lady Charlotte was among the more sensible things that's been said this evening – or probably ever – in this theatre of a house. How accidental was it, Mr Grey?'

'Entirely. Neither the quality of the wine nor the quality of the company are familiar to me.'

The sharp, aged face gave the words closer attention than their flippancy deserved. 'You seem to paddle comfortably enough in these shallow waters of radicalism.'

'Just a vague acquaintance really.'

'You wear your shipbuilding and your radicalism rather lightly, I think.'

Roscarrock was grappling rapidly for fluency. 'I tend to be too boring about both, I fear. My shipbuilding you may leave to me, but I'm eager to learn more of your radicalism, if it's the future it seems to be.'

'You think it's the future?'

'I know a bit about men, Sir Joseph. As Lady Pelham says.'

'Lady Pelham is an imbecile, and you know it.'

'I don't think that the success of reform in Britain depends on her.'

'Then why are you here? The others are no better than her.'

'There's you, Sir Joseph. A man with an interest in reform would put up with a lot of Lady Pelhams to listen to you. And if there's nothing better, why are you here?'

Plummer smiled thinly, accepting the point. 'Attention, perhaps, Mr Grey. The vanity of an old man who will not live to see his dreams fulfilled.' In his fake humility he looked less frail than ever. 'And money. These papier-mâché puppets will delight in supporting the eloquent and vague dreams of a feeble faded prophet.'

'And if that money should end up in the hands of. . .'

'Of men younger and fitter and better able to carry on the work, then Lady Charlotte can continue to dream of radicalism in whatever harmless shape pleases her, and never be troubled by the reality.'

'And aren't you troubled by what those young fit able men will get up to?'

The old man said nothing. He didn't look troubled and he didn't look harmless, and he continued to look at Roscarrock with the predatory eyes of a hawk.

After a moment he said mildly, 'Have you seen old Kinnaird, recently, Mr Grey?'

'Kinnaird?'

Roscarrock's blood had surged at the name – and on Plummer's dangerous lips. He realized how much Kinnaird had been lurking on the edge of his consciousness. The old Scotsman, originally the one point of clarity in a blurred world, had become the greatest of shadows. He seemed active everywhere, revered and vital, but Roscarrock's picture of him was fading. He moved in a parallel world, visible to Roscarrock only through windows like the Admiral and Reverend Forster. Who, after all, was Kinnaird?

'You know. Sir Keith Kinnaird. I'm sure you'd have met him if – as you say – you're a vague acquaintance of these circles.'

Roscarrock seemed to think. 'Kinnaird. Scottish? Man of business of some kind?' Plummer was watching his blank face closely. 'I think you're right. Met him once or twice. Don't think I've seen him for a while.' He leant forwards. 'You've probably gathered, Sir Joseph, but despite my wonderfully real perspective on the rights of man, I'm not one for social conversation with him.'

'No.' Roscarrock couldn't read Plummer's intensity. The old man was playing with him somehow, and at the same time in absolute earnest. 'But then, Mr Grey, once one is in a certain circle of the world, the question is no longer whether one is in touch with affairs that are secret, but how one responds to the suggestion.'

Plummer obviously thought he'd caught him out somehow, and the thought was enough. Roscarrock barely understood the point made, but the sense of discomfort in it resonated. He produced a quick, open smile. 'Well, Sir Joseph, you obviously know more about that and about Sir Keith Kinnaird than I do.'

The old man winced, and said seriously, 'I think perhaps I do, Mr Grey.' Roscarrock's was only a tactical victory, and they both knew it.

Plummer was willing to release him, and Roscarrock took a rapid glass of wine from a footman and a deep breath of air from an open window. He contrived to avoid Plummer for the rest of the evening, but adopted the old man's lines on Kinnaird word for word with everyone else he spoke to. Most knew Kinnaird, and many had spoken to him about politics in Britain and France. But then, what else did one speak about?

Whatever his professional impact, Tom Roscarrock was without knowing it an overnight literary phenomenon.

Having offered a polite goodnight to the steward at his club, an unusually anonymous building on Pall Mall, Rokeby Harris sat down to write a short note. He described Mr Grey physically, he summarized the conversation and, emphasizing that he was shifting to speculation, he made a short assessment of Mr Grey's character and role. He folded this into a letter, and marked it to an address in the City.

In the early hours of morning, Philippe de Boeldieu weaved his way to his lodgings, still clutching a glass of wine, got the key in the lock at the third attempt and made a noisy ascent of the stairs. He slammed the front door of his set of rooms, set down the glass, pulled off the lace-fringed coat, splashed water on his face, and sat at a table with new thoughtfulness and clarity. After a moment to compose his ideas, he began to write in slow elaborate strokes:

Madame de la Frenais, St James's Square, the 27th of July 1805. Delacroix. Lafleur. Comte du Guichy. Maréchal. Saint-Aubin. Plummer. Bellamy. Lady Pelham. Burdett. Hodge. Fulton. Wood. Miller. Humphreys. Strathairn. Harris. Tuff. Mrs Tyler. A new man calling himself Thomas Grey. Tall. Thirty-five? Innocent but interested in politics. Question: who is he working for?

[SS K/F/86]

Only three hundred yards across London, in a different and a more elegant room, another correspondent had sat down to describe the evening. Still wearing his coat, a small glass of wine beside him, he too wrote a location and a list of names. Then: *Fulton, the American – he has refused all persuasion, moral or financial. Your contingency directive has therefore come into effect. A first attempt tonight was unsuccessful. You will hear once his betrayal of his contract with France has been concluded permanently.* The stylish flow continued. He summarized the conversations, touching on matters economic, agricultural and political. He, too, had been struck by the new acquaintance. *A shipbuilder called Mr Thomas Grey. He is not really a shipbuilder, and it is extremely unlikely he is called Mr Thomas Grey.* The writer hesitated, and took a sip of wine. Then he added: *Could this be Roscarrock?*

Lady Charlotte Pelham sat up in bed to write her journal, a glowing face buried in a snowdrift of nightwear, pillows, bedclothes and curtains. The stranger had caught her attention as well. She acknowledged no doubts about Mr Grey's name or business. Her speculations about him had nothing to do with politics.

A little after midnight, a tall, fair-haired man half-opened the door of a room in Horse Guards building and stuck his head in. Major Ralph

Royce had had a very pleasant dinner, and was thinking of a lady rather than paperwork, but a lurking sense of guilt at the luxury of the evening had sent him into his office just to check that all was in order. On his desk there was a single sheet of paper, askew on the wood and pale in the light from the window. The anomaly of the paper demanded attention, and it surely couldn't take too long to sort a single sheet.

The eyebrows rose on the well-cut face, and Major Royce took another sheet of paper and copied the essentials of the first, addressing the new message to Mr Morrison Cope at the Admiralty. He could deliver it as he left.

EXTRACT FROM THE DIARY OF SIR JOSEPH PLUMMER

Twenty-seventh of July: Madame de la Frenais. Another tiresome performance of the masque of deceit, and I grow ever more weary of it. Somewhere within me the old spirit burns fierce and angry, but it is damped down by the painted layers of affectation and duplicity. A part of me longs to be out of London, to be left in some raw and troubled part of the land with nothing but my mind and voice and the chance to do some small but clear act of brutal progress. I long for the simple certainties and strong potential of orator Hodge, the simple certainties and strong potential that once were mine. Instead I must stifle in these political theatres, trying to tell apart the few truly committed from the host of faint-hearts and followers of fashion.

And it is an ever-murkier pool in which we swim. Almost everyone this evening, and probably I myself, was engaged in some pretence, some deception of others or of themselves. Some are pretending to be more radical than they are, some pretending to be less. Now, though, there is an ever-larger shoal of men pretending to be what they are not. I fear that fully three in ten of those present this evening had some secret and treacherous motive. Can a man be truly as bluff and crude as Tuff? What does Delacroix write, and for whom does he write it? Why is it that a man like Grey, among the fittest and most intelligent there, must also be among the most shadowed and shifting? I loathe these perversions of truth and ideal. It is a world where men are trying to betray treason, a world where names and faces lie, where words themselves are dust.

I know myself not a man of violence or anarchy, but that same simple part of me secretly hopes for some clear and definite act to cut through the fog of pretence and doubt. I have lived and thrived by my words, and I know it my duty to use my words until the very last of them to advance the cause of equality and reform in this land. But the blade and bullet and the barrel of powder have a clarity and certainty that cut through mere words. If progress grows ever slower, with the weight of resistance and conflicting ideals and deceit that do drag on it, then it will take some piece of pure, silent action to throw us forwards.

[SS M/1092/1]

My dear Gabriel,

I had your letter from Nottingham but none since and I think one lost. It heartens me much when I hear of you. Also I was thankful that you sold three pamphlets and hope that you are well for food and boots and so forth.

Gabriel, you seemed sad and angry in your letter and I wish you peace as I fear for where the devil will lead you if you stray. I hope that the great assembly will bring greater peace among men like you said and not greater violence because so many men will make a great mischief if they are not well guided. I beg you to have a care for yourself for one act of prudence will keep you for a hundred acts of spirit. I hope your voice is well.

Here Purvis is more angry now even than before and sometimes Jenny suffers because he is too much a coward to attack the King or the soldiers but Jenny will do. He is asking for a little money for my keep but there is only what I can sew for. Do not fret for this as normally his moods pass. Mrs Tunny died. Yesterday we had news from Wakefield. The coal men marched to the Mayor's house and cried We demand bread at one hapenny and the Mayor *said You are all good men and I will see you well. But some of the men began to throw stones and turfs and there was scuffling and the Captain of Volunteers cried for his men to protect him and protect the Mayor but they cried We will not fire on good and honest men but then some of the soldiers did fire and two men were very hurt. Now the Mayor is more angry and the Magistrates are like to hang some of the men but they cannot trust the soldiers now either.*

Even though Purvis is not always a good man I envy Jenny that she has him and wish that I am beside you soon. The trees are lovely in the evenings and it is pity to walk under them alone.

Your devoted wife,
~~Flora~~ Chance.

[SS M/1108/2]

＊

There were two men loitering near the door as Jessel approached it, and with surprising speed one shifted to block his path. Jessel smiled at him, which got no reaction at all, and then coughed over the rounded bulk of the shoulder and through the doorway. Lord Hugo Bellamy looked up and growled his permission for entry.

'Is Roscarrock coming here?'

'As you instructed, My Lord; here at any time.'

'Know what this place is, Jessel?'

'No, My Lord.'

'Never been here, then? Never heard of it?'

'No, My Lord.'

The Admiral seemed to evaluate this for a second. 'It's Kinnaird's lodging, Jessel. Or rather: it was.' He straightened a piece of paper in front of him, checked for new certainty in it, and then his head lifted to stare bleakly at Jessel. 'He's flown. He's absconded. Sir Keith Kinnaird has disappeared.'

Eyes wide, Jessel murmured, 'Christ...'

The news only increased his curiosity about where the elusive old man had lived when in London. A house in an anonymous courtyard within sight of the Bank of England; a pair of rooms at the top of the building, comfortable but plain. The living room was quickly summarized: the large, leather-top desk behind which Bellamy sat in grim majesty and which took up fully a third of the space; two well-upholstered chairs framing a small fireplace; a set of shelves holding perhaps fifty books, with a few gaps. Through another open door Jessel could see a bedroom.

The only decoration on the walls was provided by three large maps, of London, the whole of Britain, and north-western France. 'Not exactly a connoisseur, was he?' Jessel said quietly.

'Explains why his conversation was always so damned dull. He's taken a couple of books with him, but you can see the rest: with the exception of a couple of bits of German philosophy, it's all business. Directories, gazetteers, shipping, trade, engineering, agriculture. If you wanted the name of a north country parson, if you wanted to know the ancestry of a Provençal count, if you wanted to catch the next ship to Lisbon, Kinnaird would have been indispensable.'

'Papers?'

'Oh yes, Jessel, he had a whole desk full of papers.'

'Had?' He followed the Admiral's glare across the room. 'Oh. And now he has a whole fireplace full of ash. Not in too much of a hurry, then.'

A hint of satisfaction settled on Bellamy's heavy stone face. 'Perhaps just a bit.' On the leather in front of him he spread out three fragments of paper, each of the same irregular shape, each badly scorched around the edges. 'He has taken some papers and books with him, but he was too efficient to carry this – little pocketbook of some kind — his reflections and opinions.'

'Anything?'

'Two dozen pages survived under the grate, mostly too scorched.' Bellamy's fingers drummed once on one of the sheets. 'He certainly picked up my suspicions about him.' The hand moved to the next sheet. 'And this will interest you.' The outstretched fingers spun the single bruised page and pushed it towards Jessel.

The fair head bent down over the desk, picking at the broken words with a mutter and then skimming through an undamaged block of the meticulous script.

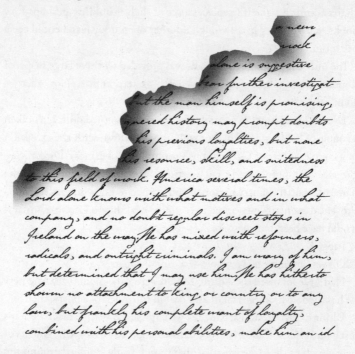

a new
nock
alone is suggestive
for further investigat
ut the man himself is promising,
quered history may prompt doubts
his previous loyalties, but none
his resource, skill, and suitedness
to this field of work. America several times, the
Lord alone knows with what motives and in what
company, and no doubt regular discreet stops in
Ireland on the way. He has mixed with reformers,
radicals, and outright criminals. I am wary of him,
but determined that I may use him. He has hitherto
shown no attachment to king, or country or to any
laws, but frankly his complete want of loyalty,
combined with his personal abilities, make him an id

[SS M/827T]

'Roscarrock, of course, My Lord.'

'Oh yes.'

'Ireland?'

'I told you to look at that name.'

Someone barked a low 'Sir' from the doorway. Jessel turned and Bellamy looked up to see one of the guard dogs standing on the threshold. Behind him was Tom Roscarrock.

Bellamy nodded, and the gatekeeper stood aside.

'Excellently timed, Roscarrock. Close the door. You can tell us about Sir Keith Kinnaird.'

Roscarrock stood on the bare floorboards, feeling the confrontation in the eyes and attitudes of the two men in front of him, wondering at the closed door and the heavy men behind.

After five long and watchful seconds, he said, 'I've spent less time with him than I have with the man who brought me supper last night. I only know of him what Jessel has told me.'

The acidity in the Admiral's words was tempered by his usual measured pace. 'Very well, then let me tell you a little. Kinnaird is eccentric, wayward and insubordinate. But he is also obsessive about procedure and rigorous in his professionalism. He roams the country working God knows what mystery and mayhem and amusing himself at my ignorance of it, but in two years he has never been a single second late for the regular council that I hold with him and certain other associates. I have known him hurry from his sickbed, I have known him hurry from Dublin, just to keep the appointment. This morning he failed.' Bellamy flexed his delicate fingers. 'Certain... procedures were immediately put into effect. When a man of Kinnaird's seniority is missed, every known aspect of his property is secured.'

Roscarrock stood watchful and poised near the door.

'Two explanations were possible. But a dead man would not have burnt his papers and removed a satchelful of books.' Roscarrock glanced to the gaps on the shelves, then back to the Admiral. 'For reasons best known to himself, Sir Keith Kinnaird has decided to sever all connection with this organization. He's slipped his anchor. He's gone.'

Like Jessel before him, Roscarrock looked around the room, for clues to a life and a mind, now less substantial than ever.

'You ever hear of a place called Tiverton, Roscarrock? In Devonshire?'

Now Roscarrock was very watchful indeed.

'Word arrived at the War Office late last night that a dragoon had been murdered there. No indication of who or why.'

Roscarrock felt and tested the balls of his feet in his boots, thought of the door and the men behind him, checked the position of the window to the left of his vision, watched for the words on the Admiral's lips.

'Kinnaird killed him. He says as much.'

This was news to Jessel too. 'He admits it, My Lord?'

Bellamy tapped the third scorched page. 'Explicitly. He'd been meeting some of his regular contacts around the south-west. In Tiverton, he saw the dragoon and decided he was an inconvenience. On some pretext he invited the man into the Magistrate's house there, which was empty, and stabbed him.' He shook his head slightly. 'There's an odd kind of pride in the description. I suppose Kinnaird was always more of a manager than a man of action.' He looked up. 'This sheet alone would hang him.'

Roscarrock's confusion escaped onto his face, and Bellamy saw it. 'Unhappy, Roscarrock?'

Roscarrock hesitated, then shook his head slowly. 'Yours is a damn strange world, Admiral. The other two pages?'

'One does not concern you. Kinnaird's private reflections on me, and I'm sure you don't need Kinnaird to fuel your wit at my expense.' He looked up at Roscarrock, discreet interest on the heavy face. 'The other does concern you – you explicitly, Roscarrock.'

Jessel had a thin, hard smile – of a secret shared, of relish at the intensity of the moment – and Roscarrock saw it. 'Tom, for those of us who had not the honour to be recruited by Sir Keith, your story's very inspiring.'

The Admiral brushed away the interruption. 'Your reminiscences and insights about America we can reserve for another day. Your Irish contacts may prove useful sooner. Kinnaird's assessment of you – filtered through my own assessment of Kinnaird – does not alter my attitude at all. I do not trust you, Roscarrock. You are the choice of a man whose motives and loyalties have always been suspect and are now to be greatly feared. But I trust none of those who work for me; I trust only your ability to do your work. We have yet to see your full talents, I think. You will prove yourself or not in my service. You are under the closest scrutiny, Roscarrock.' A pause and a disdainful glance invited comment.

'Fine,' Roscarrock said firmly. 'We know where we stand.' He did not know where he stood; his last certainties had collapsed.

Bellamy was pushing the damaged pages together with his fingers. 'Well, gentlemen,' he said to the table, 'the fox is out now. We need waste no more time bumbling in the undergrowth.'

Jessel said, 'What do we do about him?'

'The grim possibilities of what he is really up to, and in whose service, are no matter for the public. For the public, I have already put it out that he is wanted for murder.'

'The dragoon?'

'Too dull, Jessel. In half the towns of England they'd elect him mayor for that, rather than turning him in. No, Sir Keith Kinnaird has foully murdered his wife and infant son.'

'So then we leave it to the Magistrates and the militia to find him.'

'Jessel, I'd be pleasantly surprised if most of our Magistrates and militia could find the nearest privy. But this might keep Kinnaird out of mischief.'

Roscarrock said quietly, 'His network – all those unique agents – would he try to damage it?'

'It's a point but, frankly, any damage he hasn't already done he'll be able to do long before we can get to him.' The Admiral sat back, stiff. 'To be honest, Roscarrock, I'm more concerned with the use to which he might put that precious network of his. Or, indeed, the use to which he has been putting it for some time.'

'Do you think he's working for France or not?'

'You heard the conversations last night, Roscarrock. Isn't everyone?' The great head shook slowly. 'Kinnaird has always worked for his independent interest. We must speculate that he no longer believes that interest best served in this organization.' The gaze snapped back. 'Do not become sentimental. Kinnaird's treachery does not change the essential. You have problems enough with your own reputation, Roscarrock.' The eyes were cold. They held Roscarrock's for a second longer, then switched to Jessel. 'Progress?'

Jessel shrugged. 'One of Kinnaird's specials seemed to have responded well to Roscarrock – one we've not heard from in months – said he might know something about our tailor – but he's not sent what he promised.'

'The Irishman – Fannion?'

'You saw the reports from Liverpool, My Lord. He'd been there sure enough, but no traces. The Irish community has just closed in on itself – protecting their own.'

Bellamy shook his head in ponderous distaste – whether at the deficiencies of his organization or of the Irish race was not clear. But his eyes stayed locked on Tom Roscarrock.

'Your task will not get easier until you make it so. You now have Kinnaird to think of too – what he was doing, and what he is doing. The man better connected than most in the Kingdom, who's just gone bad. The man who sent us Tom Roscarrock.' Roscarrock looked for pleasantry in the eyes, but there was none. 'Never mind, Roscarrock. Perhaps the doubts of a man himself of doubtful loyalty make you purer than any of us.' He didn't look convinced. 'Finish up here.'

Then he was gone, escorted by one of the burly guards.

Roscarrock closed the door, breathed out, and turned to Jessel. 'So I'm checking the room, and you're checking me?'

Jessel smiled, but there was no life in it. 'Problem is this, Tom: not that

Kinnaird's network is even more lost to us, or in danger, but that it might not be what it's supposed to be.' Roscarrock nodded understanding. 'Think of it: all those influential and knowledgeable people, all over the country, controlled by a man whose loyalties have just drifted across the Channel.'

'So why aren't you putting the thumb-screws on me?'

'In good time, Tom; in good time. We're all dubious characters hereabouts. And like the Admiral said, the fact that Kinnaird had his own suspicions about you may be a good sign.' He started walking towards the bedroom, then stopped. 'But yes, we're watching you.'

Kinnaird had been efficient in his living and efficient in his leaving, and a thorough search didn't take long. Having looked in, under or behind every one of the few pieces of furniture and bedding, they spent another fifteen fruitless minutes looking for loose floorboards, hollow beams or panels, and re-covered plaster. A further thirty were spent riffling through the books and journals. Jessel conceived an interest in Kinnaird's business dealings – did his financial speculations illustrate his changing loyalties? Did a concern with trade accompany an exchange of allegiance? The wrappers of recently arrived mercantile reports – to Sir K. Kinnaird, at Fitzsimmons's, Fleet Street – a coffee house across town – were thrown impatiently aside as he tried to conjure potential deceits from Kinnaird's knowledge of the state of Baltic trade. Roscarrock, meanwhile, was leaning against the door, distracted early in the process by a bulky and occasionally annotated gazetteer of every port in Britain. A sharp breath from Jessel as he found another mark in a margin by an apparently uninteresting snippet of Prussian trading data, or spotted the recurrence of a company or a commodity, would shortly be followed by a hiss of irritation as the new guess collapsed and he spotted his own desperation. Roscarrock slipped the book of ports back into its place, and watched his companion. He rarely saw anger and energy in languid, sardonic Jessel, and wondered what he'd be like as an opponent.

The Irishman, the tailor and the fleet. English stability and French instability. Kinnaird's words; where did he stand now? He needed to know what game the old man was really playing, and by what rules. Without that he would never make sense of anything.

He dutifully pulled out *Morris's Register of Ships*, then pushed it back. These rooms and these books told the plain truth about Kinnaird: a man deft and knowledgeable in the currents of finance and goods and information of north-western Europe, a man well suited to business and to intelligence; a man, perhaps, who saw no difference between them. The rooms and the books told no more of the truth than Kinnaird wanted.

From the single window came the busy cries of a London morning, greetings and complaints and urgings, loud street hagglings over pennies echoing the indoor whispers of fortunes; they were as inarticulate and insistent as the gull calls that wheeled around the spires with them, and as indifferent to the obsessions of two Government agents. These noises were routines – they were both the currency and the exchange – that had changed little since the Romans first built their forum on the hill here. These noises had been London's preoccupation across the centuries, while Kings and Governments and Empires had come and gone with the Thames tide.

Temporarily bored of statistics, Jessel snatched up two of the journal wrappers from where he'd dropped them and looked for hints of origin in the paper, the style of writing in the simple address, the markings. Frustration increasingly souring his lively face, he then went back and noted down the dedications in the few books that had been gifts.

By now Roscarrock had sat down behind the desk, flicking at a wrapper, watching Jessel with growing irritation, and thinking of the man who was the one thing of value missing from the room.

Awareness of the scrutiny wasn't improving Jessel's mood either, and Roscarrock spoke as much to justify his own idleness.

'Kinnaird can't run his whole network of specials in person, surely. He's not visiting them all, all the time.'

Jessel, book open in hands, half-turned and just shrugged.

'But their information isn't coming to your friend Morrison Cope at the Admiralty, is it?'

'No.' Jessel was paying attention now, but reckoned he was ahead. 'That's the interest of this place. They could write to him here – meet him sometimes, no doubt. That's why we clamped down so quick.' He closed the book and turned back to the shelves.

'And he knows that. So what's he going to do now? Write to every contact with a new address? Too risky; too unlikely.'

'Hallo!' Jessel turned back with a small pocketbook in his hands, and threw on the desk the larger one he'd been replacing. 'Ledger of some kind... accounts maybe, stock market trades... lovely! I'll have this one.'

His mood was restored, and he looked at Roscarrock with genial concern. 'We'll have this place monitored from now on, Tom.' He watched him. 'Not happy, are you?'

Roscarrock shook his head, irritated at uncertainty. 'Doesn't work. Man like Kinnaird doesn't take risks, not with his prize network above all things, if what you say is true. And he's not going to cut loose from it.'

'Tom, he's cut loose from everything.' Jessel leant forwards. 'Don't get comfortable just because I'm a friendly face. Sir Keith bloody Kinnaird is rotten, somehow. He's halfway to Paris or halfway to hell and either way you want to concentrate on staying the right side of the divide.' Jessel's eyes flickered in thought. 'If he's thinking at all straight, he'll stay cut off from the network because the network is our best chance of finding him.'

Roscarrock wasn't paying attention. He glanced around the room. 'This wasn't panic; this wasn't flight.'

'It's not supposed to make sense, Tom.' Jessel was smiling. 'If it all made sense, they'd have to stop paying us.' He picked up two books and the small ledger. 'We're done here. Come and buy me a drink and tell me the opportunities for promising young men in America.'

Roscarrock followed him out reluctantly, wondering at the lies of Sir Keith Kinnaird.

Inspector Gaston Gabin of the Paris Police was entitled to a tiny office of his own. The stench of the Seine coming through the dirty window, and the must of timbers that never quite dried, made the space a dubious privilege. But the space, and the door, were a privilege that Gabin cherished, and the closing of that door a luxury that he considered essential to his proper functioning.

Many men who had been caught out by the speed of his activities would have been surprised by this insistence on reflection, on steady method. The Minister, too, would have been alarmed if he'd seen him closing that door, sitting down behind the small and broken desk and staring into the corner. The Minister wanted him giving orders, galloping somewhere, hurrying to produce a report. He was just back from delivering the morning report that the Minister had requested. He had taken care to arm himself with a busy list of actions completed, and lines of investigation in hand, with which to reassure the Minister.

He would have enjoyed trying to discover the spy: a most satisfying problem of deduction and elimination. Now it was a mere manhunt – routine procedural business, more intensive in labour than in clear thought. The immediate actions of yesterday had been almost tedious: the search of the room of the absconding manservant; questions about his habits and routines; the enquiries sent off about his family, and his history. The new France had excellently efficient systems for such business. At a word from him, horsemen had been galloping out of the city gates and messages flickering across the countryside by telegraph. Whether he spent a second in his office or an hour, he had the advantage of speed over little Joseph Dax, out there somewhere running like a rabbit. It was important to ensure that he had the advantage of thought over him as well – over him and over the system that must exist to sustain him, if he was as much of a spy as the Minister suggested.

The Minister was funny. A man of brilliance; a man of high intellect. But he had been genuinely surprised at the idea that his so-faithful servant should have been a spy all along. He was the former servant of arch-Royalists, and the Minister had assumed that this made Joseph Dax especially resentful towards them, and not especially devoted.

But then the Minister, like everyone else, thought that people responded to ideas. The Minister believed that the servant had responded to the ideas of the Revolution. He believed everyone had. When it turned out that his little servant had not, the Minister had to believe that he had succumbed to a rival idea – to the idea of the monarchy, as represented by some insinuating English spy-maker.

The Inspector knew that people responded to emotion. Always and only emotion, and it would have made Joseph Dax easy prey to the English, if they were as good as the Minister said. How, Gabin wondered, did they communicate with Joseph? How would they have identified him in the first place? A recommendation? Would they have found the man and manoeuvred him into that remarkable position, right beside the most powerful and feared man in the Emperor's service? Or would they have found the man in that position, and then attracted his loyalty? Had it been money he wanted, or was there some other emotional attachment? That might be important: it might help to catch the fugitive and it might help to explain how the English operated with him.

One way or another, it was always emotion and not ideas. The Revolution had been an act of frustration, not philosophy. The successful campaigns of the Emperor were the fruit of national pride, not strategy. And most times the crimes he dealt with from this little office had nothing to do with Royalist conspiracy, and everything to do with empty stomachs and empty pockets.

And now the Minister had his great plan to defeat the English. An act of political violence within weeks, in the heart of London, and then a little game played among the ships of the English navy a short while later, and then the Emperor's triumph would be complete. A great conspiracy built on the emotions.

The Inspector stared into the corner. If he were in the place of the unknown English spy-runner, how would he establish, manage and protect a Royalist agent in Paris?

———⟡———

At the corner of Fleet Street and Shoe Lane, at the western edge of the old City of London and near where it began to sprawl outwards into its newer and more fashionable districts, there stood for many years Fitzsimmons's Coffee House. Fitzsimmons's was one of the venerable institutions of the City, a place where men of business had sat and smoked their pipes and talked quietly of their affairs for generations. No money was ever exchanged over Fitzsimmons's scarred tables. But the rise and fall of colonies had been charted on them, and trading empires had changed hands in a word.

Tom Roscarrock arrived at the low, glazed door of Fitzsimmons's at the height of the mid-morning bustle, as he'd calculated. Three smart and earnest young men were pushing their way out, exchanging dreams, and he entered wedged between two large merchants who were red and sweating even before the hunched and bustling room swallowed them. He knew the sort of thing he was looking for, but wouldn't know exactly until he'd seen it, and he had to spend the shortest possible time staring curiously around.

The atmosphere suited him perfectly. No one was speaking above a murmur, most with heads bent towards each other and some with lips to ears, but the combined effect of ten cramped tables of hunched, black-coated bees was an impenetrable buzz that dominated the tiny room. Smoke hung in patches over the tables, and between them weaved and jostled servants and the impatient clientele. The two bulky merchants in front of him were bidding gruffly for a place and, as he moved this way and that to allow new arrivals or departures or the passage of another swaying tray, Roscarrock had two full minutes to scan the room and its traffic.

One part of his mind was re-testing the links of a glimpsed idea. The

Admiralty had received nothing from the Reverend Henry Forster for months. They knew where he lived, perhaps they'd tried visiting him, but he was still little more than a name, only to be accessed through Kinnaird himself or through a man chosen by Kinnaird. (That had turned out to be a dubious honour, hadn't it?) Yet Forster said he had sent a report six weeks ago.

There. The door leading to the basic facilities for those who'd overfilled themselves with coffee, presumably arranged in some dank courtyard off the back of the building, he'd deduced from the constant to and fro and those who were still adjusting their breeches as they returned. Whatever constituted the kitchen, its location was clear from servants and smell. But that kitchen was reached through a side door off a passage at the back of the coffee house, and during Roscarrock's two minutes he saw two men emerging from that passage and one entering it. Coats and manner made them undoubtedly men of business and not servants; one of the men who had emerged and then eased politely past him into the street had been slipping a packet into his coat as he went. That passage was what he was looking for.

As the two merchants pushed forwards in anticipation of an imminent table, he slipped past them and meandered towards the passage, his progress regulated by the trays that swerved in front of him and away and by the jam of chairs that scraped back and forth. Three paces short, and a servant caught his eye; Roscarrock looked through him, a busy man of affairs. As he reached the passage, it was suddenly blocked – a tall man, two drinks deftly carried in each hand. Roscarrock stepped to one side, with obvious show of irritation.

The man hurried past, with an earnest nod of thanks, and Roscarrock stepped into the passage. He couldn't hesitate now, couldn't show any lack of familiarity. His brain had to focus solely on absorbing and understanding the images in front of him: past the presumed kitchen – a glance – the kitchen indeed – now only ten feet of passage left; the passage was ending in a door – outside door, from the quality of light under it –

outside door didn't seem right; nowhere else – but now just before the door a short flight of wooden stairs up to the left, and as he took them, feet knocking hollow on each one, the man whom he'd seen entering the passage appeared at the top. A neutral nod, reciprocated as they squeezed past each other, and out onto another wooden passage; a moment's pause at the top – must keep moving – but two closed doors along the left-hand wall, a dusty window filtering stale light opposite them – knock before entering? – at the end of the passage some kind of open space.

The open space. Roscarrock walked calmly down the passage, building the picture of the space as each step brought more of it into his vision. A room: no more than ten feet by fifteen, wood floor, plaster walls, light from windows to the right and back somewhere to the left, a wooden counter running the length of the room, all the wood dark and worn, a man – servant's clothes? A clerk? – behind the counter, and the wall behind the man loomed dark with shelves. The shelves filled the wall completely from waist height to ceiling, divided into small pigeonhole compartments – one hundred? two? Many had rolled papers or packets in them. Underneath each was a label – names.

The view was instantaneously blocked. 'Good morning, sir. How are we today?' A pink, spectacled face was looking up into his.

This was Kinnaird's private system. Reports from his network of agents could be sent here rather than to the Whitehall clearing house. Perhaps those from France too. He could then choose what to forward to Whitehall.

The pink face was still inches from his, still staring at him.

'Good morning.' He was trying not to be obvious in scanning the name labels. 'My name is Roscarrock. I'm a colleague of Sir Keith Kinnaird.'

'Yes, sir. Always a pleasure to receive a colleague of Sir Keith.' The man was dapper, precise, and still blocking the way. 'How may we help you?'

The labels were alphabetical. 'Sir Keith asked me to come today, in his absence.' The clerk behind the counter had suddenly started flicking through a separate pile of papers.

'Indeed, sir. A pleasure to have you here.' Was that Kinnaird's name on a label – a label to a compartment filled with papers?

'He asked me to collect anything that might have come for him.'

Professionalism and infinite regret: 'Alas, sir, that will not be possible.'

Definitely Kinnaird's name on the label, and the compartment was filled with a mixture of single sheets rolled, and packets. 'He specifically asked. He said there would be no problem for a client of his standing.'

Regret and pain: 'I do so hope that we have not misled Sir Keith Kinnaird at any point. I was sure that he would know that we never release materials to anyone but the nominee themself, or to a nominated intermediary certified in advance.'

Roscarrock hadn't seen the sign, but in the far corner of the room another man had appeared, in the clerk's uniform of the man behind the counter but stretching it at every corner of his considerable height and breadth. The counter clerk was still riffling through papers, but glanced up once at Roscarrock.

Roscarrock smiled. 'It seems he didn't certify me in advance.'

A smile in return.

The bundle of documents was only feet from him, little more than an arm's reach, and promising so much. 'I don't want to have to go into the details of the importance of this material, and of my getting it to Sir Keith as quickly as possible.'

'I'm sure you don't, sir. I'm sure Sir Keith will understand that our procedures are designed to serve his interests, as always.'

Roscarrock gauged the distances, glanced again at the large man in the corner, now a step nearer: use the man in front of him to block the big man, lever off the man behind the counter to reach the documents, back down the passage – could he get through the mob in the coffee house in time? What would it achieve? Was it more important to read the documents or keep Kinnaird thinking that his system was unbroken?

He smiled down at the pink and spectacled face.

'I'm sure he will, Mr...?'

'Pewsey, sir.'

'Mr Pewsey. Very impressive, as he led me to expect. Good morning.'
Now he needed to get out, and quickly. These people needed to forget
him as soon as possible.

'Good morning to you, sir. I hope we shall welcome you again soon.'

Roscarrock turned and started down the passage, wondering at the
closed doors. He had to get his face away from here, and hope that his
name was forgotten soon afterwards.

'Mr Roscarrock!'

He stopped still in the passage. Had professional Pewsey weakened? Or
had he realized something that betrayed Roscarrock's lies?

'Mr Roscarrock, sir!' Footsteps behind him. Run or turn?

Roscarrock turned. Pewsey was behind him, holding a thin package.

'My sincere apologies, sir. I had not realized that you were expecting
something yourself, and my man took an age in checking, sir, an age.' He
held out the package. Roscarrock looked at Pewsey, at the package, and
back. Then he took the package with a curt nod: thin, perhaps a single
page or two, folded and sealed.

On the outside, in fine and flowing script: *T. Roscarrock, at Fitzsimmons's,
Fleet Street, London.*

<hr>

FIELD REPORT, RECEIVED THE 28TH DAY OF JULY 1805;
CREDIT ++

*As of the middle of July 1805 an itinerant tailor, name Gabriel Chance,
had been heard of in the parish of St Wulfram's, Grantham, Lincolnshire,
though it is not clear if he had visited the parish. Physical description is not
available. He had previously been in Manchester and Sheffield; movements
before that unknown. He had conversed with such men as he had met on his*

*journey, in inns and private houses. He had been inclined to speak at great
length of the rottenness of today's England, and the better world that was to
come when the old structures were overthrown. But he did not try to rouse
anyone listening to share his thoughts, nor to incite them to any specific act
of violence or unrest. Gabriel Chance would tell any listener that he was
a man inspired — the word was sometimes possessed — by a great spirit,
that he was waiting only on some final inspiration to perform a deed of
true greatness and significance, and that right-thinking men would follow
his inspiration. He had been moving on towards Ely and Newmarket, or
Cambridge, with London his final aim.*

[SS K/50/44]

❦

'We have the name of the tailor, My Lord.'

Admiral Lord Hugo Bellamy's eyes looked down in sudden and
real interest. 'That's very good, Jessel. That's very good.' In Bellamy, it
represented something like elation.

'We also have an idea of his possible movements. The name is Chance
– Gabriel Chance. He was known of in Lincolnshire a couple of weeks
back, heading to Cambridgeshire; there was no doubt of his intention to
aim for London eventually, and no doubt that he felt inspired to some act
of greatness – inspired and greatness were the exact words.'

Bellamy nodded, absorbing it all. 'Very well, then. The challenge is the
same. We know he's serious, we know we need to find him quickly. Get
to it, Jessel.'

Jessel murmured acknowledgement and turned away. 'Where did this
come from?' He turned back.

Uncomfortably: 'I don't know, My Lord. I have a shrewd guess, but I
don't know.' The confident flow had stumbled; he went on without waiting
for the question. 'It's Roscarrock. He's got the information somehow, and

he's... he's not saying, My Lord.'

The Admiral's eyes flicked hard and wide. 'He's what?'

'He just passed the information to me in the form of a new report, just as—'

'Just as Kinnaird would.'

Jessel stood silent; not a moment for wasted words. Bellamy ran a hand over his slab of a jaw. When it dropped again to the desk, it revealed a heavy and hungry smile. 'He's got awfully sure of himself awfully quickly, hasn't he?'

The glare roamed the room, and Jessel had the familiar sense of being something small hiding in the long grass.

'Does Roscarrock know which side he's on?' Jessel's eyebrows merely raised, accepting the question. 'I don't mind the side so much, as long as I know which it is. How would Kinnaird contact him, if he wanted to?' The big chest gave out one boom of a laugh, grim and curt. 'Keep at him, Jessel. Keep at him. I rather like the style of the man, but I need to know which way he faces.'

~◆~

The letter had come from the Reverend Henry Forster, using the route he normally used for his correspondence with Kinnaird. Roscarrock had read it three times before passing on the main points to Jessel, and he read it once more before burning it. After a sincere statement of affection to Roscarrock, the Vicar had added five lines of afterthought:

> *Post scriptum: Tom, if you should happen to come across Gabriel Chance, I urge you to tread gently. Before you smile at my luxuriant sympathy for such a troublesome fellow, let me assure you that my concern is largely for you. Gabriel Chance might, after all, truly know the path to the promised land, and history would*

*not look kindly on the man who hanged him before he
could show us.*

———

Roscarrock was back at the coffee house nine hours later, with darkness
to cover his activities and a strong knife to work at the locks. A minute's
observation from Fleet Street, when he'd left earlier in the day, had
suggested how the courtyards had to be laid out. Sure enough, twenty
yards down Shoe Lane from the main road he found a strip of complete
shadow between two buildings that was in fact a narrow alleyway. Shoe
Lane was gloomy enough, and a further thirty seconds tucked into the
alley entrance fully adjusted his eyes to the darkness. He began to move
further in with slow and cumbersome steps, feet slipping in the dust and
slime and tapping their cautious way over the mess of stone, wood and
who knew what other rubbish that littered the ground. From the smell,
something once vegetable or indeed animal had been left to rot nearby.

He reached the end of the alley, breathing shallow through his teeth,
and relished the chance to open his shoulders, if not his lungs. The little
courtyard was no more than ten feet square, but the amphitheatre of grimy
windows reflected a little light down into the darkness, enough to help
Roscarrock check the position of doors and windows. He glanced at his
shoulders and hands, confirming that the light wouldn't reveal him to
anyone who happened to be awake in one of those windows, and moved
quickly to the door he wanted.

For a full minute he stood with his eyes closed and one straining ear
pressed to the wood, seeking any sign of life inside. Then he eased his
knife out and began to work at the lock, trying to feel its resistances and
movements through the blade.

The lock's heavy click cracked into his sensitized brain, and he stood still
for another full minute. Then he replaced the knife, turned the handle
and stepped inside, teeth clenched in anticipation of a creak of door or

threshold. Another pause. He was where he anticipated: in front of him the passage ran straight to the coffee house; immediately to his right the stairs led up. Light from Fleet Street and the windows at the top of the stairs picked out the skeleton of the building.

From somewhere above him came faint, rhythmic breathing.

Roscarrock, taking the steps one every fifteen seconds and at their very edge, had expected this. Kinnaird and the rest of the capital's men of affairs, however legitimate their interests, would have wished them entrusted to something more than an old lock accessible to anyone with a strong knife or even boot. He took a breath, and eased one eye around the turn at the top of the stairs.

The entrance to the correspondence room was half-blocked by a door; through the door, outline edged in the grim light from outside, a pair of legs were propped up on the counter. The faint breathing was now a clear and contented snore.

Roscarrock edged forwards into the upper passage, feet finding the edges of the floor and eyes gripping the pair of legs. This would be much easier if the first of the doors on the passage was unlocked.

The handle squealed as he turned it, and the door stayed firmly closed. His whole body tensed at the noise, the irritation, and the readiness for flight. The legs and the snoring had not changed. Roscarrock released a breath as silently as he could, and began to advance along the passage again.

The second door opened smoothly and silently and, eyes flicking back to the legs, Roscarrock wondered as he stepped in what he would say if he found Pewsey wide awake and checking his books. But the room was dark and empty of life. What little light was in Shoe Lane peered through a small window into some kind of storeroom. He pushed the door to behind him, and again waited to adjust to the gloom.

Whatever he threw, as long as it was innocent enough in itself, should prompt the guilty sleeper to make a brief inspection of the premises before returning to his chair. He rejected a book as too odd to find lying around, was wondering whether a ball of string would make enough noise as it bounced down the stairs, and then found a short length of wood that was probably used to prop open the sash window. He checked the snoring, half-moved into the corridor, and swung his arm. The piece of wood took a happy bounce at the top of the stairs, and was still rattling satisfactorily down them as Roscarrock slipped back inside, pushed the door closed and dropped behind a dusty desk in case the guard checked this room too.

The guard checked the room. After a scraping and clumping through the wall, two heavy steps hit the passage floor, the door swung open and a lantern blared into the darkness. Roscarrock readied himself, one eye closed to preserve half of his night sight, for the faint chance that the guard would take his duties seriously enough to come into the apparently empty room.

The door slammed closed, and the guard's clumsy progress towards the front of the coffee house was reported by the floorboards, the locked door adjacent, and the stairs.

The guard's tour took him five times what Roscarrock needed to slip to the door, dart on dancing sailor's feet into the room of the message boxes and make it safely back again, closing the door softly behind him and taking up position behind the desk.

Sir Keith Kinnaird's message box had been empty.

Roscarrock forced himself to sit through twenty minutes of frustration, which he tried without success to turn into calculation, before he reckoned that the guard would be asleep again and felt comfortable in retracing his steps. As he slipped back out of the alley and into the limited civilization offered by Shoe Lane, he was still thinking hard, looking for a memory of Kinnaird rather than the city streets. He would not, in any case, have seen a shadow step out of the blackness of a doorway opposite the alley some time after he had gone, and the shadow resolve itself into the alert form of Philippe de Boeldieu. In dress, face and manner, all trace of the salon fop of twenty-four hours before had gone, and his expression was all hard thought as he watched Roscarrock disappear into the London night.

29th July 1805

Tom Roscarrock shadowed by the tavern chimney breast, chewing slowly on an apple.

His expression cold, fixed, he reviewed the faces of the past days: cheerful, mercurial Jessel, the hunter, and behind him the Admiral, aloof and magisterial. Then, by happy association, the vivid glimpse of Lady Virginia Strong, a seductive daydream, a siren for a drowning man. The parade of characters who populated his new world, the Magistrates and innkeepers and spies who spoke from the gloom, the writers and free-thinkers and men of business who shone in the salons. Reverend Henry Forster: a genuinely decent and moral man, applying a level of intellectual freedom and honesty that made him less rooted, less certain and less dependable than any of them. And somewhere, a half-remembered delirium of his fever, the vague and shifting face of Sir Keith Kinnaird.

In the shadow, Roscarrock smiled slightly, a smile that no one would see. He was caught up in it now, increasingly committed to this world of uncertain rules and unknown allegiances. The Scotsman had said he must sail with the wind, and that he could do, closer and stronger than most men.

With an obscure pride, he felt in himself a stubborn intent to outdo these shape-shifters and loyalty-brokers. *The loyalties I have are to dead men. The life that I would protect is drowned. I have less to lose than anyone.*

I am freer than any. I have crossed the bounds in my time.

Inspector Gaston Gabin pulled the collar of the coat up around his neck. There was no warmth in the mean little cottage. He wondered whether the old woman lying in front of him would have had a fire during the day; would she have saved her wood for evening, or even rarer occasions? No – there were trees nearby and, whoever owned them, she'd have scrabbled enough furtive kindling for her needs. But there'd been a restraint about her, a correctness; she'd have had a tight view of what she considered extravagance. So: fire for one cooked meal a day and cold evenings only. The damn cottage leaked heat. He could hear the wind darting in from the blank morning sky through holes in every window and joint.

She was like his own mother. His mother had been that type of peasant, further hardened by the Brittany winds: a little skeleton of standards to hold her up and protect her virtues, and no fat allowed. His father had been the other type: give the old man ten sous and he'd spend all ten that evening, and probably another five on account. Gabin smiled.

The mother of Joseph Dax, the runaway spy, was dead and had known nothing. He'd tormented her a little, the cushion over her brittle bird-like face, but his heart hadn't been in it. It was clear from his previous questions around the village, and his first deceptive questions to the old woman, that his quarry had not been to the cottage yet and that the mother did not know where he was or where he was going.

Gabin had tested her a little, gathered a little innocuous background. And then the old woman had died. He still wasn't sure whether he'd killed her deliberately, with one final irritated pressure on the cushion, or whether it had been an accident, or whether the old lady had finally decided to meet death herself, swallowing him in with one last airless mouthful.

Joseph Dax had found no shelter here, and now he would find none again. The sentry and the patrols would see to that. It was still possible he'd come, of course. Gabin had built a little picture of his fugitive, and independence and brilliance of thought were no part of it. The servant spy was hunted and he would feel hunted, and so he would seek shelter. Always the emotions. The messages across the police networks, the patrols and the enquiries, they were the businesslike intellectual solution to keep the Minister happy. Gabin himself would explore little Joseph Dax's soul.

The Inspector had a last look around the room, searching for any unnoticed trace of character. Then he stood and, cheerful at the prospect of warmth, stamped towards the front door. The local police could tidy up here. He had other little avenues to follow now, including the old family that mother and son had served. But first, a hot breakfast.

By the middle of the morning, the Reverend Henry Forster had finished his breakfast and was settled in his spartan study. The mornings he devoted to work – to reading, to preparing a sermon or writing letters. He enjoyed the company of his books, and he enjoyed the satisfaction that by his three hours' studiousness he was justifying a whole afternoon's walking or riding. A Bible lay open on the desk in front of him. His hands held a book on English tree varieties and their cultivation, and the book held his complete attention.

He heard the first knock, and ignored it in the hope that he'd misheard or that whoever might be disturbing him would think better of it.

But the knock was repeated. Cobb had cleared breakfast and gone for the morning; he'd have to answer the door himself.

He opened the door to reveal a rough bundle of a man, standing in the porch and obscured from the road by its walls. The man was a mess of clothing: good boots, but tatty breeches and smock, and he had a sack of some kind pulled over his head. Was he carrying something, or had it been raining?

'Yes?' Then the Reverend tried to remember his calling and not the interruption; 'Can I help you at all?'

It wasn't a face he knew – so far as he could tell, in the shadow.

'Parson Forster?' The voice was low and hoarse; he couldn't make out an accent or a class.

'Yes.'

'Have a word with you, Reverend?' It surely wasn't one of the labouring men from the village, was it?

The books were still open on his desk somewhere behind him; the fields ahead, beyond this shadow of a man, flashed the greens and golds of summer life at him.

'Yes. Yes, of course. You'd better come in.'

Fannion was moving towards the heart of England, by back rooms and barn lofts and hedgerows and hayricks. By the 29th of July he was south of Stratford, among villages too small even for one decent inn. Such places were also too small for him to reveal himself safely; there might be the occasional rustic firebrand who hated his King and his Government, but they hated strangers more.

So he'd waited in a ditch until dusk had muffled the fields, and the farmers had had time for supper, and then he followed the maze of shadows to a barn.

These fields had been the cockpit of the civil war, hadn't they? Now that would be something. A king executed and the English blowing each other to hell for once. This whole plain sat under the escarpment where the Royalists had lined up for the first battle of the war. It had, quite literally, all gone downhill from there for them. One glorious cavalry charge, discipline out the window, and Cromwell and his kind had regrouped and never looked back.

Perhaps some of Cromwell's Irish-butchering troopers had slept in this same barn. It certainly stank enough to be that old. Sometimes he got the feeling that England was slowly poisoning him, with her vast, complacent history, the stubborn comfort of her citizens, and whatever damps and diseases infested her barns. Was there nothing clean and fresh and new in the whole damned country? Perhaps he'd set fire to the straw just before he left. A nice barn-burning, now: that would cover his escape and set the farmers against the workers very neatly.

Fannion caught himself. He needed human company, soon. He needed a pretty girl, and good conversation. He stretched out. The straw was actually quite dry. He hadn't come all this way to upset a few farmers and get pitchforked to death in a ditch by yokels too stupid to be rebellious. He turned up his collar to stop the blades of straw scratching his neck; it was a good coat too, and the real criminal had been whoever left it tucked under their saddle outside a roadside inn.

Human company was definitely indicated. His destiny, and Ireland's, was not advanced by him sinking into petty theft and vindictiveness. Tomorrow night he had to be in Bury St Edmunds for the meeting, which meant a bit of horse-stealing this morning. A useful conversation that had been, back in Birmingham – they'd been good earnest fellows. Whoever was speaking at Bury would be honoured to have a real rebel with them on the stand, and he'd give them a little Cork poetry and something to think about. Then London.

The letters that had summoned him from Dublin were long gone, of course – only a fool kept souvenirs of treason. A pity his departure had been forced forwards so dramatically, before a rendezvous could be arranged. But the instructions had been clear: if he moved in the right circles – if he joined the gatherings of radical men like the Bury meeting – certain loosely described 'friends of reform' would find him. And together they would arrange to set London afire. Bizarre, that right in the belly of this fat country were people who wanted radical change so much that they'd give up Ireland to get it. And these rich rebels would be able to arrange his transport to France too, and in France there were certainly people he could do business with.

But first there must be breakfast somewhere, and a wash, and then he could take on the British Empire.

Joseph stood for fully ten minutes watching his mother's tiny cottage from the trees, lost in the aching, unattainable proximity of his youth, and because he stood and watched, he happened to see the sentry.

He had inhabited these trees, the hedges and the paths and the clearings, long before he had known any kind of home. The empty cheerful games out near the marshes, the little animals trapped and carried proudly home, were what passed for childhood. Every other experience – of poverty, of service, of loss, of Paris, of the burden of adult transactions – was a bar in the cage shutting him out of that pure, lost time.

The warmth of the cottage was a recent memory. The little dwelling had always been there – a series of large local women ready to halt his games with a slap or an apple – but when his mother had got too sick to work at the house, the old Master had let her move in. Then it became a kind of home for Joseph as well, an insight on a part of his mother he had never known, the crude wooden porch sheltering a doorway back in time.

But there, suddenly, under the oak by the road, was an alien pair of boots. They stuck out crudely, and then crossed themselves. Staring harder, Joseph could see a puff of smoke from behind the tree.

No one else was supposed to inhabit this dream. The boots gave a little spasm, disappeared, and a man emerged from behind the tree, a man in soldier's uniform, knocking a pipe against the trunk and reaching for a musket. Why did his mother need a sentry? Was she a prisoner? Would they punish her for what Joseph had done?

He had to get inside. Inside was warmth and a comfortable chair and his mother brushing at the dust on his coat with fussy hands as he stood over her.

The soldier was an invasion by the ugly adult world. He had to be careful now. Did the young Master give him any advice for this?

Lady Sybille, holding the pages for him and pointing out the words.

Now, let's have a look at this one, Joseph. This is a tricky one. What can you see here?

Half an hour later, a young woman sauntered in from the centre of the village and up to the oak tree, a coin fresh and warm in her pocket and a smile and something like make-up on her face. She kicked playfully at a big boot with her little foot, brushed the musket with torn gloves, glanced up into the dull wondering face – a cold morning, a little present from his friends in the barrack room – and led the sentry away. A minute later, and Joseph slipped by trees and hedges and shadows to the porch.

The little cottage was the coldest thing he had ever known, a terrible mortal cold that burst into his chest and would never leave him. Joseph hunched on the chair for the rest of the day beside the shrunken, bleached body of his mother, coughing great, dry sobs and crying silent hopeless tears. With dusk, the cold finally became too much, and he rose and felt his way to the door blank and blind. He was incapable now of thought or emotion, his hollow body filled with a dead, stone purpose that he could not challenge or change.

Joseph checked where the sentry was but the sight prompted no emotion; he made his silent way to the trees by hidden ditches that flowed deep and slow in his blood.

———— ⚬~⚬ ————

The moon hung low and fat over London's docks, silvering furled sails and blackening the lattice of masts and spars that held them. Strange sounds that the daylight bustle of humanity normally covered now emerged from hiding, creaks and splashes and rustles, and always the washing of the river against the city. With night, some of the stench of fish and men was subdued, as if the moon was giving fresh clarity to the breeze as well.

Buried in the shadows of a warehouse, Roscarrock sat with timbers beneath and behind him and enjoyed the old, familiar sensation of it. Even the aches in shoulders and backside felt somehow honest.

His head flicked round, though he kept his eyes on the warehouse opposite. After five seconds he said quietly, 'Keep the noise down, will you? I'm trying to sleep.'

Jessel moved forwards and squatted beside him in the darkness, looking out across the alley. 'Anything?' he murmured.

The whole conversation was in the same soft monotony, respectful of the night. 'Two men arrived half an hour ago. One left after five minutes.'

'Good. Recognize him?'

'Delacroix. The French writer who was at the reception. Can I go to bed now?'

'Fun's just starting. Come on; I've got two soldiers downstairs. We're going to do a bit of official breaking and entering.'

Jessel led the way back down out of the warehouse, steps slow and measured in the darkness, Roscarrock following and welcoming the movement in his sore limbs.

'Sorry I was late, Tom. One of our Magistrates had sent in a report he was convinced was urgent. Newmarket. No more than the sort of unhappy talk we hear all over the country, frankly. But the Magistrate is convinced they're planning something. Odd references to a big event tomorrow. The usual troublemakers quieter than normal, which is never a good sign. Unexpected voices in the wrong sorts of conversations in the inn. He's convinced they'll be burning his house down by the weekend.'

'Newmarket?'

'Exactly. Where the tailor might be headed, according to the report from your friend. That's why I bothered reading beyond the title.'

They were at street level, in the warren of muddy alleys among the warehouses. Jessel pointed them towards two shadows at the corner, shadows with muskets.

'And Delacroix?'

'We've been watching him for a while. He brings the occasional crate in – we assume from France, but everyone's doing that. Pays his dues very properly. But we don't know what he's bringing in, we don't know whether he's bringing in more than he says, and we don't know why he has a share of that storeroom you were watching.'

'Smuggling? Haven't we got better things to be worried about?'

'Quite.' Jessel grunted a greeting to the two soldiers, silent pillars in the gloom. 'The Admiral thinks maybe he's part of the French intelligence network here.'

'I took that for granted. But smuggling information in crates?'

'My guess is he's counterfeiting. And don't tell me we'd all do it if we had the chance. If the French took it seriously they could destroy this country without getting their feet wet or firing a shot. Whatever he is, this evening we're being customs officers.'

They left the two soldiers in the gloom of the alley between the warehouses, and in silence climbed a flight of wooden steps that creaked up into the moonlight. At the top, Jessel examined the door and lock and, satisfied, simply turned the handle and stepped inside. 'Customs officers,' he said politely. 'Nothing to worry about.'

The solitary occupant of the storeroom looked worried. Short and solid, with something in his stance and battered face that made Roscarrock guess he'd been at sea, he stared back at the two visitors and scratched uneasily at the scar that ran down from one twisted eye.

'I don't know you're Customs, do I?'

Jessel called one of the soldiers up to the storeroom, and explained to the still-scratching watchman that it now didn't matter what he thought he knew. He and Roscarrock began to search, while the watchman stood and fidgeted over his chair.

It took three minutes. The room contained a chair, a table, one wall of shelving filled floor to low ceiling with rolls of fabric, a short ladder propped against one of the bare timber walls, and two open crates of books in Latin and Greek. The search could largely be conducted from the doorway, but the two men made one careful tour of the small space, peering behind the rolls of material and rummaging to the bottom of one of the crates.

The watchman had both hands by his sides again and his shoulders had settled.

Roscarrock said to Jessel, 'Disappointed?'

'Not yet.' Jessel had also glanced at the watchman, and now from his standpoint back near the door he moved a careful gaze around the room. Then he said, 'What's the ladder for, would you say?'

Roscarrock nodded. 'Good question.' Jessel began to examine the floor near the ladder, and after a moment he positioned its feet on two worn marks on the boards and started up towards the top of the blank wall.

The watchman moved quickly and he moved quietly for someone of his shape and size. He was a step towards Roscarrock, hand behind him, before he was noticed; at two steps the hand was high and held a cosh; at three the cosh was halfway down towards Roscarrock's skull and Roscarrock had only started to turn. He turned fast and he turned into the advancing watchman, stopping the charge dead with his right shoulder and using his left arm to deflect the downward strike rather than trying to block it. As the watchman stumbled where he stood, Roscarrock swept his right fist up and around backhand to catch the man high on the face and send him staggering back. He took one step forwards and pushed the man down into his chair. 'Settle down, shipmate,' he said quietly.

The soldier was only now beginning to move his bayonet towards the horizontal. From his position above the room, Jessel snapped, 'By all means use that before he attacks us,' and continued up the ladder. He quickly found the trapdoor among the timber joints of the wall and reached in.

From below, Roscarrock heard a cry of satisfaction and saw Jessel pulling a sheaf of papers into the light. Then Jessel's easy laughter echoed into the cavity.

'It's French, it's illegal, and it's probably a terrible threat to order,' he said as he turned on the ladder. 'But we'll risk showing it to a professional like you.'

The papers fluttered down onto table and floor. They were all engravings of the highest quality and finest detail; the uppermost was an elegant representation of a revolutionary soldier, buried deeply and graphically in a swooning but obviously satisfied aristocratic lady.

Jessel dropped down the ladder and picked up a bundle of the pornography. 'Better take a few,' he said earnestly.

'To show Lord Hugo, of course.'

'Of course.' They left the two soldiers to guard the watchman and the storeroom, and descended the stairs into the darkness of the alley.

Stamping in silence through the squelching gloom, Roscarrock said, 'Report from Newmarket, and Gabriel Chance the tailor is going towards Newmarket. Is Newmarket anywhere near Bury St Edmunds?'

'Only a few miles, I think. Why?'

'The arrival of one tailor, however radical, wouldn't create the kind of fuss your Magistrate's talking about. But at the reception the other night, that man Hodge – the speech-maker – he asked if I was going to be near Bury. Said he would keep an eye out for me, get me an invitation if he could.'

'He's holding a meeting, isn't he?' Jessel's eyes were gleaming in the darkness. 'That makes sense! Another great rally for reform.'

'Which would be a draw for Chance the tailor, and reason for the tremors in Newmarket.'

'Lovely.' Jessel was nodding. Then he looked hard at Roscarrock. 'Maybe you're useful for our side after all, Tom.'

'Shut up and bring your dirty pictures.'

It was getting cold.

Another part of the city, constellations of candle flames sprinkling light on gold and glass in another drawing room, voices at ease and voices at play among the silks and velvets, and a fine china hand accepting a glass of wine from an admiral's sleeve.

'I'm delighted to see you here, Lord Hugo.' Words without meaning, words as mere coins of exchange.

'It is delightful to see you anywhere, Lady Virginia.' Words as duty.

Indifferent to social convention, Lady Virginia Strong lifted her glass in a silent toast. 'And how have your affairs been in my absence, Hugo?'

Bellamy found the recitation tiresome. 'Kinnaird, like some greased rodent, has gone. He's loose in the bracken. He's rogue.' The crystal blue eyes opposite him now wide in concern. 'He has left me with a man who may or may not be as treacherous as his former sponsor, but who certainly has history with radicals in America and probably Ireland.'

A new light in the eyes. 'The handsome one – rather... roughly carved? At Seldon – with the insolent eyes?'

Not a thrust to the Admiral's taste. 'Roscarrock, whether or not that's who you mean.'

'Roscarrock.' She tasted the name. 'Roscarrock becomes more interesting.'

'Indeed – perhaps even useful.' But the lady showed no further interest in Tom Roscarrock's politics.

Civility came most easily to Admiral Lord Hugo Bellamy when entirely feigned. 'Delighted to discuss my employees with you all night, Lady Virginia.' But it was not common currency. 'Feel at liberty to wake me when you wish to proceed to the main business.'

30th July 1805

FIELD REPORT (FRANCE), TAKEN THE 27TH DAY OF JULY
1805. CIPHER MALMSEY. CREDIT +

> *The Emperor and the Minister for the Navy are much delighted with the readiness of the new fleet. They are confident of its abilities. It has drawn ships and good men from other fleets, augmented by supporting craft taken from all around the French coast and fitted out to naval standard and given light armament. The Emperor will be confident of the success of the fleet, and convinced that at last he has the key to matching the Royal Navy and securing passage to Britain for the Grande Armée. The Emperor's pet name for this special fleet, his Sharks (Fr. Requins), is typical of his affection for those in the army and navy judged particularly capable of fulfilling his ambitions.*

[SS F/307/24]

The road to Bury St Edmunds led through Saffron Walden and as they trotted down its tidy, complacent main street, Jessel handed Roscarrock a sheet of paper from inside his coat.

Roscarrock skimmed the page. 'Another one of Kinnaird's specials, I assume, who you're worried might not like your face.'

'That's it, Tom.' Jessel caught him by the arm and looked directly into his face. 'Like the Admiral said: this is a good time to show you're useful, and useful to the right side.'

Roscarrock rode on.

The door he wanted was tucked into a side street. It was discreetly pillared, and had been recently painted. A brass plaque to the right of the door advertised 'Andrew Malloy' in understated style, and another below it the offices of the *Voice of the Land* news-sheet.

Roscarrock rang the bell, and waited. There was no sound of response inside. After a minute he rang again. Further down the street, someone was kicking and swearing at a jammed door. The hot, sour smell of malt hung over the town.

He stepped back off the step to look up at the house, and as he did so a curtain fell back across a bow window on the first floor.

He waited. Behind him a horse clapped lethargically over the cobbles, echoing away between the neat house fronts.

The door opened with the heavy crack of a latch.

Andrew Malloy was as smart as his plaque, a clean face behind shining spectacles over a neat and unostentatious coat. Only his inky hands showed hard work, and confirmed that this was the editor of the *Voice of the Land*. The eyes were big in the spectacles, and cold.

'Yes?'

'Good morning.' Damn Kinnaird. 'The King's roads are a weary place for the traveller.'

The newsman's expression had not changed. Eventually he said, 'I'm sure. But I'm afraid I've no idea what you're talking about.' Two paces behind him was a hefty servant, big hands rolled at his sides and watching Roscarrock suspiciously. Smart indeed.

Roscarrock's glance flicked to the door plaque as his mind checked over the details on Jessel's paper.

'The King's... I'm a friend of Sir Keith Kinnaird. He asked me to visit.'

This was the place. He hadn't made a mistake. He knew he hadn't made a mistake, because Andrew Malloy's was not an innocent suspicion. The scrutiny from the window, the servant standing guard, told of a man expecting trouble.

'I've never heard of him. You've obviously made a mistake. Good morning.' The door began to close.

'Mr Malloy, I must warn – Sir Kei—' and the door closed, dull and final.

Jessel's fair hair was clear as soon as Roscarrock stepped into the inn, and he dropped down beside him at the counter. 'I shouldn't settle,' he said curtly. Jessel looked round in curiosity. 'He's not having it. Never heard of Kinnaird, never heard of us, nothing could be further from his mind than a casual bit of intelligence work.' He leant into Jessel. 'He was warned.'

Jessel gazed back cold. 'That's not good, Tom.' The words were brusque.

'Don't come that, you miserable sod. He was got to! Either Kinnaird's told him to clam up, or he's learnt something about Kinnaird that's made him slip his anchor. Either way he's not talking, and I can't change that regardless of whether I'm a spy for Bonaparte.'

Jessel's gaze held for a further cold and unnecessary second, and dropped back to his drink.

⚊ ⚊

PROCEEDINGS OF THE ADMIRALTY BOARD,
FIRST LORD, ADMIRAL LORD BARHAM, PRESIDING,
THE 30TH DAY OF JULY 1805

The First Lord, with Lord G. Garlies, Admiral J. Gambier, and Admiral Lord H. Bellamy being present, the Board convened at twelve of the clock.

Admiral Gambier confirmed no substantive change to the dispositions of the fleets as previously reported.

There being no other business of record, the Secretaries withdrew.

[PROCEEDINGS OF THE ADMIRALTY BOARD, VOLUME XXIV]

'Well, Bellamy? No doubt you have good reason for convening us. Come to tell us you're joining the Revolution?'

'I am grateful for your time and patience, My Lord. I thought that the Board would wish to be aware of the latest intelligence from Paris. The mysterious French fleet is confirmed. It operates outwith the normal channels of command, such is Napoleon's mistrust of his senior Admirals. That fact, incidentally, explains the unusual difficulty in getting clear information about it. The ports of France have been raided for vessels that, with armament, will serve as auxiliaries. The core of the fleet is formed of some of the best ships, with the best captains, from the Emperor's conventional fleets. This is the fleet that, in combination or alone, is expected to challenge our navy.'

'Number of hulls?'

'Not known, My Lord.'

'Location?'

'Not known, My Lord.'

'I'm curious, Bellamy: do we know anything?'

'One detail, My Lord. It seems that it amuses the Emperor to refer to this fleet as his Sharks.'

'Charming. Anything else?'

'I'm afraid so, My Lord. In a coda to this report – and the real reason for my calling you today. We know from previous reports – shared with you, My Lord, – that Fouché, the Minister of Police, has some plan to destabilize the Kingdom and critically weaken the navy. We assumed he was working with radical elements in this country. It now seems that, as part of this scheme, he has sent an assassin into England.'

'Good God. I shall alert the Prime Minister; and we must keep the King at Windsor or further away.'

'I have already enacted the usual precautions, My Lord. But we think the assassin may be aiming at a military or naval target.'

'Horse Guards? The Commander-in-Chief? Or—'

'Or yourself, My Lord.'

Inspector Gabin was always irritable around soldiers – especially around large numbers of them. Their clumsy, mechanistic procedures for the simplest activity were too crude, for his taste; and the way men's faces and characters were swallowed into their uniforms and structures made them, as individuals, frustrating to deal with. It was like trying to negotiate with a landslide.

Gabin was standing in the welcome shade of a tree by the side of the road from Paris to the coast, watching the turgid proceedings of a military checkpoint. The Corporal who was with him was a cocky Parisian, who was both bored with the idea of mundane police business and convinced that an Inspector of Police was his social inferior. *Vive la Révolution*, Gabin was thinking sourly. He didn't mind the *égalité* at all – on the contrary, he thrived in it – but men ten years his junior calling him 'mate', and treating the hunt for a traitor to France as if it was an old woman missing a cow, got up his nose. For his part, the Corporal clearly thought he had better things to be doing – someone to screw or shout at, no doubt – so all in all it was not an agreeable meeting of professions.

Two middle-aged women shuffled up to the soldier stopping the road. There was mumbled chatter between the three, the soldier grumbling out instructions. The older of the two women said something louder and ribald to the soldier, but he was too hot in uniform and noon sun to respond with any liveliness. He prodded inside the sacks they carried, a gesture of thoroughness presumably for the Corporal's benefit, and then nodded them dully on their way. Beyond him, on the other side of the road, three or four other soldiers were slouching in the shade, throwing occasional glances towards their colleague to check he wasn't being overwhelmed by a Royalist horde or warning of the approach of someone in authority.

Gabin felt the sluggishness of the morning like a stifling constriction on his whole investigation. As he had had, uncomfortably, to explain to the Minister the previous day, a manhunt was a crude and chancy affair.

He'd chased down every possible connection to Joseph Dax – the Count's family whom he'd served were all dead or fled, the rest of the servants vanished into the chaos. He had acted with vigour and ruthlessness – and in the middle of yesterday's painful interview, he'd been grateful for having killed the old mother. He had used the whole resources of the state strongly and intelligently; and militarized France, with identity papers and ubiquitous soldiers and permanent state of alarm, was a powerful tool. But it only took a moment's ill-luck or incompetence – like the lapse by the imbecilic sentry outside the old woman's house – for a fleck of dust like this Joseph Dax to sneak through the efficient machine. And one slaughtered crone was hardly much return on all the effort, was it?

'I shouldn't worry, mate,' the Corporal was drawling in his ear. 'This sort of business'll all be overtaken by the war in the end, won't it?' He wanted to get on with his march to the coast, to join the all-conquering army poised on the beaches. 'Expect we'll turn up your suspect sometime.'

'That's immensely reassuring,' Gabin retorted, not taking his eyes from the road and the shifting, sweating sentry. 'You must come and advise the Minister.' He half-hoped that the Corporal would foul up in some way, so that he could relieve his frustrations by destroying him. Once he'd been back inside the old woman's house, seen the traces of Joseph's presence, he'd part-throttled the lax sentry, who would now spend the rest of his brief military career digging latrines until claimed by a fatal dose of dysentery.

If Joseph Dax was to shift from being an embarrassment to a danger, he had to reach England with whatever papers he'd stolen. Realistically, that meant the English Channel, and realistically that meant only half a dozen possible roads. Gabin now had series of checkpoints on each of them, with skirmishers deployed to stop anyone sneaking past through fields or down rivers. The fugitive could make himself hard to find, but in any case Gabin would bottle him up in France.

A man was walking slowly towards the sentry, battered hat pulled low and a satchel over his shoulder. The clothes were torn and poor, the movements sluggish in the face of heat and authority.

Gabin's eyes narrowed. It was obviously foolish to expect that he would happen to be on the spot when a sentry happened to pick up the hunted spy; but vigilance and intelligence had their rewards, and he'd relish demonstrating the realities of the world to the Corporal. He wished he'd paid attention to the servant on his first visit to the Minister.

The tattered man showed some identification to the sentry and passed on his way, hardly breaking step.

Gabin spun to the Corporal. 'What the hell is this? That's the right kind of man, travelling the right way at the right time, and your lump out there doesn't even check his bag!'

The Corporal sighed low under his breath. 'Let's go and find out, shall we?'

Five yards beyond the sentry, Joseph was in the middle of a titanic struggle with his failing heart and hysterical legs, which screamed to be running. The sweat was stinging his neck, and his eyes were rigid on the stones a few yards ahead of him as he fought to place his feet one heavy tread at a time. At the last moment, just before he reached the soldier, he'd seen the two men lurking in the shadows beside the road, and something in the face of the taller was immediately recognizable as the merciless Inspector from the house of the Minister. Step. Step. Step. From the corner of his eyes he'd seen movement, the Inspector and the other man coming for him. Run: he must run! Step. Step. Step.

Gabin and the Corporal were by the sentry, the former fighting down his frustration and allowing the Corporal to question his man. 'Soldier, that man: what papers did he present that you chose to ignore his bag?'

The sentry had stiffened to attention as the Corporal and the damn policeman had approached. He spoke precisely and formally; he recognized the posture that the Corporal was obliged to adopt for the sake of the outsider. 'Yes, Corporal; Corporal, he is an officer's servant. He travels with the army. He has the correct pass – I checked very particularly.'

'There you go, mate. You can rely on our procedures.'

Gabin scowled, watched the back of the departing servant, and turned away. Not today after all, then. He returned to the shade.

Twenty yards beyond the sentry, Joseph plodded onwards, an affiliate of the Emperor's army with several hours' seniority and the most precious secrets in Europe over his shoulder. *'Move with the machine,' the young Master had once said. 'Don't try to resist it.'* Officers, even revolutionary ones, were always needing servants. His young Major was pleasant enough, and Joseph would make good time to the coast, and get a reasonable meal or two on the way.

Step. Step. Step.

—⋅—

Roscarrock and Jessel rode into Bury St Edmunds with the last of the day's sun. The hours in the saddle had been warm and sourly silent, and both men dropped heavily into the roadway, glad to move their legs and glad to move apart.

The Fox had a large, bland frontage that promised quality but not warmth. Jessel strode into the inn; Roscarrock stayed outside to exercise his legs and get a feel for the character of a new place. He wanted action, something simple and strong, and he wondered whether this comfortable market town would offer much chance of it.

He also wanted a cold drink. Inside the Fox, among a heaving scrum of people, he found Jessel sitting with another man: a tall, good-looking officer in the uniform of the dragoons, fair-haired like Jessel but with breeding in the lazy eyelids and well-cut bones.

The chance to stretch and something to drink had, as usual, mellowed Jessel.

'This is Ralph Royce, Roscarrock. Unusually for our business, he is actually entitled to the uniform he wears.' The old warmth was returning. 'Major Ralph very kindly arranges little bits of military assistance for us.' He turned to the pleasant face waiting politely beside him. 'Ralph, this is Tom Roscarrock. Well-known revolutionary firebrand. Top man for whoever's disposed to pay him this week.'

The Major seemed ready to take it as a joke, so Roscarrock did the same. He liked the look of Royce. 'Don't let the aristo manners fool you, Tom,' Jessel was saying as they all sat again. 'Ralph's a first-class hooligan and he's only interrupted his social engagements because he fancies some sport tonight.'

They exchanged the polite, non-committal chat of men too used to lies. A woman brought stew, and all three watched her slender body sway away before starting on it.

'How many do you have, Ralph?' Jessel spoke through a hot mouthful of vegetable.

'Fifty men. Enough for your lowlife purposes.' Royce was exploring the stew with a warier spoon. 'Did she say exactly what animal was supposed to have contributed to this?'

'Any sign of our big meeting tonight?'

Royce abandoned his spoon. 'Oh, it's happening right enough.' The other two looked up. 'People have been coming in all day. Labourers from all the villages in the area, mostly, but a smattering of the better sort as well. They've been loafing through town – there'll be no free beds for you tonight – and all afternoon they've been heading out to a large meadow south of town.'

'Trouble?'

'None so far.'

'How many?' Roscarrock asked.

Royce shook his head. 'Thousands. No way of telling. We've been trawling for Gabriel Chance, tailor, like you asked but he's probably not that stupid. If he's coming at all, he's coming from out of town or he's coming with a different name.'

'But – assuming he makes himself known during the meeting – makes a speech, perhaps – we've got him.'

Again the Major shook his head. 'Not necessarily. I've seen a couple of these great mob meetings. A thousand – five thousand – men in the darkness, yes? A great scrum of men, gathered round the speakers. In the middle, you'll find a ring of picked men who'll be quietly keeping strangers away from the speakers. Even if I threw my troop at them full tilt, sabres level and damn the consequences, by the time we'd cut our way through, the ones we wanted would have disappeared.'

The inn room was heaving with men, some in the clothes they'd worn in the workshop, some in their Sunday smart, the orchestra of voices set in the constant clatter of plates and mugs. The inn would take more money tonight than in the ensuing month, but they'd be cleaning up for most of it.

Roscarrock watched the crowd, the varieties of coats and faces bunched around him, and wondered at the motives. He turned to Jessel. 'Hodge – the orator. Is he hunted?'

Jessel shook his head. 'So far he's been careful not to get carried away.'

'So maybe he wouldn't be travelling secretly?'

'Maybe.'

Roscarrock stood, and dropped a coin on the table. 'I'll try something. See you later.'

'You'll be able to find us?'

'A mob of five thousand and a troop of dragoons next to them? I should be able to pick you out.'

Roscarrock was a minute at the bar before he got a negative answer, and then he pushed his way back across the inn and out into the sudden peace of the evening. The street was busy enough, a steady stream of people even more diverse than those back in the Fox drifting southwards out of town, but the contrast with the crush and din he'd left was dramatic.

The chances of this little bet coming off were slight – Hodge only had to be late, coming in from elsewhere, lodging privately, or more cautious than Jessel gave him credit for – but it was easy enough to try. Roscarrock just walked from inn to inn asking if Hodge was staying there. The dragoons didn't think Hodge was worth searching for, and if the man himself agreed, then there was a chance he could be found.

Henry Hodge was staying at the Rose and Crown. It was the fourth place Roscarrock tried, and the immediate affirmative from the clerk came so easily that he couldn't keep the surprise out of his reply. 'That's good. Thank you.' Now what? If he saw Hodge, what could he possibly say to him that would get access to the tailor? 'Please tell him that an acquaintance from London is here at his suggestion. Grey – Thomas Grey.'

The clerk was down the stairs again a minute later, and he was alone. Hodge had already left, or he wasn't falling for the surprise arrival of someone who was effectively a complete stranger.

'I'm sorry, sir, but Mr Hodge is not receiving guests. He is resting.'

What else? Confront Hodge? Of course not. Follow him? But that wouldn't get him through the mob.

'He asked me to give you this, sir, with his compliments.'

Roscarrock took the small sheet of paper politely and as if expecting nothing else, and left. Outside, he examined it under the door lamp.

Clever. For a moment he couldn't register what it was, it being so clearly not what he'd expected. Not an invitation, not a bill advertising the meeting. Instead, it was a page torn from the Bible – and it would be one of a known sequence of page numbers too.

As Roscarrock slipped back into the Fox, Jessel and Royce were just sitting down at a different table. He hesitated, wondering at the shift, until Jessel beckoned.

Roscarrock wasn't looking forward to the banter and Jessel's lack of interest in his movements came as a pleasant surprise. 'Tragedy for you, young Tom,' he said as Roscarrock sat, and then lunged physically at a serving woman to get her attention and order more drinks. Roscarrock waited. 'Love of your life drops in from the heavens, and the good Major and I had to entertain her in your absence.'

'I'm happy you're happy, but I have no idea what you're talking about.'

'Lady Virginia Strong is what I'm talking about.'

'What? She's here?' It came out too strong and too surprised, and Jessel and the dragoon laughed in gross delight. Roscarrock smiled, rolled with the swell. 'She was distraught at missing me, of course.'

'Not sure your name came up, actually.'

'She's a hell of a way from Seldon and the salons, isn't she?' The graceful hand, the neck, the eyes were flashing and gliding in front of him again, and away.

'Don't you believe it.' Jessel was more serious, and he stopped talking while three mugs of beer were placed on the table without finesse. 'I wouldn't be surprised to find a few of the Seldon crowd here, or those we met at the Frenchie lady's. Not actually going to the meeting; not talking to anyone, no funny business. But just fancying the idea of being in the vicinity of something a little rebellious.' He leant forwards slightly. 'Then again, perhaps one or two of them might be trying to do a little business.'

'And her?'

'See, that's what impresses me, Ralph.' Jessel had grabbed the Major's arm but was still staring happily at Roscarrock. 'Here we are: Government in peril, assassin on the loose, Napoleon at the gate; and Tom's got his balls in his hand and the picture of a woman he's met for no more than ten seconds in his head. I think she fancies a little radical flirtation, Tom. Wants to see what real men are like. She knows I'm with the Admiral, and she started swooning as soon as she saw London's most handsome dragoon, so she invited me into her parlour so I could tell her a little of what's happening, and then I had to invite Ralph in so he could stare into her eyes.'

Roscarrock shook his head. 'Like I said to the Admiral: it's a damned strange world.'

'You're just jealous.' He took down the beer in one extended mouthful. 'Drink up. We've a rebellion to join.'

The evening was clear and light and warm, summer's gracious gift to farmers and to lovers, and to the organizers of radical protest meetings. The moon was up already, pale and solitary, a guest arrived too early at a party. Under the satin sky, the meadow spread peaceful and fertile from the crest of hills on the horizon, down across the river, and up again towards the outskirts of the town.

It was a time and a place for stillness and for reflection and, because it was this, the vast hive of protesters bunched dark and unruly in the middle of the plain glowered the more obscenely. On the fringes, close to, the crowd was individual men with clothes that told their trades, and faces that told their attitudes. Seen from the shelter of the trees, those people became one vast pumping organ of foreboding, a mass that shifted and hummed and threatened like some weird pregnant beast.

The troop of dragoons lurked in the edge of the woodland, occasionally lifting an indifferent eye to the mob and otherwise muttering bored boasts to each other and watching down the necks of their horses as they grazed among the roots. In the gloom, the horsemen were shadows, bodies of darkness distorting the lines of the tree trunks, indeterminate flashes winking from spurs and helmets and swords.

The crowd knew they were there. Those on the near edge would throw wary glances towards the fringe of trees, and pull them back again. Some moved away to the other side of the crowd. Neither the average protester nor the average dragoon knew precisely how the law stood – they did not know exactly what protest was legal and they did not know exactly what intervention was legal. In that uncertainty a soldier might find some relief from his boredom, and a tradesman might be crippled for life. There was no reason why the evening should not pass in complete peace; there was always the possibility of a massacre. As Roscarrock watched, there was a constant furtive movement of protesters from this side of the crowd to less exposed places.

He was squatting against a tree, back straight against its clean trunk, shifting his eyes between the vague, glimmering dragoons and the human cattle in the meadow. Jessel stood nearby, stroking his horse's mane and chatting to Major Royce.

In the middle of the crowd a few figures could be seen standing taller, on some cart or platform. Roscarrock felt the need for a telescope; Hodge he would recognize without difficulty, and he wondered if he'd be able to tell Chance the itinerant tailor, should Chance even appear.

'... so no bursts of loyal enthusiasm tonight, Ralph,' Jessel was saying. 'No side bets, no unnecessary exercise for your troopers. Our objective is Gabriel Chance and Gabriel Chance only, and I don't care if the rest of them are damning the King and singing the "Marseillaise".'

'All right, Dick,' the Major replied patiently and without much attention. He did have a telescope, Roscarrock noticed, and suddenly it flicked up to scan the crowd. 'I think I just about grasp the basics of intelligence work.' He folded the telescope and replaced it in a pocket, suddenly looking down at Jessel more earnestly. 'But I won't be able to restrain my lads if the stones start flying. They're not bad chaps and they naturally worship the ground I walk on, but they're only human.'

Jessel sighed theatrically. 'And I'd had such confidence.'

'This ain't Horse Guards, Dick. A sympathetic dragoon won't always start when you tell him to, and an angry one won't always stop.' The voice was low and intent.

'That reminds me, Major.' Roscarrock had stood, and now he stretched his shoulders and stepped in towards the other two men. 'Question I had. Between ourselves, do your dragoons ever... do a bit of work on the side?' He patted the neck of Royce's horse, then looked up into the handsome face.

Royce watched him for a moment, then nodded very slightly. 'Yes, they do, and I can't say I blame them. They'll join a mob for a penny, and rough a man up for a shilling, and they won't care who's paying.' He looked slowly around his troop in the gloom, then back down to Roscarrock and Jessel. 'The King's not that generous an employer. And not every dragoon has a lord for a father.'

There was suddenly a faint, frail call from the centre of the meadow, instantly echoed in an immense roar from the crowd, and every eye in the shadows of the wood leapt up to see. Roscarrock was still watching the Major. Then he shifted his glance to the nearest dragoon, and nodded. 'Makes sense.' He moved quietly to the edge of the woods. From the centre of the great mass of people that single call had become a thin trail of words, reaching out across the evening in welcome and inspiration.

'You off somewhere, Tom?' Jessel's voice was a hard murmur from behind him.

Roscarrock looked back for a second. 'Might see if I can find a closer view. If I get a better offer from the Revolution, I'll let you know.' He checked that the Bible page was still in his pocket, and began to walk along the shadows of the treeline away from the soldiers.

~

The 30th July

Monsieur,

Do not expect early results in the County of Durham. I have made some preparation here – I am more firmly convinced that my method will achieve results here, and I have identified the routines and the men who will facilitate my (illegible word) of the destruction – so rest assured that we will have a success at this colliery soon. But I am now sure that I am watched, and I have determined to move temporarily to another district to elude pursuit and act more freely. Look for news of me in the County of Lancashire.

Monsieur, my need for money is urgent and I beg you to act quickly. Send to our friends at the agreed place in Lancaster.

[SS MF/SH/16/8 (THE SUTHERLAND HOUSE TROVE)
DECIPHERED BY J.J., JANUARY 1806]

By the time Roscarrock had drifted into the outer fringes of the crowd, Joseph McNamara had finished. His last soaring incitement had ebbed back over the dark, bobbing heads, and under the roaring of the crowd part of Roscarrock was hearing the echoes of his speech outside the Magistrate's house in Tiverton. He began to work his way towards the centre of the crowd, ducking and slipping between shoulders and murmuring excuses as Henry Hodge stepped forwards and whipped up the roars with two waving fists.

'The American colonists, my friends, they fought for their rights and they won them. They won against tyranny, they won bravely, and they won rightly.'

Roscarrock continued to ease forwards, slowly and inconspicuously. Whenever he reached a particularly stubborn knot of arms and shoulders, he paused, listened, and waited for the natural eddies of the crowd to open a path again. Hodge spoke well, and his voice was a surprise. He had the volume Roscarrock had expected from his shape and manner, but there was a flow and a resonance that he had not expected.

'Let us not forget, my friends, that those we call American colonists, those our Government called rebels and traitors, these men were freeborn Britons like you and me.' The voice rose and fell in the sentences, making each a story in itself. 'They were our cousins; they were our brothers; they were our children.'

Rosscarock knocked too heavily into a shoulder and got a sudden glare.

'They fought on the principle that they should not be taxed if they were not represented; that they should not be obliged to support a government if they were not allowed to vote for that government. Now tell me, my friends, are we not taxed?'

Roscarrock was nearer the centre. Hodge's face was clear and shining, catching the last of the light up on his cart while the crowd below him was in gloom, reciting his catechism of the various taxes oppressing the average man. The great scrum of people was packed more tightly now, here nearer the heart of the storm; on the margins they'd been looser, milling around, unwilling to add to the discomfort of hours of standing. Roscarrock had to catch what chances of progress he could, slipping forwards in the shudders of movement that went through the packed bodies.

'You, sir! You are taxed, but do you have a vote? No! You, sir!'

The crowd seemed thinner up ahead. The transformation in Hodge was remarkable. The genial, ponderous talker in St James's Square had become a singing tempest of a man, conjuring the anger and excitement of the crowd and sailing on it.

'Our so-called rulers tell us much of the evils of the French Revolution, but they are silent about the political progress it gave average men like you and me. We have hundreds of members of Parliament, and they represent but a handful of voters. We have no members of Parliament that represent the great mass of Britons gathered here tonight, and gathered around the country.' Hodge had allowed a strain into his voice; he was feigning exhaustion as he built towards his conclusion. 'Why did the citizens of ancient Greece, why did the citizens of revolutionary France, why do the citizens of free America, why do they all, I ask you, my friends, enjoy rights denied to freeborn Englishmen?'

Roscarrock eased forwards in a shift in the crowd, and was suddenly face-to-face with a battered hulk of a man. He was an inch or two taller than Roscarrock, much bulkier, his shovel of a jaw emerging neckless from bull's shoulders and the large, flabby nose and ears telling the story of every round of the prizefights that were obviously his livelihood. Hodge's hoarse and resonant excitement was building – a march on London, a grand petition to be presented to the Government – but this great bruise of a man was giving no attention to him; he was staring out into the crowd, and right now he was staring at Roscarrock.

Roscarrock smiled at him, and glanced left and right. The man's arms were linked with the men either side of him, part of a ring of men, every one a fighter, a smith or just a damned big farm boy, and these men made a wall around the speakers.

Hodge was finishing, building a link to the next speaker, and Roscarrock was being battered from side to side by the growing roars of approval from the men around him and their waving fists of agreement. He reached into his pocket and thrust the Bible page towards the face of the fighter. The big man stared back at him. Then he turned his head over his shoulder, called something, and a younger man – better dressed and sharp-looking – hurried over. He reached over the great hedge of linked arms, held the page by one corner and scanned it, then tapped one of the rocky shoulders and nodded. Roscarrock slipped through, and the wall closed solid behind him.

He was still a few yards short of the cart on which the speakers climbed to speak, and there were men around him looking up and listening to Hodge's climax. But these men were spread out, and also better dressed. They were listening with less excitement than the mob behind them, but some were listening with more attention. Who were these men? Benefactors? Acquaintances of the better sort? Fellow radicals? Roscarrock looked at the faces around him. He'd no way of recognizing any of them. Was that one of the Parsons from St James's Square, though? He had no way of cataloguing who was here.

There was an explosion of noise from behind Roscarrock, and shouts of approval from the men around him. He'd got into the inner circle, but what did that mean? Even if they'd got lucky and Gabriel Chance was indeed coming to speak to the crowd, what was he going to do about it? He had no way of signalling to Jessel, and Jessel couldn't have done anything about it even if he had. He himself couldn't achieve anything by force, surrounded by two dozen of the largest, no doubt fight-hardened, citizens of East Anglia.

In any case, these considerations were based on the faint possibility that Chance had even decided to come here, and Roscarrock was still scowling at the futility of his position when Hodge finally hushed the crowd and introduced his 'brother in liberty, James Fannion of Ireland', and a flame burst in Roscarrock's face.

They were lighting torches as the darkness gathered around the cart, and within a minute half a dozen men were holding them up towards the speakers. As Roscarrock's eyes readjusted, he found himself two yards short of the cart and staring up into the handsome face of the Irishman that the whole British Government was supposed to be hunting. Fannion the murderer, Fannion the agitator who would set the country on fire, Fannion who'd been forgotten because they had a clue to Chance, was here tonight and almost within reach.

James Fannion seemed to be staring back at him. But the eyes were closed under the dark curls and eyebrows. It was a delicate, indoor face, with an outdoor complexion. Then the eyes snapped open, eyes with an intense life in them, glaring down through Roscarrock and far beyond, and the head lifted and he began to speak.

The crowd hadn't been sure about an Irish speaker – the applause had been polite at best – and Fannion knew it. He began humbly, with a generous tribute to Hodge, and there was little of Ireland in his accent. Then he faced their doubts full in the face. 'My friends' – and he drew the word out with a kind of pain at the loss of friendship – 'I know that many of you feel no cause to love the Irish. Perhaps your sons and your brothers have done military service in Ireland – and you wish them home as much as I do. Perhaps you're afraid of the Irish threat to your constitution.' It was clever stuff – this crowd didn't give a damn about the constitution, and in reassuring themselves on that point they'd lose some of their vaguer fears of the wild Irish. 'Perhaps you're worried about the Irish taking your jobs in these desperate times.' They weren't particularly, not in this part of the country, but Fannion was only reinforcing his honesty and integrity.

Roscarrock had never trusted oratory, had only seen it in half-drunk mutinous crewmen and village politicians – and this was why. Fannion was brilliant, and he was dangerous.

'My friends, I have not come here to tell you to love the Irish. I have not come here to tell you that these are anything but desperate times. I have not come here to curse your British soldiers – like all of us, they are most of them simple men trying to earn a penny where they can.'

Roscarrock remembered the report from Liverpool of the murdered Sergeant, Fannion the man most likely to have stabbed him.

'We are all of us victims of the same oppression – the political oppression that tries to enslave us; the economic oppression that tries to starve us. I speak not as an Irishman, but on behalf of the great brotherhood of man that knows no borders or Empires. I speak – just as Mr Hodge speaks, just as you all speak – not with the surliness of slaves, but with the fellow-feeling natural to free men across the world. In your darkness, in your struggle, you are not alone.'

Roscarrock had seen effective crews of honest men corrupted to chaos by mere words, and he was wary of words and of wordmen because of it. But there was courage in James Fannion, a hunted rebel and murderer who would travel through England and proclaim himself in the middle of a crowd, with dragoons waiting. And there was beauty in those dark, hunted eyes, and witchcraft in the words. Fannion spoke for no more than fifteen minutes, but in those fifteen he created a devastating picture of the depths of English suffering. His native accent getting stronger with every rolling phrase, he expressed over and over his sympathy, the sympathy of all people enslaved and free, for the English. He expressed his wonder that in the face of such oppression, the English people had kept their peace and paid for war against fellow sufferers in America, in Ireland and in

France. Prudently, poetically, James Fannion was preaching rebellion, and Roscarrock saw only a predator's face on the platform.

'I am only a guest here, my friends. I have no wish to provoke those horsemen in the trees there, with sabres in their hands and the King's pennies in their pockets. Instead, I should congratulate them and their Government for the most brilliant deception. Like the Kings of France, they have convinced proud people to fight each other, instead of fighting together for the rights that are theirs. If I was the British Government, I should fear some great explosion from the people, but the British Government does not fear. The British Government has avoided the fury of the people, and for that I congratulate the Government. The British Government has avoided the liberty of the people – and this is a liberty that is not even theirs to offer or withhold, it is a liberty to which we are born, and still we do not feel its absence. Some radical men will tell you that this is a Ministry of fools; I say this is a Ministry of geniuses, for the meek acceptance of the British people is nothing short of miraculous.'

Unlike McNamara's call and response, unlike Hodge's direct questioning and stirring of the crowd, Fannion was provoking no dramatic reaction. His words prompted growls and shouts of agreement, and now some grumbling anger. He had the power to make the crowd his ardent followers, and instead he was making them out to be fools. He could have made himself the head of a riot this evening, and Roscarrock couldn't work out why he'd just made himself unpopular.

'My friends, if you expect me to preach rebellion you will be disappointed. My respect for your Ministry and your dragoons is too great. If you burn Bury St Edmunds tonight, you will find you have achieved nothing in the morning. But I will say just this. Should the sleeping volcano of the English people burst forth in one devastating bid for freedom, I shall not be surprised. Should your just and peaceful petition to London be met with indifference, and soldiers, and the Riot Act, I shall not be surprised. Should your resentment and frustration be shared by the people of London, a city that loves liberty more than it loves kings and governments, I shall not be surprised. Should your protests provoke the over-reaction of the Ministry, I shall not be surprised. Should you decide, at last, that your liberty is the one thing you have left to give to your children, I shall not be surprised. Should you carry your burning desire for freedom right down Whitehall and hurl it against the muskets of the soldiers and the dead walls of your unelected Parliament, I shall not be surprised. And should all this create some natural explosion of the honest English people, I shall not be surprised. And I promise you, my brothers of the world, that should the English rise to reclaim their true liberty, the Irish would be beside them. We have shared your oppression; we share your dream of freedom; and we will share your glory.'

He didn't even produce a crescendo. The last empty word was hardly off his tongue when he turned and began to climb down from the cart.

Now he saw it. In the half-hearted shouts and grudging applause, Roscarrock saw a bitterness that would not be dissipated in a night. Fannion could have roused a cheerful riot, and the crowd's passion would have burnt out by morning. Instead he had skilfully stoked an anger and a shame that would burn slow and long, and he'd done it without a word that could count as sedition.

Roscarrock was trying to peer through the glare of the torches into the darkness on the other side of the cart. Hodge's face he could make out, a troubled face, but where was Fannion? Was that him, replacing a shapeless, soft-brimmed hat on his head? There was another figure standing upright on the cart now, but Roscarrock ignored the words, another exaggerated introduction of another speaker. Would Fannion leave now?

Of course he would. He had nothing to stay for – he had no interest in the thoughts of English radicals, he'd had the effect he wanted, and he'd get out while the dragoons were still watching the crowd. Then the man on the cart said how much pleasure he had in introducing Gabriel Chance, and Roscarrock swore aloud at his own impotence.

When James Fannion had started to speak, the torches had glared oddly in the blue evening. Now the sky was black, and the orange blazes around the cart were the only light, flaring up to the speakers and splashing out to gild the first circles of the crowd. Weirdly lit from below, Gabriel Chance seemed small and frail and surprised. Looking up at his face, grotesque in the shadows, Roscarrock knew that his voice would have trouble reaching the ring of bodyguards, let alone spreading out into the night-muffled mob.

Across five thousand men, there was silence. A flicker of wind rasped at the nearest torch.

He had it all – everything Lord Hugo Bellamy wanted. Find me the tailor and find me the Irishman, the Admiral had said, and Roscarrock and Jessel and who knew how many others had been trawling England to hunt them. Now Tom Roscarrock only had to put out his arm to touch the tailor; and the Irishman was just a few steps away. But, becalmed in the vast and radicalized crowd, he was helpless – and if anyone there realized who he was, he'd be torn apart.

'I am only a man!' The voice pierced his brain and seemed to drive down to his gut. It was high and slow, every vowel somehow forced and painful, and there was no doubt that it was ringing across the meadow to the outermost stragglers of the crowd. 'But one man may contain all the freedom of a better world; one man may share all the dreams of a better world; and one man may achieve the better world.'

This was the Reverend Forster's prophet, the man to show the way to the promised land. And Roscarrock could do nothing about him. Meanwhile, Fannion was disappearing into the darkness.

Still the voice sang into the night. 'This better world exists, and it is ours. It is the world promised to us by God, and it is the world to be found in the pure heart of every one of us. All that we need is the path to reach what is in us, and the courage to follow that path.'

The crowd was silent. Glancing around, Roscarrock saw the attention on every face, men of business and men without work, farmers and carpenters and weavers and shopkeepers and labourers from miles around staring equally dumb into the torchlight. It had to be Fannion. Jessel would see that Chance was talking; Jessel would be able to pick him up as the crowd dispersed. Fannion was leaving now, and Roscarrock was the only man able to follow him.

'Every man here knows the obstacles to his true freedom: the child crying for food; the mother sick with fever; the loaf that cannot be bought; the men with the votes and the men with the muskets. If we bow before these obstacles, we shall remain forever slaves, building bricks without straw in Egypt.'

But he couldn't follow Fannion on foot; even if he could track him through the crowd, one dark head among a thousand, the Irishman would be out of the press and away long before he could get to him. Even if he could get to him, what then?

'I know my path. I follow it, though I do not know what obstacles I will find nor how I will overcome them. But I am certain that in overcoming those obstacles I am beating a path to the Lord. I am doing his work. He has not prepared a better world for us merely to taunt us or deceive us. He has prepared a better world for us because it is our birthright, and we shame him if we do not devote our lives – if we do not offer our lives – to make that journey.'

He had to get to a horse, and he had to guess where the Irishman would head. Roscarrock skirted round the cart, took care to avoid Hodge, and checked that Fannion was no longer in the immediate group staring up at the haunted music of Gabriel Chance. Then he pushed into the crowd, regardless of where Fannion was, driving for the outside as fast as he could.

The voice of Chance followed him into the darkness: 'Liberty is not something to be awarded to us by our betters; it burns within us, and we must choose to fuel its fire. I will give my life to this glory, because without it my life is nothing. I recognize these Kings and Magistrates and laws not at all, because they are obstacles in the Lord's path. The Lord has told us himself: all nations before him are as nothing. He bringeth the princes to nothing; he maketh the judges of the earth as vanity. He raised up the righteous man, and gave the nations before him, and made him rule over kings. To them that have no might he increaseth strength. They that wait upon the Lord shall mount up, with wings, as eagles.'

A storeroom in a barracks in Colchester, rarely used, a few wooden boxes and barrels gathered in the darkness, forgotten picture frames and other indistinct shapes hiding against the walls. The feet of four men in soldier's boots had brushed through the dust; four improvised stools had been pulled close; a bottle was being passed round between the half-uniformed shadows, and the sparkle when it caught a freak of moonlight through one cobwebbed grille was the only illumination.

'I don't fancy being flogged to death.'

'You fancy dying in a ditch?'

'Is that a threat?'

'It's a fact of your life, mate, is what it is. We're all in this, now, and once you're in you're in for good, one way or t'other.'

'The officers is too scared to push us any further now.'

'They're not scared, but they don't know what to do.'

'They're trying to find out what happened.'

'No one's stupid enough to go for that cheap reward and get the same treatment Franks got.'

'So we should lie low.'

'So we should cut their throats.'

'You're not serious.'

'I tell you, mate, I'm sick of lying low. My whole life I've been starved and chased and bullied by one bastard or another. One little mistake and I'm stuck in the fucking army, and they're still starving and chasing and bullying. I've had enough, see? If I don't break the habit, it's going to be me that gets crippled or hanged or shot one of these days, right or wrong.'

'I'm all for changing the system, but what's cutting the Colonel's throat going to achieve?'

'It might take the smile off his face.'

—◆—

Ahead, ghostly as they flickered between the trees under the chilly moon, two riders were moving at a walk towards the town. The intermittent glimpses between the black bars of tree trunks showed that one wore an odd, loose hat.

Roscarrock's eyes hardened in the darkness. He'd guessed right. The Irishman didn't want to disappear into unknown countryside and risk a race with trained horsemen over open ground. He was heading for the town, comfortable in the calculation that in the event of trouble he could disappear into the crowd that would head the same way, or duck into one of a dozen inns, alleys or open doorways. Roscarrock eased his horse to an equal walk and charted a convergent course against the two riders, glancing at the ground to avoid noisier leaves or stone.

He was forty yards behind them. Should he just follow? Was that the Kinnaird way, the Comptrollerate way – to trace the net, to illuminate the bigger picture? But by all accounts, the Irishman was a uniquely valuable prize, an essential link in treason's chain. The Admiral had expressly sought his capture.

But how? Roscarrock looked around him again – for Jessel, for any of the dragoons, any one man to help him, at least to take the Irishman's companion out of the calculation. But he was alone on the slope, Jessel on the other side of the field, probably struggling to restrain the soldiers from relieving the boredom with a bit of a charge.

So it was him, him alone, with the night air in his nose and the rhythm of the horse's tread against his thighs, and still he didn't know how he was going to tackle two riders. Instinctively, somehow, he had nudged the horse into the bouncing staccato beat of a trot – to follow or to attack? –

and then behind him came the faint, foolish cry of a bugle, then shouts, and then chaos.

The madness was immediate. Roscarrock's isolation in the darkness, and in his utter concentration on the movement of his horse and the path of the men ahead, was shattered by the metallic call to the charge, by the distant animal cries of the dragoons spurring their horses and themselves to the attack and then, rippling towards him, the calls of fear and anger from the crowd, rising as a wave of alarm and confusion and then frantic movement. God knew what had prompted the dragoons – what the hell was Jessel doing? Had it been boredom, had someone thrown a stone or just a word? – but it didn't matter because now he could hear the soldiers thundering into the crowd behind him, and as he swore and looked forwards again, he saw the Irishman's attention drawn inevitably by the noise, saw the looks from the two men, saw the exchanged glance, the sudden wrenching at the reins, saw the horses leap forwards towards the town. Pursuit it must be, and Roscarrock kicked his horse to the gallop, pursuit if he wasn't swallowed up by the frightened mob surging behind him. The trees began to blur beside him, the light of the town flashing between them, and he prayed for even ground for the charging horse he could no longer control, because the slightest drop would take the beast's leg away and send him diving into one of the great trunks.

The Irishman was halfway to the town – he wasn't even galloping now – and somewhere in Roscarrock's brain there was admiration that the man had the daring and the self-control to ease his horse and draw less attention to himself. Roscarrock tried to match him, pulled the horse back to a canter, again tried to find space for calculation, and then from off to his right there was a single, high-pitched scream.

He turned instinctively, and the horse slowed and pulled around with him. There'd been only one woman in his mind today, and some wilful trick of his brain said that the scream came from Virginia Strong. He stared into the evening, horse shifting urgent beneath him, saw the graceful figure, the golden hair, the white throat that had reached out to him. Damn the woman! Why the hell did her foolish dalliance with excitement bring her here? To the right, on the outskirts of the town, a group of women had been standing, watching the meeting from a distance with who knew what interest or scorn. Now they were a broken group, shifting and nervy as they watched their menfolk scattered by the dragoons. Close by them was that single figure, and the same glance that showed Roscarrock the height and hair that just had to be the lady showed him the tension between the group and the individual, the taller figure frozen and unnatural like an animal at bay, the mob of women edgy and restive. Damn her! Roscarrock pulled the horse to the right, and kicked it angrily into the gallop again.

~ ~

Moving now at a trot and able to keep a regular glance over his shoulder, James Fannion saw the unknown rider haring away and risked pulling up for a moment to assess the unexpected movement. He'd seen it all – the sudden trembling of the crowd's fringe even as he heard the bugle, the disintegration of the group, individuals stepping away, whirling and staring like startled deer, like all the crowds he'd seen over the years; as the shouts rose and the first stones were thrown back at the horsemen, he'd seen more and more of the fringe first stagger and then run, seen the whole cauldron suddenly boiling with movement. The moonlight made the dusty mob wild and ghostly, and for a moment he fancied himself alone and pursued by a weird grey army, thundering towards him with unearthly wails. But he knew that the chaos was his cover, that his horse gave him distance and respectability, and that the town was near.

Now there was this new movement, a rider where there should have been none. A curious townsman? A stray dragoon? Now the stranger was away, riding like the wind towards a restive gaggle of people near the poorer end of town – but he wasn't riding for the gaggle, he was riding for a lone figure near them. Fannion stared at the inexplicable tableau: the small crowd, the solitary figure nearby, the horseman riding headlong towards... towards her; for it was a woman, no doubt of it – the group were women – and now one was throwing something, a few were moving towards the outcast... God, what was she doing there? Then with thunderous steps the rider was on her and she reached up as he reached down, swung lithely up onto the horse, and away into the darkness.

Fannion gave the odd incident another second, and then at a word from his companion turned away and resumed his brisk journey into town, the storm of shouting following him as he rode.

His stolen horse and the surge of blood to his head had carried Roscarrock through the crazed gallop, had brought him to the lady's side in a frenzy of hooves and shouts and swooped her up behind him, and had taken them thundering away over the shadowed and broken ground. In less than a minute they were on a flat track, then a road into town, buildings growing up around them and a civilizing light beaming from windows and slowing them to a trot. Roscarrock was too hot and angry to feel the press of Virginia Strong's body against his back, and the firm hold of her arms around his waist and chest.

Suddenly her lips were at his ear, her words blowing across his cheek. 'I should get off here, I think. People will start to talk.' He could hear the smile in the words, and it riled him.

He helped her down, and slipped down beside her.

'I'm most grateful.' She held out a fine hand, which Roscarrock gripped on instinct and then dropped. 'It's Mr Roscarrock, isn't it? Tom. I'm Lady Virginia—'

'I know who you are, My Lady. What the hell were you doing out there?'

'I... I'm sorry.' She didn't seem very sorry. 'I wanted to see—'

'You wanted to see a bit of radicalism close up. You thought that a dark cloak would keep you anonymous.'

'Those women—'

'Are not stupid. They also have hungry children, and husbands who've just been charged by the dragoons, and when they see a rich stranger obviously out of place, they're suspicious and hostile and I don't blame them.' He was detached from his own viciousness. Fannion was getting away. 'God's sake, woman!' She blinked at the unfamiliar brutality. 'Don't you people realize that out here – away from your damned salons and champagne – it's real? The suffering and the sedition and the violence – it's actually happening to real people.'

She was exulted rather than cowed by her escape, but Lady Virginia Strong didn't like being scolded. 'I suppose it's natural that an habitué of Seldon House should have sympathies with the radicals.' The blue eyes were bright and high. 'I approve.'

Roscarrock glanced around them. The first skirmishers of the crowd were starting to straggle into town, out of breath and wild-eyed. Somewhere, a pane of glass smashed. 'The more I see of the gentry,' he said, 'the more I trust the mob.'

She seemed to breathe him in, to a face shining with life. 'Lord Hugo tells me he doesn't know whether to trust you.'

'My respects to you both, but I don't give a damn.' He swung up onto the horse. Then he looked back down at the exquisite figure standing mud-flecked in the street; the wind had blown her hood off again, and strands of golden hair trailed away into the darkness. An argument had started among a group of men nearby, and another window shattered the night, much closer now. 'Will you be—'

'Thank you, Mr Roscarrock.' She smiled, and nodded graciously. 'I shall be fine. My horse is close by.' She was pulling her hair into order, and reached back to lift the hood. 'Thank you for a most invigorating ride and discussion.' The beautiful features, framed by the darkness of the hood, shone for a moment and then turned away.

Roscarrock shook his head, and kicked the horse to a canter.

― ⁓ ―

FIELD REPORT, TAKEN THE 30TH DAY OF JULY 1805

Joseph McNamara: the rich all parasites; the poor victims the world over; the King a weak and foolish old man powerless and unwilling to stop the abuses of his Ministers; Parliament a corrupt theatre; the price of bread used as a weapon for oppression.

Henry Hodge: practical wrongs of the unreformed Parliament; theoretical wrongs of the unreformed Parliament; the American colonies won rights still not granted to British working men; the French revolutionaries secured rights ditto; the few disproportionately represented in Parliament, the majority unrepresented. A people's march in London, and a petition to the King.

James Fannion: the great brotherhood of man across countries; the equality of suffering — Irish and English labouring men; Irish sympathy for English workers; French ditto; all the Irish ask is fellow-feeling; only Government deception forestalls rebellion.

Gabriel Chance: the better world promised by God; the essence of man, and his inherent relationship with God; Government and Governors barriers between man and God; paradise to be gained only by breaking through the bonds of oppression.

[SS O/162/227]

― ⁓ ―

Bury St Edmunds was burning. From two points over the rooftops smoke was coughing up into the night, and a bright crown of flames visible high up to his left indicated a roof that had caught. As Roscarrock passed entrances to particular streets or alleys, the stench of burning billowed out at him. Now, as he hurried the horse through the chaos of the roaming angry and the hurrying scared, he passed a group of a dozen men hacking at the timbers of a barn with axes, and dragging sacks out into the street. They didn't want to destroy the whole town, but selected merchants would suffer for their high prices and unpopularity. There was a shout behind him, a sudden hammering of hooves on the roadway, and he turned to see three dragoons charging down towards the looters. The men scattered, dropping sacks and tools and bolting for doorways and alleys, all except for one who stood his ground and tried to face down the charge with axe ready. But he mistimed his strike and his movements, and the massive barrelling shoulder of the lead horse smashed him back into a wall before the sabre wheeling above could do worse damage. Roscarrock hurried on.

He raced to the entrance to the town that Fannion would have used because he could do nothing else; but he knew it was futile. The Irishman would have escaped by now or, if he was sensible, buried himself in the chaos. Roscarrock wasted time asking after two riders and a hat at the nearest inns and sentries, and finally allowed sense to catch up with him. From a pair of patrolling dragoons he found out where Major Royce had stationed himself, and from the Major – sitting tall and still on his horse amid the mayhem, glass of wine in hand, directing his men with a nicely judged mixture of incitement and restraint and all the time conducting a conversation with two local officials – he found out where Jessel had headed.

The town would not suffer badly. This was not a co-ordinated protest. This was confused groups of men in the darkness, dealing with the anger and shame of being poor and being attacked by taking it out on whatever symbols of authority or unhappiness they passed. The skirmishes between the groups and the roving dragoons would continue until tiredness and cold took over and everyone's blood had settled. Then it would be up to the Magistrates to decide whether to make some examples or to let the evening pass as a regrettable explosion of tempers.

Jessel was standing in the middle of an attic room, head bent to avoid the roof timbers and eyes intent on the pieces of paper that he was passing from right hand to left. Behind him, a dragoon was hunched by a crude wooden bed, pulling at bits of bedding and furniture without conviction.

Jessel's glance flicked up as Roscarrock appeared on the stairs.

'We missed him, Tom. But we'll get him.'

'Fannion?'

'Chance.'

'He was staying here?'

'Owner's a tailor. On a night when everyone's a radical, how else would a radical tailor pick his bed? He's hooked it in the panic – must have made for the hills as soon as the dragoons attacked – left a bundle of philosophical pamphlets behind him, and some letters, by the bed.' He held out a handful of small pages.

Roscarrock flicked through them as Jessel had done. The diary of a woman missing a man.

'From his wife, obviously.' Jessel grunted.

'Any detail on his plans?'

A negative grunt. 'No addresses on any of them. But he's been in Sheffield, which has got problems at the moment, and Nottingham – they say the slums of Nottingham are the worst in the whole British Empire. Tinder for the troublemaker.' Jessel tapped the soldier on the shoulder, muttered at him, and the man stood and clumped across the attic and away down the stairs. 'Nothing on where he's going. Owner says they hardly exchanged a word, what with Chance doing a runner.' Jessel had turned away to scan the bare room, and was addressing the rafters. 'I think he was expecting a few coins in rent.'

'Leave him a pamphlet. Did you hear the speeches, Dick?'

Jessel sat on the rough bed, and it bowed dangerously under him. 'Enough of them. Chance is trouble. All that God stuff is a fine way to make fellows feel good about themselves when they're pulling down the Magistrate's house. Who can be a rebel when he's doing the Lord's work?'

From outside there was a sudden squall of shouting, and a faint scream. Roscarrock handed back the sheaf of envelopes and notes. 'Chance is remarkable, but he's away with the angels. Fannion is the dangerous one.'

'He's a killer, but I thought he went pretty flat tonight.'

'Don't you believe it. Listen to the chaos outside. They're not doing that because Gabriel Chance promised them the Lord. They're doing it because they're furious that an Irishman told them they hadn't got the nerve.' Roscarrock sat back under the eaves, surprised at how James Fannion had affected him, and his fist softly thumped at a beam. 'I had him, Dick.'

Jessel's eyes flicked wide.

'I was on his tail, moonlight and open ground and a good horse and I had him. Then Lady bloody Virginia bloody Strong had to go and get herself lynched.'

Jessel was startled. 'She's safe?'

'She's safe. Got her out just in time.'

There was a low chuckle from the bed. 'Terrible thing when lust gets in the way of duty. But I think the Admiral would prefer it this way. You'll get your Irishman soon enough.'

Roscarrock frowned at the bare boards, and then looked up. 'Jessel: I'm assuming she's not just some feather-headed aristo out for a rough radical flirt.'

Jessel considered him for a second, and shook his head.

'She works for the Admiral – for us, yes?'

A smile. 'I don't think that one works for anyone. Free spirit. Not sure if there was ever a husband, but she either murdered him or gave him a heart attack.' He stood. 'When she's not in your saddlebags, Tom, she's in France. One of our finest. Fearless, brilliant' – a grin over his shoulder – 'and persuasive, as you'd imagine.' He started to stamp down the narrow staircase.

31 July 1805

Grasmere, the 27th day of July

My dear Sir Keith,

Our poor Gough is dead, and you must blame me for this saddest of losses before you curse any greater power. I know that you were particular about the lad and bade me have a special eye to him, and so much greater is my haste in writing to you, and so much greater my shame that I was not more pressing in my warnings to him on that last glad fresh morning of, as it now seems, all of our lives.

The circumstances are briefly told. He had determined that April morn to walk over the mountain that the local folk call Hell-vellen. In rising so high out of the plains of man he has reached quite another vale, and we are the worse for it. A local militiaman named Eyles was to have guided him, but apparently never appeared – indeed, the fellow still cannot be found – and with my entreaties to care blowing around his ears like the breeze of that clearest day, dear Gough determined to make the walk attended only by his terrier. Hearing nothing more of him, I foolishly assumed that he was safe arrived and away and, in that quiet private way of his, had felt no need to communicate with me; in life as in death so do the young leave the old behind. Not one hour ago I heard of the discovery this morning by a shepherd of his body — dead of exposure or of a fall, we may never tell. Nature herself has claimed back as of right this proudest emanation of her power and beauty; his faithful hound stayed beside the corpse those long, cold weeks, last bond of life, eternal bond of the truest souls that transcend life.

This was to have been the century of the young; but they are burning out like meteors and leaving it to the old to trudge in darkness. The passing of my poor brother, and now dear Gough, leave me cold and alone.

A power is gone, which nothing can revive.
Not for a moment could I now behold
That fell, that sea, and be as once alive.
The feeling of my loss will ne'er be old.

If you are acquainted with his kin, I beg you to offer them my most sorrowful condolences for this promise and joy that is gone, and tend you my own respects and deepest sympathy.

W. Wordsworth

[SS M/1096/2]

'Damn the dog.' A Lowland Scots hiss into the gloom. 'And damn all poets.'

Sir Keith Kinnaird in a doctor's parlour in Oxford, a handful of letters piled neatly in front of him and a spartan breakfast going cold around them.

He read the last of the letters. The one from Wordsworth was folded carefully and pushed into an inside pocket of his coat, then he carried the others to the fire, watching until the last corner of script browned and blazed and shrivelled to ash.

Gough was dead, and a man calling himself Tyler was loose in the land. The chaos was spreading like a plague, and the Scotsman's face frowned and aged at the threat.

Gough was dead, and his portion of the covenant of the Comptrollerate-General must be entrusted to another.

———

By the evening, as indifferent flurries of rain sputtered out of a cold, sour evening, James Fannion was warmly established in the Red Lion inn in Colchester. They wouldn't be looking for him here, and he could afford a decent room, and a wash, and a little while staring across the inn counter at the serving woman. She was plain enough, but cheerful with it, and that suited him fine. There was a plan now, a plan with his hidden hand pulling the strings, and in exactly a week he would see London on its knees.

Yesterday had been entertaining, and the new certainties of warmth, and a bed, and a plan, had cheered him. Against expectation, he'd liked the English crowd. Stubborn and slow as donkeys, but they were thoughtful enough, and he had to respect that even if they were harder going. He'd spent his life fighting the English, and he'd killed a handful when the need had arisen; but he'd never really met many.

The serving woman was back from the other end of the counter.

'Now, you see, Mary, here's my problem.' The maid leant in happily towards the easy chat. 'I'm supposed to be in town to stay with a cousin of mine – a soldier he is – fine man, very popular with the ladies, him with his uniform. But – and here's the problem – he's a lovely-looking chap but he's not my type, and here I am sitting in your inn, and you looking after me so pleasantly.'

Mary giggled. Christ, if the Dublin specials could see him now. It was painful stuff. They both knew it.

Mary said emptily, 'Oh, you ought to go and find your cousin, I reckon,' and adjusted the shoulder of her dress.

'Mary, you're probably right. You're showing me my duty and you're a good woman for it.' He laid a hand on her forearm, fingers close to the promising heave of her bust. Christ and all his saints. 'Now, if you was a cousin of mine too, say, then...' – he looked up, and sighed – 'but you're right. You're right. Where would I find the soldiers, would you say? Where do they drink? I don't want to hang around the barracks – find myself kidnapped and off to the war, and you back here waiting for me.'

She giggled again. 'The soldiers are mostly round the Balkerne Hill. The officers don't like it so the soldiers do. There's a few pubs: the King's Head, the Marquis, couple of others. Cheap, and they can get – you know... other entertainment.' She looked down at the counter for a second, and Fannion tried to produce a bashful smile.

He put his other hand on her wrist. 'If I want entertainment, Mary, I know where...' He stopped, sighed heavily. 'But hell, I'm a slave to duty, that's what I am. Mary, you're a wonder. Be waiting for me, when I come back a general.'

Fannion offered a silent apology to the ghosts of Ireland's bards, and stepped cautiously out into the night.

The speakers had known what they were about too. McNamara was a chancer and a charlatan, but good with a crowd. Hodge had no strategy, but he was a serious thinker and, from Lord knew where, he'd found real rhetorical skill. And the tailor, now; he was something else. An honest-to-God prophet. He'd only heard a few lines, but Fannion replayed them to himself as he sauntered through Colchester. There was a kind of holiness there, something he'd only seen in poets and priests, and then only far from the cities.

There was something else: a... bitterness. As a professional, as a prophet, or just as a man, Gabriel Chance felt thwarted somehow. That might be useful.

Faintly, he caught the rhythmic rattle of marching feet from around the next corner. It was getting louder, the stamp of boots echoed by the lighter clatter of muskets and webbing. Soldiers, and coming his way. Fannion hissed in a slow breath. He had to keep going. They would not be looking for him. Two soldiers appeared at the corner and swung ponderously and began to tramp towards him, and then it was four and finally six, a patrol striding towards the lone Irishman. He forced his legs forwards towards them and his face into indifference. One of the men had a heavy moustache, and Fannion saw only the surprise of the man he'd stabbed in Liverpool.

He contrived to glance incuriously at the soldiers as they crunched past him. The reason they would not be looking for him was that Colchester was a military town, home to thousands of soldiers, and an Irish rebel would have to be a lunatic to show his face there. There would be other patrols. He was here to meet soldiers, to talk to them. Maybe he'd show what a little Irish lunacy could do.

Really, these English radicals were quite something: so civilized, and so organized. A little of that in the '98 rising and he'd have taken Dublin in an afternoon. First the letter of invitation, then the conversations last night, all so polite and reasonable. We're selling the country to Napoleon and we thought you might be interested in lending us a hand, old fellow. Mightn't he just? Instructions for J. Fannion all worked out – not instructions of course, merely suggestions, delivered with the pleasant certainty of centuries of imperial control. A couple of errands, a couple of conversations, and on the 6th London would collapse in chaos. And Gabriel Chance, the unassuming angel, at the heart of it all.

He almost missed the Marquis. In a dark and stinking back street, the dark and stinking inn was easily missed, a low and shambling ruin of timber and plaster with little light and no paint. He stood back, checked the last traces of lettering on the rotting sign that was now propped against the porch, and stepped down into the inn.

He was looking for a man called Foley, and it would be a delicate and tiring night of work, perhaps more than one night, to find him and meet him and become his friend and make him a traitor, all without getting arrested or discreetly beaten to death in the dirty garrison town.

A part of his mind was still fixed on the previous night, on the man on the horse behind him, and the woman.

1st August, 1805

In the early afternoon, Roscarrock was sitting with his chair tilted comfortably back against one of the walls of a coffee house on Drury Lane, where the poorer district in which Jessel lodged skirmished with the fading fashions of Great Queen Street and Lincoln's Inn. Another fruitless meeting during the morning, and now he was watching the ebb and flow of faces and coats, busy men and idle men, trying to convince himself that the smoke and the stink were spray and salt, when Jessel dropped dark into the chair in front of him. The fair hair was awry and the face was grim.

Roscarrock eased his chair forwards, waiting for Jessel to find the words. Eventually Jessel's stare broke, and he glanced away and then straight back across the table. 'One of these days, Tom Roscarrock,' he said low and plain, 'I'll have to know who you are and what you're doing.'

'Tell me when you do, because I'm as sick of this half-world as you are.'

'I don't believe it. You have to know more. Kinnaird knew more about you, and he obviously didn't know it all.' For a moment the voice was almost pleading. 'Tom, it doesn't matter how wrong you've gone in the past; it doesn't even matter what your game is today. We can and we will use you, if you play straight with us.'

Roscarrock stayed silent.

'What is Kinnaird doing? Are you helping him?'

'I've told you. He's more of a mystery to me than he is to you.' Roscarrock shifted in his chair, straighter, limbs ready. 'Now either you like that, or you let me walk out that door right now and forever and neither of us'll be too sorry. Or draw your blade.'

Jessel checked the position of his chair relative to the table, glanced at Roscarrock's torso, then back to his eyes. 'Honestly, I'm thinking about it.'

'We've lost someone else?' Eventually Jessel nodded, once and slow. 'Another dead fieldsman? Friend of yours?'

'No.' Jessel was almost smiling in his anger. 'A friend of yours.'

Roscarrock was very still indeed.

'The Parson up at Oakham. Forster. Henry Forster. Kinnaird's special, just like you. The man you spent all those hours alone with.'

Roscarrock was ice. 'He was alive when I left him.'

'He's not anymore. He's lying dead in a half-burnt parsonage. Bit of local trouble? Coincidence?'

'I liked him.'

'And Kinnaird liked you. Now Forster's dead, and Kinnaird's gone, and someone's chipping at the Comptrollerate-General piece by bloody piece. Looks like Kinnaird's closing down his network for good, doesn't it?'

Roscarrock was still watching, frown nagging at his forehead. Setting out the words firmly, he said, 'I do not know.'

Jessel really was smiling now. 'Look at it this way: either you're helping him, or as one of his network you'll be dead yourself pretty soon.'

'The thought had occurred to me.' The face and voice were brisker. 'Are you done with the interrogation? I'm back to Bury St Edmunds tonight. Come if you like; see if I send a letter to Napoleon on the way.'

'Bury St Edmunds?'

'The tailor; the one Chance was staying with. He was lying.'

Jessel's face opened in interest. 'More private information?'

'Chance has been on the road for weeks, right? He must be travelling with more than a couple of pamphlets and his wife's letters. But there was no bag in the room, no sack.' A servant stopped at the table and Jessel waved him away irritably, face not leaving Roscarrock's. 'Chance is used to quick exits, surely. He'd have to be. So when he goes to the meeting, he takes his knapsack with him. Just in case. He's not worried about a couple of pamphlets left behind, and he's forgotten that he's had the letters by the bed to read over.'

'So maybe he's settled his score with the tailor. Doesn't mean he's told him where he's going. Doesn't mean he would take that risk with anyone he stays with.'

'It absolutely means that. The only way the wife's letters – unaddressed, every one of them – could reach him is if he tells each landlord where he's going next, and the letters get forwarded down the chain as they come. You read the letters. He'd taken them out to re-read them himself. Chance and his wife are close, and if he was taking the precaution of having his bag with him, he'd take the precaution of making sure the tailor knew how to forward any letters that came.'

Jessel considered it, then nodded. 'Very well. Good. Might work.' He stood up, and his fingers drummed once at the table. 'Have fun with your tailor, then. I hope you both survive the day.'

Away from its main bar-room, the Marquis tavern degenerated into a rambling series of parlours where off-duty soldiers, or the poorest of Colchester's citizens, could retreat to drink in private or risk a meal or pass ten minutes with a girl. Late that Thursday evening, Private Foley knocked at the door to one of the little rooms, opened it and stepped aside to usher in three of his comrades. They stepped in warily, eyes low and looking all around themselves, before settling on the figure of a man in the gloomiest corner, face in shadow.

Foley had a final furtive look outside and then shut the door, snapping the bolt across. Then he sat, and the other three did so more cautiously. There was no movement or sound from the dark man in the corner. One of the soldiers, older than the others, said sourly, 'This your mystery friend, is it, Foley? Let's have a look at you, then.'

There was a pause, and then the man in the corner leant forwards into the glow of the single lamp. It was a dark curled head and a handsome face, with a pair of large and strong eyes that moved carefully from man to man.

'Got a voice, do you? Got a name?'

The stranger nodded. Then he said quietly, 'I do. And I'm very careful with both of them.'

'Oh, aye?'

'Aye.' Again the careful scrutiny of each man. 'You're lucky men. You've only got to haul me off to your Colonel or the local Magistrates and you'll be heroes. Maybe a little reward. I'd consider that carefully, if I was you.' The face fixed on the older soldier. 'My voice is an Irish voice, and my name is the name of a known Irish rebel. I'm trusting you because I believe what your friend here says about you. But you can get me hanged tomorrow morning if it takes your fancy. I'd consider that carefully, if I was you.'

'I'm considering it, mate, don't you worry.'

'If it makes you feel more comfortable, you can call me James. I don't plan on asking your names. If you're the quality of men I think you are, we've no need to be fooling around with blood oaths and declarations of loyalty.'

'No one's hanging anyone, Irishman. What's your business with us?'

The stranger sat back against the bench, face moving in and out of the shadows as he talked. 'Firstly, I suggest we agree what we're not. I am no kind of philosopher; I'm not preaching brotherly solidarity; I only care about a free Ireland. I have no interest in the freedoms of Englishmen, as long as they're not exercising them in my country.' The soldiers watched the display of honesty cautiously. 'On your side, I suggest that you probably don't care whether the Irish live in peace or all starve to death tomorrow. You've got your own battles to worry about.'

The older soldier – he was probably a corporal, the stranger decided – nodded slightly, an unattractive smile lurking. 'That's right, mate. I'm a little too poor for philosophy. And no, we wouldn't give a fart if Ireland sank under the sea tomorrow. You can all go to hell, for all I care, and too many English soldiers have caught fever or a knife in the back in Ireland for us to want to stay there one day longer than necessary. I guess we can agree on that.' The Irishman smiled politely. 'Right. So it sounds like we both have a problem with the British Government, doesn't it?' A nod from the shadows. 'And don't think this is radical hot air. Politics don't interest us.' Next to him, Private Foley grunted agreement.

One of the other soldiers – he was barely more than a boy – felt that he wanted more of a share of the conversation. 'It's not getting flogged to death is what interests us.'

'Flogged to death?'

'First it was Willie Watkins. They flogged him so he'll never stand properly again. Just for talking. And then it was Corporal Tubb – someone informed on him – and they flogged him almost till he died and now he's been discharged sick and he'll probably die.'

The Corporal next to him put out a slow hand and gripped his forearm; it was restraint rather than reassurance.

The stranger leant forwards, his face suddenly glaring in the light. 'There was an informant?'

'Was,' the Corporal snapped quietly. 'There isn't anymore.'

The stranger smiled as he understood. 'Perhaps you won't be dragging me to the Magistrate after all. I didn't realize just how deep you gentlemen were in. And I hadn't realized what conditions were like.' Another quick smile. 'Always having been on the receiving end of the British army, so to speak.'

'You'd better believe it, mate.' The Corporal spoke slow and insistent. 'It ain't all medals and pretty girls. None of us wants to be here. Some was crimped, and—'

'Crimped?'

The Corporal smiled heavily. 'You get drunk, or knocked on the head, or invited upstairs by a tart, and next thing you're in cuffs and the Magistrate's swearing you in as a soldier. Kidnapped, if you like.'

The Irishman shook his head. 'Christ, no wonder you were always such miserable sods with us. We might have had a little more sympathy.'

The Corporal chuckled. 'Course, the rich don't get kidnapped, and when they get balloted for the militia they can buy their way out. No choice for the rest of us. And once you're in, well... pay – food – discipline: all fucking horrible.'

'If they was as quick and generous with the shillings as they is with the lash...' Foley started.

The Corporal pressed on. 'When the navy mutinied over pay and conditions in '97, Government gave in. Handshakes all round and Rule bloody Britannia. When soldiers protest—'

'Like the Artillery at Woolwich, or the Irish Regiment in Exeter.'

The hand across again, and irritation, '— they just get cut to pieces by the dragoons.'

The Irishman was nodding in slow sympathy. 'The whole bloody system is corrupt,' he said heavily. 'The whole thing stinks. Your man Foley here and I fell to talking about it last night, but I just had no idea.'

'No. No one does. But don't expect us to be raising the flag of liberty and reform on your behalf, mate, because we've no wish to be sabred to pieces just to prove a point.'

'Right, right.' The Irishman was nodding, apparently heavy with thought. 'But your hands are in the mangle now, aren't they? Someday soon they'll have you for killing their sneaking informant, won't they? I guess you must be worried that sometime soon one of your mates is going to decide he's better off doing himself a favour and betraying you, right?' The Corporal's grim glare showed that he was well aware of this; the boy's wide eyes showed that he wasn't. 'You can't go backwards now, can you? You have to find a way forwards.'

'Don't get carried away, mate. We can take care of ourselves, and we ain't joining no revolution.'

'Course not; course not. When you act, it has to be quick, and it has to be proper, and it has to deal with all your grievances. You don't want to fight the system; you want a new system.' The Corporal was nodding warily. 'Full redress of complaints, free pardon for anything you've been forced to do along the way. Like the sailors got at Spithead.'

'Right. But that's never going to happen, is it? Country's run by corrupt politicians and fat admirals. They're never going to do us any favours, are they?'

'There must be a way.' The Irishman was leaning forwards on the old, stained table, concentration gripping his face. 'Foley says you're posted to London this week.'

'Right. Government's worried about protests.'

'They want you to fight against the people you've most in common with, don't they?' The Irishman's face was sour. 'It's sick, so it is.' Again the thought. 'But maybe those politicians and admirals have got a bit too clever for themselves this time. Maybe they're taking you for granted, and they've calculated wrong.' There was interest in the four flickering faces opposite him. 'You see, some friends of mine have got plans for the 6th of August in London – not Irish, not radicals, just people who think the system needs to change and those people responsible need to be held to account. They've got plans for Tuesday – mate, I'm trusting you not just with my life here, but with lots of lives – plans to end the brutality and the unfairness and the pointless fighting and the corruption.' He looked earnestly around the rank little room. 'Frankly, they need a bit of maturity and stability in their plan – that's what you bring – and in return this could solve everything for you in a day.'

The Corporal was staring hard at him. 'Keep talking.'

'It shall be the 6th – Tuesday.'

'I see. Can it be stopped?'

'No.'

'Should we expect a little bloodshed?'

'It's entirely possible, but irrelevant. The impact will be as strong without deaths, but if there are many it does not matter. Everyone involved is expendable.'

'A little blood might help the effect, wouldn't you say?'

'I would. But the effect on London and on the Ministry will be as catastrophic either way.'

'Excellent.'

2nd August, 1805

On the morning of the 2nd, Joseph smelt the sea for the first time. It came slowly at him out of the mist, an empty, alien smell that unsettled him because he could neither recognize nor grasp it.

He passed a cold hour huddled on a bench opposite the merchant's office, an army blanket clenched around his shoulders and the leather folder under his coat. It was so hard to think. A vicious wind was snapping up the street, edged with icy drops of water from the sea. *Silly Joseph.* He had to be so very careful; that was right, the young Master would want that. But he was so cold and so hungry and it was so hard to think.

The young Master, teaching him how to deal with an emergency, how to escape: *Crowds of people are your best disguise, but individuals are your greatest danger.* Why couldn't he just disappear into the countryside? Why couldn't he go back to Doudeville? Normandy wasn't so far. Would the Minister and the Inspector really want to waste all that effort trying to find one little Joseph in the middle of the fields?

His mother's cold, sad face on the pillow. The Inspector would never stop; he would destroy France to find little Joseph.

So he must escape France, and to escape France he must walk into the office of Du Maurier Frères – Marchands and ask at the counter. But to do that he must step out of the crowd; he must become an individual, and talk directly to another individual, and if that individual was working for the police after all, or if that individual was just not helpful, then he would be finished. He pulled the blanket tighter, and tried to bury his neck in its folds.

It was so cold. *Come on, Joseph.* Lady Sybille would want him to be brave. He stood up, and flinched as the wind stung his ears. Across the street, so cold, trying to burrow down into himself. It would be warm in the merchant's office.

But he must be a servant, not a beggar. The young Master: '*Anonymity is your best disguise, Joseph.*' So, on the threshold Joseph stood as straight as he could, pulled the blanket from his shoulders even though his neck burnt in the wind, and rolled it under his arm. *Proudly now, Joseph. The old Master going to the guillotine.* He stepped into the merchant's office.

This could be the man. What had the message from Paris said? Joseph Dax was a servant, travelling alone, unlikely to have resources for comfort. An enemy of France, carrying vital documents. Watch all departing ships and shipping offices for such a man trying to escape to England, or to anywhere from where he could travel on to England.

Slumped on a chair in the corner of the merchant's office, Jean Brel watched the little man step forwards into the room, and look around himself like a rabbit. The rabbit was trying to understand how the office worked. Brel shifted his substantial weight on the chair which had been his for two hours now, too hard and too small for him, and shifted the news-sheet up to cover more of his face. He'd put on a shabby coat instead of his police jacket, and the office was busy enough that he shouldn't be noticed.

This creature was a servant at best, and he was alone. Might he try to get to England? Of course he wouldn't do so directly, not here in daylight. Where might he ask for? Portugal? Lisbon, perhaps – a booking on behalf of his Master?

The little man had taken one deep breath and was now moving forwards to the counter. Brel folded his news-sheet, and stood slowly, rubbing his rump. He sauntered over to the noticeboard next to the counter, and began to examine details of transports down the coast.

The little man had to wait for someone else in front of him to finish; he stared directly ahead of him. He didn't look like a spy. There was no cunning in the eyes, no strength of mind in the face. Just a timid servant scared to talk to his betters.

Brel paid great attention to the dates of cargo sailings to the German states.

The little man reached the counter. Brel leant his head towards him, eyes not leaving the timetables that blurred in front of him. What was he saying?

'Please, sir – I am asking about the times of coaches to Paris.'

That certainly wasn't it. Wrong man; no spy after all. This office had nothing to do with coaches, anyway, as the clerk was saying. Waste of time, this was. Brel turned, hoping that his chair was still free. It was uncomfortable but it was better than standing all day – or, worse, having to keep watch from outside.

'But sir, Monsieur Trichet assured me you would know about coaches to Paris.'

The chair was still free, and Jean Brel ambled slowly towards it and tried to make himself comfortable. He looked quickly around the room, wondering if the distraction of the idiot servant had made him miss anyone more promising. Nothing. He unfolded the news-sheet again. The servant was back at the door now, with the clerk's curse in his ear no doubt, and he looked broken beyond despair. Probably expecting a beating for fouling it up so badly.

The chair creaked ominously. Brel rebalanced himself, and his mind drifted away from the forlorn rabbit. Stew for dinner today, surely?

Behind the counter, the younger Du Maurier was murmuring hurriedly to a servant. 'Yes – the man with the blanket under his arm. There is no doubt; the phrases were precise. Watch that lump of a policeman; if he moves for the door you must get to him immediately and delay him – you think he's someone else and you have information about the sailing for Hamburg. And you' – to another servant – 'out the back now, and follow that servant. Do not approach him until he has travelled at least fifteen minutes and is completely away from here; make absolutely sure that there is no one in sight when you approach. When you are sure, give him the details for Labiche's boat at the outer jetty tonight; nothing more.'

———— ✦ ————

The core of the Admiralty building – like the institution – is seventeenth-century formality, panelled rooms and cold stone corridors. Jessel was waiting outside one of the meeting rooms when Lord Hugo Bellamy emerged, and as the Admiral strode off down the corridor, he fell in step at his shoulder.

'I may turn revolutionary just to avoid all these damn meetings. How do you do today, Jessel?'

'Adequate, My Lord, thank you.'

'The petition comes to London on the 6th, and the Admiralty assume that any serious trouble – the tailor, and Fannion the Irishman – will be related to that.'

It was a statement, and Jessel didn't bother to interrupt.

'And I have told them that our French assassin may be related, as part of a wider French design, but that we cannot be sure.'

Jessel kept pace, and waited.

'The convention, Jessel, is that you give me information, and not the converse. What about Kinnaird? Where is he and what is he doing?'

Jessel's mouth twisted in discomfort. 'We have nothing, My Lord. He is clearly active. He is getting at his agents where he can. But we can't tell what his objective is.'

'Grim, Jessel. Grim. Keep at it. And Roscarrock?'

'Bury St Edmunds. He thinks he can find out where Chance the tailor is going.'

The Admiral stopped and stood still in thought. 'Intrepid sort of fellow, isn't he, Jessel? I do hope we can confirm him on the right side eventually.'

Jessel just grunted. 'Any more as to that?'

A slight shake of the head. 'Nothing definite, My Lord. Enquiries in America, but it will take weeks to get anything of who Roscarrock knew and what he was doing there. Enquiries in Ireland: there have been Irish Roscarrocks, and they've been directly connected with radicalism and the rebellion, but—'

'Hasn't everyone?'

'Quite so. But we've no way of knowing when Roscarrock was there and what he was up to. Perhaps he just… knows that world, My Lord.'

'It's clear from what Kinnaird knew that Roscarrock has radicalism and mischief in his past; Kinnaird didn't spook easily – if he was worried about this man, he's worth worrying about. He might be tempted to radicalism again.'

'But we employ him still? The Admiralty wouldn't be surprised by that?'

'Jessel, the Admiralty would be horrified to know half of who we employ; that's why I don't tell them. The closer Roscarrock is to radicalism, the more he can say and do about it. I'm using him, Jessel, not putting him up for my club.'

'He may be active already – if Kinnaird has gone bad—'

'Regardless of Kinnaird.' Bellamy started to stride forwards again, and Jessel hurried after him. 'He may be doing something on his own account regardless of Kinnaird. But is it for reform, or is it for France?'

'Quite, My Lord.'

'Jessel, we need to be able to show my Admiralty colleagues that we are trying to stop a revolution this week.' The two pairs of feet thumped heavy and insistent along the corridor. 'Energy, you hear? Action.'

'My Lord.'

3rd August 1805

FIRE IN SAFFRON WALDEN

NEWSPAPER PREMISES BURN

A FRESH ASSAULT ON THE LIBERTY OF THE PRESS?

We learn of a serious fire in Saffron Walden yesterday, the 2nd of August. The conflagration, the timing and origins of which remain undiscovered, caused severe damage to the offices of the *Voice of the Land* news-sheet. It is not known when this organ will next be publishable given the loss of press equipment and scarce paper.

There is some uncertainty about the only inhabitant of the premises, Mr Andrew Malloy. Mr Malloy, also owner and editor of the *Voice of the Land*, has made no comment on the destruction of his property and his whereabouts remain unknown. We have long known Mr Malloy as a wise commentator on the social and agricultural difficulties of his district, a prudent advocate of an improvement in the conditions of his fellow man, and a brother in the cause of the freedom of the presses. It is devoutly to be hoped that he has come to no injury in this sad incident. Neighbours suggest that he was absent from the building for a day or more before the blaze, and we trust that he will emerge shortly to resume his former activities and status.

[THE BURY AND NORWICH POST, 3RD AUGUST 1805]

Late in the afternoon of the 3rd, Tom Roscarrock was seen to walk slowly into the coffee house on Drury Lane. Tiredness was crowding behind his eyes after two days' travelling, his thighs were dull and stiff after the hours on horseback, and he scowled at those servants and customers who slowed his path to the corner table. He let out a soft hiss of discomfort as his saddle-sore backside settled on the chair, and growled for something hot to drink.

Gabriel Chance, itinerant prophet, was heading directly for London – and might already be in the capital. As Roscarrock had reckoned, the tailor of Bury St Edmunds, briefly Chance's host, had been lying when he'd claimed to have no idea where his fugitive guest was headed. Roscarrock had implied that he knew more than he did, and had implied that he was more predisposed to violence than in truth he felt up to after a day's travel, and the tailor's breathless denials had collapsed in five minutes. Before heading off to address the crowd, Chance had told his host than any letters coming for him should be forwarded to the Mermaid Tavern in Hackney.

After such an investment of time on the road, it had felt underwhelming.

Roscarrock had thanked the tailor politely for his newfound honesty, and equally politely described the range of terrors that would be exacted on him by an outraged Government and a vengeful God should he fail to forward any future correspondence for Chance to Mr Morrison Cope, at the Admiralty. Then he'd turned his horse back to the south again, and London.

Bury St Edmunds had showed little trace of the rampage of a few nights before. The misrule of those few dark hours had been absorbed by the town and forgotten by the inhabitants. He wondered how many men were still slumped in gaol waiting for the Magistrates to decide whether the unrest was better punished or quietly consigned to history.

It felt good to be out of the press of streets and into fields again. He'd stopped for supper at a roadside inn, but it had been so grim and dirty a place that he'd slept out under the warm stars instead, horse tethered to a tree and the soft swell of a grass bank comfortably under his neck.

But Gabriel Chance was not staying at the Mermaid Tavern in Hackney. Roscarrock had gone straight there, as a travelling and sympathetic friend of the tailor keen to catch up with him. The indifferent ignorance of the surly individual behind the counter as to Chance's presence or even existence – coupled with the nagging possibility that two days' effort might only have produced another lie from the tailor of Bury – had hit like the seasickness he hadn't felt in twenty years.

Roscarrock had stalked out of the Mermaid quickly and gracelessly, anger scalding the tiredness that ate at him. He had checked how the roads lay around the tavern, then found an unobtrusive spot under some trees and watched the building for an hour; but there was no sign of hurried departure or any reaction at all to his interest in Chance.

The Mermaid seemed too elaborate a lie for the tailor in Bury to have conjured himself or concocted with Chance. In which case, sometime after leaving the attic room to go to inspire the crowd with his holy sedition, Chance had decided to change his plans. Or had he been prompted to by someone else? By the dragoons' attack?

Roscarrock had only started to think clearly at the end of his vigil outside the Mermaid Tavern, watching Hackney's drowsy afternoon activities drifting past him, the routines of the village and the first returning travellers from the markets in nearby London. By changing plan, Chance had cut himself loose from the frail lifeline of his wife's letters, and he'd have needed strong reason to do that; Roscarrock had a sense of their importance to the itinerant prophet. In fact, he surely wouldn't cut himself loose: if the landlord at the Mermaid hadn't been asked to forward any letters, then Chance would have to come back to collect them. Jessel would need to post a watcher in the tavern.

The change of plan, the abandoning of his system, and the proximity to London all suggested that Chance was now focused on some specific action, and that his timescale was shortening. What, beyond the presentation of a petition to Parliament, was planned for the 6th?

As Roscarrock had stood up, brushing the dust off his thighs and reaching for his horse, one final possibility had struck. If Chance had been intending to stop in Hackney, rather than disappearing into London just a mile further on, then it was for a reason – for someone to meet. That person or people, and that meeting, might still be here.

At the Dolphin Inn, where he and Jessel had met Phil, the informer, Roscarrock left a message for the Government spy. Then he'd hauled himself back onto his horse, and ridden on to London and the coffee house.

Roscarrock hadn't lost hope in the possibility of progress. But, slumped back against the coffee house wall, gazing through the bumps and evasions of the circulating customers and servants, mouth soured and head unrevived by coffee, he'd been too tired even to consider it.

So when Phil's face suddenly distorted itself against the coffee house window and peered in, Roscarrock found it hard for a moment to convince his brain that his visit to Hackney and the squashed features through the glass were both real. He dropped his indifferent glance back to his empty cup, and waited.

Phil slipped in as if part of the street dust. He had not opened the door himself, and those who had done so did not seem to give way as they left, but Phil was inside as the door closed. Roscarrock let the front feet of his chair drop loudly to the wooden floor, and still he didn't look up.

'You waiting for anyone, mister?' Now he looked up, and Phil was standing above him indicating the unoccupied chair across the table. He shook his head.

'Got your message, Mr, er, Grey.' Roscarrock just nodded. Phil sat as if making no more than polite conversation, voice low. 'Mr Albert not here?'

'Audience with the King.'

Something flickered around Phil's prim mouth.

'You're right, Mr Grey. Something's on tonight.' Roscarrock's tiredness evaporated with the words. 'Meeting of our little reforming group in Hackney.'

'Had you planned to tell us about it?'

'Honestly, Mr Grey, the meeting's a one-off. No messing.' Phil was in his professional business manner, and Roscarrock believed him. 'I wouldn't have known about it – not everyone's asked, I think. But after you tipped me off, I asked a couple of acquaintances, casual-like, and it turns out there's a group coming together.'

'Who? The hotheads?'

'You could say. Don't know who exactly, but Ted Wass'll be one, him as was after muskets when we met last time. And here's the thing: we're meeting in no normal place.' Roscarrock just looked the question. 'Basement of the old church. Ten tonight.' There was life in Roscarrock's eyes now, anticipation near his face. 'Want me to go? You and Mr Albert going to be keeping an eye?'

'You go. And yes, we'll keep an eye.'

Phil leant forwards, and there was none of his usual fluency. 'Serious, Mr Grey: you need to look out for me. If this is getting bigger, then I'm—'

'We'll look out for you.'

———

On the 3rd of August, the Vicar of St Wulfram's Church in Grantham received a letter from the Bishop of Lincoln. It informed him that certain influential local residents had raised significant concerns about his attitudes on grounds both social and theological – there were no specifics in the letter, and certainly no mention of the Vicar's regular discussion meetings with the late Reverend Forster and others. The Bishop was naturally extremely worried by this situation, particularly at a time of such disquiet nationally. The Vicar was consequently relieved of his position in the parish of St Wulfram's, with immediate effect, and ordered to London for consultations on whether, and where, he might appropriately find a position in the future.

A week later, the Bishop would receive a short reply from the Vicar's housekeeper. The note said that the housekeeper did not know what the

Bishop's letter had contained, but that she felt obliged to warn the Bishop that there would be a delay in response because the Vicar was currently undertaking a tour of north country churches expected to last several weeks, and was not contactable before his return.

—⁓—

London's bells had already clanged nine across the great hive of the city before Jessel reached the coffee house. He'd gratefully swallowed a mug before one of the servants brought him the message from Tom Roscarrock. Jessel glanced at it, swore loud enough to silence the whole room, and ran for the street. It would be ten at the earliest before he could gather any soldiers, and even then he'd be well short of Hackney.

—⁓—

In a stone chamber below the world, seven men were considering revolution, like children debating whether to steal apples. One was a blacksmith, two were shopkeepers, one was a weaver, one considered himself a writer but was unemployed, one was an itinerant tailor, and one a Government spy.

Phil, the informer, was affecting a slouch in a whining chair, but he could feel every muscle screaming his worry. He'd met these men before, most of them. It had never been a particularly friendly group – he didn't make friends easily – but it had always been what you might call respectful. There'd been a civility – a sort of tradesman's politeness – to their empty discussions; even drink had made them congenial rather than heated. Tonight was different. Wass, one of the shopkeepers, was brutal angry about something – business, or family perhaps, it wasn't clear – and snapping at anyone whose drive didn't match his own. Phil had heard from one of the others that Miles, the weaver, was on the verge of losing everything, and desperation showed in his face and his words. They were all edgier, and the weird setting wasn't helping.

The old church had been pulled down just a couple of years before, too small for the growing population. But the tower still stood, vast and odd over the village. The rest was a wasteland of fallen stone, left while they decided what to do with the site and dwindling night by night as fragments of church were carted away to become new bridges or houses or walls. Among the foundations of the church there had been a storeroom, and it remained beneath the rubble, accessible if you knew which truncated blocks of carving to squeeze between and which boards to lift. Phil had known the place – done a couple of deals himself down in this convenient dungeon – and these men knew it well. They'd crept here individually and in pairs with the first of the darkness, uncovering lanterns only as they hunched down the worn stone steps; now the lanterns made distorted shadows of their plotting in the corners and picked out nasty, glistening streams of moisture on the walls.

'Tuesday might be the chance to—'

'I've had it with "might be", mate.' Wass spat the last word, vicious. 'We've been talking for years, and it hasn't done nothing. Go on talking for years more; it'll do nothing.'

'It's last chance for me.' Miles, sullen and empty.

'I can't be waiting on a bunch of Suffolk peasants. We have to make sure that this march of theirs changes things once and for all.'

One of the lanterns flickered suddenly, and the faces flickered with it and the shadows behind them shivered. The seven were gathered around a long thin table, the only significant furniture in the storeroom apart from a crude cupboard in the corner. Sitting on a mixture of chairs and boxes and lumps of stone, the conspirators glowed in the gloom.

'Maybe it—'

'I told you, mate. No "maybes"! Maybe isn't cutting it anymore.' Wass turned to the little man sitting silent and compact next to him, and his voice softened. 'What do you say?'

Phil was sitting at the other end of the table from the little man, next to the big cupboard, and watched him uneasily. This was their special guest;

this was the tailor, and the tailor unnerved him.

Gabriel Chance said, 'Passivity and fear can be crimes against the Lord's will, as much as oppression and the denial of our rights.'

'Damn right. There've been petitions before and they've done nothing.' Wass looked around the gloom. 'The march has to become a proper riot, and that means the Suffolk boys have got to be panicked, and that means the soldiers have got to be panicked first.'

The blacksmith said, 'My cousin's a porter at the Admiralty. With him, we could arrange a little surprise maybe. That would get them panicking all right.'

Phil listened to the words rolling slow from the face, watched in alarm the madness blooming.

'You mean killing?'

'Maybe I do and maybe I don't.' The blacksmith was incapable of haste. 'Scare them, anyhow.'

'I'm not sure I want viol—'

'Well I do, and we're all in it together now.' Wass reached for the object on the table in front of him. 'Violence is just what's needed.' He grabbed at the object, and Phil's eyes widened. This was the blacksmith's contribution to the lunacy: he'd brought two swords with him, and they shimmered like waiting snakes on the table. Not normal swords, either, not sabres pinched from a couple of drunk soldiers. He'd made these himself, according to the limits of his skill and his imagination: two heavy, crude broadswords.

Wass gripped the cord-wound hilt of one of the swords with both hands, and lifted it a few inches from the table with difficulty. 'What do you say to violence, Mr Chance?' His eyes stayed on the blade of the sword.

The tailor's face was white, even in the lantern light. 'If it is necessary to advance the Lord's work, then we must not shrink from it.' He spoke as if he could not control what he was saying – as if the words came through him regardless of his own thoughts.

Phil had listened to Chance with bewilderment and worry: bloke was mad, obviously; but it was dangerous mad. Phil had been in more riots than he could remember, and more than a couple of conspiracy meetings, and in the end they usually came down to the fact that men would do all kinds of stupidity if they were in a group and angry and if possible a bit drunk. This was different. This was preaching holy logic, and it was giving justification to Wass and his ridiculous mediaeval weapon. Unconsciously, Phil shuffled his chair backwards a fraction, and knocked against the decrepit cupboard.

The sword clattered down onto the table, and someone hissed in irritation at the noise. Wass glared at them. Phil watched from the corner. Madness, and he was trapped in it. Bloody Government. Barely enough shillings for his boots, and here he was cornered in a cellar by a bunch of lunatics with homemade broadswords. There was the crazy-wary shine in the eyes now; he'd seen it before. The moment of discomfort and collective doubt when they all realize that a joke's going too far; the moment when they giggle foolishly and walk away feeling lesser men, or when they plunge ahead. He'd seen it in petty thieves, he'd seen it in radical plotters, and he knew it in himself. If they should ever find out that he was playing for both sides, well – in the state Wass was in, and the blacksmith – they'd... Phil felt sick. He'd felt it before, and he'd survived. But a man's luck had to run out sometime.

The man next to Chance whispered to him, and Chance nodded, and whispered to Wass.

Wass nodded. 'Mr Chance has to leave now, gents. He's got ways to go still tonight. Sure we're all grateful he was here.' He turned to the little tailor, speaking with reverence. 'Godspeed, Mr Chance. We'll meet again, I think.'

Phil was breathing more evenly. Chance's departure might serve as an interruption to the building excitement, might let things calm down a bit.

Chance stood, slowly and delicately, and turned towards the steps. Then he stopped, and looked back at the huddled group. He put one hand lightly on Wass's shoulder, and began to speak. 'My brothers, to see the promised land and not to strive for it is the devil's counsel. It is not merely faintheartedness, but betrayal. I am a man of words, and not action. It is my greatest shame. I have travelled this country, gorging myself on the wrongs done to our people, and I have failed to find a way to use my energy for good.' He looked genuinely uncomfortable. Phil watched in amazement. 'Among you here, you true men of action, I am honestly humbled.' He gave Wass's shoulder a little pat. 'I know you will not fail, because your hearts are strong. I know you will not fail, because the Lord is with you, and is calling to you.'

Phil glanced around the shadows, and felt fear again. Deliberately or not, Chance had tipped them over. Before, it might have been a joke, something to step back from tonight and feel silly about tomorrow. Now it was a crusade, and none of the men in the cellar would be able to step back.

Now Chance had disappeared into the darkness. Where the hell were the Government men? They'd been wanting Chance for weeks; were they waiting outside? He peered up into the gloom that had swallowed Chance, trying to catch the faintest suggestion of sound. They must have had time to get to Hackney by now. After all this effort, were they going to miss their prey?

Had they even believed him? Phil shifted his focus back to the table, his fellow conspirators, and his stomach heaved and his chest flushed cold. Wass was staring at him with some dark triumph in his eyes, and his hand was back on the sword hilt.

The others hadn't moved, or changed expressions, but they were all watching Wass as he started to speak. 'Before we go on, gents, something else we need to settle.' He dragged the sword towards him, scraping clumsily over the table. 'Now that it's just us, so to speak.' Phil was following the roughly pointed and sharpened blade tip. 'Seems like one of our number hasn't been straight with us.' He was still staring at Phil, certain of his triumph, and the eyes of the other men were dancing between them. 'Seems one of our number has been a bit too keen to spread the word. Well, Phil? If that's your name. Why don't you tell us what the plan is?'

He stood up, dragging up the sword hilt and then lifting the blade in his other hand so that it held level, pointing straight at the informer.

You've been here before. You can do this. Phil stayed sitting, opened his hands, used fear as natural surprise in his face. 'Ted Wass, what the hell are you talking about?'

'Government spies is what I'm talking about!' Wass took a solid step forwards, blade still pointing the way to Phil's heart. The men between them stepped hurriedly back against the wall, chairs and boxes scraping clumsily with them, confusion in every face. 'Seems you've done it before, looks like you're doing it again.' Now the blacksmith had picked up the other sword, holding it comfortable and firm in one fat hand.

Phil was up too, and backing. ''Fore God, Ted, I don't know what you mean.' This was it: alone, forgotten by the Government, dying in a cellar like the rat he knew he'd always be now. His chair fell under him; the swords moved another step nearer; frantic, he untangled his legs from the fallen chair, stepped back again, one arm finding the cupboard and the other slapping cold against the cellar wall.

'Oh, I think you—'

Then the door of the old cupboard exploded outwards and Tom Roscarrock stepped into the room, knife steady in his left hand and a pistol in his right.

'I've come to join the Revolution,' he said after a moment.

The faces in the room just gaped at him, staggered and stupid, Phil beside him the same as his mind tried to deal with the successive shocks.

'You was a bloody spy then!' The blacksmith, sword still firm, halfway round the table.

'Course he was!'

'And what—'

Under the blacksmith's words Wass had snatched at a chair and flung it towards Roscarrock; it was slow and clumsy and Roscarrock slipped easily to the side as it clattered against the cupboard, but as he moved he stumbled against Phil, lost balance, Phil pushing him away to avoid the stretching knife hand, and the blacksmith was charging at them with sword swinging. Roscarrock found his feet on the swaying deck and raised his arm and the cellar smashed in noise as he fired.

Galloping forwards, the blacksmith was no more than a foot from the rigid pistol barrel when it came up straight and the blast caught him full in the face. His head snapped back and he dropped like an elephant, the brutal sword that he'd forged clattering down with him.

The succession of shocks and the explosion of the pistol froze the room, stupid and deaf. Then Wass picked up his grim glare from the body of the blacksmith and took half a step forwards. 'Now you've just your knife, you bastard, and I've still got the sword. So let's see you!'

Roscarrock shifted the blade to his right hand, pistol to the left as a cosh, glanced at the rest of the group, kicked the chair away, checked his ground. Wass was coming on, steady half steps and the sword gripped two-handed in front of him. Roscarrock glanced at the furious face, then concentrated on the blade and the arms that held it. He had to catch the first sign of the charge; would the sword swing? Could he get inside the swing or could he deflect the first blow of that massive blade?

There was a sudden scuffling from the darkness, again the faces flicked around in confusion, thumping feet on the stone steps and the shadows became Jessel, launching himself into the room. Wass was still turning to face the new threat when Jessel pushed down the arm that held the broadsword and drove a sabre into the exposed chest. Wass gave out one long moan of last pain, and seemed to shrivel in on the blade that held him, and then as it pulled away he collapsed frail to the floor and gave up his life in breathless chokes. The Lord had called to Ted Wass sooner than expected.

Jessel said, 'Did I interrupt?'

'I had it under control.' Roscarrock was watching the exultant face.

'In which case I'm sorry we weren't a little slower in getting here.' Three soldiers had appeared from the gloom of the stairs, and at a gesture from Jessel they began shepherding the remaining plotters with their bayonets.

Roscarrock was already striding around the table towards the stairs. 'Come on. Chance is getting away.'

'It's in hand.' Jessel held up an arm to slow his colleague. 'I'll show you.'

From the back of the room, still slumped against the dank wall in alarm, Phil called out, 'Mr Grey!' Roscarrock turned. 'You – you were looking out for me after all.' Roscarrock just nodded. 'Thank you.' Phil gaped for the words. 'I... I sort of thought you didn't really care.'

'I don't. But that doesn't mean you deserved to die tonight. Besides, I had to get after the tailor.' He turned back to Jessel.

Pushing up past the scattered boards at the top of the steps and through the clumsy stones, Jessel said softly, 'Quietly now. I'll show you.'

'What the hell's going on?'

'Quickly now – and quiet, right?' Jessel began to jog away from the ruins of the old church and along to the first corner. As they came closer to it, he slowed and held up a cautioning arm. Then he led them a careful step around the house end, checking that they were in darkness.

Two hundred yards away a man on horseback, moving away, was visible among the moonlit shades of grey. 'Chance,' Jessel murmured. 'Now watch.' Halfway between them and the pale, plodding horse, the shadow of a man became distinct from under some trees, and began to follow, stopping and starting and changing speed as he tried to read the pace of the horse and reacted to stretches of open ground or greater darkness. Jessel's hand came up again to maintain the silence; after thirty seconds he whistled a single note. From some yard or alley nearer by, another horse thumped quietly into the street and began to follow too.

'What's happening?' Roscarrock spoke low and insistent. 'We should be on him.'

Jessel led the way back around the corner. 'The esteemed Home Office is happening, Tom. Orders and decisions, now that we've done all their work for them. Chance is felt not a significant threat on his own' – he continued over a single hiss of exasperation from Roscarrock – 'and so we are to follow him and see who else he meets. Play this right and we can roll up a whole net of plotters.'

They were back under the great blank face of the tower, lonely and uncomfortable without its church beside it. Jessel continued past it to another turning and half a dozen horses being tended by a soldier.

Once mounted, Roscarrock said, 'Risky though.'

'Yup.'

'He could be the assassin that the French have sent.'

'Yup.'

'Jessel, I'm serious: they'd better be damn sure they know what they're doing. We've lost Fannion completely, and we're not grabbing the one remaining connection we do have to whatever's going on – a man who's certainly trouble and could even be fatal.'

There was a grim smile in the gloom. 'Yup.'

'Jessel.' Jessel's head turned again. 'Thanks for getting here when you did.'

''S'all right. Thanks for finding Chance; that's twice now.'

'Can't promise it a third time.'

They nudged the horses into the slow walk back to London.

———— ～ ～ ————

Sir Keith Kinnaird in London: snatched glimpses of him, through the sun-scorched window of a coffee house or behind a pillar in a candle-blazed reception room, seconds of illumination in twenty-four hours of shadows.

A room off a courtyard off a street near the Palace at Westminster. The lines on the gnarled face deepening in concern, the web getting thicker so that the face seems to darken. Alleyn, the Lawyer, had died again – a relapse into the pneumonia that had clutched him three months before – and this time there would be no gaunt Scot reaching down to conjure him back out of the gloom. That left Garrod, Roscarrock and Christiansen.

Three dead men against the Comptrollerate-General.

4th August 1805

The Home Office watchers lost Gabriel Chance exactly twelve
hours after they had found him. As their department's report of
the day shows, the subject was observed entering St Michael's Church
on Cornhill. Twenty minutes later the same figure was seen leaving St
Michael's and walking casually up Cornhill and then Bishopsgate. He
walked for an hour, without obvious destination, but tending towards
the east. Ambling among the stalls in Well Close Square, he suddenly
turned into an alley and started to run. He was, though, being followed
not by a single Home Office agent but by a team, some keeping ahead of
him and some on parallel streets. He was seen again almost immediately
on Cable Street, and at this point an agreement forced out of Wickham
at the Home Office by Admiral Lord Hugo Bellamy came into effect: if
the fugitive tried to escape, or showed any other signs of knowing that he
was being followed, he was to be taken.

Unfortunately, when two Home Office men scrambled to their feet still
fixed to the man they had just wrestled into the dust, they found that they
had not been following Gabriel Chance, but Gabriel Chance's coat and an
unemployed Irish labourer by name of Kirwan. After an uncomfortable
two hours with Home Office and Comptrollerate-General officials, a
bruised and desperate Kirwan could do no more than confirm that a
dark-haired, good-looking fellow countryman had paid him a shilling to
put on another man's coat and hat and draw off someone following that
man – of course he knew it must be criminal business, but he'd been
told it was just a little thieving, and who wouldn't take a shilling to help

an Irishman in need in alien, threatening London? A tighter description confirmed that the other Irishman could have been James Fannion, but Kirwan knew nothing more. He got a week in the cells just to pay for the frustration and embarrassment of those who'd lost Chance. The owner of the Spitalfields slum room where Gabriel Chance had spent the night also spent an uncomfortable interview with the authorities; he knew nothing whatsoever about his erstwhile tenant, but he also got a week in prison from the angry Home Office men.

Roscarrock didn't need Jessel to open his mouth to tell the story – the expression on the normally pleasant face was enough. He swore once at the sky, short and vicious, and shook his head in fury.

～

The sloop *Seahorse* slipped into Folkestone with the dawn, an insubstantial emanation of the clearing mist. She tied up at the quietest, most distant part of the harbour, silent grey men moving around the deck with the competence of generations.

In the course of the next hour, the Captain of the *Seahorse* received two visitors, and the crew kept themselves out of the way until both had come and gone. The first arrived shortly after the boat was secured, a tall man with a scarf around his face and an official pass in his pocket who stopped silent on the edge of the jetty until the Captain strode to the ship's rail to meet him.

'The life of a sailor must be lonely,' the tall man said.

'But the life of a sailor is free,' the Captain replied.

'God save the King.'

'God save the King,' the Captain said, and handed over a leather satchel.

The tall man nodded, turned, and disappeared into the mist. The contents of the satchel, re-addressed to Mr Morrison Cope at the Admiralty, would be with the Comptrollerate-General of Scrutiny and Survey by lunchtime.

The second visitor ambled along the jetty towards the end of the hour, and stepped over the rail with surprising skill for someone of his bulk. He greeted the Captain genially, and accepted the offer of a drink. As he walked to the Captain's tiny cabin, he glanced through one of the hatches into the hold, where at least two dozen barrels fresh from France were carefully stowed. After a gentle empty chat, the visitor pulled a thick notebook from a pocket and said, 'What have you got, then?'

'Dozen barrels of wine. From Lisbon.' The Captain nodded to a little table, with a single sheet of paper and a small but heavy bag.

The customs officer signed the paper noting the arrival of a dozen barrels of wine from Lisbon, made an entry in his notebook, pocketed the small but heavy bag and left as cheerfully as he had come.

As soon as he was gone, the Captain walked through the sloop to where the crew were sheltering out of the wind. 'All right,' he said quietly. 'Unload.'

The men stood immediately and without discussion, and moved to the hold. The Captain beckoned to one, a small man who came uncertainly towards him.

'Where are you headed?' the Captain asked. The little man just shrugged, and shook his head in discomfort. 'Oh, hell. Er – *où... allez-vous?*'

Joseph peered at the clumsy French and clutched at ideas. Where was he going, after all? He had escaped France, thanks to these strange and organized Englishmen, but what was he supposed to do now?

'*Londres?*' he said after a while.

'London.' Louder: 'Lon-don. Say it. *Essayez*: "London".'

'L – Lun-dern.'

'London. Who – er – *qui?*'

Another shake of the head. The young Master. He must try to find the young Master. Had the young Master ever told him how to do this? He had told him never to use his name, that was important. He must remember that. Eventually: '*J'sais pas. L'Ambassadeur de la France?*'

'All right. Try it. *Essayez*: "French Ambassador"; "French"... "Ambass-a-dor".'

The memory of Lady Sybille repeating words with him flooded Joseph with pain – but a pleasant ache of familiarity as well. After a few goes he got the phrase close enough to make the Captain feel he'd done what he could to help.

'All right,' he said again, and shook his head in doubt at the idea of the little man setting off alone into England. He looked at the lost face for a moment, and then pulled out a handful of coins and thrust them at him. 'Now – *allez* – help – *aidez... les autres*.'

Uneasily, Joseph moved over to where the crew were using pairs of poles to shift the barrels onto the jetty. A minute later a cart clattered down towards the *Seahorse*; four men jumped down from it, unhitched the horse, and turned the cart with practised fluency on the narrow jetty. Then they began to take the barrels from the edge of the jetty and load them on. The process continued for a few minutes, the men on land with the short journey to the cart catching up on the sailors hauling the barrels up from the hold.

Joseph, palms burning as he struggled with his end of a pole, stiffened as a hand dropped onto his shoulder. It was the Captain again, beckoning to him. Another of the silent crew moved quickly to replace him at the barrel. The Captain pointed along the jetty, and Joseph followed the finger to see two soldiers a hundred metres away, tramping ponderously towards them.

'Quickly now, mate.' Joseph started to panic at the confusion of words and uniform. '*Vite*. They've started checking crews, for some reason. *Vite* now.' He grabbed Joseph by the collar and dragged him towards the rail.

Joseph gaped helplessly. What were they doing? Was he being arrested? Was he being thrown into the sea?

The Captain was gesturing him emphatically onto the jetty. '*Vite*, for God's sake. You – *vous* – *avec les autres*.' He was pointing at the men loading the barrels onto the cart, and pushing at Joseph, and at last Joseph understood. He half-fell onto the jetty, all elbows and knees, then pulled himself upright and together. He looked back at the Captain, and gabbled his earnest thanks. The Captain nodded sincerely. 'All right, mate. *Bonne* bloody *chance* to you.'

The gang loading the cart accepted Joseph with the same wordless indifference that had so scared him in the crew. He was part of some silent, efficient machine. He felt small and yet somehow warm.

He didn't understand what was happening. He didn't know why these helpful Englishmen should be protecting him from English soldiers. He didn't know of the Comptrollerate-General's irregular ships, nor of the sentries that had been posted to stop an assassin. But by the time the English soldiers, a brusque young Captain hurrying ahead of a stolid Private, reached the *Seahorse* and jumped down to question the crew, as the last of the barrels was being passed onto the jetty, the little Frenchman had become an English dockworker.

Thus Joseph Dax, leather satchel still strapped under his coat, came from the office of Napoleon's Minister of Police to the shore of England, and thus the old habits of the Comptrollerate-General for Scrutiny and Survey overcame the procedures that the organization had recently imposed to intercept just such a man.

Gabriel Chance had followed the peculiar instruction to visit St Michael's Church as the edict of inscrutable fate. He knew now that he was in the hands of some larger power, which would lead him along a path that he could not discern but could not avoid.

When, though, after a few minutes sitting serenely on a pew among the pallid echoes of the church, he saw James Fannion beckoning to him from the shadows, he went warily. He did not protest when Fannion pulled off his hat and coat and threw them to another man, but he looked up into the face of the Irishman not knowing whether this powerful angel had determined on his destruction or his triumph, whether he was another of the eternal bullies of his childhood alleys or the long-awaited hero of his daydreams.

They waited fully fifteen minutes in the darkness at the side of the church. Then the other man left the church wearing Chance's hat and coat. Another ten minutes, and Fannion led the way out through a side door and away into the bustle of London. For a mile they walked in silence, Fannion following a mazy route through streets little and grand and regularly scanning for pursuit, Chance following.

There was an unusual respect in Fannion. He rather liked the little tailor, and knew him as the essential tool of his plan, but the west of Ireland brings you up to tread very carefully in the face of spirits beyond your understanding. Only once they were in the park did Fannion seem to relax. He stopped suddenly and grabbed Chance in a handshake. 'Mr Chance, sir, it's a pleasure to be with you again. Please forgive all this bustle and incivility: for the agents of this tyrannic regime you are a prize beyond rubies. I'm sworn to protect you, and I have to go a little careful myself.'

'You are... wanted for crimes?'

Fannion looked grave. 'I don't have your enlightenment, Mr Chance. But in my small way I've been trying to help people where I can, to move them forwards against the oppression of this Government, and it's earned me an ill name with the oppressors.' Chance stared up in wide-eyed compassion. Fannion tried to read the gaze, and failed. He beckoned them on again. 'We should keep moving; we'll see them if they try to follow, and they'll never hear what we say, but we should take every precaution nonetheless.'

'Are we in such danger?'

Fannion was striding ahead, Chance hurrying to keep up, and now the Irishman grabbed at the tailor's sleeve as he walked. 'Mr Chance, I cannot stress enough how much of a threat you are to these warmongers. The Admirals are robbing England to starvation to pay for their aggression, and the Generals are kidnapping every healthy lad to throw into the field.

They thrive on this war. A man like you, preaching peace and progress, is the one thing they fear. And they're right to do so.'

'The resentment of the people is growing. They will throw off the tyranny.'

Fannion stopped, and again his dark eyes gazed down into the tailor's. 'The people are lost, Mr Chance. They are lost without a leader, and without a sign.' The gaze broke, and the dark eyes looked out into the distance. 'We have come to a crisis, Mr Chance. The tyrants, the warmongers, they are at their strongest, and the people can do nothing to resist them. One victory for Britain, one slaughter of poor Frenchmen and our own forgotten lads, and all hope of reform will drown in blood. In their vile glory, the Admirals and the Generals will have the power to crush anyone who tries to argue for a better world.' He looked down again. Chance was still absorbing him. 'We have just days. Tuesday must bring this corrupt Government to its crisis, or this Government will destroy us all.'

James Fannion and Gabriel Chance walked and talked for two hours. Fannion talked about Ireland, and about the activities and attitudes of the British Admiralty. He probed the reaches of Chance's philosophy and dreams. He checked the effect of the new arrangements he'd given Chance in Bury St Edmunds, and gave him further directions for where to stay and what to do in London. His first question, though, had been about none of these things. After his desperate warning to the tailor, there'd been a moment of silence, and then into it Fannion had said pleasantly, 'Tell me, Mr Chance, do you have a family at all?'

Chance had opened like an oyster, and talked as he'd never talked.

~

That evening, Tom Roscarrock was in polite society again. Jessel was busy elsewhere, and the Admiral's instructions were no more than a terse exchange in a corridor as he was leaving and Roscarrock was arriving. He listened with impatient sympathy to Roscarrock's opinions about the

Home Office, and cut him off when he tried to complain about another fatuous evening among the quality.

'But – My Lord – Chance and Fannion are loose and in London.'

'What of it? Have you a trace of them? Do you plan to wander the streets calling their names?'

'At least let's get into the Irish community. The Tailors' Guild. Let's—'

'Roscarrock, the French have sent an assassin, and somewhere off the coast a whole French fleet is waiting to strike. These—'

'Fannion and Chance are already here! They could—'

'What could they do, Roscarrock?' Bellamy got irritated by interruption, but never angry at disagreement; perhaps it came of knowing everyone else to be an idiot. Roscarrock wondered if Jessel had said that Chance the tailor was less of a threat. 'I want them found, but a few more speeches and murdered sentries aren't going to bring down the Government. Napoleon's secret fleet could, and it will do so if we don't find it very quickly. You'll damn well do as you're instructed, and listen to the French community here tonight. Who knows? Perhaps some of the great thinkers may know about your little tailor.'

Roscarrock felt he was being kept out of the way – presumably while they investigated him. How much had the old maverick Kinnaird written about him? What parts of his past were Jessel and the Admiral digging up? He'd been a new and unknown quantity to them, and Kinnaird's flight and the continued damage being done to the Comptrollerate-General's network could only be increasing their suspicions about him.

But in this world of mirrors and illusions, they thought that a traitor Roscarrock could still be useful to them. What had he said to poor Reverend Forster? No one better than a rebel to explain sedition to the Government. And no one better than a traitor to illuminate treason. If the Comptrollerate-General thought his loyalties were doubtful, Bellamy would reason, so might others whose loyalties were doubtful; and such people might talk a little more freely.

He'd have a little room for manoeuvre, then. The Comptrollerate-General would keep Tom Roscarrock in play.

———— ❦ ————

'Monsieur is unhappy?' She was French, surely under twenty, clean and fresh and pretty as a flower in the morning, and Roscarrock felt that if he so much as touched her his rough old corruption would rot her instantly. He said something gallant, and went to get two drinks.

It was a different room in a different townhouse on a different square, but otherwise essentially the same gathering he'd been to a week before; the same currents, and many of the same landmarks. The French girl had recently heard the story of General Metz and wanted to retell it: the old Royalist lion, still in hiding and waiting for the opportunity to lead a popular reaction against the new order in France – a reactionary, of course, but wasn't it so terribly romantic? Roscarrock handed her on to an earnest young journalist, not without a little regret, and turned to find Lady Charlotte Pelham pushing towards him.

'Mr Grey! I am so pleased to find you here. How is the mood in the city?'

Another man was hovering near them – the French fop he'd spoken to the previous week, now in a different but similarly elegant coat – De Boeldieu.

Roscarrock barely understood the question, let alone knew how one was supposed to answer. Fortunately Lady Charlotte had only the vaguest idea of how a pretend shipbuilder's world overlapped with finance. 'Considerably less charming than here, Lady Charlotte.'

She managed to combine a little gasp with a continued flow of words. 'My husband – he has his business interests, as you know – well, I have never seen him so flustered.' Roscarrock was more interested in the character of a man married to Lady Charlotte than his business interests. 'You will understand these questions of finance – I'm afraid I don't – but my husband speaks in terms of the gravest crisis.'

'London is resilient, Lady Charlotte. But we face a test of nerve, I'm sure.'
Then she was gone, fixed on the next face to fall into her vision.

'You really think London's resilient?' A man standing next to him.
Roscarrock tried to put a name to the face; he'd been at the other reception
– Burdett, the politician deprived of his seat.

'I was more concerned with Lady Charlotte's nerves. I'd defer to you
on London's.'

Burdett took the invitation seriously, and his eyes searched for the words.
'London is... a big, spoilt child, Mr Grey, prone to fever. Fundamentally the
child may be healthy, but it is fickle and vicious and liable to outbursts of the
wildest emotion. A burst of radical enthusiasm and a drink too many and
London's apprentices could throw over the Government in an afternoon; a
failure of nerve by the men of business, and the apprentices won't need to
because a complete financial collapse would render the Government irrelevant.'

'Are you worried about Tuesday, then: the march and the petition?'

Burdett gave a humourless smile. 'That would depend on where I stood,
wouldn't it?' The smile went away. 'Tuesday could be a revolution or a
picnic, and no one will know until it happens. A word, a volley, and the
city could erupt. London's nerves are shot, Grey. It wouldn't take much
to set off the apprentices or the men of business. What do you hear of this
special fleet of Napoleon's?'

Roscarrock was more interested in how on earth Burdett had heard. 'I've
been out of town a little.'

'Just gossip. But I know a few men in the Admiralty, and there's behind-
doors talk in Parliament, and whispers in the salons. The Emperor has
some new fleet that the Admiralty weren't aware of; a new weapon. This
could shift the balance of power at sea and put Napoleon across the
Channel.'

'The French have yet to manage a single significant victory at sea.'

'Oh, I agree. But they've only to do it once, haven't they?' Someone had
caught his eye, over Roscarrock's shoulder. 'That's the sort of thing that's
got London on edge, anyway. Would you excuse me?'

Roscarrock spoke to a barrister for a few minutes, enjoying the uncompromising honesty of his reasoning, and then a Suffolk parson whom he asked about what had happened in Bury St Edmunds. Another pause, and lace-edged fingers touching his wrist.

The fop: 'I did not wish to interrupt before – you were talking of tiresome things like ships and finance and so forth.' A nervous smile: 'You do not remember me, perhaps, Monsieur Grey, and there is no reason why you should. De Boeldieu.'

'Of course I remember, Monsieur; hard to forget a man of your elegance.' De Boeldieu had liked that. 'Tiresome? You aren't interested in a serious threat of invasion?'

'I cannot stop it, so why should I worry about it?'

'It would turn the world upside down.'

'Monsieur Grey, I have already lost one whole world.' De Boeldieu spoke as if describing a minor wager that had gone the wrong way. 'Country, family, all gone. One learns that one can survive very well, if one is flexible. One has simply to adjust one's priorities.' The lace wrist clutched at an idea in the air. 'For example, in a London ruled by Napoleon, an English patriot would feel discomfort; but a dependable shipbuilder might do very well. Is it not so?'

'I wonder, Monsieur, whether you understand English patriotism.'

'Mm.' The Frenchman's dark eyes were fixed intent on Roscarrock. 'Are you so sure that you do?'

Relief arrived in the unlikely form of Sir Joseph Plummer. Roscarrock excused himself from De Boeldieu's word games, greeted the old philosopher politely, and asked him his expectations of Tuesday's petition.

'I have learnt to expect nothing in this world, Mr Grey. Nothing is usually what happens. The petitioners are well meaning, and their cause is just. In a truly civilized country their democratic march would be observed with pride, not embarrassment and fear.'

'Will the petition do anything?'

'Will they persuade this regime to change? Of course not. But who knows what chain of events may unfold? The Home Office will worry; they will call extra troops into the city to keep order. That may either subdue or provoke protest. London is on edge because the Emperor is waiting to cross to Dover and Nelson, the idol of the small-minded, is too far away to do anything about it. It's a hot summer, Mr Grey, and there's a lot of dry tinder about.' The predatory squint came back into the old eyes. 'Have you seen our friend Kinnaird recently?'

The game was tiresome, and Roscarrock's reply brusque. 'No. Have you?'

'Yes. A couple of days ago.'

'What?' He'd associated Kinnaird's flight with a complete disappearance. 'Where was this?'

'You seem surprised.'

'I... I'd thought he was away travelling.'

'Perhaps he was. In Coventry, on this occasion. I was making one of my periodic journeys away from London – to see what's really happening in this poor country. We found ourselves in the same inn. A short conversation. He was interesting himself in the possibilities of radicalism among the metalworkers of Birmingham. Clever man, Kinnaird. He actually thinks, you know? I'd thought that was going out of fashion.'

Kinnaird was suddenly real again, but still so slippery. 'Did he say where he was going?'

'Here and there, he said. Tying up some loose ends. Housekeeping – that was his word.' Sir Joseph tilted the arid face towards Roscarrock. 'I've always assumed Kinnaird to be an intelligencing man of some kind – working for one Government or another, or just on his own account. But it's bothered me much less than the duplicities of the salons. If one must have spies around the place, let them be men of prudence and thought, like him. You would agree, Mr Grey?'

Roscarrock was spared by another onslaught from Lady Charlotte, with a journalist to present to Sir Joseph. Roscarrock turned his back on the group, and found himself two feet from the golden beauty of Lady Virginia Strong. His first instinctive glance took in her body, the simple string of pearls falling around the smooth swoop of her exposed neck, and at last the elegant lines of her face. She was watching him with something like amusement, and it annoyed him.

'I was coming to your rescue,' she said softly. 'Return the favour, so to speak.'

Roscarrock nodded slightly. 'I was a damn sight more comfortable on that horse.'

'To tell you the truth, so was I, Mr R—'

'Grey, Lady Virginia. Thomas Grey.'

The teeth opened in a wide smile of pleasure. 'Grey. Well, that's perfect.' She leant forwards, tongue caught between her teeth as if ready to strike. Roscarrock noticed for the first time the cold white flash of a scar between the pale eyebrows. Very deliberately, she poked him once in the chest. 'I am determined to bring you out of your anonymity, grey Thomas.'

Her finger stayed where it was against his shirt. Roscarrock gripped its delicacy in his own rough finger and thumb, and lifted it gently away. 'I like my anonymity. It's the last warm place I have left to hide. An anonymous man is a free man.'

She scowled prettily. 'That sounds like Kinnaird talking. Didn't all those grim aphorisms drive you mad?'

'I didn't understand many.'

'I think Kinnaird was the one man I've ever been afraid of.' She was suddenly more serious, and it made her seem younger and more vulnerable. 'Turns out perhaps I was right.'

Roscarrock watched her with interest; the seriousness was the opening of a door onto an unexpected landscape.

'It's a ruthless world, Tom, and I make no complaint about that. I play that game and I play it well. But Kinnaird's was a ruthlessness of the emotions. Everyone in our world is indifferent about human life, but he—'

'Was indifferent about human passion as well?'

'Exactly.' She lifted her head, the door closing. 'You put it very delicately, but you needn't worry about my feelings. Whether it's me, or some drudge of a maid downstairs, or any other woman, men's desires are essentially the same.'

'But Kinnaird is immune. And you're afraid of that?'

Her eyes drifted up in thought, then dropped to Roscarrock's face again. 'My parents died when I was very young. I grew up with a bitch of an aunt who thought I was an inconvenience, and beneath the refinement of her own children.'

Roscarrock smiled gently. 'Kinnaird as governess; I can see that.'

The shining blue eyes were wide, the face open and earnest again. 'I've always wanted a father – one who would respect me.' She gave a tiny nod to herself. 'That's it. Perhaps that sounds strange.'

He shook his head slowly. 'It doesn't. I've always wanted a father of any kind.' She was watching him with warm interest. 'I met a Parson the other week. He was estranged from his family, and from the career he should have had, but he'd found Kinnaird. Jessel hated his father, but finds the chance to be loyal to this organization. I certainly can't imagine the Admiral having parents – he must have been born aged forty.' He shrugged. 'We're all orphans and bastards.'

'And whores.' She said it quietly but firm.

Roscarrock shrugged. 'Nine tenths of the country are on the brink of starvation. The other tenth think Napoleon will be in Kent tomorrow. Who has room for principles?'

She smiled, and Roscarrock beckoned a servant for more wine. Around them, the rattle of chatter and the blending of bodies continued. When the servant had drifted away, Lady Virginia said, 'And what has bastardy and whoring told you this week?'

He watched her eyes for a moment. How much couldn't she know? 'I'd found Chance, the philosopher tailor, but the Home Office have lost him again. Personally I thought there could be no malice in such a man, but he's now almost certainly working with the Irishman, Fannion, who's an unscrupulous machine of malice. There's an organization to Chance's movements now, and that suggests something specific is planned and imminent. It's likely to involve the march and petition on Tuesday the 6th, but without Chance or Fannion we can do nothing but flood London with soldiers and pray.' He scowled. 'The soldiers become part of the problem, and I'm not a man for prayer.'

'I heard what you did the other night. Getting into that meeting – and you had to kill a man.'

'I take no satisfaction from it. He was misguided, and I had no choice. We were both victims of the times, and I got lucky, this time.' Roscarrock took a mouthful of wine, as the faces came at him again. 'And it could all be irrelevant, because at any moment this unknown French fleet could appear off Dover and put the Emperor on the road to London.' He watched her face, enjoying and wondering at it. 'Your side of the business, I think.'

She nodded, and in her turn considered him for an instant. 'The Emperor refuses to trust his Admirals. Perhaps he's right. So he relies on grand schemes of his own. Unfortunately for us, that means that the Royal Navy has even less chance of predicting what's happening, and none of our normal channels of information can tell us anything useful. This is purely Napoleon, and Fouché – his Minister of Police; vile man – and certain selected others. But everyone I speak to over there is alive with the idea. At last, a brilliant naval combination to defeat the Royal Navy! I've met men on the fringes of the navy, or politics, and they actually like the fact that the movements of this fleet are a secret; to them, it's proof of their Emperor's genius.'

Talking business, she was focused and earnest, and part of Roscarrock's brain watched the performance in admiration. 'These people you meet,' he said, 'they're happy to talk to you?'

She shrugged. 'They're men, and they're French; they're much more interested in my sex than my nationality. Besides, Tom: France is crawling with rogue Britons – merchants, deserters, adventurers. They have receptions in Paris just like this one, the nationalities and the loyalties just as mixed; I move between them.' She lifted her jaw and smiled at him, enjoying herself. 'You're going to lecture me about the dangers, and comment on my unladylike behaviour.'

Roscarrock shook his head mildly. 'I'm a Cornish orphan who's spent more time at sea than on land; gentility doesn't mean anything to me. Besides, most of us'll die before we're fifty from one sickness or another; you might as well make yourself useful.'

'Exactly!' She lifted her shoulders and chest in a great open breath. 'I... I crave this excitement, Tom, this work of ours.'

'That I understand less.'

'I want to live!' She threw a glance around the room, the murmurs and the fine clothes. 'Don't you feel so much more alive than the rest of these people?'

Roscarrock spoke quietly, tolerant of her energy. 'On the contrary; I feel more dead every day. This world of yours is killing me with its deceptions and shadows.'

She pouted. 'You're one of Kinnaird's, after all. Just an old Puritan.'

'Lord, no. Life's too short to wait for your pleasures. And I'm looking forward to getting back to life.'

'And what are your pleasures?'

She watched him thinking, enjoyed the rough lost smile, the prospect of his honesty. 'The silence of the sea,' he said after a moment, looking into her face again. 'The wind on my face, a hot mouthful of rum in the rain, hair spread on a white pillow.'

She breathed out a connoisseur's satisfaction. 'A royal duke gave me the finest silk dress in London. A French count wrote me a concerto. But I think that's the most beautiful thing I've ever heard.'

'That's just your unhealthy taste for adventure talking. Besides, we're a long way from the sea.'

'I'm sure there are pillows nearer at hand.'

An upstairs room: a snatched candelabrum twinkling in a mirror and glowing in the fabrics of curtains and a fat bed, two glasses of wine, a trail of shoes and skirts, and Tom Roscarrock undoing the laces of her corset with deft fingers, face full of the shine and scent of her hair.

'You're the first man I've known who could do that. I should have spent more time with sailors.'

The corset fell away with a whisper, and he turned her to face him, eyes firm in hers. 'You should see me with a knife.'

◆ — ◆

Rokeby Harris had turned down the evening's invitation, and so had missed the opportunity to observe and comment again on Tom Roscarrock's performance in high society. Instead he had enjoyed a pleasant supper with a pair of like-minded men – careful, serious ideas and old, complacent jokes – and it was past midnight when he reached for the front door of the house where he lodged.

It opened before he could touch it, wide and sudden, and the widow who was his landlady gazed out at him. 'Oh, Mr Harris sir, I'm so glad you're here at last.' She wasn't prone to fluster; it told him immediately that something was wrong, and the compassion in her eyes told him that he was the victim. 'A burglary, sir, and we've never had one, not in twenty years. I... there's a...' and then confusion overwhelmed her again.

'Very well, Mrs Dunn.' Through the open door Harris could see the flight of stairs leading up to his rooms, and he gave them a last baleful glance of regret. Then he looked at the old lady and said, quiet and brisk, 'Mrs Dunn, I'd be obliged if you'd have an eye to my books.'

Then he turned, stepped into the street and, with his former landlady staring after him, walked quickly into the darkness.

◆ — ◆

Roscarrock, naked, walked to a table, poured a full goblet of wine and sank half of it.

Lady Virginia Strong was enthroned in pillows, one arm thrown wide and the rest of her limbs stretching the sheet that dusted the rolling waves of her body, watching the play of muscles in Roscarrock's back.

He turned to the bed again, taking the rest of the wine more slowly.

'You're looking at me like a horse you might buy. No' – she tilted her head back, and the blue eyes narrowed and glittered – 'like a horse you've just... ridden... to a victory you didn't think was possible.'

'No, I'm just... intrigued. Your timing.'

She frowned, and then the fine bones opened in amusement. 'You mean: why now? Why not that night in Bury St Edmunds?'

He grunted. 'Something like that.'

'Breathless maiden, new-delivered from deadly peril, not to mention a bracing ride on that terrible horse of yours?' She breathed a soft giggle. 'Poor Roscarrock: I believe that you could make all Napoleon's secrets an open book; but you'll never understand women.'

5th August 1805

On the 5th— we were still in Vigo, of course – the women were ugly as sin and desperately bad-tempered, but I had a charming villa there – I sent out a frigate. The Didon, it was. She went north, towards your Channel, looking for zacharie, Allemand and his fleet.

I may tell you that I prayed. The good revolutionary, he is not supposed to pray, but in Napoleon's France there is a god and that god is success. I had my dreams of glory – who would not, on a warm Spanish morning, with a plump little maid bringing breakfast and the greatest of fleets down in the harbour ready to move at one's command? Mostly, to be very sincere with you, I prayed for freedom. I hadn't seen much of it, you know? There was not much égalité in the distribution of the liberté, and no fraternité that a civilized man would care to mention. I prayed to the great god success, because success would free me of the constant irrational interference of the Corsican.

I knew what he thought of our navy. I knew what he thought of me – let me have no false pride on the subject. Now, at last, it was me, and the sea, and Allemand, and together we would show what we could do without all these peasants and clerks with their envy and ignorance and meddling.

All very simple: the *Didon* will find Allemand and his fleet; I will follow on her signal, with my grand fleet. Your poor Nelson, he is nowhere still at this point, and together the fleets of Villeneuve and Allemand will cruise into the English Channel, pick up the Corsican and deliver him to England for his imperial triumph. Then we will be calling it the French Channel – perhaps even the Villeneuve Channel. Ah, the dreams of a sunny Spanish morning!

Then too there is this plan of the butcher Fouché. I must tell you that I had found out enough about it by this point. The man is a swine, of course, but brilliant, and this plan – my God! Still you do not comprehend it, I suspect. Me, I had pushed, and hinted, and bribed, and made the logical deductions, and I know I didn't have everything because Fouché is like that, but I had enough. Astonishing. The extraordinary events in France, the extraordinary events in England – my God!

Dangerous knowledge, of course. To know these secrets of France – especially the secrets of this Fouché – is like a weak heart: it can kill you at any time, you understand me? But on this day, ah, what do I worry? I will escort the Emperor onto English soil – perhaps myself step onto English soil first to hand him down from the boat. Ah, glory!

[SS G/1130/14]

Joseph was shivering all the time now. Sometimes he was gripped with a violent shake at the back of his neck that frenzied his head and arms, as if a big wet dog had snatched him up for sport; mostly his limbs and chest were weak, his muscles like water, his hands somehow distant and unable to grip.

He was lost in England. He guessed he was in England, but he had no way of telling. He could only assume that the Captain was English and had landed in England, but he did not know what English sounded like or what England was supposed to look like. All he knew was an alien landscape. The buildings were built differently, the fields were laid out differently, and the few people – whom he'd avoided as much as possible – dressed differently. There were more dogs around the houses. Usually they barked; once he'd been chased.

No, he must be in England, because several times he had gripped himself, walked hesitantly up to some other lonely traveller, and muttered helplessly, 'Lun-dern?' and the traveller had nodded and pointed down the road. But the road was muddy and never straight like French roads, and there was no way to know whether London was a few leagues over the hill, or only to be reached in a far future by some immense voyage over the seas.

This morning the sun shone, at least, and he felt better in its light and warmth. He had allowed himself a few minutes' rest sitting against a tree by the roadside – the bark was familiar, so maybe they had some of the same trees in England. In his left hand he cupped a precious pile of scraps, begged from the back door of a tavern – a humble, open face and hand, and a dumb mime to his mouth. The fat man had scraped the remains from a plate into his surprised hands, a few lumps of meat, he didn't know what kind. Then the fat man had looked at him as if considering a death sentence, before handing him a piece of cheese.

He was only guessing that it was cheese. It tasted hard and dull. But that would maybe fill him up better, and it felt good to be chewing. The Captain had given him coins, but he didn't know what they were worth or what he should do with them. It seemed better to protect them for an emergency, and not risk being tricked.

He had walked such a long way. The whole world seemed to have walked such a long way. Once there had been peace and the big house and the old Master and his Lady, and Lady Sybille teaching him his letters and the young Master and all the other servants, and then there was so much blood, and they were all gone, just the young Master teaching him, but the young Master was frightened and unsure as well, and now there was just poor Joseph, escaped across the sea, lost and feverish and begging for hard, dull cheese.

The thin satchel, strapped over his shoulders and flat against his back, was a cold slab that was pressing in towards his spine. Sometimes he flinched at its chafing, tried to escape its grip. Sometimes it felt like it was all that was holding him together.

Inspector Gabin knocked at the Minister's door, and unconsciously pulled himself to a soldier's straightness and took in a deep breath. He'd had uncomfortable interviews before; perhaps he would have them again. But a man had to die sometime.

A single word from inside. Another breath. He'd made a point of breakfasting well; one never knew.

'Minister, I asked for this meeting because I considered it important to report failure as promptly as I would do success.'

Minister Fouché watched him from under the pale eyebrows.

'Minister, it remains possible that our many precautions have kept the spy Joseph Dax contained in France. But I must draw to your attention the chance that after this time he has somehow escaped France.' Bayonet-straight. He tasted the morning's meat on his teeth. 'Minister, I acknowledge this as my failure alone.'

Distaste worked its way around the Minister's lips. 'It is not your failure, Gabin. I judge my men carefully, and I did not select an imbecile. Your industry, your precautions, and your ruthlessness have been appropriate.' A thin smile, wholly without life, crept through the face. 'You must endeavour to become a little... luckier.'

Gabin nodded once and slowly. There would be another dawn or two after all.

But there was a new, vicious energy in the Minister's face. 'I think that's enough of your laboured humilities for one day, Inspector. I need your energies, not your apologies. This game has barely started.' Fouché stood, and Gabin stiffened instinctively. 'Our little fiction about an assassin may yet neutralize the spy. In any case, his papers will tell the British nothing.' The Minister stepped towards him, and made as if to prod at him, but stopped. The Minister didn't seem to like physical contact. 'Adjust your perspective, Gabin. Observe, and learn. Tomorrow we will see... a little bit of theatre in London, an outrage to paralyze their Government. Then the Emperor's Sharks will deal with their Royal Navy, and he will cross to England at his leisure.'

'I hope that I may be of some small service in this, Minister.'

Fouché settled back into his chair, and looked up cold at the policeman. 'I know you will, Inspector. Have no doubt in the matter. For our success to be complete, part of this game must be played here in France. You will deploy all of your abilities, Inspector. I trust we will see a little... luck, on this occasion.'

It invited no comment, and Gabin gave another formal nod.

'The heart of our ambitions, Gabin, is a man called' – the Minister took the name one unfamiliar syllable at a time – 'Ros-car-rock.'

For a week they had been on the road, travelling in fives and tens, slowly, cheaply, and on the 5th the men from Suffolk began to arrive in London. They were no more than two hundred, the most inspired or the most desperate of the thousands who had swarmed around Bury St Edmunds, those with no master, those with a master who was unusually tolerant or unusually hated, those whose only master now was a cause. In London they found the dirtiest places to lodge, begged or bartered for new boots, slept. They found sympathetic landladies who would give them hot stew for free. One or two had friends in London, or contacts in radical circles, or a link through their guild. London's reforming politicians visited the more civilized of them in fuggy city taverns. London's loose young men – the dockers, the apprentice boys in weaving and tailoring and half a dozen other trades – clustered after the day's work to the places where the petitioners were staying, hoping for a fight or a girl.

Jessel passed the 5th of August bustling backwards and forwards across the city, co-ordinating investigations and searches, sending agents out among the radicals, the tailors, and the Irish, meeting Government spies and men of the shadows who would tell a good story for the price of a drink. Roscarrock was with him sometimes, or in meetings or visits of his own, or back in the coffee house, chair tilted and head solid against the wall and staring into the storm as a half-finished mug went cold in front of him. He was watching Chance in his head, the Chance he'd seen and heard and the Chance he had to imagine, listening to what he said and watching him move and trying to follow him into the restive mass of humanity that was London, the greatest city on earth.

The men of the West Suffolk Militia, from Colchester, were quartered six to a room in Battersea, south of the river where the lodging was cheap but close enough to where they might be needed. Their officers were delighted at the possibilities of London, and glad of the chance to escape their surly troops, and so orderlies were kicked and uniforms brushed and boots polished and the officers hurried across the river into town for dinners and assignations and the preening pleasure of a night on the town. They left the troops in the care of the Sergeants, confident that they would drink and whore themselves into docility as cheaply as possible, and so make no trouble.

So, by and large, they did. But for two platoons the evening of pleasure – pouring watery beer into themselves and taking turns with the world-worn riverside tarts – had the desperate abandon of a last night on earth. After years of stagnation and passivity, tomorrow the world would be turning a little and they would be part of it. They had talked each other up into the dare, as men will. Now they exchanged poses of courage, phrases of earnestness and defiance, playing magnanimity with their pennies and conquest with the bored whores.

An Irishman had sauntered among them this afternoon, earnest and conspiratorial and respectful of the uniform and bearing that set them apart among their fellow men. He had patted a couple of men on the shoulder, looked deep and hard into some of the faces, and had huddled conversations with two. In the taverns, no one talked of what they would be doing tomorrow; in truth, no one knew exactly. So in their little groups they stood each other drinks and spoke as men of action are supposed to speak, and in their moments of solitude they faced their apprehensions and their dreams. Many looked forward to nothing more than an act of companionship, a grumpy protest in which they would follow their friends and their seniors as usual. That couldn't really be wrong, could it? They'd be all right together. Some picked at the scars of past wrongs, family sufferings and personal humiliations that would be avenged on the cruel world tomorrow. Some clutched at futures. The barracks politician listened to his speech to the mob, the cheers and the brilliant future. A young man with schooling looked at the Admirals and Generals listening soberly to his arguments and nodding at a hard-won compromise. A poet heard his song of liberty, first on his own bold lips and then echoing around the streets. Men saw their inner heroism enacted at last on those who had kept them in impotence. At least one man dreamt of blood – anger and violence and blood that would wrench him clear out of the shame and frustration of his world. No one saw the dragoons.

Jessel strode into the coffee house ready to make up a day's lost food and drink. Hours of dynamism across London had put a little swagger in him, and as he walked between the tables towards Roscarrock, he snatched at a servant and began to list his requirements with a wolf's pleasure. Eventually released, the servant hurried away, and Jessel grabbed a chair and swooped into it and launched into an aggressive pleasantry.

He stopped still at Roscarrock's raised hand and distant eye.

'He's met Plummer.' Roscarrock spoke as if surprising himself, and at last focused on Jessel.

'So have—'

'Gabriel Chance has met Plummer. Poor old Reverend Forster said that Plummer had visited him and some of his local acquaintances, and he used a phrase: "Liberty is a fire inside us, and it's up to us to... to give it fuel" or something; it was obviously a line Plummer had used, anyway. Then Chance used almost exactly the same line in his speech at Bury St Edmunds. No way they could each have made that up independently. Chance and Plummer must have met when Chance was coming south and Plummer was on one of his tours of the provinces.'

'Doesn't mean he'll contact him now.'

Wine arrived, and a large pie, and Jessel plunged into them while watching Roscarrock.

'Maybe not. It looks like Fannion is looking after Chance's movements now, so maybe he's buried in some Irish slum room your people have never heard of. But maybe Chance is feeling lonely and lost, despite Fannion. Maybe he wants to make the most of his time in the city.' He pulled Jessel's fork from his hand and speared a lump of meat for himself. 'I've heard Chance a couple of times, and he's not going to find much stimulation in the average London tavern, is he?'

Jessel was still chewing rapidly. He added a mouthful of wine, and nodded.

'But Plummer is radical royalty. He's enough of an old wizard to appeal to Chance's mystical side. I can't think of anyone else capable of impressing Chance or of offering him any meaningful sympathy.'

Jessel shrugged, and tried to excavate something from his cheek with his tongue. 'Fine. As good a waste of time as any other. I'll check where Plummer lives.'

———✦———

The Three Kings Inn on Eastcheap did a brisk trade that evening, thanks to the presence in London of those marching, those who wanted to see the march, and those who were supposed to be stopping it. While the landlord beamed at the pennies crossing the counter and kept a close eye on the stumbling soldiers, James Fannion was upstairs enjoying the company of the man's youngest daughter. She'd mischief in her eye and a trick or two in bed that belied her age, but she was girl enough to have fallen for the cheapest charms of the poet. Fannion lay back on her mattress, as she played with his hair and pushed her fresh peach of a body against his, and he smiled at the tomorrow he had created.

He wasn't worried about the landlord. He wouldn't be sleeping here tonight or ever again, so what the landlord discovered or the daughter confessed wouldn't touch him. A second luxurious tumble with the very healthy young woman beside him and he'd disappear into the night, first to look for a good supper and then to find Chance. The tailor had a call he'd wanted to make this evening, and that was all right by Fannion, but after that he needed the tailor to be alone. He'd told him not to sleep tonight – the danger of betrayal and discovery too much, look how close the authorities had come already, twice. By the small hours, he wanted Chance tired and lonely and wandering the unfriendly metropolis; he wanted him thinking too much, in the hours of the dead.

There was a sudden nip at his ear, and Fannion's head snapped round. The girl stared back at him, brazen. In the silent hours of the morning, he would find Gabriel Chance and stand him some drinks and talk to him some more and set him on the path to chaos. But now Fannion the predator grinned slow and hungry at the girl.

———

It was late by the time Jessel got back with Sir Joseph Plummer's address, and later still when they reached the narrow house on Fleet Street. Evening London had become night-time London, the happy constellations of lanterns replaced by gloom, the strollers and the seekers of entertainment replaced by tired streetwalkers and furtive beggars, the shadow world of the criminal and the desperate.

Plummer himself answered the door. Roscarrock wondered whether democratic instincts or relative poverty made the old hawk do without servants; perhaps he'd just happened to be in the hall.

For a moment he stared at the two men on his doorstep, arrogant and waiting. Then the face twisted in curiosity; 'Mr... Grey, surely?'

Roscarrock made to speak but Jessel was pushing towards the old man and past him. 'Our apologies, Sir Joseph, but we must trespass on your privacy tonight.' He strode into the hall, and his over-loud voice echoed up into the house. 'Government business.'

The calculating eyes hadn't left Roscarrock. Now they sagged with the face, and a sigh of something like disappointment as they drilled into him. But then, wolfish, they heralded the faintest smile. Whoever was enjoying his hospitality this evening, and whatever it would cost him, Sir Joseph Plummer had another little victory.

Now he turned to address them both. 'You are welcome, gentlemen, of course. I am always willing to support the activities of a legitimate government. A glass of wine for you both, perhaps.' Jessel and Roscarrock watched him, uncertainly. 'But if it's Gabriel Chance you were hoping to meet, gentlemen, I'm afraid you're out of luck. He left me but half an hour ago.'

Gabriel Chance wandered London alone, and as its streets grew darker and emptier, he assumed this was merely the imprint of his spirits on the world. He had been chosen, surely he had been chosen, but where was his glory? His life had become a gloomy alley, without exit. The further forwards he walked, the more he explored, the more the chilly night closed around him.

He could turn and run. If he ran hard enough, perhaps he could find light again. He blinked the thought away. It was an illusion. The lights had whispered into extinction behind him. Behind him was the world of mediocrity and failure – the unprofitable products of his clumsy hands and the pity of his neighbours – and to return was a living death.

Sometimes he could hear his wife's voice. The memory of her seemed to glow at him. Surely Flora had not flickered out in the night sky. But she was too far behind him. He could not face her now. To have come so far, and to have to go so far back again, to go back to those two barren rooms with nothing, this was a final failure; to spend his eternity watching the hunger and sadness and futility reflected in Flora's face, this was surely hell.

He wanted to scream the world to destruction; he wanted to set his lungs on fire and explode in one endless cry that would shatter the darkness and flood the world with light.

Somewhere near him he heard movement, voices, or just grunts, a man and a woman. The Lord had promised a better world for these people, a way to the light. His life must mean more than failure and insignificance. His spirit, his certainty, the conversations he had alone in the fields, these told him he was meant for a purpose. He was the plough; he was the comet; he was the flood.

Flora would tell him he must be realistic; Flora would tell him that she loved him for his visions, but that she loved him as a man just as much, in the tarnished world of day. He would be realistic, then. He would grapple with the world of the real, the world of the men and the women in the gloom. A man had come to him with a message; a man had come to him with a path. He, Gabriel Chance, could be the man to blow the trumpet and destroy the walls of the old world. The Lord offered the light, and he had chosen Gabriel Chance to clear the path to it.

In this new day, Gabriel Chance would show the world who he was; he would show the way. The dawn was coming, and he was the dawn.

Around him and ahead the buildings stretched up into the darkness.

6th August 1805

The events of Tuesday, the 6th of August 1805 are a matter of record. The summer night melted quickly, and London's early skirmishers were busy in the dawn. The hawkers of oranges and pies took their first steps of the long day, enjoying the warmth of the morning and the easy feel of their still unladen trays; the peddlers of ribbons and religious tracts soon followed them, making for favoured haunts in the city or towards the fashionable west. The first songs and curses rang around the market streets, and already the roads from Surrey and Essex were delivering the goods that would fill the stalls. Men who had not slept, busy copyists and feverish invalids, watched the rising light with primitive wonder. Nightworkers – watchmen and thieves and lovers – slouched homewards, sour and sated. Sleepy, battered scraps of boys brushed the dung and debris from the better streets, and the last whores drifted away with the dust.

In Battersea, just over the river from the palaces of King and Parliament, the soldiers of the West Suffolk Militia were bawled and kicked awake before six, heads aching and resentful, empty bellies lurching in anticipation. In a tavern in Lambeth, among a few dozy remnants of the night, an Irishman and a tailor sat in silence; the tailor, eyes lost, sipped mechanically at a cup, the Irishman close beside with head inclined as if waiting for inspiration from him. Periodically, the Irishman would mutter some prayer or other dredged from his childhood. Soon they would take a walk, just across the river, into the heart of the British Empire.

The petitioners – the men of Suffolk, and those from neighbouring Counties they had gathered on their way – awoke in festive mood. Four or six to an unfamiliar room, among new friends, sure that the last of the days of trudging was behind them, the men were boys again and boisterous. Today was another day off work, wasn't it? For most it was their first visit to London, and its sheer size awed and excited. The name itself, two mighty booms of a bell, told a vast permanence. The greatest city on earth, right enough, and more people and power and money than a man could imagine in his wildest fantasy. Could there be a better place for a holiday? Could a man feel more free?

Soon after eight in the morning they had started to gather in the street, drifting and chatting and exchanging insults with the London men, wary at their differences in dress and wide-eyed at the height of the simplest house. At nine, Henry Hodge, the orator, appeared in a first-floor window. His words gave them nobility now as well; their cause was just, and they marched in the name of all men. Then someone from the London Corresponding Society: a welcome from their brothers in the greatest of reform movements, a request for the honour of marching beside the proud men of East Anglia. Then one of their own leaders, his words drowned by drums and jokes, and no one minded, and then shortly afterwards, with banners and music and shouting, the swarm of men began to move towards Whitehall, where the politicians and the soldiers waited.

Two platoons of the West Suffolk Militia were on a convergent course with the marchers, but in truth they were soldiers no more. Their opportunity had come after an hour's morning tedium: the rest of the regiment sent down the south side of the River Thames to be ready to cross Westminster Bridge to Whitehall if needed; a single Lieutenant left behind in charge; lots drawn, and a vengeful former pickpocket claiming the pleasure regardless; a distraction, a cosh, and the young officer was sprawled broken in the dust. They'd stood around wide-eyed then, their rebellion suddenly real. The passion could have ebbed at that moment of uncertainty. But voices of idealism and bravado had come from the ranks, faltering and then strong, and so instead the passion flowed. The old restraints were abandoned: neck stocks loosened, knapsacks thrown off, leaders elected from the ranks in the wave of enthusiasm that had swelled over the body of the Lieutenant. Now they were marching over Battersea Bridge, on the straightest line towards Whitehall, the petitioners and the centre of Government.

In the madness of millions, there was no one to notice the silent, hobbling entry to the city of a French servant in the last stages of exhaustion. But as James Fannion slipped back across the river and set his face towards France, Joseph Dax completed his journey from Paris to London.

The petitioners marched to the cheerful, chaotic rhythm of their pipers and drummers, who picked out tunes and beat according to their fancy. Some of their number straggled off as they stamped west through the city, and they picked up as many new recruits from the street boys, the idlers, the apprentices and the enthusiasts. They were a tiny number among London's countless millions, but in their own noisy cockpit, crammed and jostling between the overstretching buildings, they felt themselves a multitude and they knew themselves popular. Their cause was right and their cause was general.

From a high window in Fleet Street, Sir Joseph Plummer watched them pass. He was nervy, unable to settle to his writing; his unnecessary bravado with the Government men the evening before had impressed the ghost of his younger self, at least, but it could put him back in prison by nightfall. Chance was mad enough for martyrdom, and Plummer thrilled at the faint possibility that the strange little village saint could somehow ignite a conflagration through London's desiccated society. But the greater Chance's effect, the greater the price for his associates. The old hawk took a parched breath into his throat, sickened by his own fear. Through the window, the last of the petitioners were passing beneath him, dogged and cheerful; futile and foolish, but who knew?

The Admiralty Board convened at half past ten. No Secretaries were present because no formal business had been scheduled, but each of the participants would talk about the meeting for a long time afterwards, and so the broad thrust of discussion is known. Lord Barham opened by repeating his insistence that the Board should be together in case the wider security situation in London or the country required immediate decisions; the Prime Minister had welcomed the suggestion. Admiral Gambier questioned whether such a precaution was necessary. Sir Evan Nepean, who had seen trouble enough in a year in Ireland, said that he was happy to waste a morning if there was the slightest chance it would help to control a riot. Admiral Bellamy spoke gravely and effectively of the level of latent unrest across the nation, and the real tension at all levels of society in London. Lord Barham – who had fought his first sea action more than fifty years before – declared that he was determined that the Admiralty would provide a model of stability and reassurance for the rest of Government, and that they would not be found unready. 'When the crisis comes,' he said high and sharp, 'whether it be from the French or from the mob, it will find me on deck and in command.'

His subordinates on the Admiralty Board had nothing to say against that, and Gambier suggested that they took the opportunity to discuss the naval situation. In the distance, through the high sash windows of the Board room, they could hear the first faint approach of men and drums. No one mentioned it.

The shouts, the squeal of the pipes and the chatter of the drums came clear to Jessel and Roscarrock, pacing fretfully in Whitehall, and soon the first of the crowd that had grown up around the petitioners appeared at the top of the road. With no trace of Chance or Fannion, they had spent the morning patrolling the environs of Government, making such preparations as they could for a threat that had no form, and snapping at each other.

Now the crowd had turned at Charing Cross, in front of the King's Mews, and was starting down Whitehall into the heart of the corruption they had sworn to challenge. They'd passed detachments of soldiers on the way, and the lack of trouble had relaxed them; at the same time the jovial support of London's workless and work-skiving citizens inflated their spirits. Now the edifices of British Government soared around them: the Admiralty, and the Horse Guards building; then Downing Street, where even now the Prime Minister might be pondering their cause, and beyond that Westminster Hall and the British Parliament. That was their goal; that was the end of their trek. They would march right up to the door of democracy itself, bang on it and demand that at last their voices be heard, and then... no one knew what would happen then.

The two rogue militia platoons were marching towards them, only a few hundred yards away, with similar, muddled anticipation. They'd drunk a little; some had drunk a lot. They marched erratic and with fragments of crude song. One of the Corporals had said they had an appointment at the Admiralty, and the angry, eloquent Private who'd been elected to lead them had said they would go in partnership with their brother democrats, the petitioners, and present their demands. Other words had been shouted among them, incoherent and intoxicating – warmongers, redress of grievances, revenge, arrest, tribunal of the people, republic – and they marched with the dumb collective enthusiasm that only groups of drunk men can know. Ahead they could see greenery and open sky.

Roscarrock said, 'Where else are we vulnerable?'

Jessel shook his head. 'There are guards everywhere, detachments of soldiers in case the crowd gets out of hand; Royce and his dragoons.'

'Are you more worried about the mob, the French assassin, or Fannion and Chance?'

'I'm just... Those idiots in Hackney – the meeting under the church – they were talking about the Admiralty, weren't they?'

Roscarrock nodded. 'And we arrested the cousin who worked in the Admiralty, and he didn't know anything, but he's in gaol in any case.'

'They were talking about something in the future, not something already arranged.' Jessel's face was still uncomfortable. 'But...'

'What hasn't been checked?'

'I don't know. I'll think of something.' He glanced at the approaching mob of petitioners. 'Don't run off now.'

The soldiers had reached the parade ground behind the Admiralty and Horse Guards, hearts wider and voices louder as the world opened up around them, trees and royal parkland spreading away to their left, the buildings of Government close on their right. Just on the other side of those buildings, marching south as the soldiers marched north, the petitioners had reached the centre of Whitehall and were bunching closer together as they neared the final yards of their journey and found themselves amid the overpowering architecture of authority. Tom Roscarrock was standing in the archway that ran through the Horse Guards building from Whitehall to the parade ground, watching the approaching petitioners in the former and now glancing round to see a group of soldiers on the other side, and Jessel was halfway to the Admiralty building when a dull terse rumble bloomed under it, and every one of the hundreds of people in the vicinity stopped dead. The sound had been so short and muffled; what had anyone actually heard? Then gusts of smoke swarmed up from the Admiralty basement and over the facade that guarded its courtyard.

～ ～

Admiral Gambier's summary of French naval dispositions had been brief: Admiral Villeneuve was probably in Spain; Admiral Allemand with his small squadron was at sea somewhere off the south-west of England; the other French squadrons were still blocked in their ports.

'And our own?'

'Blockading, My Lord. Patrolling the Channel.'

'No damned good, Gambier! Allemand is loose in the Channel. Give him so much as a rowing boat more and he'll have enough to challenge one of our squadrons. Presumably Villeneuve will be pushing north to join him any day, Bellamy.'

'We believe so, My Lord.'

'And even if he doesn't, we still have Napoleon's private fleet, ready to come at us when we least expect. That fleet's the key to the Channel and to the war. Allemand alone is too small. Villeneuve we might be able to block in Spain. But if this other fleet comes at us, we'll have no choice but to weaken the force blocking Napoleon's army. And you still don't know where the damned fleet is, Bellamy?'

'No, My Lord.'

The First Lord of the Admiralty shook his old white head at the Comptroller-General for Scrutiny and Survey with something like accusation, and then the building shuddered around them and the world seemed to thump and the portraits of former First Lords of the Admiralty slumped on the wall, and a cloud of smoke billowed up outside the window and the Admiralty Board was dimmed.

———◆———

In Whitehall there was uncertainty, then confusion, and finally alarm. The petitioners who had already passed the Admiralty thought that the back of their column was under attack; those still next to the smoking building didn't know what to think, but they knew they didn't want to be where they were. In a first-floor window further down Whitehall towards Parliament, a Magistrate and an anonymous Government official shared the confusion and knew what they ought to do in any incident of doubt:

soldiers and dragoons were in place in several locations, and a signal was passed to bring a detachment across Westminster Bridge to restore order.

Even as the smoke cleared to reveal no damage to the Admiralty, the march in the street beside it was collapsing into chaos. Those at the back of the column of petitioners were drifting back up Whitehall to Charing Cross, and the impression of a retreat startled the spectating Londoners. Those nearer the front were trying to shove forwards, and soon the threat of a stampede forced the leaders of the column to begin running towards Westminster Hall. This sudden rush was exactly what Parliament's custodians had feared; frantic shouts of orders, and a detachment of soldiers was hurrying out of the building's courtyard to block the way, muskets level. The front of the column now found itself being swept towards a line of bayonets, at the same time as those behind them saw another detachment of soldiers trotting towards their flank from Westminster Bridge, and the storm of shouts and screams and hoarse commands to soldiers and futile attempts to control the panicking marchers soared, deafening and intoxicating.

In the shadow of Horse Guards arch, Roscarrock watched the scrum in anger and frustration. This was not necessary, it was never necessary, and now what could have been peaceful would mean injuries and probably deaths. The prophets of reform had led their people to another futile battle. Teeth clenched and eyes grim, he bullied his mind into self-control, looked methodically around, to Whitehall and out to the parade ground and up towards the Admiralty: this surely wasn't an accidental riot; it meant something, it was happening for a reason, and under its shadow some darker purpose had to be in play. But what, and where?

And who? Whitehall showed nothing but the mob and their falling banners and billowing dust, and he hurried through the arch to the parade ground. As he emerged, the space and light yawning over him, he saw a detachment of soldiers moving towards him and Whitehall; reinforcements, presumably, but they were moving without purpose or discipline. To his right, other movement: from the back of the Admiralty building a small group of men hurried into the daylight, well-dressed men – uniforms?

Lord Barham had survived seventy-nine years and a score of battles and he did not scare easily. But in the shock and the confusion – an attack on the Admiralty itself? – he led his subordinates hurrying out of the building, old spindly legs skittering down the back stairs and onto the parade ground. The mob was in Whitehall, and someone had said they were stampeding, so the back it had to be and a guard of Marines and a carriage out of the city.

Roscarrock didn't recognize the First Lord, but he could see the dominant figure of Bellamy hurrying the old man away from danger, and then behind them he saw Jessel running to catch up. What were these soldiers doing? They were still straggling on the other side of the parade ground. But now there was a shout, shouts, and their muskets started to waver and fall level, and they began to trot towards the handful of Admirals. Instinctively, Roscarrock started towards them; they should be coming to protect the Admiralty Board, but where was the discipline and where were the officers?

Jessel had seen them too, and he overtook Bellamy and Lord Barham and moved closer to the approaching soldiers. No discipline, no officers, and he knew them for a threat. He fumbled in his pocket and an instant later a whistle squealed across the parade ground. The Admirals, edging down the side of the square towards the Horse Guards building, stopped in confusion. Roscarrock knew what it meant, but there was still no way of knowing how everyone would move. The militiamen hesitated in the middle of the parade ground, startled and wary, then took the whistle for defiance or the last vestige of the corrupt authority they had drunk themselves into overthrowing, and hurried forwards again with shouts.

A thunder from the trees at the northern edge of the parade ground, shouts, the vicious hiss of metal against metal and Royce's dragoons gushed out into space, a fist of darkness that drummed over the ground and exploded into the terrified soldiers. They staggered, they screamed, two or three muskets were fired on instinct, and then the packet of rebels were fleeing or falling under the swooping sabres of the dragoons, and Roscarrock knew that he was watching the work of James Fannion. The noise and violence of the attack dragged out slow and stark for the onlookers, but it was only fifteen seconds before Royce called his men to order around the remnants of unrest. They stood shocked and shattered, muskets abandoned at their feet, among the screaming bodies of their wounded colleagues and the forbidding ring of dragoons.

Half a dozen horsemen cantered after those who had fled, and the brutal episode was done. The Admirals breathed gasps and exchanged uneasy bravado. Ahead of the others, Lord Barham turned and bestowed a single nod of approval on Bellamy for the precautions that had saved them all.

Lord Barham was perhaps thirty yards from Horse Guards arch, the other members of the Admiralty Board spread out beyond him. Nearer the skirmish between soldiers and dragoons, Jessel was fifty yards and Roscarrock rather further from the arch. In the aftermath of mayhem, none of them paid immediate attention to the solitary figure who walked through the arch at that moment, though his placid movement was the strangest thing of all on that day of frenzy.

The First Lord of the Admiralty noticed the fellow walking silently towards him, and thought his approach perhaps disrespectful but hardly a threat. Jessel saw the man and on some instinct started to move. Roscarrock not only saw the man but knew him, and launched himself across the expanse that separated them.

It was Gabriel Chance, coming into the light at last.

Shouts from Roscarrock and then from Jessel bewildered Lord Barham, who found himself with two men running towards him and a third gliding closer in silence. Jessel reached into a pocket as he ran and pulled out a pistol. Roscarrock was tearing over the loose ground, and still Chance walked. Roscarrock knew in his nightmare that he could never reach him. Barham was alarmed by the weird silence of the man coming straight at him, by the wide, bright face that stared at him but said nothing, and started to back away. Jessel was closing fast, pistol coming level, and Roscarrock kicked his feet faster and harder off the dust and reached for his knife as he ran. Then in the nightmare he saw Chance's arm emerge into the parade ground with a pistol of his own.

Jessel had one shot and knew he couldn't get between Barham and the assassin, now so close; he had to slow, he had to be steady if the shot was to have any hope. Still Chance was moving on, the silent serenity of a dream, and Jessel was ten yards from him and stuttering to a halt and holding his pistol level with one controlled breath, and the hammer strained and snapped forwards and only a click disturbed the parade ground.

Misfire.

Jessel gaped in surprise, stared at the pistol, round at Bellamy, and back to the First Lord of the Admiralty and the man who would now kill him. Gabriel Chance had stopped; he blinked twice and walked on, so close to the old grey man, so close to the light, and a smile broke on his ghostly face and the pistol wavered between Jessel and Barham and then settled on the old man, and the smile grew wider and more serene and then from the unseen shadows outside his vision, the shadows that were all that was left of the old world, Tom Roscarrock hurled himself forwards and knocked Chance to the dust.

Bellamy and Jessel were pulling Lord Barham away, and the rest of the Admirals were still becalmed on the parade ground trying to absorb the wild succession of shocks. Roscarrock was sprawled on top of Gabriel Chance, his knife buried in the prophet's chest. The pale, unworldly face flickered, coughed out one last frail breath of corrupted air, and settled into its perfect peace.

Above it, arm shaking on the knife and breath coming in desperate gasps, Tom Roscarrock gazed down, grim. Beneath him, he could only see the face of the Reverend Henry Forster, and that face held sad sympathy and an infinite disappointment.

In his mind, he heard the last words of Forster's last letter. Somehow, Tom Roscarrock had set himself against the angels.

FRANCE

6th August 1805 – continued

ROSCARROCK, Donal (and family) Donal Roscarrock born Wexford? 1740. Married Rachel GALLAHER Roscarrock 1765 d. 1768; married Ann CONNOLLY Roscarrock 1769. At least six sons survived to adulthood, including Donal (1766), Patrick (1770), Sean (1773). Fate of twins (1 s, 1 d) born 1771 unknown. At least two other daughters, including Fiona (1768). Donal (snr) active in Defenders and United Irishmen. Several of sons also active including three above named: Sean executed 1799 for rebellion; one other son (name unknown) killed Vinegar Hill; Patrick and one other son hunted following 1798 rebellion – file still open (Fiche no. 833). ?Familial link to traitors in Wicklow (see Fiche no. 155 on DWYER). Donal Roscarrock now habitually living Rathcoole w. Martha ?Macdonagh; status of w. Ann unknown.

Brother of Roscarrock, James, b. Wexford ?1741 and still dwelling there. Married Annie PRICE Roscarrock 1770 (eldest d. of Price, Michael of Armagh, whence fled apparently because of links with Armagh Defenders). At least 4 s survived adulthood. James and at least two sons involved in support for Leitrim rebellion and Longford unrest 1793 and (esp. son Michael) in preparation for proposed landing of French force 1796. Believed residual familial links to Armagh and Defenders.

Brother or cousin of J. T. Roscarrock, references Wexford 1765–1775, Dublin 1790, Wicklow 1793–5, and intermittently. No further reference – perhaps d. Wife unknown. 1 s D. D. 'Tiger' Roscarrock, sometime prizefighter now thought Dublin, link to Emmet insurrection 1803 unclear, 1 s P. T. Roscarrock whereabouts unknown, at least 2 other s living. Reports of sons active 1798 including Vinegar Hill.

Other associations: TANDY, Napper (see Fiche no. 78 on TONE); SIMMS, ?Jonathan (see Fiche no. 103 on ROWAN and Fiche no. 149 on HAMILTON); McBRIDE, Joseph; McBRIDE, James; CURRAN, Sarah; MacNALLY (see Fiche no. 298 on HOPE).

[SS I(D)/2/407]

It was over. He had come so far, come almost to the very end, and now, in the final doorway, Joseph was blocked. The tiredness was all-powerful now, a vast blanket on his shoulders, so heavy that his knees kept buckling, and so warming. Outside him, the night was bitterly cold.

Once again, one last attempt, his French just a whisper to the uniform buttons in front of him. 'I must enter. Must see the Ambassador. Vital. It's for France. Please. Vital.' But he kept losing the words in the folds of the blanket, and the uniform buttons glared and blurred in his dull eyes. The footman was bored of the game now, ruder, throwing out threats to this bent bundle of a man at the foot of the steps.

Roscarrock paced the landing like the uneasy deck of a ship before storm clouds, gripped the banister rail and wished for the spray on his face. The reception at the house of the French Ambassador to London, official representative of the exiled Crown, had become a celebration of the escape from assassination of the First Lord of the Admiralty and his colleagues, and Roscarrock wanted no part of any of it. Behind him was the brittle chatter of glasses, the gurgling of conversation, and he scowled at the distraction and the irrelevance.

This, surely, was not it. Surely, there was more to Napoleon's secret designs than this misguided craftsman. Surely the vanguard of the French threat was more than a handful of surly infantrymen. Where, indeed, was the French hand in any of this? Was there some part of the danger that he just hadn't seen, a whole level of the plot they weren't aware of? Why, once his blood had cooled, did the melodrama at Horse Guards seem so insubstantial?

The Irishman, the tailor and the fleet. The tailor was dead, the Irishman presumably escaped into France. The fleet was still out on the sea somewhere and, unless the Comptrollerate-General's network in France could find it, the rotten timber that was English stability would shortly receive its final, shattering blow.

From a doorway on the other side of the landing, all trace of the fop absent, Philippe de Boeldieu watched the Englishman, trying to read the tense, tired face.

———

There was a mist settling around him. Perhaps the cold in his feet meant he'd missed his step, missed the firmer grass and slipped into the shallow water of the marsh. There was a morning freshness to the air, and as the reeds swayed around in front of him he listened for the call of the birds.

Joseph was alone. Vaguely, his eyes had registered the sudden unco-ordinated movement of the two footmen. One turned and hurried into the house on some errand at exactly the moment that the other trotted down the steps and past him across the street, and he tried to turn his head to find out what the incident or attraction was, but his head wouldn't turn.

Lady Sybille was scolding him gently. He had missed something, of course.

The doorway was clear. Somewhere beneath him, his legs began to move up the smooth stone steps.

Roscarrock saw the footman bustling across the hall below him, wondering at the errand and its triviality. The movement pulled him out of his reflections and he started for the stairs. Fresh air.

Another figure appeared below him, a dark and dishevelled form sliding along the wall, and the incongruity of this dirty shape against the polish and gleam of the decorations froze him. His eyes tracked the painful movement from above, a stain on the white squares of the marble floor that kept disappearing into the black ones. He set off down the stairs.

There was sudden new movement and noise in the hall below him, and the Ambassador and Lord Barham strode across his vision, with the unhushed assurance of those who knew they could not be outranked in this place.

Roscarrock's glance shifted back. The creeping figure had come alive. The movement in front of it had sparked energy, a new clarity of action.

Was this it? To get the Royalist Ambassador as well as the First Lord of the Admiralty, and the head of the Comptrollerate-General, in one coup would be a fantasy for Paris. The impact of such a strike in the heart of London would be shattering. Roscarrock was taking the steps in twos and then threes, oblivious to all other sound and movement around him. One stealthy figure could penetrate where no band of rebels could dream. Move!

He landed on the marble chequerboard tiles with a leap and his appearance stunned the furtive creature in front of him. The forward movement stopped, a pale head came up and two dead eyes opened in alarm. Roscarrock strode towards him, knife ready, body poised.

Then in an attack from nowhere his knife hand was flung up and he was shouldered aside with a force that sent him staggering, and Philippe De Boeldieu was tearing past him trying to shape an incoherent cry of amazement into words. 'Great Gods! My Joseph – Joseph! How have you come, how are you here? Great Gods, what has happened to you?'

⸺ ❧ ⸺

At last it all felt right. Master Philippe was here. Master Philippe was holding him. Now he could sleep, if the young Master would permit...

⸺ ❧ ⸺

Roscarrock stood over the two Frenchmen, bewildered. De Boeldieu looked up at him, breathless and stern. 'Your English hospitality is a terrible thing, Roscarrock, but since this man has just by some unimaginable chance escaped from the very heart of Napoleon's evil, could you possibly manage to find him a glass of water?'

Lord Barham had heard the unrest in the hall and taken two steps back to observe, absorbing the peculiar scene with weary surprise. Extraordinary people, the French.

⸺ ❧ ⸺

Through the hot summer night, the ripples of the chaos in Whitehall spread across the city. The men of Suffolk were dispersed, their unity broken in the first confusion and by one panicked and unnecessary burst of musket fire. But small bands of them roamed the streets hurt and angry, inflating each other's stories of wounds and wrongs and looking for cheap violence to prove their resolve. Silly brawls and broken windows charted their wandering through the warrens of the metropolis. Meanwhile, the anger and the confusion were echoed by other fists and voices. Young apprentice men had been caught up in the mayhem of Whitehall, and they spread news of a Government offensive, new restrictions on rights, the permanent stationing of soldiers in the city. A dozen new protests became a dozen confrontations, hot and hasty stand-offs with soldiers and officials, machines broken and buildings set alight. In Leadenhall Market, a Magistrate found himself cut off by a mob and had to be rescued by the militia. Lord Mayor Perchard was forced to take refuge in a church on Lombard Street. The radicals and reformers of the London Corresponding Society hurriedly ran off handbills denouncing the Government's new tyranny – rallying calls for liberty, words into the mouths of the angry young men who wandered the streets venting their insecurities.

And in the prudent watchful heart of the city, the men of business listened to the reports of violence and the sound of shattering glass and hurried to their counting houses and their brokers. An attack on the Admiralty; Parliament itself threatened; French agents at work. London, it seemed, was no longer a place where a man might do business and trust in the safety of his cash box.

Joseph rested in an upstairs room at the Residence, lurching from incoherence to unconsciousness, a shrunken dirty rag on the spotless linen, Roscarrock and De Boeldieu watching over him.

De Boeldieu had gently undone the satchel and slipped it from the frail body. With Roscarrock he raced through the documents it contained, but the title and the first sheet of paper had been enough to tell the significance. From Paris to London, Joseph Dax had carried the Minister of Police's private file on the naval plans of France. Now the file was with the Comptrollerate-General's experts, men who had studied the French navies for a generation, and they would find what it revealed of Napoleon's Sharks.

As Roscarrock and the Frenchman had hurried through the pages there had been a harsh whisper from the bed, and De Boeldieu had scurried to Joseph's side. 'I read the words, Master, I read them; I knew it must be important.'

'It is, my Joseph, it is.'

'Please to tell Lady Sybille that I read the words, Master.'

Roscarrock was struggling with the French, and the sudden pain in De Boeldieu's face surprised him.

'I'll tell her.'

'I took it slowly and carefully.' The words began to drop with more difficulty. 'Your sister, will she be proud of me now?' Then he had slipped back into unconsciousness.

He had been half-awake again a few minutes later, and Roscarrock tried asking him about the unknown fleet, and about French plotting against London. But Joseph in his lethargy could make nothing of Roscarrock's French. De Boeldieu tried instead, but still the feverish face shook uselessly at ideas it could not grasp. Then he was gone once more, and Roscarrock had left to pass the precious folder to Bellamy.

The 6 August

Monsieur,

There has been an incident of blood, of which you will read more by other means than I may tell (missing word?) haste. I acted of necessity, and I hope you will not judge me hard for it. I am forced to depart the County of Lancashire. I realize you will be frustrated after three months' inactivity and I will try to arrange a colliery explosion in the County of Yorkshire in the second

*part of August to appease you. If I chance
to have some success there, I shall (illegible
word?) to Scotland for a time, with greater
discretion which I hope you will understand,
to satisfy your (illegible word?). I received
money from you at Lancaster, for which a
thousand thanks, but it was less than I had
understood and I swear to you Monsieur that
you must send to our (illegible word assume
friends?) at the agreed place in York if I am
to survive.*

[SS MF/SH/16/10 (The Sutherland House trove)
Deciphered by J.J., January 1806]

When Roscarrock returned, Joseph was still unconscious, with Philippe De Boeldieu bent over him. He wondered if they'd had the chance to talk in his absence. He pulled a chair forwards, and sat down close to the dark and watchful Frenchman. De Boeldieu watched him cautiously.

'Time to be a little more open, I think, Monsieur.'

De Boeldieu considered this for a moment, and then nodded.

'This man has brought a dossier of the greatest sensitivity from the French Minister of Police. He was so important that they created the fiction of an assassin in the hope that we would stop him. It's an astonishing achievement.' De Boeldieu remained silent. 'Who is he? How did he do it?'

'He was Minister Fouché's servant. I can only guess how he managed it.'

'You're obviously very close to him.' De Boeldieu hesitated. 'I'd suggest that neither of us wants to waste time debating what is and isn't my business, Monsieur.'

De Boeldieu almost smiled at this, and nodded again. 'Before that monstrous machine Fouché employed him – before the Revolution – Joseph was a servant to me and my family.'

'And he steals the Minister's dossier and brings it to you simply out of ancestral loyalty? Amateur enthusiasm, and then a bit of luck avoiding what must have been a massive manhunt?' Still the Frenchman hesitated. Roscarrock hissed his frustration, and grabbed at a different approach. 'You seem a little less of a dandy this evening, Monsieur. He's your former servant, you say. Very well. So who are you, really?'

De Boeldieu pursed his lips, and his eyes flickered around in thought. Then they settled back on Roscarrock's suppressed anger. 'Since the threat from Paris cannot get more severe, Mr Roscarrock, I suppose there is little danger in telling you, wherever your loyalties lie.' He glanced down at Joseph. 'I am gatekeeper to Sir Keith Kinnaird's network in France.'

'The network *de la fleur*?'

'You have heard that name?'

'Only gossip. The old Royalist net of General Metz.'

A nod. 'They are not exactly the same, but they overlap. For five years I have managed agents in my country, on Sir Keith's behalf. When Joseph obtained his position with the Minister, it was through the greatest good fortune and the most delicate manoeuvring. He became our most important agent – the royal lily of the network *de la fleur*. I do not suppose that you have seen the reports.' Roscarrock shook his head. 'I trained him well, Roscarrock. The reports he has sent over these last months will contain everything he knows.'

'Have the reports mentioned the missing French fleet?'

'No. They speak of Fouché's plan to neutralize your Royal Navy, but there is no detail.'

'What about plotting an assassination in London? That madness today.'

A shake of the head. 'Nothing.'

'There must be something.'

'Why?' De Boeldieu was hotter suddenly. 'All there is, is in the reports.

If there is confusion, surely it is in your organization. And yes, I know enough to know there is chaos.'

'Have you seen Kinnaird recently?'

De Boeldieu winced in frustration. 'Have you, Mr Roscarrock? Let me throw your own question back at you. Who are you, really?'

There was a cough from the bed, and they both turned. 'Ask him if he has any more information about special movements of the fleets.' De Boeldieu was reluctant, and the intensity in Roscarrock's voice sharpened. 'The invasion. The Emperor's Sharks.'

'Sharks?'

'Ask him! Is there anything that isn't in the reports?'

De Boeldieu and Joseph whispered, and Roscarrock could catch only some of the words.

'It's all in the reports. When he escaped, he reported the last meeting the Minister had held. There's nothing else.' Roscarrock looked down at the bed, at the closed eyes and the candle-coloured skin.

The eyes drifted open, and he tried again in his own rough French. 'What else did you hear – what else did he hear after the last meeting? Anything!'

'Do not bully him! He has suffered enough.'

'His achievement is nothing if we can't get the information from him,' Roscarrock said harsh and fast. 'Ask him!'

De Boeldieu's expression was foul, but he turned to the bed and murmured to Joseph. A shake of the head on the pillow, which De Boeldieu magnified sadly to Roscarrock.

Then Joseph began to whisper. After a moment his eyes closed, and De Boeldieu looked up again. 'A signal is to come from London, and then the Emperor's fleets will sail. That's all he said.'

'Does he mean the Sharks?'

'He did not say so.' De Boeldieu said a few words into Joseph's cold ear, and there was the faintest shake of the head on the damp pillow. 'He has not heard of this.'

'Damn it; there must be more he can tell us. To have come so far – from the centre of it all—'

Joseph made a long, shallow gasp from his throat. De Boeldieu leant down to the sickly face, and Roscarrock strained to catch and translate the words that rasped slowly out.

'Will she... think well... of me now... Master?'

'She will, Joseph, she will.' De Boeldieu's face screwed tight in pain, then released, and he took Joseph's head between his two hands. 'She had no braver or more faithful servant.'

And at last Joseph's face relaxed, and he came to the end of his journey. 'Oh go to her, my brother!' De Boeldieu whispered. 'Show me the way.' He placed a kiss on the cold forehead, and eventually turned away with a face at once angry and utterly alone.

7th August 1805

IRISH REBELS MAINTAIN EFFORT AT FRENCH ASSISTANCE

To the Comptroller-General,

Sir,

W. Tone has departed these shores for France. Our factors within his circle confide that he seeks support from the Revolutionary Regime for projected but unspecified insurrectionary activities in Ireland.

Travelling as W. Smith, under false American passport, Tone departed from the port of New York on the Jersey bound for Le Havre. He has letters of introduction for the American Ambassador to Paris, James Monroe, and others.

The passenger complement totals only ten, and all of nine save Tone/Smith are registered as citizens of France. This is a known lie in at least three cases: Thomas Prudie (19), Tadh Roscarrock (28) and a man listed as Jean Dauban (31), which we apprehend to be an alias.

The Jersey is foreseen to arrive in Le Havre within the first week of February.

30th day of January 1796.

[SS A/5/127]

Jessel walked to the Admiralty through strangely quiet morning streets. London, like a fallen woman, had worked hard to forget the humiliations of the previous day and night. The chaos had disappeared into the darkness and the cells. The sweepers and shopkeepers had been up with the first of the light, repairing and covering, washing away the debris of shame. By the middle of the morning, only the occasional board on a window or scar on a face betrayed that the events of Tuesday the 6th of August had even occurred. The extant records give almost no coverage of that day's rioting, and cannot show the resentment that lingered in back streets and workshops, and the fear that still smouldered in the banking houses and offices.

Their Lordships of the Admiralty had exercised their authority and borrowed a detachment of Marines from HMS *Edmund*, anchored down the Thames. The redcoats lurked in the shadows of the Admiralty courtyard, uneasy at unknown threats and solid ground. Two of them, competent and forbidding, stopped Jessel in the first entrance hall, and he was obliged to spend twenty minutes on a stone bench there waiting for Admiral Lord Hugo Bellamy to emerge from the depths of the building.

Hurrying to catch up with the striding figure. 'A little inconvenient for our business, My Lord.'

'We'll settle the arrangements shortly, Jessel. Lord Barham is insisting that he and his colleagues show themselves in Whitehall for work today, but he's taking no chances with security.' They crossed the courtyard, and the waiting Marines stiffened briskly at the Admiral's approach.

'His Lordship doesn't scare easily.'

'A relic from a different age, Jessel. But a brave age for all that.' Bellamy showed something to a Marine guard and they re-entered the building through a side door. 'Is Roscarrock on his way here?'

'Yes, My Lord. He's been with De Boeldieu, the Frenchman.'

'Who is more than we thought.'

'Gatekeeper to Sir Keith Kinnaird's French network, My Lord, yes. The spy was one of his, and a former servant.'

'How did the man cross the Channel and come ashore?'

'Kinnaird's network in France has arrangements to get people onto our go-betweens.'

The sharp tapping over the marble floor stopped instantly. 'He came across on a Comptrollerate-General ship?' Jessel nodded. 'Clever Kinnaird: the same system that transports our agents and messengers becomes an escape route if one of our spies is threatened.'

'The Captain showed the man how to evade our sentries on the coast.'

Bellamy strode forwards again. 'Of course. This organization is so damn clever it defeats itself. Jessel, you're supposed to be bringing that collection of pirates and smugglers under better control.'

'Yes, My Lord.'

'Do so faster.'

'Yes, My Lord.'

'We're close to the crisis now.' Bellamy stopped still again. 'Since the Frenchman is Kinnaird's man, Roscarrock is of course thick as thieves with him.' Jessel shrugged. 'Doesn't he care what we think? Has he no discretion at all?'

Jessel spoke almost fondly. 'Roscarrock is instinct and action, My Lord. He killed one assassin yesterday and was about to kill what he thought was another. Hard to control, I fear.'

'I don't want to control him. I want to see where he leads.' The Admiral made to dismiss Jessel, and paused. 'Your paths will separate now, for a time. You will co-ordinate our activities here. Roscarrock is going on a little journey by sea. The Admiralty are throwing everything into France to stave off collapse.'

Jessel nodded. 'The papers that came out of France, My Lord: was there much in them?'

Bellamy shook his head slowly, and turned away into the long cold corridor.

◆

We beg leave to report a most bewildering circumstance.

On the 6th of August two men fought on the towpath of the Leeds & Liverpool canal, adjacent Mr Long's brickyard. Witness John Rendle: 'I heard shouting and crashing and swearing'; no words recorded. Witness Rachel May: 'There was two of them, circling like dogs and then wrestling. Both men looked as they had knives. I hurried away.' Witnesses Alfred Arthur and others had seen two men first meeting, apparently incidentally, on the street near Macey's Store and subsequently walking apart but near each other in the direction of the canal path.

Testimony of Witness Alfred Arthur describing one of the men, including white patch on face, may tally with testimony of Witness Edward Mallon and others of a man lately seen around Burnley Drift pit and once chased out of the premises. Identity unknown; occupation unknown. But, following recent reports of machine-breaking and other acts of wilful destruction at mines in this and other Counties, this led to speculation that one or both men were criminals in that pursuit, who perhaps fell out over some aspect of their enterprise.

The postscript has confused the matter, and made it truly perplexing. In the early hours of this morning the body of a man was found in a stable in Plumbe Street. Age perhaps thirty or thirty-five; knife or similar wound to side; cause of death unknown but probably complications or fever resulting from knife wound. Witness testimony (Joseph Hill, Perseverance Todd) strongly states that the dead man bears very close resemblance to Richard Garrod, sometime engineer in Halifax, Rochdale and elsewhere, though fallen into difficulty as a result of a business scandal. Garrod was believed drowned in the Oakworth incident in April. His body was never found, so it is conceivable that he somehow survived that tragedy only to die in these present unexplained circumstances. What cannot be conjectured is what he might have been doing in the four months interim, and more particularly why, if alive, he did not make himself known to any of his former acquaintance.

[SS J/30/418]

Roscarrock had not visited Lord Hugo Bellamy's office before, and he only reached it on this occasion with a stolid, striding Marine on either side of him. The room was dark wood and dark wallpaper, and without much furniture or decoration. No clutter in Bellamy's vision. The few items on the desk seemed small against the large man standing behind it.

The two Marines left smartly at Bellamy's curt dismissal, closing the door but stopping just the other side of it.

Roscarrock stood in the centre of the room, glancing at the surroundings and then returning Bellamy's scrutiny.

'The First Lord of the Admiralty has asked me most particularly to pass on his personal thanks for your performance yesterday, Roscarrock. From a man like him, that is not cheaply earned.' He turned away to the single window.

Roscarrock grunted politely; he still wasn't quite sure what he'd done yesterday. Light coming over Bellamy's shoulder caught a thin layer of dust on a decanter and matching glasses on a side table; the single chair this side of the desk looked similarly unused. Men had interviews with the Comptroller-General for Scrutiny and Survey, not conversations.

Bellamy turned back from the window, face in shadow. 'Don't get carried away. You haven't won the war yet.' The sarcasm dropped heavy and without interest. He stepped nearer, and Roscarrock suddenly saw the tension and tiredness in the face. 'It's getting serious now, Roscarrock. The greatest secret in the Kingdom is this: we are on the brink. The politicians are hysterical and practising radical speeches. The merchants, the men of business, are selling everything that isn't locked in the Tower, and shipping their interests out. They'll take the British economy with them.' He was picking the details ponderously out of the air. 'The Admiralty... The Admiralty are rattled. Even if it had detonated properly, there probably wasn't enough gunpowder to do real harm, but the very possibility of it... The First Lord would fight the French single-handed, but it's starting to look as though he might have to. The Emperor's fleets need only a moment's good fortune to break into the open sea, and our chances of stopping them flicker and fall with each gust of wind. Most worrying of all, the country won't stand. The prizefighter has absorbed his last punch. One more incident like yesterday and Napoleon's grandmother could capture London.'

The Admiral's grim gaze swung heavily round, and he sat. 'An extraordinary meeting. I've never seen anything like it, Roscarrock. Anger – and fear. And that old man, staking the nation on his last throw of the dice.' He looked up at the silent man in front of him, and the old cold professionalism was back in the voice. 'Here it is, then. The Admiralty can do little more to stiffen our resistance to Napoleon. But they will do everything possible to weaken the attack, and at the very least to understand it. You are to go—'

'What do the documents from Joseph Dax say about their plans?'

Bellamy's face flashed irritation. 'They say really very little that we did not already know. A few data on dispositions and numbers of the various fleets. Detailed suggestions of Napoleon's plans for their movements, but our own men could have guessed most of that.'

'The Sharks?'

'Nothing, Roscarrock. The documents say nothing. You must look on yesterday's excitements as an irrelevance. The man Fannion has escaped to France, where he will no doubt be plotting precisely the kind of Irish distraction that will bring trouble to half the ports in England and neutralize our resistance. And despite your little servant we still know nothing about the single most potent threat to our command of the Channel.'

Roscarrock's eyes were set hard. That vital dossier, brought out of France at such desperate cost, said nothing about the Emperor's most significant fleet? He felt the fog muffling his ship again, wondered at the shadows of rocks in the murk. *I am in a world of darkness and mirrors. Facts and truths are as insubstantial as identities and loyalties.*

Bellamy settled back stiff against his chair. 'The Admiralty are looking to the Comptrollerate-General. We are the last hope of England. Every one of our irregular ships – and you never saw a wilder mix of heroes and cut-throats, Roscarrock – is putting to sea, with the most precious cargo. Every spy and spy-runner we have is going into France, and our irregulars will deliver them.' His fingers drummed once on the desk. 'And gold.' The word came out harsh. 'The Admiralty have signed over an unprecedented sum to us. Sealed and guarded wagons are rushing it to the coast to be loaded and shipped. Our agents will pay for every useful fact, every beat of a Royalist heart, every doubt in a wavering official's loyalty. We're buying time, Roscarrock, that's what it is, and the Comptrollerate-General will pay ready cash for every precious minute of it.' The eyes widened and hardened over the desk. 'The single largest shipment is to go to the leader of the Royalist resistance in northern France. Have you heard of General Metz, Roscarrock?'

A name, an idea, repeated in the salons. 'A little.'

'An old Royalist hero, who took the remarkable decision to live in hiding in France rather than escape while he could. Extraordinary figure, by all accounts. His military reputation was remarkable, and the myth that's built up around him has only multiplied his influence. It's a measure of our desperation, but the gold will convince him we are committed to his support, and with luck it will buy us a rising in the north.'

'You have an optimistic view of the affordability of French loyalty, My Lord.'

A grim smile crossed the Admiral's face. 'Oh, the price of trouble is down these days, and a hundred thousand pounds should buy enough of it.' He noted the rare flicker of respect in Roscarrock's eyes. 'Unrest in the countryside around Amiens, perhaps with a couple of French regiments starting to waver when they hear that the General is back in action, might distract the Emperor's army enough to hamper the invasion.'

'That's an expensive might, Admiral.'

Bellamy's eyes narrowed. 'Any alternative suggestions from you would as usual be welcome, Roscarrock. In the meantime, Lord Barham has approved this last chance, and he has approved the man to escort the gold. You, Roscarrock.'

The Admiral waited for a reaction, but there was none. 'Your responsibility is two-fold. Firstly, you will make contact with General Metz, and deliver the gold to him – if he accepts contact and accepts our proposal. Second, you will scour our network in France for every grain of detail on the Emperor's secret fleet: we must know location; we must know intent.'

Now Roscarrock spoke, quiet and earnest: 'I'd take any excuse to get out of London. But I have no experience of this foreign work, I don't have good French, and I don't know the spy networks.'

'Believe me, Roscarrock, I would be delighted to send anyone else. I consider your attitudes unco-operative and your loyalties suspect. But the First Lord of the Admiralty himself commands it. You are his epitome of Comptrollerate-General reliability. Besides, our best chance of finding the secret fleet will be Kinnaird's network in France – if he hasn't already sold it to Paris. The key to Kinnaird's network is De Boeldieu. And De Boeldieu now trusts you.'

Roscarrock didn't bother trying to disabuse him. After a moment's reflection he said, 'I'll need to see all the reporting that's come out of France.'

'As long as it does not delay your departure.'

'You intend that De Boeldieu comes with me?'

'I suspect he will be crucial to reaching the most useful intelligence. You should have little difficulty convincing him of the importance of this journey. He will be pleased that he and not a substitute is trying to contact his agents, and at this most crucial time.'

Roscarrock said nothing. De Boeldieu would have to be a lunatic to want anything to do with this last, desperate foray by a dying Empire, but there was no point arguing the point with the Admiral. Besides, whatever De Boeldieu's attitude to him, there was an independence and a seriousness to the Frenchman that would be welcome. Though was there any more proof for De Boeldieu's claim to be Kinnaird's gatekeeper than for his previous pretence, beyond Joseph Dax's dramatic but futile journey and the sheer implausibility of someone making the claim falsely?

He stopped in the doorway. 'You said every possible spy-runner.' The Admiral looked up. 'I assume that means Lady Virginia Strong.'

A grave nod. 'She should even now be in France. She too is hunting Napoleon's secret fleet, and she's tracking your Irish friend, Fannion. We must learn whether he makes contact with the French Government, and what he plans. Fannion – General Metz – and the Emperor's Sharks: our future is in the balance.'

Roscarrock shook his head in distaste.

'Roscarrock, I cannot make it a distraction from your other tasks. But she may well be moving in the same districts as you. Keep watch for her, you hear me? And bring her safe out if you possibly can.' Roscarrock nodded. Bellamy's lips soured. 'She too asked, most particularly, for you.'

RECEIVED BY THE OFFICE OF MR MORRISON COPE AT THE
ADMIRALTY, FORWARDED FROM HACKNEY.

My dear Gabriel,

I got your letter and was so mighty pleased at it. Your
hand is so familiar to me and when I see it I think always
of us sitting together and you teaching me the letters and
when I see it I see your face and your mind and your
smile. It worries me when I hear that you are followed by
the Government men, and I know you are not as carefree as
you pretend. I care nothing for the trickeries and the secret
friendly hands you tell of, for you always taught us that deceit
is deceit and an offence against the great pure truth and it is
like the scorpion that stings itself. I am glad you have found
men who have received the light from you and who hearten
you. I hope that they are good and trusty men, and I pray
that together you may go forwards to glory like you say.

Here we are well and life goes on.

It made me cry to hear from you and I wish you here.
You seem so far away and I know you have further to go
before I might see you again. I pray that the good Lord keep
you safe until we meet.

Your loving wife,
Flora Chance

[SS M/1108/3]

Ten years before, the ancient port of Newhaven had endured the indignity of capture – by rioting militiamen from Oxfordshire. The town still showed the scars: cracked and pocked walls, and mysterious furrows on the green where the artillery had dispersed the rebels. The place was oddly quiet today, meditating sullenly on the past.

Roscarrock and De Boeldieu, tramping side by side in discontented silence, found the sloop *Jane* at the end of an old jetty away from the centre of the port. As he looked up from the stones at his feet to the two soaring masts, something in Roscarrock started to breathe again after a long stifling. The seawater nuzzled like a faithful dog at the ship's side, and the air had the thrilling emptiness of smell that promised freedom and the pure, uncompromised challenge of man against nature. Roscarrock suddenly felt his weeks of absence from the sea – the longest he had been on dry land since he learnt to walk, and the longest he had been out of sight of that vast expanse of truth.

Their last few steps along the jetty were beside the *Jane*. Roscarrock liked the look of her, for speed: she was sleek and sharp, and the long bowsprit projecting out towards the empty sea only accentuated this. He didn't, though, much fancy the thought of a heavy Atlantic swell in her. One step up and he swung smoothly over the rail and onto the deck, De Boeldieu scrambling behind him.

A small dark man crossed the deck. Roscarrock said, 'The life of a sailor must be lonely.'

'But the life of a sailor is free.'

'God save the King.'

'God save the King. Roscarrock?'

'Yes. Captain Miles Froy?' A nod. 'Permission to come aboard, Captain?'

'Aye. Are we waiting for anything more? I've got the wind and not much more of the tide.'

'Has our cargo arrived?'

Froy nodded once. 'In the hold this half hour.' His words and movements came soft and economic, and Roscarrock was reassured by it.

'Then as you judge.' His attention caught, Roscarrock knocked thoughtfully at the ship's rail.

The Captain saw the movement. 'Cedar.'

Roscarrock looked up with interest. 'Bermuda?'

'Yes. You know ships, then.'

Careful. A shrug. 'Book learning mostly. Helps in this trade.'

A grunt, and the Captain was off giving quiet orders for departure. Roscarrock scanned the deck: compact, and very tidy. Lashed down near the tiny raised quarterdeck were two irregular canvas-covered lumps. Cannon: nine- or perhaps twelve-pounders – enough to make a noise and get out of trouble. In the hold, he found an unhappy-looking Marine trying to stand to attention by a pile of wooden boxes. He probably wouldn't know what was in the boxes, but he'd know enough to be intimidated, and Roscarrock wondered if the crew had been goading him a bit. They were too professional for real mischief, but to the Marine they probably looked rough enough to knock him on the head without losing any sleep about it. Roscarrock thanked and dismissed him; they wouldn't be needing a uniformed Marine, and the young man hurried off gratefully. Roscarrock was left with the pile of boxes that had now become his responsibility, and wondering at the madness.

They were at sea less than half an hour later, and it was only that long because of the two figures who came hurrying along the jetty as the crew were getting ready to cast off. The first of them waved his presence to the *Jane* when he was still fifty yards away.

It was Jessel. He reached the sloop, greeted a wary Froy, and climbed aboard. Behind him, a burly soldier came up with a chest in his arms. Jessel pulled the chest from the soldier, and sent him away down the jetty.

For a moment Roscarrock thought that Jessel was coming with them. His colleague grinned at him and disappeared into the ship, staggering ungainly behind the Captain with the chest in his arms. But he was back a few minutes later, without either Froy or the chest. He grabbed at Roscarrock's arm.

Roscarrock was unsettled, and didn't know why. He realized that the reappearance of Jessel, and the urban confusion that he represented, was tarnishing the freshness of the sea. 'Final orders for the Captain,' Jessel said, and added cheerfully, 'Thrown up yet?'

'Not until I saw you.'

'Can't stand boats. Hate it every time I have to get on one. How's your Frenchy friend?'

'Trusts me even less than I trust him.'

'It'll be a lovely voyage, then.' Jessel looked into Roscarrock's face, and suddenly he was serious. 'Take care, you hear, Tom? Whatever you are, you're not ready for that slab yet.'

'You too. Make sure England's still here when I get back.'

Then Jessel was away across the deck. He made for one of the crew – the First Mate, tall, bearded and watchful – and spoke privately with him for a minute. Then he was away over the rail with a final, pleasant wave, and the jetty was moving away from the sloop's side, and then Newhaven began to shrink, and soon they were clear of the headland and Roscarrock felt the force of the sea and the breeze plucking at the ship.

'You look unhappy, Mr Roscarrock.' His head snapped round: De Boeldieu. He hadn't heard the Frenchman coming up behind him, and it hurt his pride. 'Are you not well?'

'I'm fine,' Roscarrock said tersely. De Boeldieu nodded indifferently.

He stood next to Roscarrock at the rail, and looked towards the disappearing coast. After a moment he said, 'You say you learnt about sailing from books. But you jumped onto the ship – and you move around it – like a dancer.'

Roscarrock glanced at him. What did it matter anymore? 'I've sailed some.'

De Boeldieu didn't press the point. 'I thought you were seasick, perhaps.'

'I'm at last feeling a little less landsick.'

'Your mouth was open like a dumb donkey.'

Roscarrock smiled. 'I was thinking. Doesn't come easily. Or just a sailor's superstition, perhaps: last-minute disruptions never bode well.'

'Surely the more experienced a sailor you are, the less you have need of superstitions.'

'The opposite.' Roscarrock heard his own earnestness, and hesitated. The Frenchman was watching him.

Kinnaird knew everything about him, and De Boeldieu was Kinnaird's man. 'I was born in a community that was more sea than land. And when your livelihood and your life depend on the sea, you develop every kind of crazy belief to keep the sea on your side. I could tell you a dozen things that you mustn't bring on a boat, say on a boat, or see on a boat.'

De Boeldieu smiled, and put a hand on his shoulder. It was the first suggestion of pleasantry between them. 'My friend, you are a spy, trusted by no one, in charge of a cargo that most men would kill for, with a crew that I would fear more than most men, travelling to a country where they will hang you simply for your nationality. What can possibly go wrong?'

❦

All around the coast of south-eastern England, from the Thames Estuary to the Isle of Wight, the irregular ships of the Comptrollerate-General for Scrutiny and Survey were putting to sea. They left by quiet jetties and forgotten inlets; they left by dawn and by dusk. They carried brave and desperate men – men as varied, as eccentric or disreputable, as the crews that ferried them. They carried gold, and the last hopes of an Empire.

❦

It was a small crew, and Roscarrock did not warm to them. They were good enough at their work – excellent, indeed. But there was no spirit in them. He had a fair suspicion what they got up to when they weren't running errands for the British Government, and he'd hauled more than a few illicit cargoes over moonlit Cornish sands himself. But even among the most debased men, there'd been a comradeship, a mutual dependency in the face of constant threats to life. Too much business had hardened and frozen the men of the *Jane*.

Froy, the Captain, he liked the look of as a seaman, but the man was too quiet and distant from his crew. Aloofness worked in a man-of-war with hundreds of men aboard, but not in a sloop with a dozen. Men needed to respect and even fear their Captain in a little ship as much as on a large, but they also needed to feel he was one of them. On the *Jane*, orders and reports all passed through the sour and acerbic Mate, Griffiths. He wondered if crew and Captain had not been long together.

Roscarrock dropped into the hold and had another look at the boxes. There were exactly twenty of them. For what they carried, they seemed small and insubstantial – no more than a foot square, thin panels of wood, and without fancy metalwork or indeed any marking. Each was sealed, so any attempt to tamper with it would show, but otherwise they were only nailed shut. He scrambled the full length of the hold; this was the only cargo.

He wondered what Jessel had told the Captain about the boxes, and what the crew knew. Crews didn't like transporting things they didn't know about, and you could usually reckon on someone having a peek in the small hours to assuage curiosity and calm superstition. The boxes were obviously important, and even if they didn't know exactly what was in them, the men would know that it was very valuable to someone. They'd have to be getting a fat wage for the voyage, and the promise that they'd be hunted to the ends of the earth and given all the tortures of hell if they tried to borrow their cargo. At no stage did Roscarrock imagine they'd be doing it out of sheer patriotism.

He hauled himself up out of the hold, murmured a greeting to two of the crew he passed near the hatch – it would do them good to know he was keeping an eye on the cargo, but there was still little to stop them dropping him over the side if the fancy took them – and went to find De Boeldieu.

The Frenchman was dozing below deck, sprawled against the side of the boat with his head cushioned against a blanket. One arm lay across the bag he'd brought with him. The hilt of a sword showed through its open folds; Roscarrock wondered if De Boeldieu had left it showing deliberately. It was the first time he'd really had the chance to observe the man. He'd put on rougher, plainer coat and trousers for the journey, but his thick brown hair and fine hands hadn't lost the signs of the attention they normally received in London. The skin was wine-warmed, and De Boeldieu was running to fat a little, too. Even if the fop was a pretence, the Frenchman obviously lived well enough.

Sitting back against a bulkhead, Roscarrock pulled a paper from an inside pocket of his coat and skimmed it one last time. Then he tore it into fragments, and put them in an outside pocket. They could disappear into the Channel next time he was on deck.

'Anything about me in there?' Roscarrock looked up at the words. De Boeldieu was watching him carefully.

'Yes, I'll be knocking you on the head just after midnight.'

'Ah, excellent,' De Boeldieu said soberly. 'I shall have time to sleep a little.' The face and body shifted uncomfortably, and Roscarrock wondered if the Frenchman himself suffered from seasickness.

'We're heading for the mouth of the Somme, as you suggested.' De Boeldieu nodded. Instinctively, Roscarrock checked they were alone, and lowered his voice further. 'Two little tasks, then we can go home. Napoleon's secret fleet: we must talk to as many of your agents as we can about it. And we must make contact with General Metz.'

De Boeldieu whistled. '*Le Vieux Taureau*? Just like that, we will contact him? I told you: our networks overlap, but we have never met him.'

'I've been given a password, and I'm sure your people will have ways to reach him. What did you call him? Old Bull?'

De Boeldieu nodded. 'A nickname from the army. Nowadays, the people doubt whether he exists. Until now we have not wanted to contact him. He is a weapon to be used sparingly. The Government use his name to justify their repressions. Loyalists use him to justify their hopes. If you have some code from the old days, perhaps this will appeal.' He sat back and his cheeks puffed out. 'But this is serious business, Roscarrock. *Le Taureau* is a legend. His record, his reputation... his inspiration, you understand? If there is one man who might rouse France...' He shook his head. 'But now – he is a ghost. I doubt – Oh!' The eyes widened, and the Frenchman smiled grimly. 'I understand now! You will use your boxes to persuade Monsieur Le Général to make a little distraction to save poor England.' He shook his head. 'I am sure he will be delighted to oblige.'

Roscarrock scowled, irritated that he had no good argument to put against De Boeldieu's sarcasm, and trying not to think about how he would put the suggestion to the General even if the man did exist. 'I'm more concerned about getting into France in the first place.'

De Boeldieu flicked a disdainful hand. 'There are procedures. You will see.'

'You've travelled on a ship like this before?'

'Many times. I am invariably seasick, but it is a very clever system. An initiative of our friend Kinnaird, of course.'

'I've heard. Our private fleet of irregulars – fishermen, merchantmen, smugglers – the best sailors, and ready to run risks for a price. How many are there, do you know?'

The Frenchman shook his head, and then winced as his nausea flared. 'Two dozen? More? I don't know. I have rarely been met by the same Captain more than once.' He glanced around their little, lantern-lit space. 'Is this a good ship?'

'Fast, certainly. More flexible with the wind – she can sail very close. But not very steady, I'm afraid.' De Boeldieu tried to produce a brave smile. 'Monsieur' – the smile faded at the new severity in the word – 'how long have you known Sir Keith Kinnaird?'

A moment's thought. 'Five years? More.' The flushed face leant forwards. 'But never well, if you understand me. He is not that kind of man.'

'What do you think has happened to him?'

Philippe de Boeldieu gave an enormous, theatrical shrug. 'Oh, as to that, I know everything and nothing. He has made his calculation, as always. That is all.'

Roscarrock considered this.

'And you, Roscarrock: are you asking me because you do not know, or because you do know but you want to find out how much I know?' A frown fell on the Englishman's face. 'It is a pretty game, is it not?'

⎯ ⁘ ⎯

In the silent seclusion of his windowless office, Fouché placed two pieces of paper beside each other on his desk and let out a long hiss of satisfaction. No one else had placed a foot in this room, not since the betrayal by the servant Dax. The office, and the mind, of Napoleon's master of secrets was a lonely landscape; the activities, and the satisfactions, were beyond the comprehension of average men.

At last the navies of France were operating as they were supposed to – in concert with each other, and in concert with his plans. Admiral Allemand was at sea with his ships, cruising west of France and within striking distance of the English Channel. And now – at last – Admiral Villeneuve knew this and Admiral Villeneuve was free to manoeuvre. No British blockade was in his way. Perhaps it had been worth letting Villeneuve know a little of the plans after all; such confidences played to the man's aristocratic vanity, and if aristocratic vanity was required to float the Emperor's fleets effectively, then the Revolution would bear it. It was now only a matter of a few days before Villeneuve was at sea and united with Allemand. Together, they would sail for the Channel, and then Fouché would put his Emperor into London.

All that remained was to draw off enough of the Royal Navy to guarantee that Villeneuve and the invasion transports were unhindered. At the same time, Fouché would preside over the final destruction of the Comptrollerate-General for Scrutiny and Survey, and the last taste of betrayal would be washed away forever.

It was time. A message to Gabin, already near the coast, and then he would set off himself. He must be close to the Emperor, and close to the action. A signal was coming out of England, and that was all he was waiting for now.

———

Darkness had swallowed the summer evening before the *Jane* glided closer to the coast of France. Only the necessary crewmen were on deck, and the Captain himself was at the wheel. De Boeldieu was directing one of the crewmen as he prepared a lantern, and Roscarrock was watching the Frenchman and trying to calm the storm of his thoughts. Around them, the sea glistened in the night, a vast pit of black snakes seething over each other.

'Roscarrock: take her a moment, would you?' Roscarrock nodded and stepped to the wheel, and Froy moved to the side of the ship. He scanned the gloom, peering for the shore and the currents. 'A point to port,' he called softly over his shoulder. Roscarrock smiled, and turned the wheel as instructed.

Froy continued to watch the darkness for some moments, and then returned. 'Book learning?'

'Book learning.'

Froy replaced him at the wheel. 'Don't worry, Mr Roscarrock. We're all liars of one kind or another.'

Roscarrock chuckled low into the darkness. It had pleased him to confirm the Captain's suspicions, and he judged it would go no further.

The *Jane* dropped anchor. At eleven o'clock, De Boeldieu stood the lantern on the ship's rail and uncovered it for five seconds; then he covered it for another five, and uncovered it again; a third time, and then without hesitation or discussion he extinguished the lantern and returned below deck.

The performance was repeated at half past the hour, and again at midnight. Going below for the third time, De Boeldieu murmured, 'Can we afford to spend another twenty-four hours here?'

'I doubt it.'

The Frenchman shrugged grimly and ducked down into the relative warmth.

But in the first glow of the dawn a fishing boat came out of the Somme estuary, and made for the *Jane*. Signals were exchanged, the fishing boat came closer, and De Boeldieu just nodded at Roscarrock. Five minutes later, after a final glance into the hold and a brief exchange with Froy – the restrained murmurs of men speaking their own private language – he was stepping down into the fishing boat after the Frenchman.

The *Jane* pulled up her anchor and drew away from the coast, to wait. The fishing boat, with two new men among her crew, began the routines of the morning. Thus, heaving splashing, ungainly lobster pots out of the water on slippery ropes and trying to get a grip on the barked Picardy slang, Tom Roscarrock came out of the sea mist to France.

Sometime during the night, he had answered the biggest question of all, the question he had been asking for weeks, and the implications of the answer were still eating at him.

8th August 1805

ROSCARROCK, Tom, identified Taunton 15th July 1805 (Vivary Arms), Bristol 17th July 1805, Wootton 18th July 1805 (Five Bells), Newbury 19th July 1805 (Rachel Stafford).

[SS X/41/12 AND VARIOUS]

A helpful wind pushed the fishing boat up the Somme estuary, between the sprawling banks of brown and swampy sand, and in the late afternoon Tom Roscarrock stepped onto French soil. The single step from the boat to the dark stone of the quay represented a new level of alienation and danger, and he was glad to focus on the chores of tying and tidying the boat and bringing the lobster pots on shore. He watched De Boeldieu making the same step, saw the little ritualistic kick that the Frenchman gave his native ground, and wondered again at his life of exile and deception.

The boat kept them busy for an hour, helping at the age-old chores with the fisherman and his crew, two slow and hefty sons and pair of sharp and equally bulky cousins. Then they disappeared with them into the little fishing village. St Valery-sur-Somme looks out over the first bend in the river, a dark and ancient warren of close-packed flint houses, and it swallowed them easily.

De Boeldieu did the little talking that was needed, and he kept it to a minimum. Roscarrock guessed that his companion's educated accent would stick out as much as his own voice. Most of the movements and transactions were silent, and he had the impression of a practised routine. On both sides of the Channel there were men prepared to blur the boundaries between the nations, and not ask questions.

There was a murmur between De Boeldieu and the old man, and suddenly the fishermen had disappeared down an alley, and the two interlopers were alone. Roscarrock was instantly more watchful, but had to trust the Frenchman. Fifty dank and shadowed yards further on there were two horses, and a minute later they were trotting south out of the village. Roscarrock had followed every movement in silence. It made sense that they weren't staying in the village after all; he knew the raw communal life of an isolated fishing village, where everyone knew everyone else's business, and it was no place for two spies.

The packet handed to a French military policeman of the Imperial Gendarmerie in Étaples, south of Boulogne, was a single sheet of paper folded and sealed. The few words on the outside gave no indication of the contents, but they included one phrase that moved the packet speedily to regional headquarters and a second phrase, familiar only to senior officers of the Gendarmerie, that moved the packet on again very speedily indeed.

When, on the evening of the 8th, Minister Fouché stepped with sour, sagging eyes from his coach after a twenty-four-hour journey from Paris, this single piece of paper was in his hand before his second boot had touched the ground.

He had been expecting it. The outside phrases were irrelevant to him; at last the seal was broken, with a single impatient finger, and he looked inside. A thin smile grew on the pale and weary face, and Fouché snapped out, 'Messenger!'

The inside was blank, but for a neatly written name: St Valery-sur-Somme.

———

In the middle of the evening, a single figure walked with the last of the sun towards the crumbling farmhouse where Roscarrock and De Boeldieu were sheltering. Roscarrock saw the approach, and De Boeldieu was quickly beside him at the window. At the gate that enclosed the dusty yard the man stopped, and seemed to scrape at the ground with his heel; then he withdrew forty or fifty yards to a tree.

'Keep looking out all round,' De Boeldieu said, and then walked out into the yard. He reached the gate, glanced at the ground where the man had scraped at it, then did the same himself before walking back to the house. The other man advanced to the gate again, checked the ground, and looked up and nodded. De Boeldieu came forwards again, the man entered through the gate, and they embraced, quickly but sincerely.

They walked five circuits of the increasingly gloomy yard, talking quietly, De Boeldieu's arm around the man's shoulders for some of the time. The other man handed over a folded paper. A final embrace, and he passed back through the gate and disappeared into the night.

De Boeldieu reappeared. 'A friend.'

'I hoped so.'

'Some information on the dispositions of the army up at Boulogne, which we can pass back. A little local gossip. We are safe enough here for a few days. The people in the farms around here do not trust authority of any kind; it threatens their world, their little rural habits. Any strangers and my friends will hear of them.'

'Safe enough to light a fire, then?'

De Boeldieu thought, and nodded. 'I have sent some messages – arranged some meetings.'

'The General – Metz?'

'I have started the process, as you asked.' Roscarrock nodded, and started to pile kindling in the ancient stones of the hearth. 'It will not be easy, my friend. The Old Bull – you do not simply knock on his door.'

'I understand. I gave up on easy a long time ago.'

De Boeldieu smiled, and nodded, and found two decaying chairs. 'And I have told our local network of friends to keep watch for this Dutch acquaintance of yours, Mrs Sophie Van Vliet.' He kicked a log towards Roscarrock. 'I may assume that I would know her as Lady Virginia Strong?'

Roscarrock gave it only a second's thought. 'You may assume that.'

'Very good at what she does, my friend. But she stands out, I fear.'

Roscarrock sat. 'Is that regret I hear?'

'Oh no, no, not in the least.' De Boeldieu shook a fierce negative finger. 'She is not my type, that one.'

'You can obviously afford to be a damn sight choosier than the rest of us, then.'

A little shrug. 'My tastes are elsewhere. Besides, when I go to bed, I like to think there is a good chance I will get up again.'

Later, the glare of the fire playing with the rough lines of his face, Roscarrock said, 'Philippe, tell me about your family. What happened to them?'

The Frenchman turned and examined him for several moments, then looked back into the fire. 'My father was a wonderful – what is this excellent phrase you have in English? – "old fool"?'

Roscarrock smiled. 'Old fool.'

De Boeldieu nodded. 'Actually, it's quite significant – that phrase, that type of phrase.' He continued to nod as he looked at Roscarrock, and waved an instructive finger. 'Seriously. This ability you have, both in manners and language, to laugh fondly at authority, this may yet save you a great deal of bloodshed. But my father – my father was indeed an old fool. An old-fashioned, absolutist, monarchist, reactionary aristocrat – utterly devoted to his servants, every dozen of them, completely loyal, would have died to protect them, never missed the birthday of the most insignificant of them, insisted on their comfort and health as badge of our own family pride – but thought it inexplicable and insane that they should have any opinion in the matter. He made no attempt at all to escape or compromise with the Revolution. He stood erect before their citizens' tribunal, used language I had never heard from him to describe every one of them and their ancestry back for untold generations; and from nowhere he produced arguments, of a sophistication and a clarity and a – a poetry – that I had never dreamt he possessed, to dismantle and condemn their bastard ideals. He all but asked outright for an invitation to the guillotine, and when it came, he took it with a grace and a style that I shall always aspire to.' Philippe took an enormous breath, eyes staring away into the flames.

'Did you ever have the chance to tell him any of that?'

A shake of the head. 'It was not necessary, nor would he have cared. He wasn't trying to impress me. No, I didn't change my previous opinions of him, if that's what you mean, but I found something to love him for. At the end, the very end, I understood what history and family meant to him – and what they must mean to me.' Roscarrock went to speak, but De Boeldieu would not be swerved. 'My mother was beautiful, graceful, really rather stupid – or at least completely unthinking – and loyal. I can remember not one single word of significance ever uttered by her, from my earliest memory to when she walked to her death, slapping off the hands of the functionaries who assumed she would have to be dragged, praying to the God in whom she never doubted, silently and proudly following the husband about whom she felt approximately the same.'

Roscarrock kept his eyes on the fire. Then, softly: 'And Lady... Sybille? Your sister?'

Philippe de Boeldieu shrugged at the night, shook his head, sucked at the air for words. 'She was all that I was not. She was the son that my parents deserved. Intelligent, active, committed and strong. I should have hated her, but there was nothing in her that was not to love. She was better read in philosophy than most of the revolutionary leaders, she understood the attractions and strengths of reform better than most of the reformers, and its seductions and dangers better than most of the monarchists. When the crisis came, my father made sure that she was away at one of our distant estates. He probably couldn't be sure whether she'd fall to the Revolution or join it. But it found her in any case. Any of our servants, whatever their views, would have died to defend her. Seven of them did so.' His hands were clenched on his knees. 'She killed herself rather than be taken. Only Joseph survived to tell. He and I have been trying to be worthy of her ever since.'

As promised, Admiral Lord Hugo Bellamy called that evening at the First Lord's Residence at the top of the Admiralty building. After the cool, formal fashion of the rest of his rooms, Lord Barham's study was darker and more personal, souvenirs of West Africa and the West Indies crowding the books.

'Anything yet, Bellamy?'

'Not yet, My Lord. Almost all of our people should have reached France by now. It will take time to get any news out.'

'You have systems in place, of course.'

'The Comptrollerate-General ships will rendezvous with some of our regular brigs and frigates. Flags and semaphore, of course; we can relay any essential intelligence back to England tolerably quick – most obviously any news of this fleet of Sharks.'

'We're pissing into the wind, Bellamy, aren't we?'

'My Lord.'

9th August 1805

CROSS-REFERENCING FOR PLACE NAME ROSCARROCK AND
EQUIVALENTS

*ROSCARROCK, Godstone (Surrey) – hill of this name, regular
environ for Francis Monk or Francis Munk or Black Monk,
highwayman and sometime J/20 (d 1799), vide J/20/86,
J/20/92, J/20/134 and once site of seditious meeting (28th
November 1804, vide J/20/296 and X/24/7)*

*ROSCARROCK, Wadebridge (Cornwall) – farmhouse, hamlet
and hill of this name, twice meeting place of smuggler
Simon Hillyard, subsequently X/51, vide X/51/27, X/51/31,
M/10/7/27*

*ROSCARROCK, Boston (America) – temporary lodging for
Thomas Paine, two nights March 1775, vide A/3/41*

*ROSCARRICK, Falmouth (Cornwall) – sometime home of
Henry Hope Martin, thief and smuggler (and sometime casual
factor), vide J/133/209, X/53/18, M/482/50*

*ROSCARRICK, Lisburn (Belfast, Ireland) – site of 20th of
June 1797 meeting of Defenders, vide I/X/12/83*

[SS M/1309/2/12 DRAWN FROM GAZETEER SS 1/17 BELIEVED LOST]

In the first soft, animal stirrings of the morning, a little man trotted through the dew to the farmhouse on a horse that was obviously too big for him. He hesitated on the edge of the yard, hands still on the reins of the borrowed horse, until De Boeldieu had shown himself and murmured some private word of reassurance.

De Boeldieu introduced Roscarrock as 'a colleague', and the little man as 'Monsieur Jean', and no one enquired further. The two Frenchmen murmured slowly and gravely, apparently of community affairs in one of the nearby towns. Monsieur Jean spoke cautiously and precisely, and in an attempt at emphasis he two or three times produced a phrase in English for Roscarrock's benefit. The French had been slow and formal enough for Roscarrock to gather that the man was some kind of local official, and to pick up basic messages on the poverty of the villages, the resentment at so much military activity in the region, and the busyness of the police.

The little man excused himself after half an hour; he had received a sign of their arrival late last night and had wanted to take immediate advantage, but now he must hurry to work so as not to break his normal routines. De Boeldieu escorted him to the door. He told Monsieur Jean he looked tired; Monsieur Jean should get some rest.

De Boeldieu had assumed responsibility for making what he could of the basic food that some invisible friend had left, and started to work on a breakfast. 'Mood in the district,' he said in summary. 'Some interesting details about police procedures and the military and the state of things. But we will be getting nothing on your mysterious fleet from such a man.'

'Your friend Joseph brought out the Minister's private copy of French naval plans. If they didn't contain anything on it, it's going to take a very special agent to do better.'

'This business has touched my professional pride,' De Boeldieu said, and he was serious. 'Now, my Prometheus, may I beg of you a fire? An indifferent soup, like an indifferent liaison, may be much improved with a little warmth.'

❧

CONVERSATIONS OF ADMIRAL P. C. J. B. S. DE VILLENEUVE, RECORDED THE 30TH DAY OF NOVEMBER, 1805

On the 9th we put to sea from Vigo. Ah, what a moment. My fleet, this greatest fleet, and our destination the south coast of England. I was in the Bucentaure, of course. You're not a sailor, are you, my friend? You wouldn't understand this, I fear. The young Lieutenant here, he would sympathize with me. Designed by Sane himself, finest Shipbuilder of the age. The first of her class, eighty guns and sleek, a true-bred Arabian horse galloping towards England. We were twenty-nine ships of the line, and many frigates and corvettes beside. Ah, that sight. Shadows in the Spanish sun that lit my way.

Now, at last, it is so simple. No more Napoleon, no more waiting, no more obstacles. I am at sea. I have France's greatest fleet under my command. Your British blockade is nowhere – for the first time I feel the sea my own. Soon Allemand will join me, and we are greater still. To Boulogne, collect the Emperor – 'Ah, Excellency, might I have to honour to invite you to step into England?' – and because of Fouché's plan the Royal Navy will be too weak to stop me.

Of course, I am thinking of the brute Fouché and his plan. A lot depends on him, and his network of agents. If his spies have not managed to disrupt and distract the Royal Navy as intended, then even with Allemand we might not be strong enough. But Fouché is efficient: you might not have him to dinner, but for all his comic opera titles he gets a thing done. And now I am a little more comfortable, you understand, because what Fouché and the Emperor do not know is that I am rather better informed than they think. In La Royale, our French navy, we have had our networks since long before these revolutionaries have come along thinking that they change the world. Now the Minister Decrès and I have a private arrangement by which news will reach me of whether Fouché's extraordinary scheme has succeeded or failed.

Ah, that moment. The land falling away through my cabin window, and all the politics with it. Ahead, the open sea and glory!

[SS G/1130/15]

━━━◦◦━━━

They grew tetchy with the hours of enforced idleness, with the unspoken fear that, despite De Boeldieu's network of friends in the nearby farms, they might at any moment hear the thunder of hooves or the tramping of a squad of gendarmes, and with their mutual suspicion. De Boeldieu declared that they would try the soup cold for lunch, since the occasional descent into barbarousness offered variety, and only scowled when asked whether he took the same approach to his liaisons.

In the early afternoon a beggar slouched up the lane to the farm. De Boeldieu watched carefully, then smiled, but still told Roscarrock to keep a lookout on all the approaches to them. He opened the door to the yard. 'If this is what I suspect,' he said, 'I shall need the code word or code phrase you have been given to reassure the friends of General Metz.'

'"The air of Picardy."'

'The air of Picardy? Charming. Well, let us see what this beggar wants.'

'If he's in real trouble, we can offer a hundred thousand pounds in gold, or all the cold soup he can eat.'

De Boeldieu studied Roscarrock's face for one grave moment, then smiled and stepped into the yard.

Roscarrock watched the two men talking over the farm gate, trying to weigh De Boeldieu's affectations and his intrepidity.

The Frenchman was back after a few minutes. 'I have made references, comparisons, and jokes about the air of Picardy, and I am beginning to sound like an imbecile. Nothing.'

'Perhaps this isn't one of the General's contacts. Perhaps he wants to check us before he gives acknowledgement.'

'"The air of Picardy"? That exact phrase?'

'The exact phrase. I got the impression they'd got it like that from some file.'

There was a cough from the doorway. The beggar had ambled across the yard to them. De Boeldieu gave a final glance of frustration at Roscarrock, then headed for the door. Halfway there he stopped, his face opened in sudden enlightenment, and he shot another glance of irritation over his shoulder. He muttered something to the beggar, and reached into his pocket. While he rummaged fruitlessly, he began to whistle. Watching the search eagerly, the beggar joined in the tune. Finally a coin was produced and changed hands; the beggar bit at it, winked, and shambled away across the yard.

De Boeldieu closed the door. '"Picardy" is an old country tune, for the love of God! Lord, when Napoleon rules in London, perhaps then I will have masters of quality.'

'Will General Metz see us?'

'I doubt we are at that stage yet. But we move well.'

'When do we bring the gold ashore? Can your fisherman friend be trusted that much?'

De Boeldieu nodded. 'He knows that France is at stake, and he would die for her, his sons with him. I do not know whom I fear more, the French police or your English pirates on that boat.' A moment's thought, and a decision. 'But tomorrow we must be on the road I think, and the day after. We have not much time.'

'In that case I must get out to the *Jane* tonight. Then our old fisherman can take sick, and his sons and some of your other friends can keep an eye on the boat in harbour. To any right-thinking French policeman, it would be insanity to leave all that gold moored in the open like that.'

'To us all, my friend.'

⚓

The door shut smooth and firm behind him, with the distinct click of an expensive mechanism, and James Fannion found himself out in the corridor again, alone in France and wondering what exactly he'd achieved in the conversation that had just concluded.

He had trekked right across England, into the black heart of her bloody Empire and out again, death and chaos in his wake and the dreams of a free Ireland in his soul, and now he had at last met the one man in Europe who could realize those dreams. Fouché, the butcher of Lyons, the Emperor's ears and the only man to know the Emperor's soul, the man who answered to no one but Napoleon himself and could command the whole apparatus of the revolutionary state, and as slippery a bastard as James Fannion had ever encountered.

He'd turned off the Cork poetry. Fouché, it was rapidly clear, was extremely shrewd and as cold as death, and would have no time for philosophy or romance. Fannion had offered him an Irish rising at a place and time of his convenience and no questions asked. Co-ordination with a French landing obviously the condition, a free Ireland and be on your way the price. He'd offered him the key to the back door of the British Empire, and the pale Minister of Police had thanked him politely and said how satisfactory that would be and wished him a pleasant evening.

Fouché had respected him, he'd seen that clear enough. It was there in the Minister's careful scrutiny of him; damnit, it was all over the man's cautious words. Fannion knew his own skill and impact, and if Fouché was half as sharp as his reputation suggested, he would know exactly what this Irishman was capable of. Fouché had known that Fannion was making a genuine and serious offer, and he had answered seriously.

Fouché had other horses running, that was obvious. But tomorrow they would talk again, these serious men. In the meantime, he was a solitary Irishman in the middle of a vast French encampment. The women were wretchedly starved and nowhere near as pretty as he'd been led to believe, and he hadn't had sight of a decent meal for days.

———

Inspector Gabin had set up his headquarters in a mill one kilometre upriver from St Valery. Working on the assumption that the network of Royalist and British spies was as effective as the Minister had suggested, it would be imprudent suddenly to turn a fishing village police office into a circus. The mill was close enough to St Valery and the main roads, and a regular traffic of people would be less obvious. His men wore the rough rural clothes of the local people, and he kept the number at the mill to the minimum; its routines would continue as much as possible.

The power of the Minister applied to the normal police structures had given Gabin a very satisfactory machine, and he found himself growing alarmingly complacent in it. In addition to the network of policemen and informers across the district, he had a squad of men under his direct control. He had a grenadier Lieutenant acting as liaison with the military, which he couldn't see being a great deal of use but made everyone involved feel more important. He had three cocky chasseurs to act as mounted couriers, supplementing the police systems and keeping him in closer touch with Boulogne and, through the telegraph tower near Abbeville, even Paris.

A brisk young Normandy policeman, who had presented himself as the Inspector's deputy thirty seconds after Gabin had arrived in the middle of the previous night, now stepped smartly into the storeroom and awaited permission to speak.

A nice little despot he was becoming. Gabin's thoughts of an aggressive career in Paris were now alternating with visions of a senior post back in Brittany – responsible for the corner of the country he knew best, lots of young men running around to satisfy the politicians, and little interference from Paris. He smiled at the young man. 'Tell me.'

'Report from the village of Friville, Monsieur L'Inspecteur, to the south-west of here. Barthe, the Mayor's clerk, went home from his office early today; he has kept his borrowed horse and seems to be loading it for a journey.' There was a faint haze around the man; the whole building swam in flour dust.

'On which he will have set off by now. I trust he is being followed.'

'Of course, sir.'

The 'sir' was nicely done. 'Very well. Wait until he is clear of the village, somewhere nice and private, and then take him. We must contain this problem.'

━━━━•❧•━━━━

Roscarrock pulled himself up onto the deck of the *Jane* shortly before midnight. Boule the fisherman seemed both content to put himself at their disposal for the duration of their stay, in return for whatever combination of pride and gold De Boeldieu had established over the years, and to be an exceptional sailor. Sailing close inshore at night is an extremely risky enterprise – Roscarrock had done it himself a few times – but sixty years spent more at sea than on land had brought the old man into a unique harmony with his element. Hunched, scowling and silent, he stared into the night and seemed to hear and smell the currents. Even the minimal lantern signals from the *Jane* felt superfluous.

Griffiths, the dour bearded First Mate, met him at the rail. Roscarrock grunted a greeting. 'Captain awake?'

'Captain's dead.'

Roscarrock's eyes went wide and hard. He straightened to his full height, and gazed into the truculent face, and waited.

'Captain drank. Last night he had a heavy one, and by morning he was gone; must have tipped over in the darkness.' The face was impossible to gauge in the night, but he seemed to be waiting for the reaction.

Roscarrock didn't believe a word of it. But the fate of poor, isolated Miles Froy had to be irrelevant. 'Looks like you're Captain now, then, doesn't it?' he said.

The only issue now was whether the private or business scuffle that had killed Froy was going to affect the vital role of the *Jane* – and whether he would get off the sloop alive and back safely into Napoleon's France.

There was a grunt from the dark face, and Griffiths seemed to relax. One positive: if Griffiths and his confederates had just wanted the gold, they'd have been halfway to the Indies by now and not cruising the French coast for Roscarrock. Which also made it more likely that Froy had been killed in some personal affair.

'I need the boxes ashore tonight. Can you get the crew to start transferring them immediately?'

Griffiths nodded briskly; he'd been anticipating a less businesslike Roscarrock.

Roscarrock waited for him to start the crew going in the hold; as he'd calculated, the man was still enough of a First Mate to supervise the tricky trans-shipment of the cargo. Then he slipped into the darkness of the ship, listening hard for the whisper of steps behind him, and made for the Captain's cabin. Dimly, confusion was wrestling with the first, frail strands of another idea.

There were two chests in the cabin, which was no surprise. Every cabin on every ship had chests in it – for books, for instruments, or for clothes. Most sailors lived many years out of a sea chest before they had any kind of home to call their own. The first of these two was older, larger and locked. Roscarrock assumed it contained the life of the late Miles Froy, and he knew how small that life would look.

The second chest was average in size, as such things went; perhaps as big as three of the boxes of gold coins being passed over the side in the darkness above him. A single man could reach the two handles at the ends, and could just carry it depending on what was inside; certainly the soldier and then Jessel had carried it alone at Newhaven. The timber wasn't as solid as on normal sea chests, but there was a lock – with a key in it. Curiously, a line of small holes had been drilled into the side of the box, just below the lid.

It wasn't even locked. Roscarrock took a single breath – of anticipation, of a theory facing its test – and lifted the lid.

Visually, the contents were unremarkable. A candle lantern was fixed to a wooden shelf at one end of the chest. Next to it was a length of wick cord. Other than that, the chest was filled with a black powder.

Roscarrock breathed out, and closed the lid. With no definite purpose in mind, he locked it and pocketed the key. There was no doubt that Miles Froy would have known what was in the chest – no captain would have accepted such a thing otherwise. But he wondered at the range of contingencies that might have caused the Captain to use a substantial dose of gunpowder with a time-delay mechanism, and once again he wondered at the activities of the Comptrollerate-General for Scrutiny and Survey.

10th August 1805

A REGISTER OF WORLD-PROOF HEARTS: OUR GREAT
FAMILES OF THE CATHOLIC FAITH BY HENRY CRABBE,
PUBLISHED PARIS, 1754 (EXTRACT)

*ROSCARROCK (ROSCAROKE, ROSCARRICK) John
Roscarrock dwelt in Cornwall in the Sixteenth Century of
our Lord, and was known for a man of a good and faithful
disposition. He is buried in the Chapel that bears his name in
the Church of St Endelion in north Cornwall. His son Nicholas
Roscarrock (d. 1634) achieved distinction for his composition
'Saint Endelienta', and owns undying merit for his account
of the Lives of the Saints, altho' perchance his greater service
was as the sworn friend and associate of the Blessed Cuthbert
Mayne (mart. Launceston 1577) when in the University of
Oxford in that Holy Circle which included Gregory Martin,
Edmund Campion and Humphrey Ely. For his Faith Nicholas
Roscarrock suffered confinement and tortures in the Tower of
London, among the echoes of the hymns of so many faithful
men, but endured to continue his service. This family of
Roscarrock have been known for true believers through times
of plenty and times of hardship and held fast to their Cornish
rock as they held to the One Religion.*

[SS M/1309/2/10]

The following morning De Boeldieu and Roscarrock rode through the first glow of the mist towards a farm five miles off. Word had come from the beggar. Kinnaird's network and the web of protection around General Metz had found each other, as London had hoped.

Roscarrock had told his companion about the disappearance of Captain Miles Froy, and sat patiently through the reaction. 'Allow me to be clear, my friend; the fine professional crew of our ship of escape – our one link with safety, the ship on which all our hopes depend – have just murdered their Captain? Truly your organization overwhelms me.' Roscarrock was starting to find reassurance in the exile's dark bravado. 'I think, Roscarrock, that as a good Frenchman I shall renew my loyalty to the regime in which I now look likely to spend the rest of my life. Tell me, what will you do?'

Behind them, in the dark, huddled quiet of the fishing village of St Valery-sur-Somme, they left one hundred thousand pounds in gold bobbing gently against one of the jetties.

The farm of Lamarque sprawled over a shallow bowl in the Picardy landscape. The fields of grain glowed gold in the morning; they'd be harvesting any day now. But today the labourers they saw were picking at little chores – sharpening tools, repairing a cart. Three times they were stopped as they rode in, De Boeldieu murmuring select phrases to the man who had gripped his bridle while Roscarrock watched the hefty peasant invariably in attendance.

They were met at the farm door by a man in his thirties, tanned and good-looking. 'I am Lamarque,' he said curtly. 'You are welcome to my house. Have you had any breakfast?' De Boeldieu's face lit up.

Lamarque's wife, prettiness hardened by years of farm work and child-rearing, brought bread and cheese and wine, and left them alone in a whitewashed parlour.

Stiff in his wooden chair, Lamarque continued to speak with quiet efficiency. 'Firstly, please, you will tell me who you are. I have of course little way to know if you are telling the truth, but honesty will help us.'

De Boeldieu glanced at Roscarrock, and received a tiny nod. 'I am Philippe De Boeldieu, of the Boeldieus of Yvetot and Argentan, hereditary Counts of Charente, the Cotentin and of the Vacetian Islands.'

'Not I think in current possession of those lands, Monsieur.'

'I am temporarily in exile.'

'And working for the Government of Britain.'

'And working for the restoration of a legitimate government in France. This cheese is excellent, by the way.'

The door opened with a crash and an old man stumbled into the room. He was tall and thin, his bald head gnarled and browned by two generations outdoors. He slouched towards the fireplace, one foot dragging behind him. The two visitors watched him for a second, then looked back at Lamarque.

'My poor old uncle. He hears little, understands less, and will betray nothing. You may speak freely.'

Roscarrock was watching the old man as he settled in the chair by the unlit fire and began to doze. He wasn't as old as he seemed: fifty at the most, and sinewy rather than frail. Perhaps the trouble was mental rather than physical. Every peasant family had its simpletons, and a decade of horror had left internal as well as external scars. He looked back at his host. 'I'm Tom Roscarrock. I work for the Comptrollerate-General of Scrutiny and Survey, of the British Admiralty.'

'The name of that organization is almost a myth to men like us, Monsieur; it is rare indeed to hear it spoken.'

'Monsieur Lamarque, you could get me hanged just for my nationality; there's no point being coy about my address.'

A respectful nod from the farmer. 'And you have approached my friends and I, because...?'

Roscarrock spoke in slow and careful French. 'We believe that the peace of Europe depends on the restoration of stable government in France. For now, that means that Napoleon Bonaparte cannot be allowed to defeat Britain. Everything possible must be done to distract and weaken him.' He paused. There was no response from Lamarque. 'We believe that you share this attitude. We believe that the one man who can inspire such resistance is General Metz. We believe that you can help us contact General Metz.'

There was silence in the room. Lamarque tapped his lip reflectively. Then he said, 'General Metz is a ghost now. He is a dream.'

'Perhaps only a dream can save France now.' De Boeldieu was more earnest than usual.

Roscarrock: 'We believe that the General can be real again, and that he must be real again. If he does not inspire a reaction against Napoleon now, the opportunity will not come again. This is the last chance for Britain as well as for France. Britain will give every possible support to the General.'

'In what form would that support be?'

'In the form of gold coin. Guineas. Lots of them.'

A nod. 'We are not mercenaries, Mr Roscarrock.'

'But idealism can be expensive, can't it? Besides, you need to know we're serious.' Roscarrock's head came forwards. 'Britain is on the brink, Monsieur. If Napoleon is not slowed or distracted now, he will conquer us easily. If he conquers Britain, it is the end of resistance in Europe. Napoleon will rule France and the Continent untouchable, and his descendants will follow him.'

Then De Boeldieu was speaking, a sudden torrent of emotional French that Roscarrock had no hope of following. The old man stirred for the first time, gave a loud sniff from the depths of his trance, and resided. Lamarque listened impassively to the speech, and when it finished gave only another thoughtful nod.

'And if the General decides that he wishes to discuss this with you?'

Roscarrock was still watching the uncle. 'I had hoped,' he said carefully, 'that we could have reached that point already.' He turned to Lamarque. 'We can arrange a place that we both consider safe.'

'And if the General wishes to see the... resources?'

'They can be brought to this district in the same period.'

The farmer paused to consider. Then he stood. Roscarrock and De Boeldieu did the same, uncertain. 'I guarantee that the General will consider your offer, nothing more. If he is interested, we will contact you. If not, you will hear nothing. Do not come to this farm again.'

There was another loud sniff from the old man. Two very blue eyes opened in the brown face, and stared out into the room.

'You are the young De Boeldieu?' The voice was as sharp and strong as the gaze.

'Sir, I am the only De Boeldieu.'

The walnut of a face wrinkled and peered. 'You were a fop: a dilettante, a waster.'

De Boeldieu scowled in irritation, and then pulled himself straight. 'With God's will, those good days will return.'

The old man pressed on. 'But now you live as a hunted man, sneaking between hovels of the countryside.'

De Boeldieu's grace was fading. 'There's been a Revolution, *Grand-père*, or didn't the news reach here?'

The crystal eyes regarded De Boeldieu sternly. 'The Count, your father, would be very surprised at you, young man. And very proud I think.'

De Boeldieu turned and left. Roscarrock gave polite thanks from them both, shook hands with Lamarque, and then stopped in front of the old man's chair. 'I look forward to seeing you again, Monsieur le... Oncle.' He nodded respectfully, and a minute later they were passing back through the lane of swaying grain.

'The old man?'

'I think so too,' De Boeldieu said.

'But will he act?'

News of the mortal scuffle by the new canal in Burnley did not reach Sir Keith Kinnaird for several days, and then only in the form of a report on the report, scanned quickly in a room looking down onto the mail-coach stand at York as the gasping horses were led away. But the details were clearer to him than to anyone.

M rpt from B—y (Lu) tells of canalside scuffle involving one + suspected industrial spy/wrecker, and subsequent d., presumed related, of man provisionally id as GARROD, previously believed d. Lord Oakworth.

[SS K/17/98]

The second of his dead men was dead to him as well as to the world.

Garrod, the Engineer, had been testing the Comptrollerate-General's activities in the area of industry and manufacture. He had got too close to a French secret agent of destruction. It had been an unnecessary distraction, and now angry, earnest, wounded Garrod was dead.

That left Christiansen and Roscarrock; the Schoolmaster and the Sailor. Two dead men against the Comptrollerate-General.

And now Roscarrock had gone into France. His single-mindedness, his courage, and his storm-forged sailor's wits had carried him further than anyone could have imagined possible, right to the heart of the Comptrollerate-General.

And now, because of him, the Comptrollerate-General was more vulnerable than at any time in its history, and with it the stability of the Empire.

By lunchtime they were in Abbeville, upriver from St Valery and the first crossing point on the Somme. De Boeldieu's contacts had found them good horses, but they rode them loose and slow so as not to draw attention to themselves. The Frenchman did all the talking whenever there was anyone else around, and amused himself with high-handed attitudes to his servant Roscarrock. On the outskirts of the town they found the Auberge de la Tour, and within it a bland, soulless room that De Boeldieu had picked deliberately, and settled in one corner.

After half an hour another man came in, bought a drink, and sat at a table near them. Fifteen minutes more, and polite phrases were exchanged. De Boeldieu offered the man a drink, and he joined them.

Paul Desmoulins was a navy Quartermaster based in Boulogne but working all over the region to manage supply for the vast machine of consumption that was Napoleon's Army of the Ocean Coasts, and the fleet of transports and escorts that would convoy it. The circumstances allowed no more than polite formalities and a gentle murmur of chat, but Roscarrock could see the warmth with which the trim officer gazed at De Boeldieu when he first sat down. The loneliness of the men they met in these days manifested itself differently in each case, but it burnt strong.

Desmoulins was pedantic and a little pompous, but Roscarrock could see De Boeldieu staring hard as he tried to store the quiet stream of facts coming out of the official's mouth. He described the disposition of the army, much of which they'd already heard, but which could have changed and might offer clues to the plan of invasion itself. He described the location and condition of ships, the movements and the embarkation rehearsals. He described the massive effort to amass food and military supplies for the invasion fleet, and what this meant for the durability of the force. He described what he knew and what he'd heard of the French navy in its various ports and at sea. He said nothing about the Emperor's Sharks.

Roscarrock began to murmur questions in a slow, stiff French that had De Boeldieu checking the room in concern. What had Desmoulins heard of a private fleet of the Emperor? A special fleet? A special mission? How could such a fleet be sustained if not through his organization? Was there someone like him elsewhere, an equivalent, who would know of supply and disposition?

Desmoulins knew nothing of this. He made suggestions about how the fleet might be manned, and sustained, and where it might be based, and what it might be doing. But he was more pomposity than pedantry now. Roscarrock felt his own frustration, the sour flush of disappointment that this daring and dangerous foray away from the coast was proving irrelevant. He could see disappointment in De Boeldieu's eyes too: this was the key naval source in Kinnaird's French network, but Kinnaird's French network was not delivering on the single question that most mattered to the British Empire.

De Boeldieu thanked his old comrade. 'You look a little tired, Paul,' he said softly, and his hand rose as if wanting to touch the other's arm. 'You should get a little rest.'

The navy Quartermaster frowned. He licked his lips, and glanced at Roscarrock. Then he gave a formulaic dismissal of the suggestion, thanked them for his drink, and left.

De Boeldieu wandered to the counter and knocked on it, trying to rouse the landlord to offer food. Roscarrock watched him go, and he was still watching him as he sat again.

'Whatever it is, we were better to have brought some of that damn soup.'

Roscarrock ignored the comment. 'You're closing the network, aren't you?' he said quietly. De Boeldieu watched him carefully over the table. 'Closing – perhaps just suspending. But that's what you're doing – this phrase you use. Yesterday morning you told your official friend, Monsieur Jean, that he looked tired and should get some rest, and today exactly the same phrase again. I couldn't think what it meant. Monsieur Desmoulins is going to turn deserter, isn't he, and make for the hills? Same with Monsieur Jean.' He leant forwards, and hissed: 'Why, Philippe? What are you up to?'

Philippe De Boeldieu folded his arms, and said softly, 'Because I do not know what is happening, in England or in France, and I will not risk this network while I wait to find out.' His head tilted as if seeking an alternative view. 'And yes, Mr Roscarrock, I include you in my doubts most certainly.'

'Kinnaird's network – your network – these men may be all we have left.'

'These men cannot save us, Roscarrock. They do not have the answers you need – the story... the story is beyond them somehow. There is nothing they can do to stop this fleet, and I do not see they should risk their lives while we wait for it to come.'

Roscarrock sat back, and pawed at one side of his face with a slow hand. 'Did Kinnaird tell you to do this? To cut us off?'

'It's simple,' De Boeldieu unfolded his arms and clasped his hands neatly. 'If Kinnaird was somehow still good, he would want me to do this; if he is bad, I do not care what he thinks. Either way, I must take responsibility for the network myself.'

Roscarrock chewed on this. Eventually, still watching the Frenchman, he took one deep breath and said, 'All right, Philippe. The next meeting? Here, or do we move again?'

'Here. I would not dream of missing whatever poor rodent the landlord is currently scraping up from his yard for our lunch.' He shifted in the chair, and resettled himself. 'Maybe this time we find some more about your fleet, yes? This should be your agent who reported the Sharks most recently, I think.'

'You've met him?'

A shake of the head. Roscarrock held up a finger as the landlord approached with two bowls, dropped them onto the table, and left. 'No. I am not the only man – or woman – who meets these people.' De Boeldieu looked down into the grey broth, and shivered. 'I just have the highest standards.'

Source 'Malmsey' was a man in his thirties, nervy, arrogant and well-dressed – under a coat that was dirty and too large for him. He insisted on speaking English. He introduced himself as a close acquaintance of Marshal Soult and navy Minister Decrès, amongst others, then launched into a description of a supper he'd attended in Paris three evenings previously. He offered colourful character sketches of his notable companions, and a beautifully balanced generalization on the mentality of the conversation.

De Boeldieu interrupted him: where was Minister Decrès now?

Malmsey didn't know: Decrès, like so many of the Emperor's Ministers, was an ornament and not an organ of his Ministry.

De Boeldieu asked about the disposition of the French fleets. Malmsey didn't know, brushed away the question. Roscarrock wondered if De Boeldieu's antipathy was pique at having to deal with an agent who wasn't part of his own network.

The stilted conversation continued, De Boeldieu's blunt questions disrupting the flow of the spy's fragile wit.

Roscarrock realized that the dirty coat was Malmsey's attempt at disguise. He started with questions of his own, speaking in French to try to encourage the man to greater discretion. In the most recent report from Malmsey – Malmsey perked up – there was talk of the Emperor's Sharks. What more could he say about the fleet?

The spy smiled at his French, and continued in English: he did not know, of course, about these details of fleets; his reports covered strategy.

'But in the report you said the Emperor was pleased, and confident, about the fleet; you described how it had taken resources from elsewhere in the navy.'

'But this fleet, it is secret! Who can know such details? I have heard only a very few references – a word here from an admiral, a word there from a secretary of Decrès – they do not know much themselves, of course, but they confide in me.'

'Monsieur, your report was very specific.'

'Oh, the technical details were from her, your very lovely colleague with whom I spoke. She was seeking my judgements, as one familiar with the politics and the strategy.'

Lady Virginia Strong, presumably. But where had she got it from? 'In the report, you called the fleet the "Emperor's Sharks".'

'Oh, yes! It is amusing, this name. I had not heard it before. But this is most typical of the Emperor's style.'

'Who would know about the details?'

'Decrès will know something, but perhaps not details. No doubt there are clerks who could tell you of the details of supply. If it is so secret, Fouché himself must know what is happening. In the great chamber of imperial activity, most men have at best a simple candle. Fouché has the lantern; Fouché is the lighthouse. If you could find his plans, you would know everything.'

'And the assassination that was mentioned, you know nothing of that?'

'No, I have not heard of this.'

The conversation stalled rapidly. De Boeldieu was brusque; Roscarrock was absorbed in all that he had heard and read. The man in front of them, realizing their disenchantment, tried a final summary of the brittleness of society around an over-centralized and secretive Government, then subsided, surly.

De Boeldieu and Roscarrock waited fifteen minutes after a rather crestfallen Malmsey had hurried out, and then left themselves, unspeaking. De Boeldieu led them immediately into a network of back alleys, a different route to their horses. A short distance, and he started to murmur his thoughts on the meeting. Then Roscarrock, listening close, saw the sudden stiffening of his face, the surprise, and followed his gaze down the alley. Appearing around a corner was Malmsey: for some unfathomable reason, he had come back to the vicinity of the meeting and was walking towards them. He stared in immediate discomfort when he saw them, and hurried on, head down as he neared.

The briefest shared glance, and Roscarrock and De Boeldieu continued past him, keeping up a murmured conversation. Soon Malmsey was behind them, and they walked on. But they couldn't miss the sudden shout of surprise, had to turn back to look. Malmsey was at a junction of the alleys, backing away towards them. As he retreated, his whole body rigid and alarmed, another man followed him, stepping uneasily forwards as Malmsey stepped uneasily backwards. They stared at each other, panicked and uncertain, and then the newcomer pulled his coat aside, apprehension and malice fighting on his face. In an instinct of action that surprised his observers, Malmsey snatched forwards at the other's waistband and pulled out the knife and stabbed its owner in the stomach. Then he was retreating again, stumbling and confused, weaving towards Roscarrock and De Boeldieu with pleading hysterical eyes.

'An informer! He's a police informer! We know each other from years back!' Roscarrock got only a few words from the desperate gabble, but enough. He and De Boeldieu were checking all around them, and then De Boeldieu had grabbed the flailing man by the shoulders.

'What are you doing back here?'

'I doubled back – in case I was being followed – so they could not easily follow—'

'Amateur!' A vicious spit from De Boeldieu. 'Moron. And—'

'That's Nicolin – the spy – he's a police spy – he must have recognized—'

'And now he's seen all of us.' Roscarrock spoke over his shoulder, halfway towards the man on the ground. The man was a rolling, groaning bundle, hands clutched to his gut and covered with his blood. It was a terrible, clumsy wound; the spy could have many hours of suffering before he died – and time enough to talk.

Roscarrock looked at De Boeldieu; the Frenchman gave him the slightest of shrugs, a face of resignation and pity.

Roscarrock shook his head grimly. He stepped forwards, and knelt beside the informer. As gently as he could, he pulled the knife from the man's gut. Then he placed his hand over the man's mouth, and stabbed him in the heart.

Malmsey watched this horror, and as Roscarrock rolled the corpse into the ditch at the side of alley, he turned to face De Boeldieu again.

'You killed him, you miserable bastard.' De Boeldieu's face was deadly. 'And probably us too. Now get out of here.'

'But – can't I—'

'No.'

Malmsey stepped away reluctantly, glancing rapidly at the various alleyways. 'This way.' Roscarrock was near them again. 'The way you were going. Don't stop, don't make sudden turns or detours. And lose that stupid coat as soon as possible.'

Wide-eyed and small, Malmsey scurried into the warren of back streets. Roscarrock and De Boeldieu had a final glance for any sign that this melodrama had been observed, then strode away to recover their horses.

Two British spies, now party to the murder of a police informant, they stood at the French roadside.

Roscarrock said, 'The coast?'

De Boeldieu pointed an elegant finger to the left.

'The next meeting?'

The finger pointed right. 'Amiens. Halfway to Paris.'

Tom Roscarrock looked at his companion's sour, stolid face, and smiled maliciously at him. Then he pulled at his horse's neck, and set off through the dust towards Paris.

'I don't care if the imbecile is dead!' They'd never seen the Inspector like this. 'He deserved to die! I'd have killed him myself if the English hadn't saved me the trouble.' Gabin had one substantial fist wrapped around the remains of a collar, knuckles pressing into the man's throat. Now he pushed the gasping face away with a final roar of frustration, and turned to the other policemen in the room. 'Your informer is irrelevant, you hear me? I don't care if all your informers drown in the Somme tomorrow.' His boots kicked up flour dust as he stalked around the pale faces. 'Let me explain: on the one hand, the glory of France, the triumph of the Emperor, the triumph' – he stabbed a heavy finger at his ambitious deputy – 'of those who deliver him success. On the other, the life of a gutter spy. Now, you tell me if that matters.' The voice was calmer now, but the heaviness seemed more ominous. 'Bring me another informer. Bring one now, and I'll kill him myself if that'll help you understand this. It is vital – it is vital!' – he almost screamed the word – 'that the Englishman Roscarrock is free to operate. If the incompetence of this morning causes a restriction in his movements, then we are all, my friends, finished.'

Yesterday a deputation of merchants and banking men, styling themselves the Defenders Of Sound Money And Good Trade, were received by the Senior Secretary to His Majesty's Treasury, Mr Huskisson. Their discussions have not been made public, by agreement of both parties. Nonetheless, their themes may easily be assumed by those familiar with the recent trends in economic debate.

The scarcity and the unnaturally high price of gold, consequent to the extreme and prolonged expenses of war and a regrettable tendency to hoard coin, have become commonplaces of complaint among men of business in recent years. An exaggerated discretion by His Majesty's Treasury on the state of the nation's gold reserves has not encouraged confidence, nor has the continued failure to mint the new guinea coins planned following the Union with Ireland five years ago. Gold and confidence are ebbing from London and from Britain, with the predictable and most harmful effect on prices and on stability.

The late public disturbances were a grievous blow to confidence. In combination with the precarious state of the war, they have raised a tumult among even level-headed men of business as well as having an inflammatory effect on the mob. Gentlemen, well before the close of the London season, are shutting up their houses in town and retiring with their families to farther country estates or for prolonged periods of travel abroad. The Duke of Beaufort has, without precedent, cancelled his annual reception. Loyal financiers and merchants sentimental for London's continued pre-eminence as a city of trade as well as liberty will have prayed for some practical resolution in yesterday's meeting. The rest are already shifting their activities to neutral lands and seeking means to accommodate their fortunes to the rise of Paris.

[THE TIMES, LONDON, 10TH AUGUST 1805]

11th August 1805

Roscarrock and De Boeldieu slept at the vilest tavern they could find, a little off the main road. There was too much traffic on the road to be able to spot an observer. Later the next morning they reached Amiens, drawn into the sprawl of complacent townhouses and grim slums by the white mass of the cathedral that soared over the city, its vast, tiered frontage dwarfing the earthly buildings and busy finials scraping the sky. Again they stopped short of the prosperous centre and waited in a forgotten tavern of the outskirts. A one-legged landlord slumped on a stool behind the counter; just one other customer, sitting upright in a corner and playing patience with a greasy deck; silence, under the slap of the cards. Faintly, as they sat and drank and waited, Roscarrock had a perverse urge to rush to that great whale of a building at the heart of the city, just to prove that he was capable of escaping this life in the margins.

Half an hour after they had arrived, the patience player ambled across the flagstones and asked if either of them fancied a game. De Boeldieu grunted agreement, and the man sat. He was a big man, stocky but not fat, staring sombrely at the world from a heavy, jowled face. He shuffled for piquet, and De Boeldieu cut. By the time that the stranger had pulled a squat pencil from a pocket and started to tot up the first elements of their scores on the tabletop, the three of them were talking softly.

De Boeldieu checked that the man behind the counter was still out of earshot. 'Monsieur Jacques is the landlord of a tavern in Paris,' he said quietly, 'and a man with many excellent contacts. He is a scholar, and a well-known card cheat.'

'A scholar?'

The heavy face swung slowly to Roscarrock. 'In the end, bottles were cheaper than books.' He turned back to his cards. 'Besides, books live longer in the memory than wine. Tell me, Monsieur' – he leant intently towards De Boeldieu – 'I must know; have you heard anything of little Joseph?'

De Boeldieu stopped fiddling with his cards. 'He made it to London, and—'

'To London?'

'All the way to London. He died in my arms.'

Monsieur Jacques shook his head slowly. 'To London! I did not think he would get to the end of the street.' He pulled absently at a card. 'Great hearts grow in the strangest places.' A grunt from De Boeldieu. 'Monsieur, I have a few pages of notes which I will pass you next time I deal. I am afraid there is little substance to them.'

De Boeldieu's eyes stayed on his cards. 'What about the Emperor's secret fleet? Napoleon's Sharks – what do we know?'

There was a grumble from within the man's throat. 'Gossip: a little; from the navy, and from the police. Facts: none. Fouché is very excited, though.' He scrawled another number on the table. 'His wife is in her forties and fattening by the day, and Fouché dines regularly with Madame Messines. That dry insect of a man fancies himself a philanderer; at least it makes Madame feel influential and allows me to get useful insights from her footmen. She asked him whether he wasn't worried by the Royal Navy. He apparently said, "Ships? I have some English souls, and their ships follow."'

'It's your lead, my friend.' De Boeldieu examined his cards again. 'But nothing on the planning for this fleet?'

Monsieur Jacques laid his first card. 'Nothing at all, Monsieur. I have three different sources who confirm that Fouché has some great plan involving such a fleet, and the defeat of the British, but I can get nothing on the details of the fleet or its movements.' He shook his head ponderously. 'I have never met such an unbreakable secret. Fouché is a humourless man, but he's very pleased with his plotting at the moment. That worries me more than anything, Monsieur.'

The tricks were taken rapidly and without interest. Roscarrock said, 'I assumed that the unrest in London was influenced by Paris.'

The large man looked momentarily at him. 'Oh, that is certain. Fouché is most entertained at how Britain weakens herself. This outrage you experienced in London last week, I have no doubt that he knew in advance that it would happen. The last report from Joseph showed this also.' Roscarrock nodded. 'And the details of the events – the rebellion by the soldiers, the load of gunpowder that is enough to frighten but not to destroy – he retells these things with great amusement. There was an Irishman, I think? Fann...?'

Another nod from the Englishman. 'Fannion.'

'Fouché proposed a toast to the events in London after he had heard of them. "A week ago I did not know the name of this Irishman," he said, "and now I am in his debt." He said he was looking forward to meeting him.'

'That's very interesting.' Roscarrock's face was dark and intent; he shook his head, trying to absorb the points. 'He was going to meet the Irishman?'

'He suggested so. He has left Paris now.'

'You have impressive knowledge of Fouché – even after Joseph had escaped from his service.'

A little smile appeared within the heavy jowls. 'We cheat, Monsieur.' Roscarrock frowned in interest. 'We benefit from the jealousies of the Government. The French navy distrust the Emperor and his plans, and Decrès – the Minister – hates Fouché. The sailors are unhappy that soldiers rule the Empire. They are worried that Villeneuve and the rest of their fleets will be sacrificed unnecessarily. So the navy have one or two spies who report back to them on Fouché and his activities. What they don't know is that some of this information then reaches me. I have spies who report on the spies. It's most convenient.'

They spoke about Joseph again, about the man who had hunted him. Over the second hand of cards, De Boeldieu asked about Paris and former acquaintances. Over the third, he prodded again for insights on Napoleon's fleet and Fouché's plotting. The fourth hand passed in silence, just the flick of the cards in the lifeless tavern, and Roscarrock saw the frustration in De Boeldieu's face.

By the end of the fourth hand, Monsieur Jacques had won. He gathered up the cards, and looked at the two men opposite him sombrely.

Roscarrock said, 'You look rather tired, Monsieur Jacques.'

De Boeldieu's face darted round to the Englishman, then away more slowly. He nodded. 'He's right. You should get some rest, Jacques.'

Monsieur Jacques digested this. He nodded once at De Boeldieu with heavy finality, then stood and walked away with the greasy pack of cards buried in his big fist.

Outside, De Boeldieu said wearily, 'And he too knew nothing of these Sharks.'

Roscarrock spoke pleasantly. 'I didn't expect he would.' De Boeldieu's face spun to him, looking for the insult. 'Now, are we off to interview the Empress, or can we get back to the coast now?'

They rode in silence at first. De Boeldieu threw occasional glances at his companion, and eventually spoke. 'My friend, our disappointments continue to grow, but you are become more serene. Is the situation of Britain somehow less desperate than I understand?'

Roscarrock thought for a moment. 'No, the situation is very grim indeed. Without clear information on this magical French fleet, there is every chance that the navy will be unable to stop a French invasion. We are the only people who can get that information out, and we are in the middle of France with much work ahead of us.'

'And we don't even know the information! Yet you are calm.'

Roscarrock was watching the horizon, face inscrutable and hands easy with the reins. 'Kinnaird once told me that there would come a time when I might have to be myself again.' He smiled privately. 'I think that time is very near.'

———～———

Jessel knocked softly, but the Admiral's head flicked up irritably. He was looking worried, Jessel thought – less certain than he had always seemed.

The heavy eyes just watched him. 'This summary has finally been collated, My Lord: Roscarrock.' He passed over the pages, rolled tight.

Now there was interest in the eyes – almost a hunger.

'As we suspected, there have been several Roscarrocks of interest in Ireland. No Tom Roscarrock that we have records of, but a whole family of that surname active in Wexford and Dublin. Radicals the lot of them, certainly, and at least three brothers were part of the United Irish movement in '98. One killed at Vinegar Hill, one executed, one escaped. They were too smart to get involved in Emmet's rising two years back, but one or more of the Roscarrocks keeps appearing in reports about the continuing local unrest until it finally died down last year.'

Admiral Bellamy was nodding very slowly. 'That's fascinating. Where's this from?'

'Our files, and additional researches with Dublin and Belfast.'

'Anything else?'

'Yes, My Lord.' Jessel was letting his own excitement show now. 'America: again, there's nothing clear, but a Tadh Roscarrock – God knows how they pronounce that – sailed from the colonies to France in '96, at the same time as the Irish representatives trying to get support for their rising. New York to Le Havre on the *Jersey*, January 1796. Age twenty-eight, which would be about right. Then – this is just an accidental observation by our clerk, My Lord, but one rather wonders – a Thomas Ross sailed from America to Dublin in 1801.'

'Once things had died down a little.' A nod. The Admiral stared fierce into the distance. 'Damnit, Jessel, could our man really be one of this crew? That would be something else, wouldn't it?' The gaze refocused.

'Unfortunately, this is a week late to be of practical use to us. Whoever he is, he's loose in France, and we can only wait to see what he's up to.'

———————

Inspector Gabin arrived back at the mill in the middle of the afternoon. The meeting with Minister Fouché had been brief and typically direct. The Emperor was becoming increasingly distracted by the reports of Austria's mobilization in the east. Diplomatic protests would do for the moment, but soon he would have to consider a punitive reminder of who now ruled in Europe. It was more imperative than ever that the invasion of England happened quickly. Minister Fouché had insisted to the Emperor that a few more days would see the final success of his plan for the neutralization of the Royal Navy. Minister Fouché had stated to Inspector Gabin, with ominous clarity that invited no debate, his expectation that the Inspector would successfully conclude the St Valery part of the operation accordingly. Inspector Gabin had given his assurance, and left.

'Monsieur l'Inspecteur?'

Gabin looked up into the worried face. At first he'd thought the lad was a true-blooded revolutionary – there were a few around still – but he'd turned out to be just an old-fashioned, ambitious little sod.

'I am sorry to disturb you.' Gabin tried to look more encouraging; perhaps the young man was not, after all, reporting another failure. 'It's probably trivial. But you insisted that we should share every detail of these people.'

Gabin nodded, then held up a finger; it would do no harm to cultivate the local man. 'A lesson in police politics, my young friend, since you seem like a fellow who wants to get on.' There was no reply, but the brightening of the face told everything. 'Incompetence and failure and disloyalty will cost you, and rightly so. But never be afraid to seem stupid. Some genuinely rather stupid men have made impressive careers for themselves. And half the time stupidity is just lack of guidance. Sometimes, indeed, stupidity turns out to be brilliance.'

'It's just local gossip, really, but you asked for every detail and discrepancy.' Gabin waited; this looked like it was going to be stupidity after all. 'The farmer Lamarque; where the Englishman visited.' Gabin tried to maintain the encouragement in his face. 'He has a wife, and two daughters, and his old uncle. Well, I was going through the reports, and it's just that one old lady we were speaking to said in passing that Lamarque's uncle died ten years ago.'

Now Gabin smiled for real.

⟡

De Boeldieu and Roscarrock were the rest of the day on the road back from Amiens, and the muffling peace of the summer evening had covered the land by the time they reached the outskirts of St Valery-sur-Somme. They were sore after a day in the saddle, and had long ago run out of things to say to each other. They avoided the centre of the village, but De Boeldieu stopped them at Marceau's, a rambling and decrepit hovel passing itself off as a tavern. He went inside, leaving Roscarrock inconspicuous under nearby trees, keeping an eye on the horses and trying with a clumsy hand to restore normal circulation to his legs.

De Boeldieu was back within a minute. 'Two messages. One good – the General will meet us – officially this time, I guess. Tomorrow night. We must decide where.'

Satisfaction cracked Roscarrock's tiredness. 'Good. That's good. Can he come to us at the farm? It's closer if he wants a look at the gold.'

'Very well. I'll ask. The second message is perhaps not so good.' De Boeldieu's usual flamboyance was flattened by exhaustion; he thrust a scrap of paper into Roscarrock's hand. 'Ah, my Roscarrock: even in France, the ladies, they reach out to you.' The words fell heavy. Roscarrock was trying to decipher the handwriting and the French. 'From my friends.

Their ears, their eyes, they are well spread. Your friend Mrs Van Vliet – the fair Lady Virginia – was noted in an hotel in Étaples this morning. She was heard to say that she was heading for the town of Rue, in connection with some unfinished business of her late husband.' Roscarrock's jaw had tightened. 'Does that phrase mean something?'

'It does. It means she needs help, and badly.' Roscarrock shook his head, and reached for his horse. 'That damn woman draws trouble.'

'She draws you, my friend. She is an elegant blonde woman with a most charming figure, and she is a spy; there has been no greater force for trouble since Eve.' He put a hand on Roscarrock's arm. 'I cannot go, my friend. I have business here this evening and through the night.'

'I know. Better this way.' He was pulling himself painfully up onto the horse again.

'Oh, I interrupt your liai—'

'Just tell me where on earth Rue is.'

'I'm serious, your French is not—'

'I have to go! She may have vital intelligence about the Sharks. And—'

De Boeldieu patted him on the knee. 'And I understand, my friend. Maybe there is a bit of the Frenchman in you.'

Roscarrock scowled. 'Philippe, is there any chance of a fresh horse?'

'From Marceau? Are you deranged? That man cooks any mammal that enters the district, and not well.'

<hr />

FIELD REPORT, WRITTEN THE 11TH DAY OF AUGUST 1805

Chatham. An attempt was last night made on the life of Mr Fulton. As his coach progressed from London towards this place, it was accosted while crossing the Bexley Heath. Two horsemen emerged from the scrub and ordered the coach to stop. Though this desert place is notorious, their indifference to the coachman, their failure to make any reference to

*valuables, and their lack of any bags to carry off their gains, lead me strongly
to suspect that these were no highway robbers. I was riding separately behind
the coach according to our practice and, as they approached it, I engaged
the men with pistol and sword, ordering the coach to drive on. The assassins
loosed three wild shots at the coach as it escaped, but then did not linger as I
advanced. The American is peevish but unharmed, and I have him fast and
well-protected in the town here.*

[SS X/42/61]

The little town of Rue was north of the Somme estuary, and Roscarrock
cantered towards it in the last of the light, easing his horse to a trot
as he got closer. Fortunately De Boeldieu's directions had been good,
along with the horse that he'd procured by some triumph of influence
or larceny.

He rode through slowly, getting an idea of the town and where Virginia
Strong might be staying. A line of dull stone and plaster frontages huddled
under a fantastical tower in the centre, its miniature turrets shaming their
ordinariness and disappearing into the deep blue sky. Fortunately there
was only one establishment on the main street that would be acceptable
for a Dutchwoman of quality or an English spy accustomed to moving in
high society, and Roscarrock tried to mark the pattern of side streets and
shadows around it as he passed.

He reached the far edge of Rue, and tethered his horse in an alley where
there was less chance of it being seen or stolen. Then he made his way
back towards the centre on foot. The hotel Lion d'Or was unlikely to
have a tavern room dingy and inhospitable enough for a spy to remain
unobtrusive, so he'd have to find somewhere outside where he could watch
and wait for a sign of the lady.

He was still some distance short of the hotel when a coach overtook him, rattling and lurching on the uneven road. The coach was closed, which made for a basic comfort – but not at all ornate, so probably not privately owned. Perhaps a public passenger coach, then – and Roscarrock tried to remember how far Étaples was from Rue, and how long the journey would take. No form of idiosyncrasy or bravado was beyond Lady Virginia Strong, but travelling as a grieving and prudent Dutch woman she was much more likely to travel by coach than horse, and there would not be many coaches during the day.

The coach stopped outside the hotel, with a final stamping of its horses' feet and creakings of its strained springs. The driver dropped heavily into the roadway, the little door opened and he helped down a tall figure in full cloak and hood. She moved quickly to the door of the hotel but, as the driver pulled it open and she turned to thank him, the light from inside shone brilliant on her face and a golden frame of hair under the hood. Something kicked inside Roscarrock, and then he scowled at his own susceptibility.

Others were getting down from the coach now; it might be continuing to Abbeville tonight, but the travellers would be given the chance of a drink first. Roscarrock was suddenly aware of someone near him. He'd heard the brisk beating of hooves, but his attention had been on the coach and that shining face. The horseman had stopped only a few yards beyond him, in the middle of the street, and was now watching the hotel as intently as he had done.

Roscarrock slipped further into the shadows, and watched the horseman.

The last of the passengers having descended, the coachman climbed up again and the vehicle lumbered a short distance out of the way of the hotel entrance. The horseman watched this, and then kicked his horse into a cautious walk. Roscarrock waited. Just across the street from the hotel, the rider turned into an alley. Roscarrock waited a little longer, but there was nothing more to see. He crossed the road himself and disappeared into the back streets.

There were days when Virginia Strong felt that she was gliding over the world, and she loved them. Too much of life was defined by the structures and rules of others. The restrictions of society, of conventions, of governments, were those of just another frigid governess and she first writhed against them and then created a life where she only conformed when it suited or amused her. This was such a day – of life, of pleasure, of gliding. No one could touch her, as she moved between England and France. Today she was Dutch, and it meant nothing. She could have been Italian or Turk and still she would have soared down the French coast, unrattled by the coach, unhindered by the soldiers, untouched by the war and the world. She could even have been English to the boy downstairs if she'd wanted to; she would have found a justification, a way to make it first attractive, and from there to make it acceptable. To be French would be hard, even if you wanted that restriction of identity and loyalty. But to be acceptably not French, that was easy. An Englishwoman, with a Dutch name, speaking French: she sailed through Europe as she chose, a spirit free of restraint and identity. She was not an English spy; she wasn't an English anything. Nor was she French, nor Dutch. She was neither heroine nor traitoress. She was neither impudent nor undignified. There was no wrong place to be, no wrong thing to do. She was a free creature of the world, moving as she pleased.

The practicalities of life were tiresome: the long registration process with the rather pretty young man behind the desk; having to come down again to complain at the linen, to command laundry, food, hot water. But she stood outside herself through it all. Climbing back up the stairs, this free creature of the world was looking forward to washing herself and eating a hot meal. When she locked the door and turned to face her room, Tom Roscarrock was standing by the bed.

She stifled a gasp. Then she walked quickly to him and kissed him on the cheek.

Roscarrock frowned. 'Your message said you needed my help.'

'Help, never,' she said. 'You... always. I think someone's been following me.'

'They have.'

'They could be outside now.'

'They were.' She frowned. 'They're now unconscious, gagged and tied, and under a pile of straw in a stable. We should be going.'

The tiniest flash of wonder flared in her eyes and mouth. 'You're mighty competent, Tom Roscarrock. Getting in here like that, too.'

'If I can manage your corset, a shed roof and a window aren't much of a challenge.'

She undid the clasp at her neck, and pulled the cloak back off her shoulders. Under it she wore a simple white dress in the French style, tight on her breasts and showing her hips as she walked to a chair to drop the cloak and kick off her shoes and then came back towards him.

She stopped in the centre of the room, as if finding her place on a stage. Then she looked at Roscarrock and, as though suddenly free of some great constraint, her face opened with an exhilaration that she could no longer suppress. Her eyes shone wide, her hands covered her mouth in a final moment of disbelief, and then dropped to release a long breath of excitement.

'I met him, Tom!' There was no affectation or control in the voice now. 'Napoleon! The Emperor himself – I met him.'

He nodded his genuine respect, and watched the unfamiliar honesty with interest. 'What's he like?'

'Small!' She shook her head at the recollection. 'An amazing man, truly. All that nonsense people have talked about him... But he really is extraordinary. A clarity, a conviction, and a... a drive. I'm not sure he's as intelligent as they think, but he's harnessed the whole power of France simply by being quicker to seize a chance than anyone else – and by sheer charisma. I just don't see the old societies of Europe being able to produce a man to challenge him.'

'And his secret fleet?'

'I have it all.' She waited for the reaction.

He smiled. 'Honestly, I never doubted it.' She flickered with interest at his sincerity. 'Kinnaird's network, the rest of the Comptrollerate-General, they couldn't do it. But you did.'

'Tom, I think you're actually impressed.'

'You know where the fleet is?'

'It'll be gathering within the next two days. As soon as I can get the message out, our navy can move to intercept them.'

'Of course. We should be going.' He turned towards the window, then hesitated. 'I hope the associate of Emperors will not mind clambering over an outside privy to escape.'

She frowned. 'We're not going now, surely.' He looked the question. 'We can't get anywhere, on land or sea, in pitch darkness.'

'At least I can hide you somewhere else in town.'

'I'm staying! I have no desire to spend the night in one of your stables.' Behind the petulance there was professional calculation. 'Whoever's after me thinks I'm safely under watch here. Better to let them think that, than risk drawing attention to both of us, which we'd surely risk if we had to steal a horse or ride together.' She lifted one delicate eyebrow. 'I am... a little distinctive, Tom. Besides, this is much the most comfortable place to spend the night.'

He observed the performance. 'De Boeldieu calls you the greatest force for trouble since Eve. I'm liking that man more and more.'

She was wary. 'Are you sure which side he's on?'

'I don't know which side I'm on myself. He and I have a healthy relationship of affection based on strong mutual distrust. Tell me about Napoleon's Sharks.'

She pouted, but it was too girlish an affectation for her elegance. 'I'd romantic notions of you, Tom Roscarrock. Perhaps you've been corrupted into bureaucracy after all.' The glittering eyes and fidgeting body still burnt with her excitement.

'Wouldn't you rather pursue your romantic notions after you've escaped to England and saved the Empire?'

She was breathing hard, an animal after the chase. 'This might be our last night on earth; who wants to talk politics?'

Her exhilaration would not be contained, and as Roscarrock kissed the scar above her nose, and pulled the dress away from her shoulders and let it breathe down her body to the floorboards, he rediscovered another part of himself. In a world where death waited in every shift of wind and waves, a man took his pleasures as he found them. She was right in that, at least. Every aspect of existence in the last weeks had become a veil: loyalties, affections, and even identities were distortions. He must start with what he knew. He was a man; he would sustain his life for as long as he could, and while alive he would truly live, by his beliefs and his instincts. He pushed his fingers into her hair, pulled her face up towards his, and his other hand moved down firm over the small of her back and on towards the swell of her rump.

They made love outside the ruled world, rolling free and wild, waves over the rocks, water eroding stone, each confident in their own secrets and an equal spirit. Later, lying on her side with the sheet still tangled around her legs, watching his profile and the rise and fall of his chest, the fierce marks of her possession still plain across it, she said, 'Who are you?'

The profile turned to her for a second. 'I'm waiting for someone to tell me.'

She poked him in the side. 'Don't play with me.' More gently: 'Kinnaird knew that you'd been in Ireland; America.'

He pushed his head back into the pillow. 'All right. My family is Irish, though I've spent most of my life out of the place. The Roscarrocks are from the south-west of the country: Cork and around. My father disappeared when I was young – we were always told he was taken by the British, but I guess there was some Irish politics mixed up in it as well. You'll never have heard of Conor Roscarrock, but around Cork they still sing of him.' He glanced at her again; she laid a hand on the muscles of his stomach. 'I was the youngest. My mother I think wanted to keep me out of the worst of it. So I was schooled away from home, and sent travelling. America, when I was older. It was an exciting time to be there – a new country creating itself. I listened to politics, and learnt to distrust it. I worked for a radical printer, McCulloch, for a while; travelled in the interior. I've spent a lot of my time in Cornwall – we've links there, and the Cornish think they're a nation apart, which suited me. I'm a citizen of the sea as much as anywhere. I call myself an orphan, but that's a statement of politics and geography more than anything.'

It came like a release.

Lady Virginia Strong was nodding, and finally smiled. 'I knew it,' she said. 'You're another free soul.'

He smiled, trying the idea, then sat up. 'It'll be light soon. I must go.' He was looking down at her, enjoying the swelling of her breasts under the sheet, the candlelight in her eyes. 'You'll be well here? I'll send someone when I've got you a boat.'

'I'll be fine here.' She lay serene, face haloed by the hair that spread over the pillow and crept onto her naked shoulders. 'Tonight was about finding you. I may have work to do still. Did you find your General?'

'I found him.'

'And the gold?'

'Safe ashore and hidden.'

There was another flash of wonder in her face. 'Of course. All ship-shape with Tom Roscarrock.'

He dressed quickly, and moved to the window. 'We should get you out of France quickly. No delays or games for you.'

She nodded seriously. 'Yes. Perhaps you're right. Send your man quickly.'

'Of course.' He smiled at her, and carefully raised the window. 'There's a danger, of course,' he said, 'that when the navy move to intercept the Sharks, they'll leave the way clear for Napoleon to invade anyway.'

She peered hard at him then, then nodded and smiled slowly. 'In the end, Tom, we must let the Empires fight it out. We have lives of our own.'

12th August 1805

Marceau's had none of the attributes of a tolerable hostelry. It was, in truth, nothing more than a single room in Marceau's crumbling house. It was cramped, dingy, stinking and inconveniently placed for all but the few who travelled out of St Valery on the road to the under-populated district that included the farmhouse where Roscarrock and De Boeldieu were based. It had no counter and no tables, very rarely offered food, and for drink nothing but rough local wine and some firewater brewed up by Marceau's brother in the shed.

But De Boeldieu trusted Marceau to a point, and this faith was reciprocated. De Boeldieu was vouched for, silently and irrevocably, by the confidence of other men whom Marceau respected. A stranger, however powerful or rich or friendly, would never be welcome at Marceau's; but a man who was accepted would be protected. Roscarrock knew the place from a dozen villages of the far south-west of England. He himself was accepted by extension, a silent man who looked fit enough not to be trifled with.

It was never lively, and at seven in the morning Roscarrock had the place to himself. He chewed slowly on a lump of rough bread that Marceau thought might take the edge off the rough wine, and waited for De Boeldieu. The Frenchman had said he was going to be busy during the night, and they travelled to and from the farm together whenever possible; it minimized the number of movements around the place, and gave a chance of protection.

De Boeldieu walked in half an hour later, by which time there was only one other drinker. Roscarrock looked up, but his colleague ignored him and walked straight to the counter and the lump of a man behind it. With movements that could not be seen behind him, he placed a coin on the counter and a finger on his lips. Marceau gaped stupidly, and Roscarrock watched as discreetly as he could.

Then De Boeldieu spoke, in strangely slow and deliberate French. 'Marceau, I am going to the farm. If anyone is coming after me, he will know what to do.' Marceau's eyes flicked in bewilderment towards Roscarrock, but Roscarrock's gaze had dropped and he was now entirely absorbed in a mouthful of bread. De Boeldieu turned and walked straight out again.

If anyone is coming after me? Roscarrock took a slow mouthful of wine. There was someone after him; it was the only explanation for the bizarre performance and odd words. Roscarrock took another mouthful, and sauntered to the window. Sure enough, just after De Boeldieu had disappeared with unnecessary haste around the first bend in the road that led towards their farm, a man on horseback emerged from an alley on the edge of the village and trotted after him. A young man; rough clothes but a good horse, and concern on his face as he focused on the corner where De Boeldieu had been.

Roscarrock returned to his chair, and bolted his bread and wine. The other customer had paid no attention to any of it.

A minute's canter and Roscarrock caught up. De Boeldieu's pursuer was keeping one bend between them, and Roscarrock did the same. That probably meant that the man knew where De Boeldieu was headed, so wasn't worried about sudden detours.

But the man didn't know the road well enough. As Roscarrock eased slowly around a bend, he saw a long straight stretch in front of him. Ahead, De Boeldieu had stopped, and was looking in his pockets for something. The pursuer had found himself exposed on the road and had stopped too, wondering whether to ride past or retreat. When he looked back for the possibility of concealment, he saw Roscarrock trotting towards him.

Roscarrock slowed as he passed. '*Bonjour,*' he said amiably, and then swept his fist up and around under the man's chin. It was a clumsy strike, but enough to tip the man off balance and topple him into the roadway. Roscarrock was on him a second later, reaching for the knife to hold at his throat, but the man kicked his legs away and they were both scrabbling at each other in the dust. Head struggling dangerously close to a set of heavy horse feet and a pair of hands clawing for his throat, Roscarrock managed one good punch to the side of the man's head and they rolled apart. They stood up together, swaying, hooves thundering behind them as De Boeldieu raced back to close his trap. The man hesitated between fighting and running and Roscarrock hit him twice, feet dancing over the ground as the other staggered back. The man managed one instinctive strike in return, and Roscarrock lost balance for a second, but as his opponent turned to escape, he was on him again. He grabbed him from behind in a bear's hug, and they grappled clumsily for a moment, feet scuffling in the dust as they spun, and then there was a word of protest and a long choke of pain as De Boeldieu drove his sword into the man's chest.

Roscarrock let go his grip, breathing heavily, and the body dropped loose to the ground. 'We're not interrogating him, then?' he gasped out. 'You could have finished me with that thing too.'

De Boeldieu's face was grim. 'Perhaps I should! They're all over us, Roscarrock!' It was a new De Boeldieu, angry and brutal. 'That man can't tell me anything I don't already know.' He held his sword high and level, the blade at Roscarrock's throat. 'What in hell are you doing, Englishman? What dirty game are you playing?'

Roscarrock knocked the sword away. 'What do you mean, "all over us"?' He'd caught his breath, and his brain was starting to race.

'The countryside is alive with informers and policemen! Everywhere we go we are watched. And so we are contaminating the whole damn network!' The words came in a torrent, clumsy and tumbling in De Boeldieu's haste. 'They are rolling us up, Roscarrock! Jean, the Mayor's clerk, was arrested. Ducroix, from the first evening, has disappeared. There are two other men we can't find out about. God knows what has happened in Abbeville and Amiens. I can only pray that by warning them to disappear I have saved enough.' He grappled for the words, and then in an incoherent instant of frustration he punched Roscarrock in the face. 'This network took a generation to create. You are destroying it in a day!'

Roscarrock stood fully upright again and rubbed at his battered cheek. His eyes were lost in the distance of the landscape. De Boeldieu started to speak again, and he raised a hand to silence him.

'They're rolling—'

'Philippe!'

De Boeldieu stood and seethed.

At last Roscarrock looked square at him, and there was new gravity in his voice. 'I understand it now. God, I understand it all now.'

'What does that mean?'

Roscarrock was still thinking hard. 'It means I understand what I was doing in England. It means I understand why I was sent into France.' He actually smiled. 'It means we are all puppets, my friend, of the cleverest man in Europe.'

'Fouché, you mean?'

'No. No, Sir Keith bloody Kinnaird.' He looked sadly at De Boeldieu. 'You told them to shut up shop, to get away. Maybe they changed routine – panicked – and are getting picked up because of it.'

De Boeldieu glared at him. 'Yes, Roscarrock, that thought had occurred to me, thank you so much.'

'Can we get word to the General not to come?'

'I do not dare communicate with his people outside the normal channel. He comes tonight. Besides, can your precious British Empire afford for him not to come?'

Roscarrock nodded. 'Very well. Three things, Philippe.' De Boeldieu looked at him warily. 'Philippe, I can't ask you to trust me, but – you can ignore me if any of these things harms your network. First, I need to talk to old Boule, the fisherman, now. I'll meet him in any place you choose, any rules. Second, Fouché's people must have a base near here. Find it.'

'Just like that?'

'There'll be new people around; unusual movement. Your network must be able to locate it.'

De Boeldieu nodded modestly. 'Very possibly, if they don't cut my throat first. And third?'

She'd been reluctant to leave France until she heard that the gold was ashore and the General coming to get it, and then she couldn't wait to move.

'Lady Virginia. She's in Rue, at the Lion d'Or. Get one of your people to her now. Get her to the river, and get her on a boat out of France.'

'Very well,' De Boeldieu said slowly. He found a spark of himself. 'In the name of a chivalry that I hope France will someday recapture, we will get her out.'

'In the name of nothing. Like you said, she's trouble. She's a complication. And tell your man that once he has got her to a boat, he is to get clear; get well away. The same with the crew who get her out to sea: once she's delivered to the *Jane*, they must disappear.'

'You really trust my people so little?'

'I don't trust anyone anymore.'

On Monday the 12th of August, the Admiralty Board met in emergency session again in London. No Secretaries were present. 'Preliminary details on the Emperor's special fleet at last, My Lord.'

'Not before time, Bellamy. Well?'

'The fleet is thought to number some twenty ships of the line, with support.'

'Twenty!'

'They have been dispersed, which is why we have not accounted for them. When gathered, they will make for Brest, where they will drive off or destroy our blockading squadron, releasing Admiral Ganteaume's ships.

Admiral Villeneuve, coming up from Spain, and Admiral Allemand, who is already on the high seas, will likely rendezvous there as well, making—'

'Making a fleet three times larger than we've ever faced. Great Gods, it would be unstoppable.'

'Yes, My Lord. Even if one of those combinations is unsuccessful, the French will have enough of a force to enter the Channel and protect the invasion.'

'Then we come down to it, gentlemen. We must defeat the French piecemeal, before they combine. Bellamy, what time do we have?'

'A very few days, I fear, My Lord.'

'Nelson's ashore now, isn't he? Gambier, can he get to sea in time to stop this?'

'If we are talking of only a few days, My Lord, then he certainly cannot.'

'Then you must tell Cornwallis and Keith to have the bulk of their ships ready to move out of the Channel immediately we know the gathering point for the Emperor's Sharks. We must get to them before they can combine.'

'That means drastically weakening the blockade on the invasion ports, My Lord.'

'We have no choice. Your analysis, Bellamy?'

'My Lord, the other French fleets are blocked; Villeneuve cannot be found, and hopefully is still nearer Spain than England. If we can locate the new fleet, we should strike it at once.'

'Bonaparte is presumably waiting on the success of his manoeuvre before launching the invasion, so we have to trust that we have time if we act immediately. The last throw, gentlemen!'

It was late in the afternoon when Inspector Gabin got back to his temporary headquarters at the mill. There had been no developments or surprises in the nearby villages. But his people were in place; the net was ready. Within twenty-four hours his success would be complete – perhaps within twelve. The sore rump and the empty belly came with the salary.

One of his policemen met him as he dismounted. There was a visitor for the Inspector – waiting in the storeroom. Gabin passed the reins to the policeman and climbed the stairs, intrigued. As he entered the large first-floor room, the mill labourer was leaving it; terrified into co-operation and silence, the man had continued to receive and process St Valery's grain under the indifferent scrutiny of the policemen. Seeing the Inspector, he hurried away down the hollow steps.

There was a policeman just inside the door, who nodded to the end of the room where a man had made himself comfortable among the bulging grain sacks.

Gabin was expecting no visitor; his informants did not call like this. The man in the gloom wore no uniform, and did not look like an official. Gabin muttered, 'Has he a weapon?' The soldier had checked thoroughly. The man had no weapon. 'Very well. Leave us.'

He walked towards the man. Hard-wearing, anonymous clothes. Nothing fancy; working clothes. But somehow unfamiliar to the Inspector – foreign. A good face; a strong face, with dark eyes that watched him calmly. Gabin continued to scrutinize. A fit man; tall and in good health.

Gabin pulled out the chair from his makeshift desk, and sat down near the stranger, close enough for conversation, far enough to avoid a threat. Very slowly, he smiled. 'Monsieur... Roscarrock, I imagine.' A nod from the stranger. 'It is a great pleasure to meet you. What is it I am required to say? "The storm blows strongest from the west." That is the phrase, is it not?'

The man said nothing; then, slowly, he too smiled. 'And you will be Inspector Gabin, perhaps.'

'You have heard the name?'

'The spy Joseph Dax reached London.' The policeman's face soured momentarily. 'He told us of the man who had hunted him. You have heard of me, too?'

'Oh, little Dax is not the only spy in London, Monsieur Roscarrock. Now, what accounts for the pleasant surprise of your visit?'

'I heard you were looking for me.'

A friendly smile. 'Oh, Monsieur Roscarrock, I was not looking for you. I was watching you.'

'Of course. It's General Metz you're really after, isn't it?'

Gabin watched the man opposite him carefully. A very able man indeed, clearly. 'Yes. Now we know his identity, we have him.'

'He's so important to you?'

Gabin considered the answer carefully. 'You are not French, Monsieur Roscarrock: you cannot know his spell. He is worth one of your fleets. He is an invasion in himself. While he is free, he is a memory of an old France, and a dangerous hope of a return to it. His capture will send the contrary message – that there is no chance of going back. It will end all thought of domestic resistance. You understand that we were looking forward to meeting you all tonight.'

'At the farm, presumably.' Gabin nodded. 'Which you still propose to do.' A slight shrug. 'You're taking a risk of course – all that clear ground – the chance of an open fight. But perhaps there's no alternative.' Gabin waited silently, appraising. 'You're surprised that I'm so co-operative? Why? Everything you've heard from England has told you that my loyalties are... ambivalent. If you had that code phrase for me, you must have known it.'

'So ambivalent that you wish to help the arrest of yourself?'

'Inspector, I have only one concern tonight: I wish to live until morning.' He rolled his shoulders. 'I have no interest in the domestic politics of France, and not that much in those of England.'

'You? An agent of the legendary Comptrollerate-General?'

'These are difficult times, Mr Gabin. The wise man recognizes what is inevitable, and works out how to survive with it. Any man who has stayed alive through the last fifteen years in France knows that.'

Gabin smiled, nodded in acknowledgement of the point. 'We've an old saying where I grew up, Monsieur Roscarrock' – he produced a mouthful of weird syllables – 'it means, approximately that it is not—'

'It is not necessary to enjoy it, but it is necessary to survive it.'

Now the policeman was surprised. 'You – you know Breton, Roscarrock?'

'No. But I know Cornish.' Roscarrock was thoughtful. 'Perhaps we're closer than even I imagined, Inspector.'

'You are a Cornishman! I start to understand a little more about you.'

'You're going to arrest the General whatever happens. Thanks to my movements here, you can identify and destroy the Royalist and Comptrollerate-General networks in northern France, and capture the gold. I just want to survive that process.'

'You have perhaps some suggestion to increase the chances of this? I should warn you that the General is really the only person we want to capture alive. Someone like yourself...'

Roscarrock considered this. 'I have a suggestion. Two suggestions.'

There was a note from Roscarrock at Marceau's. De Boeldieu skimmed it, and frowned, then read it through more slowly. The change in plan was undesirable, and further communication with the General's people a risk. But there was a kind of sense in the suggestion, and the tone was emphatic. Fifteen years of deceit had passed since De Boeldieu had been able to relax in the trust of other men, and the loss was an open wound. He slipped back into St Valery to pass a message to the farmer Lamarque.

He was on the road to their own farm half an hour later; Roscarrock had said not to wait for him. He trotted solitary between the walls of grain, torn as usual between the two Frances. This land was his: he knew it and loved it and was an emanation of it, and to see it and smell it and taste its flavours was to recapture old identities and certainties. But it was a new France now, a France that had estranged him from his roots, destroying his family and his way of life, and hunting him as if he were vermin. Now he moved through France in a kind of fever, as if his body was reacting against himself.

There was a short flat explosion from the ground immediately ahead – a musket? – and the movement of something in the ditch. De Boeldieu tried to reach for the sword in his saddlebag but the horse was rearing and skittering and turning, and by the time he pulled her to order and had her steady, four men had risen from the grain with muskets levelled at him.

CONVERSATIONS OF ADMIRAL P. C. J. B. S. DE VILLENEUVE,
RECORDED THE 30TH DAY OF NOVEMBER 1805

Very well, it is now the 12th of August. My twenty-nine warships and zacharie Allemand's five are converging at last. We are both at sea, we are both free, we are completely undetected by your Royal Navy. After many months' confusion, soon, we will combine, and together we will be able to fall on your coast wherever we choose and you will not stop us.

This is the nervous time, you understand me? The waiting time. We old men, my friend, now we may relax in our long chairs. For the Lieutenant here – Lieutenant, this is before you, and you will come to know this feeling. The uncertainty. The emptiness of the sea. All of those magnificent ships and their brave men totally in your hand. A miscalculation, a moment of error, and you are responsible for more deaths than any General could contemplate.

Ahead of me, somewhere, is Allemand, and my eyes are like the eagle's as I search the sea for him, I myself the lookout boy. Then, sometimes,

I look behind myself also, waiting for a fast ship to bring me news from Paris of Fouché's plan.

[SS G/1130/17]

❦

The mill, the gentle rush of water beside it, the flat and pleasant countryside under the soft evening, these all suggested an innocent and peaceful France. But Philippe de Boeldieu saw only the stains of evil on the scene. Hands lashed together and to the saddle in front of him, he could ride but not escape. Around him were four other riders; his captors. The two men he could see idling by the doorway ahead would, he assumed, be policemen or police spies. The mill itself had become a tower of oppression, a new Bastille. Inside he looked to find only enemies, and the final betrayal of his hopes and his trust.

He was pushed upstairs at sword point, and into a large, spartan storeroom: wooden floor, a great many filled sacks, a lot of dust, and two men. On a plain chair nearer him was a solid man of average height and a blank, innocent face. Small dark eyes flashed in the lantern light and turned to his arrival with happy malice. This would be Gabin, the policeman who had hunted Joseph.

Comfortable and laughing on a throne of sacks, the other man was Tom Roscarrock, and the last faint hope of Philippe de Boeldieu died.

The policeman spoke pleasantly. 'You are welcome. I am delighted to see you here.' De Boeldieu just scowled. 'Please make yourself comfortable like your friend.' De Boeldieu threw a brief look of contempt towards Roscarrock, and stood still. Gabin smiled. Roscarrock, unable to follow all of the rapid French, sat back among the sacks.

'I think, Monsieur, that I am speaking to Philippe de Boeldieu, son of the last Count of—'

'I am the Count of Charente, and my descendants will follow me in that title. The unhappy period of your illegitimate regime will pass, and I pray that I may see the true France restored.'

The policeman smiled politely. 'If that time comes, Monsieur, you will find me as true a servant to that regime as I have been to this.'

De Boeldieu shook his head vehemently. 'You have sold yourself to this dictatorship, Policeman, and you will be destroyed with it.'

A shrug. 'Very possibly. Monsieur Roscarrock and I have been sharing the wisdom of our ancestors in Brittany and Cornwall, and they would make the point better than I can. We are practical men, Monsieur, realistic men. You would be more comfortable if you would share our view.'

'If you two are realists, then I am proud to be an idealist.'

Another shrug. 'If you insist. To practical matters, nevertheless. Thank you for sending your message to the associates of General Metz, changing the arrangements for tonight. We—' De Boeldieu's shoulders dropped and he stared hatred at Roscarrock again, his fears confirmed. 'Yes, Monsieur, Roscarrock sent you that message as part of our agreement. The General will not go to your farmhouse tonight; instead he will go straight to the fishing boat where you have been storing your gold. My men will be waiting for him, of course. We will capture the General and the gold in one coup, and a much more contained and certain operation it will be. Very sensible – an excellent suggestion by Monsieur Roscarrock.'

Three sudden steps and Philippe De Boeldieu launched himself at the complacent figure on the sacks, trying to reach face or neck regardless of the cord that bound his wrists. Roscarrock wriggled out from under him, pulled him up to his feet and pushed him away.

The policeman had stood quickly. He waited until De Boeldieu had subsided. 'Monsieur, if you do not remain calm, I must bind your legs also and have you under closer guard. If you co-operate, we can do without bindings completely and pass a more pleasant night together.' Gabin sat down. 'My men will be in place on the boat as soon as darkness comes. You will wait here with me until I receive word that the General has arrived there. So we have several hours together, I think, and I hope we can all be comfortable. Then I shall complete the arrest of the General, and subsequently of the rest of your network of spies and traitors in this country. Until this week, we could not trace a single spy of your Comptrollerate-General; by this time tomorrow I shall take them all.'

De Boeldieu closed his eyes, trying to escape the nightmare.

They passed six hours in the spartan storeroom. Gabin tried pleasant conversation, but neither of his companions was in the mood for it. He came and went, checking arrangements or receiving reports or perhaps resting elsewhere. But always there was a policeman by the door with a musket. De Boeldieu had accepted the untying of his hands with the same expression he would have used walking to the guillotine; he refused to move any closer to his betrayer, and eventually sat down on the bare boards, his back stiff against the wall.

For most of those six hours, Tom Roscarrock slept.

13th August 1805

With the first pale suggestion of dawn in the sky, a figure hurried into the mill. Gabin, impatient, was in front of him at once. It was his ambitious deputy, excited and proud. 'Monsieur l'Inspecteur: our observers watching the harbour have reported the arrival of three men. They were heading for the fishing boat.'

Gabin's heart bloomed in his chest. The plan was actually working.

'By now, Monsieur, they will be in our hands.'

'Well come on, then! Horses!' Gabin thumped up the stairs to the storeroom. 'Gentlemen, you must excuse me for a short while. The General is in our hands, and I must welcome him appropriately. We will return within the hour.' He muttered to the guard by the door, and left as rapidly as he'd come.

Roscarrock settled back against the sacks, watching the guard. De Boeldieu slumped against the wall again, staring at his boots on the dusty boards.

'Philippe.'

De Boeldieu turned one wary eye towards the Englishman.

'Philippe, I'm sorry.'

Bitterness broke through De Boeldieu's restraint. 'You're sorry! How can you begin—'

'Calmly, my friend, please. The guard here does not seem to understand English, but he would get interested in a fight.' The voice was measured, pleasant. 'I'm sorry that I couldn't tell you what I was doing today. You're a good man, and I needed your honesty to convince the Inspector. But because you're a good man, you deserved better.'

Confusion led De Boeldieu into the conversation he swore he wouldn't have. 'What are you talking about?'

Roscarrock checked the guard again. The man was only half-awake, leaning against the wall at the far end of the storeroom. 'I had to get here myself because I needed to be here on my terms. I had to get you here because this was the safest place in all France for you. I also knew I would need your help.'

De Boeldieu just shook his head, bewildered.

The voice continued low and calm. 'I shan't ask you to trust me. Loyalty's too common a currency now – it's cheaper even than gold and human lives. I can only ask your help in getting out of here and saving the General and as much of the network *de la Fleur* as we can.'

De Boeldieu stared bleakly at him. Eventually he said with resignation, 'Well?'

'If I gave you a sword and a distraction, could you deal with that guard?'

The Frenchman's face burnt scornful in the lantern light. 'You forget yourself, Englishman. The world has tumbled with revolutions and treacheries, but I am still a Count of France.' He glanced at the guard. 'Without a sword it will be a little more difficult, but...'

Roscarrock got up slowly, and the guard opened his eyes fully and stood straight. Roscarrock acknowledged the gaze companionably, and began to rub his back. 'We're looking for a grain sack with a white cross on it,' he said to De Boeldieu in the same even voice. He bent to rub the circulation into his legs; the guard subsided against the wall again.

'We are?'

'It has a sword and knives in it. I had it delivered to the mill this afternoon.'

Dimly, a little of De Boeldieu's spirit was starting to glow in the cold morning. 'I still don't know who or what you are, Tom Roscarrock, but you do bring a little colour to a man's life.'

'We need to hurry.'

De Boeldieu had stood, and copied Roscarrock's performance of stiff limbs. 'We do?'

'Any moment now, Inspector Gabin is going to discover that his faith in me has been badly misplaced.'

⌇

Gaston Gabin was trying to keep his horse at a steady trot, but it kept slipping to a canter and he knew his own excitement was responsible. He wasn't usually so emotional – but surely it was understandable. To crown the destruction of the English networks in France with the capture of Metz – the Old Bull himself... He allowed the horse to push its head in front of the others.

Ahead, in the darkness, there was a faint shout. Gabin glanced beside him; the others had heard it too. It came again, nearer and stronger. 'Inspector! Inspector!' Gabin cursed the indiscretion, and the interruption to the smooth skill of his success. Out of the black mass of St Valery, a policeman was running towards the horsemen silhouetted in the dawn.

'Inspector!' A desperate gasping for breath from the man as he grabbed a bridle for support, and the beginnings of an obscenity from Gabin. 'The fishing boat: she's – she's sailing away!'

Gabin's world began to crumble. He kicked the man aside, and galloped for the shapeless village.

⌇

De Boeldieu was leading them towards the village and the coast, but on a different road. Roscarrock tried to make himself coherent over the thundering of their hooves. 'We have to warn the network – now. There'll be confusion for a short while, and they must use it. Those you haven't already warned off must disappear before morning. If they're under observation, we'll have to hope that they can slip it. Gabin will have told his people not to close in until the General's capture has been confirmed.'

'What's happening to the General?' De Boeldieu was faint in the onrush of air.

'He's getting away to sea, I hope.'

'How?' De Boeldieu suddenly veered away to the left, and Roscarrock followed.

'I told old Boule to get his sons aboard the boat, along with the cousins and any other large citizens he could think of. When the police arrived this afternoon to set their ambush, they'll have been ambushed themselves.' The Frenchman was slowing now as they approached an isolated farm. 'It's all been about the General, Philippe; the General and the network. Like you said, we've been watched almost from the moment we stepped ashore. Gabin was waiting for us to land somewhere near here, and as soon as he'd found us, he could follow us.'

'He let us move around?'

'He didn't care about us. He wanted to use us: we were leading him to the network of British agents here.' The horses slowed to a walk. 'Where are we going?'

'Someone we haven't met yet – so hopefully he's not under watch. He will pass the word.' The farmhouse loomed white in the grey dawn. 'When did you realize all this?'

'This morning. Then I knew they'd be wanting the General. He's the great prize. At the farm, there'd have been a massacre: the General arrested, and anyone with him slaughtered. Assuming the General's identity had become known, we had to get him out of France. That meant the fishing boat. I had to change the arrangements in a way that the General would accept – but also Gabin. That was this evening's performance.' They dropped from their horses under the blank wall of the farm. 'Sometimes it's useful when everyone thinks you're a traitor.'

De Boeldieu knocked at the rough planks of the door, hard and rapid. 'And now?'

'Now we have to get a boat ourselves, and fast. Joseph said that Fouché was waiting for a signal out of England; you remember?' He smiled grimly.

'I realized yesterday that we were that signal.'

'We were the signal?'

'Now a signal is coming out of France, and it means the deception of the Royal Navy and the invasion of England. I have to stop that signal.'

* * *

Inspector Gabin was in a nightmare of panic and failure. By the time his horse skittered onto the dockside in St Valery-sur-Somme, his men hurrying after him in confusion and timidity, the fishing boat was a faint sail among the sandbanks. There was nothing now to stop General Metz making the open sea and freedom from France. Only then did the Inspector grasp the full extent of the deception, and after a last futile glance at the sail against the pale sky, he wrenched his horse around and headed back into the narrow streets, yelling at his bewildered followers to get to the mill. A vestige of the old Gabin was trying to consider and to understand this man Roscarrock, but the old Gabin was a faint voice next to the harpies of hope and apprehension that screamed in the impassive head.

When they got to the mill a few minutes later, they found only dead men. Dimly, Gabin clutched at the possibility of recapturing the deceivers, of securing some prize for the Minister even though the General had escaped. In the nightmare, he heaved at the gasping horse and led his shattered party back towards the village once more.

* * *

Roscarrock and De Boeldieu had hidden their horses on the outskirts of St Valery and crept into the village through silent, misty back streets. There was no sign of Gabin and his policemen as they made their cautious way towards the waterfront. A last twist of an alley and the estuary opened in front of them, an instant expanse of light and space.

The mouth of the Somme was filled with untended fishing boats. Pressed close to a wall on the waterfront, Roscarrock scanned the jungle of masts rapidly. As many boats as a man could want, but none of them capable of being readied for sea in less than an hour or sailed by only two men.

'Time is passing, my friend' – De Boeldieu, murmuring in his ear – 'I don't want to risk trying to find another contact with a boat – not after what's happened, and with Gabin likely to arrive. But we might find somewhere to hide until we can find a boat.'

Roscarrock shook his head, eyes still moving over the water. 'We've run out of time, Philippe. If nothing else, we'll have to cut one of these larger boats loose and hope to drift out, but...' There! A low shape on the far side of the estuary. 'That might do us. Some kind of single-master – I hope so, anyway.'

'You can swim that far?'

'I gather I'm about the only person in the whole Admiralty who can swim at all.'

'And if it's no good?'

Roscarrock pulled off his boots. 'I'll swim to England. Give my best to the Emperor.' He smiled earnestly. 'I'll be back, Philippe.'

'I believe it. You damned English have been coming back for five centuries.'

A mooring rope hung from a stone bollard on the edge of the quay, and Roscarrock straddled it and made to lower himself into the water. Then he looked up again. 'Philippe, I didn't have time earlier: Joseph's information – what he brought out of France to you, using your system – it explains everything.'

De Boeldieu stared in surprise, excitement replaced by confusion. 'But there was nothing in it!'

Roscarrock smiled grimly. 'Exactly.'

'Exa— I don't understand.'

Another smile, at the bewilderment. 'It explains everything. If I can use it properly, it's just possible that you – and poor Joseph – will have saved Europe.'

'I just don't see—' He picked at the idea. 'Saved Europe, eh?'

'Something for your father, perhaps.'

A sniff, and a smile. 'The old fool would never have given a thought for Europe.' De Boeldieu's eyes were deeper for a moment, and he nodded. 'Sybille, though: she'd understand.' He glanced back along the quay. 'Be quick now. I want my breakfast.'

Roscarrock slipped down the rope and dropped without a splash into the chilly water of the estuary.

Gaston Gabin and his small band of men had raced madly through the streets of St Valery, the Inspector sending individuals off down side streets as they ran. There was no sign of the fugitives in the lifeless village. A minute after he'd arrived in the outskirts, the Inspector was hurrying out onto the amphitheatre of the waterfront, casting feverishly around the quays and the moored boats for any hint of movement.

There was nothing. The quays were deserted. Nothing moved on the boats at anchor.

The Inspector breathed, trying to decide whether this was good news or bad. Surely they couldn't have got to the waterfront, got a boat and got away in so short a time. No, they were still in the village somewhere, or they hadn't got here yet. Perhaps they were hiding out, until the confusion had died down.

Hooves and footsteps and heavy breaths were gathering behind him. He had the time now, and he had the advantage.

The waterfront of St Valery-sur-Somme spread out in two encircling arms. One stone quay stretched round to the west. It was from the far end of this that General Metz had put to sea – less than an hour ago: the thought scalded Gabin's mind. Another curved to the east, under a gloomy frontage of shuttered shops and houses, and then projected out into the estuary. Throughout the day these quays were busy streams of activity, of flapping fish and spread nets and brusque trade. For now they were silent, just shadows and stone.

Gabin sent two men out along the western arm of the harbour – one to watch from the end of the quay for any boat trying to slip out towards the sandbanks and the sea, the other to investigate a fishing boat tied alongside. The rest he left with his deputy, to be put to patrolling in the village.

The initiative was his again. He was on his own ground, and they were the fugitives. With prudence, he would contain them here and then locate them.

Gabin began to walk steadily along the waterfront, bringing first his emotions and then his thoughts under control. He thought of the mystery that was Tom Roscarrock. He also thought of the Minister of Police. The Minister would be livid that Metz had escaped; but, after all, out of France he was no longer a problem. With the Cornishman and the aristo, Gabin could deliver the British network in the region. Meanwhile, Fouché's bigger plan to distract the British fleet and secure the invasion continued unaffected. There was freshness in the morning again, and Gabin began to step with greater confidence.

Something had moved. Something on the edge of his vision – an irregularity in the stillness of the estuary. He stopped on the rough stones, and stared out across the crowd of boats. There! A movement again, on a small boat on the far side. Gabin began to walk more quickly towards the eastern arm of the harbour. As the quay curved out from the village he saw the boat again: a tiny flat shape on the water, but surely that was a figure crouched low in it. He hurried on over the age-worn stones, the blank frontage of buildings and shadowed doorways to his right and the murmur of water to his left. Again there was movement in the little boat, an oar – two oars – emerging ungainly from the sides.

Then a man stepped out in front of him, and Gabin stopped.

It was Philippe De Boeldieu, one hand folded behind his back, the other resting light on his sword hilt, a startling portrait of aristocracy on the grey and anonymous waterfront.

'Good morning again, Inspector.' The voice was quiet and cold, a new voice of authority. 'We have business today, I think.'

Gabin took in the poised figure, relaxed and ominous. His first thought was that he had not, in all the madness, had any breakfast, and his whole body seemed to sigh. 'Business?' he said softly.

'I am a servant – the emissary of Joseph Dax.'

'You set him as a spy, and he died escaping the treachery that you had created.'

De Boeldieu nodded. 'That is quite true, Inspector. But I am here to seek his vengeance for his mother, Marie Dax. She was promised the support and protection of the Comtes De Boeldieu for as long as she lived. I owe a debt of honour to her memory, for a France that did not care for her as she should.'

Inspector Gaston Gabin just nodded. Then he grabbed at his knife and his pistol; he had the knife in his left hand and the pistol swinging up in his right, but death was on him, with lightning flashes of agony to one side and then to the other, and he was staggering back with useless arms and burning pain and then, with one last glide, De Boeldieu's sword pierced his heart.

～ ━ ～

Faintly, there were shouts from the waterfront, and Roscarrock allowed himself a glance over his shoulder as he heaved at the oars. There was nothing – he put his back into another smooth stroke, and looked again – De Boeldieu was out on the quay – he kept peering awkwardly at the village as he rowed towards it – and then he saw figures emerging onto the waterfront, pointing, and again there were shouts.

De Boeldieu saw the men too; he stepped towards them to check, then looked back into the estuary. 'Roscarrock!' he yelled. 'Get out – go now!'

Roscarrock ignored him, and bent to the oars again, kicking down with his legs to drive every pound of momentum he could get.

'Roscarrock!' Another mighty heave at the oars, and the boat swooped forwards over the water, and Roscarrock looked back again. The figures were running along the waterfront now, and there were more emerging behind them, muskets waving as they moved.

'Philippe! Jump, man! Get into the water!' A hundred yards.

De Boeldieu hurried to the end of the quay. 'Get out, Roscarrock! Save Europe for me!'

'Jump, you fool! I can pick you up.' Eighty yards.

'Roscarrock, listen to me! Go!' Roscarrock missed a stroke, and the boat slewed slightly. He yelled his irritation and took another mighty pull at the oars. 'I'll drown, and even if I don't they'll pick us off with their muskets. You must listen!'

'No!' Seventy yards, the burning of the muscles in his back and the thump of the oars against the water, another smooth heave, sixty yards.

'Roscarrock – Tom! You must listen to me! You will lose everything we've fought for if you don't get out now. I can buy you the time. Listen!'

Roscarrock turned and looked over his shoulder again, and he listened. He held off for a stroke, and then with a cry of frustration pulled on the right-hand oar alone so that the boat turned slightly and he could see De Boeldieu more easily.

'Tom, you must go now! You know it.'

He felt the cold in his sodden clothes. 'You can still—'

'Go, you romantic idiot!' De Boeldieu pulled his shoulders and head up. 'This is my country. I belong here. You do not. Go and do what you must do for your Britain; leave me to fight for my France.'

Roscarrock's shoulders sagged in despair. Then he looked up sadly. 'You're the possibility of a better France, my friend. Give my respects to your father.'

Philippe gave an elegant wave from the quay. 'God speed, my brother! I hope that one day soon you will find yourself.' Then he turned smartly on his heel and, an aristocrat striding proud before the mob, the last of the Comtes De Boeldieu advanced towards the hurrying soldiers with hand on sword and head held high.

———◆———

Over the south of England, the morning of the 13th of August rose fresh and cloudless. It was so clear that, from the coast of Devon in the south-west, a man with a telescope could just make out unknown sails moving on the horizon, more than twenty miles off.

When the Admiralty Board met early that morning, Admiral Lord Hugo Bellamy had early reports of these unknown sails beginning to gather to the south-west. Confirmation of their rendezvous point and likely movements was expected during the day. The Admiralty Board sent orders to Admirals Cornwallis and Keith to prepare to abandon their blockade and move to meet the threat.

Still Admiral Villeneuve sailed north, waiting for a sign that the distraction had worked, waiting for the chance to slip into the English Channel, waiting for glory. On the beaches of Boulogne, Napoleon's Army of the Ocean Coasts was waiting too, for the moment when the Royal Navy's weakness would allow it to hurry across the small strait to victory. In London, on the English coast, and on the coast of France, men listened for the hurrying feet of a message, or watched the sea.

———◆———

The little sailing boat carried Tom Roscarrock out to sea, alone in the gulf between France and England. He was no stranger to oars, and their hard, steady rhythm had swept him clear of St Valery-sur-Somme, the last defiant stand of Philippe De Boeldieu dwindling behind him as he stared towards it. Once among the open sandbanks at the mouth of the Somme, he'd raised the boat's single sail and caught a little wind, enough to carry him away from France and the chaos he had created. Slumped against the transom, the tiller tucked under his arm, he realized how hungry he was, and how very tired. He'd tried to sleep in the mill, knowing that this day would bring the crisis, but there was a deeper weariness in him that a few hours among the grain sacks could not ease.

Another half of an hour, and he saw a sail: a small pale triangle against the horizon. A fisherman at anchor? Then as he got closer he saw two masts, and realized that it wasn't the mainsail of a smaller boat but a bit of canvas raised to keep a larger boat steady. Still too small for a navy frigate, though. A French naval craft of some kind? His own little sail carried him onwards, and as he got closer, Roscarrock's face grew grim.

It was surely the *Jane*. For some reason – some other passenger, some other task – the sloop had waited.

Of all ships on the sea, he had wanted it not to be the *Jane*. He had calculated that she would have moved quickly to pass on the message about the Sharks; he had calculated that not having the sloop for himself would cost a few extra hours, but still enable him to stop the conspiracy. His task was suddenly a lot less simple. He could not avoid or outrun the sloop.

If it was the *Jane*, there would have to be more deaths – and one death in particular. And the *Jane* it was.

Then he understood why. The sloop would not carry the message herself. She would relay it via the navy frigates patrolling further off the coast. That meant flags or a meeting, which meant daylight.

In the distance, over the top of the sloop, he could see sails now. That would be the frigate. There was something else. Another small boat was moving alongside the sloop – probably a fisherman. As he watched, two ropes were thrown up to the *Jane* and for a moment they were pulled hard together. In that moment, a figure had clambered up onto the side of the fishing boat and was reaching for outstretched arms on the sloop that hoisted him up and safely aboard.

Another agent of the Comptrollerate-General? By the time Roscarrock drew close, the fishing boat had pulled away and was adjusting her sails for her onwards journey – either back to France or on to the lobster grounds. On the *Jane* there was new movement: they were pulling up the anchor and raising sails.

Now there was pointing on the deck, and he had been spotted. As he drew close, he raised a hand in greeting, and steered for the stern of the sloop. Closer still, he dropped the sail of his little boat, and let momentum carry him alongside and down the length of the *Jane*. He glanced up two or three times, trying to gauge the reaction to his arrival, looking for one face in particular. He tied up to the stern, under the windows of the Captain's cabin, and already he could feel movement as the wind caught and her sharp lines began to cut through the water.

A rope thumped against the stern beside him, and Roscarrock scrambled up onto the tiny quarterdeck at the back of the sloop. The first face he saw was Griffiths, the former Mate and presumably the murderer of Miles Froy. Roscarrock started to speak, but Griffiths had been content just to check who he was, and now turned and stepped back down to the main deck to keep an eye on the crew. As the back of his head dropped away, it was replaced by a form opposite in every way. As Roscarrock finished coiling the rope, the face and then the chest and then the whole, swaying body of Lady Virginia Strong appeared at the top of the short flight of steps. The morning sun glowed in the golden hair and the delighted face.

'Tom! I didn't dare believe it.' She grabbed him by the arms, stopped, checked behind her, and kissed him quickly on the cheek.

Roscarrock grunted a greeting. The kiss burnt on his face.

'Even after that night in the hotel I still wasn't sure, Tom. I didn't know which way you were really working.'

'But now?'

'How could you be here if you weren't with us? What happened to De Boeldieu?'

'He's dead. Gabin too.'

She shrugged, and turned. 'There's someone I want you to meet.'

Roscarrock moved forwards carefully, something inside him enjoying the movement of the deck beneath him while his mind raced, and started down the steps. As he did, a figure in a dark landman's coat – the figure he'd seen scrambling aboard just before his own arrival – turned to him.

The face was so out of place that, for an instant, Roscarrock couldn't register it. The rich curls, the strong cheeks, the dark eyes: it was James Fannion, an Irish rebel on a ship of the Comptrollerate-General for Scrutiny and Survey. But really, how surprising was that after all?

By the time they were level, Roscarrock's momentary incredulity had been replaced with a new sharp realization: if he was to stop the invasion – if he was to stay alive – he had to act very quickly indeed. He contrived a rough smile, and gripped the Irishman's hand.

'I've become what you might call a close observer of your work, Fannion,' he said evenly. 'You're an exceptional man.' Fannion smiled, and for the first and last time Roscarrock saw the seductive power of the poet's eyes.

As Roscarrock turned away, Virginia Strong was behind him. He examined the face again, part of him enjoying the absolute beauty of the bones, the skin, the shining eyes. Again, he managed a smile.

'Have you passed on the location of the Sharks?' He had to act quickly, and he had to pray to the god of the sea for a last mighty measure of Cornish luck.

She nodded towards the Royal Navy frigate shrinking behind them, a mile away now and heading in the opposite direction. 'Signalled to the *Unicorn* half an hour ago.'

He felt the key in his pocket. 'Good. Then our mayhem is complete.' She nodded again, excitement in the remarkable eyes. 'Enjoyed yourself?' She smiled. 'Always.'

He watched her for a moment more, with something like wonder. 'Right. I haven't slept in a week. I'll see you when it's all over.' And he ducked back under the quarterdeck, towards the Captain's cabin.

They watched him go. Around them the crew were busy with the eternal tidying of the ship. Sails set and checked, the *Jane* was gliding now over the water. Virginia Strong watched it all, and turned to the sea again, loving the wind for bringing sharp life to her face and tugging at her hair. Then Fannion was beside her.

'That's the fellow you were telling me about – the one who chased me that first night we met?'

She nodded. 'That's him. Oh – he is from Ireland, originally; you said you knew the name.'

'Where in Ireland?'

'Cork. There was a whole family of them: Conor Roscarrock and his sons, all of them tall and wild like Tom, no doubt.'

There was a thumping from behind them, and then Griffiths's angry voice. 'Roscarrock! What—' More thumping, heavy steps. 'Roscarrock's blocked himself in the cabin!'

Virginia Strong said, 'He's just—' but Fannion had grabbed her by the arm.

'There are no Roscarrocks in Cork, Virginia.' The dark eyes, the shaking head, the insistent voice tried to communicate his urgency to her bewildered face. 'No such man, and no such family.'

'Captain!' A shout from up on the quarterdeck. 'Astern – look!'

They hurried up the short flight of steps, Griffiths, Virginia Strong and Fannion, impatient with each other and their confusion. 'There!' They followed the crewman's pointing arm. Thirty yards behind them, forty yards, was the small sailing boat, dropping further behind with every second of the sloop's forwards movement and the firm rhythm of the man at the oars pulling in the opposite direction.

Fannion, confused, and trapped in a course of events over which he no longer had any control: 'Who in hell is he, then?'

And Lady Virginia Strong, with the first suggestion of doubt and a last gasp of wonder as she gazed across the water: 'Tom?'

Then the stern of the *Jane* blew itself out of existence, and the sea surged into the weakened decks, pulling the sloop down into its darkness.

THE DOOM BAR

From the deck of His Majesty's Ship *Unicorn*, Captain Angus Folliott had seen the destruction of the *Jane*. Shortly afterwards, his men were pulling a rough-looking individual up out of a sailing boat that appeared to have emerged from the disaster.

The man raced up the rope to the ship's rail like one born to the sea, and when he stood to his full height Folliott could see that his face had the same texture of the oldest of the *Unicorn*'s hands. He was tired, unshaven, and dressed in worn and simple clothes, but as he demanded to speak to the Captain he spoke with urgency and command. The ship's First Lieutenant glanced uncertainly towards the quarterdeck. Folliott gave a curt nod, and a moment later the stranger was at the foot of the steps below him.

'Permission to come aboard, Captain.'

'Granted. The First Lieutenant will provide you with—'

'I need to speak to you, Captain, immediately and in private. It concerns the signal you have just relayed to the Admiralty, and the safety of the Empire.'

Folliott's eyebrows rose a fraction. He observed the tall stranger a second longer, then led the way below decks.

In the gloomy privacy of the Captain's cabin, Roscarrock had a second to size up Captain Folliott as he sat and removed a chart from the table and his visitor's line of sight. The thin face spoke breeding and disdain faster even than the voice. The stiffer type of officer, by the look of him, but you didn't get to command a Royal Navy frigate without experience and exceptional judgement.

He had to hope for both. Folliott started to speak, but Roscarrock cut him off. 'My apologies, Captain, but time is critical. In a moment I'm going to ask you to cancel the signal you just sent describing—'

'How on earth do you know—'

'Captain!' The voice was quiet but hard. 'Delay could put Napoleon on Dover Beach. I will tell you all I know, openly and honestly, and you must judge.' He took a breath. 'My name is Tom Roscarrock. I am an agent of the Comptrollerate-General for Scrutiny and Survey, in the Admiralty. That name is largely unknown, but I suspect that the Captain of a frigate may have heard rumour of it, or at least have an idea of the activities of a secret department of the Admiralty.' There was silence from Folliott. He knew. 'You have just relayed a message from that sloop, via other ships in the fleet, to the Admiralty. The signal, originating from Comptrollerate-General spies, gave a location. That location is supposed to be the rendezvous point for a fleet of previously unidentified French ships. Again, I suspect that a frigate Captain entrusted with Admiralty communications and the most sensitive inshore patrol knows something of this.' This time there was the slightest of nods from the austere face opposite. 'As soon as the Admiralty receive that location, they will take ships from our squadrons blockading Napoleon's invasion force in an attempt to defeat the new threat before it can combine with any other French fleet. Do I summarize fairly, Captain?'

A cautious Folliott, calculating. 'You do.'

Roscarrock leant forwards. He had to convince, immediately. 'This new French fleet does not exist, Captain. It is a phantom, created out of false intelligence reports with the deliberate aim of distracting the Royal Navy and allowing the invasion. Thanks to the bravery and endurance of a remarkable man, I have seen the naval dossier of Napoleon's Minister of Police. That dossier contained not a single word about this fleet. That's not because it's so secret; it's because it's a fiction.'

'This is fantastical.'

'Isn't it? But what's really fantastical is the idea that a whole fleet could be created and crewed and supplied and steered without a single documented reference. You know better than anyone how complicated it is to send even a single ship to sea.'

Folliott sat back in his chair suddenly. 'But – one moment – that's nonsense: we've—'

'You're going to tell me, I suppose, that the sails of this fleet have already been spotted. How many ships of the line? How many warships, Captain? None so far, I imagine. Just a few, sketchy reports of sails. And London are now so panicked about the new threat that they're diverting ships from the blockade squadrons on the basis of those reports alone.' Folliott was silent. 'Those sails are all sloops and schooners, one- and two-masters, and they're not even French. They are irregular ships of the Comptrollerate-General for Scrutiny and Survey, sailing under corrupted Captains.'

Roscarrock breathed out, trying to read Captain Folliott's face.

'There is no way you can believe all this on the word of a complete stranger. So you should suggest to the Admiralty that a reconnaissance be made of this new fleet before a single ship is diverted from the blockade of the French invasion forces. Those that have already been diverted must go no further. If I'm wrong, you can throw me over the side and no harm done. Frankly, I could do with the rest.'

'If you're wrong, they'll have lost precious time in stopping that damned fleet. Once it moves, it could get anywhere.'

'That's a better risk than leaving the French army uncovered. One other thing: I don't know who to trust anymore; your message must be sent on regular Royal Navy channels, as personal for the First Lord of the Admiralty. Mention my name if you want.'

'The First Lord of the Admiralty has heard of you?'

'I saved his life last week.'

Captain Folliott drummed his fingers on his chart table, for what seemed to Roscarrock like an age, and his eyes neither moved nor blinked.

Eventually he said, 'What happened on that sloop, Mr Roscarrock?'

The question surprised Roscarrock. He considered the Captain's face for one crucial moment. 'I destroyed it,' he said quietly, eyes fixed on the Captain. 'The Comptrollerate-General equips its ships with time-delay mines: gunpowder with a simple fuse mechanism, for offensive use or in case they're being captured, I presume. I killed an Irishman – a rebel, a murderer and a betrayer of the common man, though he'd probably say much the same about me. I killed the sloop's Mate – he'd killed his Captain as part of this plot a few days before, but otherwise I'd nothing against him.' Folliott frowned slightly: treason was one thing, but discipline at sea was sacrosanct. 'I killed perhaps a dozen crewmen, corrupt men who'd spent most of their lives drifting on the wrong side of the law – along with most other English sailors I've ever met. And I killed a woman...' – his gaze broke now, and he searched for the words – 'a creature of great beauty, who thought that if one had no real loyalty, one could never really be a traitor. Part of me wishes she was right.' He looked at the Captain again.

The Captain was staring at him still. He started drumming his fingers again. Then suddenly he took a breath, and called, 'Marine!' There was immediately movement outside the cabin door.

'That's an unattractive truth, Mr Roscarrock, or an unnecessary falsehood. Either way.'

The door was open, there was a thump as boots and musket-butt stamped to attention, and Roscarrock could feel the expectant presence behind his shoulder.

Folliott glanced up, then back to the strange man opposite him. 'Marine! Send for Mr Ancombe, now. I shall be on deck in thirty seconds, sending a signal of the highest priority.' The door closed.

Roscarrock breathed out very slowly. The gaunt face watched him.

'You're a man of the sea I think, Mr Roscarrock.'

He nodded.

'But not of the Service.'

He shook his head. 'The sea is my country, Captain. I haven't the discipline for your service, nor the certainty for your rank. I admire you, but even if I had your qualities I couldn't give my loyalty as you do – absolutely, and to an indifferent master.'

The Captain's eyes narrowed. 'I have Scottish blood in me, Roscarrock. I need no homily on the deceptions of the British Empire.'

Roscarrock smiled, acknowledging the point, and the two weary pairs of eyes watched each other, and something relaxed on the Captain's mouth.

Again silence, and then again, softly, the fingers began to drum on the table.

'What on earth are you, Mr Roscarrock?'

'Someone I hope you'll forget, Captain.' Roscarrock suddenly felt the weeks of tiredness. 'I'll save that Empire today, with your help, and once I'm done I want nothing more to do with any of it. I have a life that I'm anxious to restart.'

❧

CONVERSATIONS OF ADMIRAL P. C. J. B. S. DE VILLENEUVE, RECORDED 1ST DAY OF DECEMBER 1805

And what of Fouché's great deception, and of dear Villeneuve? On the 19th of August we are still pushing north. The English Channel and the English coast are closer every moment. But on the 19th it all changes. We meet a Danish ship. The Captain is brought before me that I may interrogate him. A surly fellow. It is the second time in a day that he has been stopped and interrogated.

Oh? Who else is in these parts? An English ship? Now I am on my mettle, of course. I seek to learn something of the English movements. But it had been but one English ship, and what I learn is more significant. This Danish Captain tells me of the news that is passing from ship to ship through the Royal Navy.

A man has escaped from a shipwreck with an extraordinary story and a message. There had been rumours of a new French fleet, but now it is confirmed that these were precisely rumours and nothing more. Perhaps there had been a few ships, but they were small and of little consequence, and perhaps they have been destroyed now by some of your British frigates.

Are these details being signalled by your midshipmen? I do not think so. Somehow this story is spreading on the currents. Sailors are great tellers of tales. But my unhappy Danish Captain tells me of the one formal message that is indeed spreading by flags across the English Channel and the eastern Atlantic: all of His Majesty's ships are to remain at their present station.

That is all I need to hear. It is clear that Fouché's so-brilliant plan has failed. His phantom fleet, created in rumours and false reports spread by traitors in British intelligence, has not distracted the Royal Navy. Your ships will maintain their complete blockade of their invasion force at Boulogne, and all of the other blockades too. I, poor Villeneuve, will have no assistance and I must risk attack for every league that I sail closer to the Dover Strait and then I must fight my way in to the Emperor and then fight my way out again with his army. Is this sensible? Of course, I order the fleet immediately to cease sailing north.

What happened to those ghost ships, my friend? Ah, a little shrug. They disappeared into the fog again, I think. They must have realised very quickly that they were not distracting any significant Royal Navy fleet, and they began to slip away. [Interjection: two were tracked by Royal Navy frigates, but they escaped. Individual men were traced.] Ah, and those men, they suffered a little, I think. And then perhaps they had accidents. Or perhaps their employment was renewed with greater stringency. The sailors, well, a sailor is a sailor, and if you captured any of the sailors of this ghost fleet, your press gangs will have been grateful. But only two ships and some individuals? The rest, they vanished into the forgotten coves of your south-western shores, or into the infinity of the Atlantic, did they not? For a time they were English ships, and for a time they were French ships, and then they were gone again.

The French navy, we were busy too in those uncertain days. Our spies in Fouché's Ministry of Police were most active. Quickly they confirmed the failure of the scheme, and so Decrès knew of this within hours. With lightning speed a message was travelling to me at sea, in French navy code. Clearly there was no success, no glory, to be found in those crowded waters, not even one single chance of it. Just one more failure for the Emperor's unloved and untrusted navy. Within a week, I had our fleet back safe in Spain, and the Emperor's last dream of invasion ebbed with me.

[SS G/1130/20]

In his office above Fitzsimmons's Coffee House, adjacent to the room of pigeon-holes, Mr Pewsey was working methodically through a column of figures in a ledger when one of his clerks knocked and entered.

'Mr Pewsey sir, beg pardon.'

'Baines?'

'Beg pardon, sir, but there's a lad here with a delivery. For one of our gentlemen.'

'Well? Have it brought up.'

'Sir, we can't, sir. The lad's just here with a note from the dock. It's... it's a fishing boat, sir. French one.' Pewsey's eyes widened behind the round spectacles. '"Fishing boat, passengers and cargo. For Sir Keith Kinnaird, care of Fitzsimmons's Coffee House." That's all he can say, sir.'

Again the fields of Boulogne shuddered under hundreds of thousands of boots, but they were marching away now. The Army of the Ocean Coasts was a thing of history; it was the Emperor's Grand Army now, heading south and east towards new and astounding triumphs. Behind them, the invasion barges slumped and rotted on the sand. The vast stores of food, of boots, of clothing, of supplies and equipment for armourers and engineers and cooks, were packed up again or burnt or sold or looted. The long, bright columns of men tramped up the hill and away, looking ahead into the Continent and never back at the sea. The little finger of wood promising to show the way 'To England' had disappeared, but few noticed. The citizens of Boulogne watched the soldiers disappear into the dust of Europe, waved cheerful or tearful goodbyes, began to reckon up – the profits and the spoils, the unpaid bills and the damaged furniture and the pregnant girls – and to pick through the debris. Another army had come to the coast, and gone. There would be others.

From the tower on the cliff, Napoleon Bonaparte took a last look at the impassive wall of the sea, still pockmarked with English sails.

He was searching for the next success; behind him, the Minister of Police was reciting with cold pedantry the last failure.

'Elements of the plan miscarried, Excellency, and I have not slept for analyzing my shortcomings. But if Admiral Villeneuve had continued, there was still—'

The Emperor turned; Fouché knew when to shut up.

'Better is required, Fouché.'

'Your disappointment is my shame, Excellency.'

The walls of the tower's high chamber, and the great table, were decorated with new maps now – central Europe, northern Italy, Austria – and the Emperor's fingers moved over them like a blind man tasting a woman's body.

'Have we gained nothing?' he asked absently.

'We know more about the divisions in London, Excellency. At the very heart of the British establishment are men and women working actively for your victory – traitors in positions of authority. Their time will come again. Excellency, it remains my deepest ambition that – after victory in the east – you will turn again towards the west and that you will ride in triumph down Whitehall.'

Napoleon looked up carefully into the pale eyes. He reached out a slow hand, and pinched his Minister of Police by the cheek; Fouché fought down his irritation. 'Keep at it, Fouché. I have only begun to remake Europe.'

The Emperor released the Minister, and turned away to stare into the maps.

On the 19th of October 1805, Admiral Villeneuve would finally sail out of Cadiz harbour to face the destiny that he had long avoided. The *Bucentaure* was still his flagship, and the combined fleet of French and Spanish warships included the *Santísima Trinidad*, the most powerful ship then in existence. Two days later, Admiral Horatio Nelson and the British fleet caught up with Villeneuve off a Spanish headland called Cape Trafalgar. Nelson, on HMS *Victory*, surged into the line of French ships and engaged the *Bucentaure* personally. After two hours of devastation, which would see most of the French and Spanish ships destroyed or captured, Villeneuve surrendered.

On that same afternoon of the 21st of October, as the cannonballs gouged clouds of splinter and flesh out of the English and Allied fleets, an explosion at Hebburn Colliery near Paisley killed thirty-five men.

The Battle of Trafalgar made Nelson a legend and Villeneuve a prisoner. It guaranteed the British Empire for a century, and ensured that France would never be more than a Continental power. Villeneuve would spend some months as a captive in England; Comptrollerate-General records show some but not all of the conversations he had while in the hands of the British Government.

Shortly after his return to France, Admiral Pierre de Villeneuve would be found dead in a Normandy hotel room, with multiple stab wounds to his chest. The verdict, given under the authority of the Minister of Police, would be suicide.

The dirty, slurred cackling of two departing drunks in the darkness, and the screech of an unseen, unloved name-board back and forth on its iron hooks, told Jessel he'd reached his lodging. His face screwed up as he took in the rotting wood, the indifferently whitewashed stone. It was a vile place, and he foresaw immediately the maggoty bread and the infested mattress that would take him through the next hours. But there was no alternative in the wretched little harbour village, and in the wretched little harbour village he had to be, again, for the morning would bring a climax.

The inside was all that the outside had warned of. But among the mixed human smells Jessel caught malt and cooked meat; the basics might be well enough. The drunks had been the last of the customers; the two benches were empty, only the few drained mugs and the sodden, scuffled straw telling of previous trade.

As Jessel closed the door behind him on its crude latch, a man turned around from the dying fire. The landlord, obviously: a big, shambling, bearded wreck, crude and rotten like his inn. Jessel saw it all in the hot, ravaged face and the way the man moved. First there was hostility; the inn was closing, a solitary drinker no compensation for disruption to the man's indifferent and base existence. Then the dark, greedy eyes saw the glint of gold in the stranger's fist, and the stranger smiled to himself at the trivial criminal sidelines that no doubt kept the man solvent.

The beer was rough and the meat grey, but both were warm and welcome at the end of a long journey. The landlord mustered up some bonhomie for a promising guest, and stood nearby watching Jessel intently.

'You have a name, landlord?'

Instant wariness, and again Jessel smiled to himself. He wondered if he'd get the truth. But the man had relaxed, and continued to gaze at his guest.

'Hillyard, sir. Henry Hillyard.'

Jessel looked up at him, searching the coarse face for a second. 'Hillyard? I seem to know the name.'

'Do you, sir?' The landlord picked up an empty mug and looked back at his guest. 'Do you indeed?'

* * *

The sun was climbing higher out of the sea now, and it created simple sweeps of colour: the endless dull blue of the water; the great expanse of yellow sand; the brown of the angry cliffs.

Admiral Lord Hugo Bellamy hated the world outside London. He hated the lack of comfort and civility and conversation, he hated the brute simplicity of the people, the clumsy buildings whose lumps of wood and stone seemed to shape their inhabitants, the endless wastes of empty landscape, the wet, and the eternal, all-pervasive cold. Rural life meant only the chilly barbarities of his school, the isolated sterility of life with his provincial family, the endless wait for damp and disease to carry one off enlivened only, and not much at that, by the macabre and primitive festivals of the country people. For every fifty miles one travelled from London, one could reckon to step back a century of civilization. Which put him currently somewhere in the Dark Ages.

Not for the first time, he cursed the name of Tom Roscarrock. Three bone-sore days in a coach, foul inns with their grim staff and grey food and the weird noises of the night, a wind that blew sharp and constant from the north, had carried him to the far south-western extremity of England – and it felt like a different country. Then the trek across the sand this morning – fully half a mile? – to the wreck, as he had been instructed. Alone, as instructed. This wasn't a different country, but a different world: he was floating somewhere between the land and the sea, adrift with only ghosts for companions.

Next to him, the vast black fingers of the shipwreck clutched out of the sand, the timbers dank and crumbling. It didn't take much imagination to see one's own ribs rotting alongside them.

He had the suspicion that his boots were leaking, moisture creeping in from the damp beach. This was the meeting place; but where was Roscarrock?

Actually, there were benefits to being free of the city for a few days. Too much unintelligent tension, too much muttering and wondering as people waited dumbly for fate. Britain had avoided disaster by a hair, and so there were the lurches of hope and the certainty of another alarm and, like a man with the ague, the nation continued to sweat and to writhe. The conclusion was inevitable. The fever would never let up, until the inevitable crisis. One could only accommodate oneself to it. But he was tired now – tired of it all.

A figure in the distance – a man walking – towards him across the sand – and eventually he recognized Roscarrock. Bellamy smiled slightly, wondered at the interview to come. If Roscarrock had survived, then Roscarrock must know a good deal.

At last they were face-to-face: the mighty figure of the Admiral, out of uniform but smart and imposing, and the lean and watchful man who had gone from London into France and come out alive, death always in his wake. It wasn't clear who should speak first.

Eventually the Admiral started to speak, aloofness and cynicism ready on the large face, but Roscarrock cut him off. 'To answer your question, you're here because I wanted to show you the real world.' Confusion – a hint of scorn – on the face opposite. 'You're an admiral. I thought it was time you saw the sea. Look at it.' Indulgently, Bellamy glanced over his shoulder. 'I've spent most of my life on that; the chances are I'll die somewhere out there. Men have always lived and died on the sea. Lads from all the villages hereabout, they come out of the estuary, on fishing boats or with the press gang, and they pass their short lives out there. Down through the centuries the sea has been the whole world for every family, and it won't change. Men die out there because of the clash of Empires, they die because of treachery, and sometimes they die simply because whatever force moves the wind and the waters decides that it's their time.'

Bellamy bit back his irritation; there was obviously more to come than this romantic fancy.

'It's the decisions of men like you that send men out there, and I wanted you to see what your work really means – the death of ships like this.' He nodded at the splayed ribs of the wreck. 'I wanted to get you out here, away from your civilization and your certainties. I wanted you marooned between the land and the sky. I wanted you adrift, just as I've been adrift these last weeks. I wanted you out here, Bellamy' – the hard eyes pulled away from the wreck and gazed into the Admiral – 'because you're the black heart of conspiracy. And once I realized that, I wanted to look into your eyes, for the first and the last time.'

Eventually, Bellamy said, 'Well?'

'You haven't denied it.'

'You sound disappointed, Roscarrock. You clearly believe this notion, and I fancy there's little point in denying it – out here, to you.'

Roscarrock shook his head. 'That's not it, Admiral. You're waiting, aren't you? You're still waiting to find out where I stand. That's all you've ever wondered.'

The Admiral waited.

'I haven't stopped asking myself the same thing. From the very beginning: why Tom Roscarrock?' Bellamy was frowning now. 'What use was Tom Roscarrock to you, Admiral? I couldn't get this out of my head, and only when I realized the answer did I see your treachery.'

He glanced out to sea. 'The world is full of romantics – good and bad, man of war and man of peace, patriot and rebel – Plummer, Fannion, Chance, the men who marched with the petition and the men who risk their lives in the navy – every one of them with some kind of ideal, some kind of dream, some kind of delusion.' The eyes came back. 'But not you. You're pure calculation. You've taken a good hard look at Britain, and a good hard look at Napoleon, and you know who's going to win.'

A faint smile waited on the Admiral's face.

'I had the same conversation with Rokeby Harris in a London salon and with a French policeman in a watermill: it's all about survival, and in the end treason is a man simply adjusting himself to the prevailing wind. You sold yourself to Fouché, with Virginia Strong as your go-between. Fouché would get Metz and the Royalist networks in France, enough gold to cripple the British Treasury, and the Royal Navy distracted for one crucial day. You would get a comfortable future, and perhaps some of the gold that's been slipping across the Channel over these months.'

Bellamy frowned, and Roscarrock spotted it. 'You don't like the idea that you're a mercenary? Why not? It's a very practical calculation.' He breathed in and out deeply, ordering the thoughts. 'Movement in and out of France is illegal – but the navy wouldn't stop Comptrollerate-General ships sending gold on the orders of the Admiralty. They have the freedom of the seas, and when Virginia Strong brought the message out of France that Fouché was ready to roll up our networks, some of those ships were ready to play at being Sharks for a few vital hours.'

'My boots are getting damp, Roscarrock.'

'The Emperor's Sharks were an astonishing idea. But I'm a sailor – unlike you and Fouché – and the more I heard about them, the less substantial they became. It seemed unlikely that you could hope to divert the Channel squadrons on rumour alone, so there would have to be at least a few sails to push the Admiralty to act, and I couldn't see where they'd come from. Then I found myself on a Comptrollerate-General ship in the middle of the night, surrounded by skilful and unscrupulous sailors, and at last I knew. Your private fleet would give Fouché his gold, and with it the network *de la Fleur* and Metz, the figurehead for resistance in northern France. It would give him his distraction. And it would give you a jealous little victory over Kinnaird, wouldn't it?'

The flicker of a frown again on the heavy face.

'Sorry, Admiral. Calling you emotional is worse than calling you mercenary, isn't it?' Roscarrock hesitated. 'I almost admire the sheer scale of your treason. Most men would wonder at selling a paper or a ship; you were delivering the Empire. It's a mighty imagination you have. And it wasn't easy, was it? For this whole plan to work, you had to get London – and especially the Admiralty – into a mood of hysteria. Only panic would cause them to send all that money into France; only panic would cause them to divert ships from the blockading squadrons. That same panic would help to undermine the country's resistance to the invasion. Neither you nor Fouché wanted the state to collapse, but it was essential that you had enough chaos and fear. So you created that mad Tuesday of the petition.'

He shook his head in wonder. 'I couldn't get over how insubstantial that day was. That mixture of everyone's worst fears – reform agitators, rebellious soldiers, the Irish, an assassination – which came together so powerfully and meant nothing. It took weeks for you to find the right pieces and bring them together. That's what Jessel was doing for those weeks, and what you had me doing too, wasn't it? Not trying to identify an existing conspiracy, but trying to find the ingredients to make a new and fantastical one. You had rumours of Gabriel Chance, but you had to find him and manipulate him. You invited Fannion from Ireland, but then something went wrong with the arrangements and you had to find him too. The petitioners were a welcome addition; those idiots in Hackney added a little colour. It all started to come together at the great meeting in Bury St Edmunds. Chance and Fannion finally appeared. Jessel sent the dragoons into the crowd to fuel the resentment, and to create enough chaos for Chance to escape and for Virginia Strong to meet Fannion to explain what was wanted. That's what she was doing, wasn't it? After she'd distracted me when I was on the point of getting to him.'

Still the smile. Some distant part of Admiral Lord Hugo Bellamy was enjoying the process of thought, and the extent of his own mind. 'A little embarrassed, Roscarrock? All this planning – the creation of the conspiracy – there's no proof that it wasn't a French plot.'

The words came out like a musket volley, long-planned. 'If Napoleon's Sharks didn't exist, then half of what you said to the Admiralty was outright fiction. The reports about the secret fleet were planted by Virginia Strong; no Frenchman ever mentioned the name "Sharks". Fouché never identified a Comptrollerate-General spy; he only found out about Joseph when Virginia Strong told him that we had reporting on his private meetings.' Roscarrock shook his head slightly. 'I learnt some things in France, Admiral. Fouché clearly knew that something was going to happen in London and roughly when. He had details of the plot – the insufficient load of gunpowder, for example. But it's inconceivable that he wouldn't have known of James Fannion's identity until just before the event, if the conspiracy was being managed by Frenchmen. If the details weren't being arranged by the French, then they had to be coming from the Comptrollerate-General. And that's the only credible explanation for what you and Jessel and Virginia Strong have been doing. Most of all, it's the only explanation for what you had me doing.'

Another deep breath. Above them the sky lofted blank and white. 'Kinnaird's jealous and obsessive and he was worried about you from the start. His agents wouldn't talk to you, assuming you even knew who they were. This was paralyzing your plan: it was making it harder to bring together a credible conspiracy in England, and it meant you had nothing to offer Fouché in France. Then I appeared, and I was the answer to your prayers, wasn't I? A man picked by Kinnaird, but cut off from him. Men who would never talk to Jessel were prepared to give me a chance. Reverend Forster. Rokeby Harris. De Boeldieu and his people.'

Roscarrock looked at his boots, at the estuary and the sea, and up again. He hadn't talked this much in weeks; perhaps ever. 'At last, I knew why you were using me. You were turning the Comptrollerate-General inside out: exposing its agents and using its assets to help a French victory. I led you to Chance. I led you to the meeting in Bury St Edmunds. And when you sent me into France I led Fouché to the network *de la Fleur*. I got you the information you needed in England, and if Gabin, the policeman, had lived, then Fouché might have got more of our people in France. But in his last hours, Philippe de Boeldieu saved them.'

Lord Hugo Bellamy cleared his throat. 'I've been extremely patient, Roscarrock. You still haven't given me the one fact I don't already know. Don't you know where you stand? Haven't you decided?'

Roscarrock looked at the wreck, and then the sea beyond it, for a long time.

'Got some bad news for you, Admiral.' And he smiled, dark and slow. 'That was the other reason you were interested in me, wasn't it? Not only was Tom Roscarrock the key to Kinnaird's network, but his obscured and radical past meant that if he started to find out what was really going on, his natural sympathies would make him even more helpful. For you, I was ideal. Only problem is: I'm not Tom Roscarrock; Tom Roscarrock doesn't exist.'

The Admiral was suddenly wary.

'Now, a false name is hardly a surprise. If you'd found out about it when I first appeared, you'd hardly have cared and your plan would have continued unchanged. But the more you checked, the more real Tom Roscarrock became, and the more his identity appealed to you. Poor, fragile Virginia Strong finally got the full story of Roscarrock's troubled past, and it convinced her that I was a radical free spirit after her own heart. Unfortunately for her – and for you – it was fantasy.'

He prodded at the sand with a boot, and watched the water starting to pool at the bottom of the little hole, then looked up again. 'You're worried now, Admiral. I can see it; even you. You don't care about me and you don't care about Roscarrock. But if Roscarrock doesn't exist, then where did he and his past come from? And the answer is your nightmare, isn't it, Bellamy? The nightmare I can see growing in your eyes now. The answer is Kinnaird. The answer is that Kinnaird has beaten you.'

The Admiral's chest pulled in a slow breath, and the face settled grim. He glanced towards the estuary and the cliffs, but there was still no sign of man or boat.

Roscarrock saw the glance, and something flickered momentarily at the corners of his mouth before he continued. 'Again: why me? It took me a long time to work out what I was to you. It took me even longer to work out the second, greater question: what on earth I was to Sir Keith Kinnaird. I joined an organization in the middle of a civil war. Kinnaird's doubts about you had grown to open distrust and hostility. He still didn't know what you were doing, but whatever it was he didn't like it. Comptrollerate-General agents were starting to turn up dead. Kinnaird didn't know that this was Jessel removing those who found out the wrong things or asked the wrong questions, but he knew the ship was terribly adrift. The organization that he had saved and rebuilt was being eaten away, and Kinnaird had to act. That's why Malloy the publisher wouldn't talk to me, and disappeared. It's why Rokeby Harris has gone, and a dozen other parsons and writers and men of business. You didn't know what was happening; you tried frightening men like Harris and

Malloy and you'd probably have killed them if they hadn't escaped you.' He paused. 'Just like you killed the Reverend Henry Forster.'

The face opposite sat hard and watchful.

'And in the middle of all this, Kinnaird made time to identify and recruit a new agent – and then send him to work for you. Partly, I suppose, he thought I'd be a distraction. With me, your own plans started to move more comfortably, and you could waste time trying to find out who I was. But there's something else, Admiral. It's what means your failure is complete, and it's what means I'm going to destroy you.'

Interest – almost amusement – on the heavy face, and again the glance towards the rocks and the estuary.

'Kinnaird had the vision to see that he could defeat whatever your plan was, from the inside. He created Tom Roscarrock, and he sent him into your plan. He knew that you'd find Tom Roscarrock useful; he knew that Tom Roscarrock would get drawn deeper into the plan. He faked references to a radical past, to distance me from him and to make me even more interesting to you. I said that you were turning the Comptrollerate-General inside out. Kinnaird's genius was to turn your plan itself inside out, by creating me and setting me loose in it.'

Bellamy licked his lips. Still the promise of a smile lurked there. 'You agreed to this, Roscarr— What is your name, really?'

'You'll never know it, Admiral.' A shake of the head. 'Can you imagine any man would have agreed to this madness? I cared for Kinnaird and his problems no more than I cared for you. But Kinnaird didn't pick me by accident.' He smiled. 'We come back to the same old question. Who is Tom Roscarrock? Or, since we know who Roscarrock is and isn't, who am I? I've been asking the question as much as any of you, because it turned out Kinnaird knew something about me that I didn't even know. He told me there would come a time when I would have to be myself, and I had no idea what he meant. This was his brilliance. He found a man who would be absorbed into your activities with no sense of their right or wrong and no sense of self beyond the mask of Tom

Roscarrock, but a man who carried within him a spark of identity that would explain everything.'

He kicked at the sand again. 'In case I didn't find out that something was wrong, Kinnaird even sent me a message, in those faked diary fragments. He didn't kill the dragoon – the one you sent to kill him. I did – and only I would know that.' A flicker of confusion opposite, a shifting from one foot to the other on the uneasy sand. 'It was a strange and unnecessary lie; but as well as diverting attention from me, it was Kinnaird's little hint to me that everything else I was hearing was wrong. From the diary onwards, you were on the wrong track and I was on the right one. Kinnaird didn't know exactly what was happening, but he knew that I, glowing inside Tom Roscarrock, would find out. Like one of Jessel's time-delay mines, I would continue to operate unknowingly until the moment when everything made sense. The moment when I would see, at last, what I was doing in the middle of your chaos, and would turn on you. Virginia Strong was right, you see: I don't give a damn for any of it – for you or for Fouché, for Napoleon or the bloody British Empire, for patriotism or treason. But that little spark was the real reason he chose me. And it's the reason you die today.'

He glanced at the Admiral's intrigued and patronising face. 'You're looking confident still, Admiral. I wonder why that is.' He made another hole in the sand with his boot, the water seeping in more quickly this time, and then gazed about him at the sea. 'I'll tell you a little story, and it's all you'll ever know of me. As you've gathered, I'm a sailor. Not an occasional sailor, but a man born to the sea. And I'm Cornish. Not Irish, but our little secret down here in the south-west is that we know we're a whole world away from London and we don't have to fight for it. Sometimes I've been a fisherman, and sometimes a trader, but always a sailor. Finally, I was First Mate on the ship of a friend of mine. Friendship's a rare luxury in a Cornish fishing village, Admiral, especially for an orphan bastard. But Simon Hillyard was a truly good man and over the years we talked and we trusted each other and we built our own little world. We shipped cargoes around the coast; we smuggled a little. Laws and borders don't mean much down here, and we did what we needed to live. Simon, as Captain, looked after the business and the dealing, and I ran the crew and the ship and didn't ask questions about what we were carrying or the cloaked and hooded men who paid the bills.'

The sky and the sea sprawled around them, two small humans lost in the wildness. 'Then, a month or so ago, we were wrecked – just up the coast there. I don't remember much of it – putting out to sea with the Captain in a foul mood, the storm almost immediately, the sheer staggering noise of it all, the ship losing control, breaking up against the cliffs – but I survived by a miracle, and I was the only one.'

Again he stared into the water. 'The men I knew, they're all around us now, in the water.' He smiled, grim. 'You're wondering now, aren't you, Admiral? That was my past, before the Comptrollerate-General, and it was a past I thought I'd lost. And then I found myself sailing to France, on an irregular ship crewed by independent competent men who didn't ask their Captain too many questions about who or what they were carrying across the boundaries of the world, and I understood it all. We'd been a Comptrollerate-General ship. I'd run errands for the Comptrollerate-General, and I'd never known it.'

The eyes were wide and hard. 'One day, Jessel must have tried to push our Captain to do something he refused to do. And Simon knew too much to be allowed to refuse, so one of Jessel's evil chests of powder with the delaying fuse was set down in our hold just before we sailed, and it blew out our tiller, and that's why my shipmates are now just ghosts in the waves.'

The Admiral's glance flicked up inland, and then down again. He nodded slowly.

Still the deathly smile in front of him. 'More bad news, Bellamy: Jessel isn't coming to save you.' The first suggestion of a frown on the Admiral's face. 'He's been your guarantee, like always, hasn't he? I knew he wouldn't stay in the same place as you last night, because you rightly assumed that I would check whether you were coming alone as instructed. To be ready this morning, there was only one tavern Jessel could have stayed in. I know the place, as it happens. The landlord is a vile man, a great, broken brute of every possible vice and crime, who has lived a life without a single aspect of decency or humanity. He fits in fine around here, of course; we're almost fond of him. Old Henry's one redeeming quality – and he tried hard to hide it – was his attitude to his son. He beat him until he was too big to beat, and he never stopped cursing him for a fool, but in some dark place deep inside he loved the boy for his independence and his learning and his making a success for himself. Strange world.' The Admiral's frown was harder now. 'The landlord's name is Henry Hillyard. His son was Simon Hillyard – my friend, and my Captain, and the man who drowned out here because he refused to be corrupted by you. Dick Jessel's eaten his last meal, Admiral, served by a man from whom he stole the future, and his only hope was a quick death.'

Another heavy nod, and eventually Bellamy said, 'Mm. I see.' Another pause, and the eyes never wavered from the man in front of him, as the mind continued to work. 'You and Kinnaird seem to have managed things very cleverly. I rather think this will turn out to be a successful episode for the Comptrollerate-General after all.'

'Still calm, Admiral? Still calculating? Now he's beaten you, Kinnaird will want to use you, won't he? Find out what you know. Turn you so that you can work against Fouché. And you wouldn't mind that.'

A little shrug on the big shoulders. 'The thought of being subordinate to the whims of that shrivelled old wizard I find appalling. But your recent exploits have made London a rather more stable prospect for the time being. So, yes, it seems that I shall accommodate myself to Kinnaird and his scheming.'

'I'm sure he'd like that as much as you'd hate it. The man's extraordinary, isn't he? In the middle of it all, when he could barely hope to keep the Comptrollerate-General going and stave off invasion for more than a week, part of his mind was still planning months and years ahead. When Gabin, the French policeman, met me he used what he thought was a code phrase that I would recognize. It was gibberish – meant nothing to me. My guess is that Kinnaird had identified half a dozen people whom he suspected of being Fouché's agent in London, and that he let each of them discover a different phrase to use should one ever meet the mysterious Roscarrock. Now he'll know who the spy is. Remarkable.'

He was looking into the wreck, and shook his head in wonder. 'So I'm sure he has plans to exploit a prize like you.' The eyes snapped up. 'Unfortunately, he's going to be disappointed. I don't work for Sir Keith Kinnaird or for anyone. I'm here for myself, alone, and that's why you're going to die instead.'

The Admiral was baffled, scornful. 'You envisage us fighting some sort of duel out here on the beach?'

'No, Admiral, I envisage you dying, and me finding a life again. Your final lesson in seamanship for the day. This isn't a beach; it's a sandbar. Exposed at low tide; surrounded and then covered at high tide. This bank has been death to many ships and sailors over the centuries. They call it the Doom Bar.' He glanced around them, at the encircling water and the tiny patch of sand on which they now stood. 'Round here, the tide comes high and it comes awful fast. It's a terrible thing even to those who know it well. Perhaps, Admiral, you weren't looking at the sea. Or perhaps you thought Jessel would be here with a boat, like someone has always been for you. But there's no one else now. It's just us, and the sea. And I can swim, and you can't.'

Hugo Bellamy looked about himself, through eyes that flickered with unfamiliar fear, on a world that now was changed terribly. He saw the unavoidable sea all around him, and he saw the eyes of the man in front of him, bleak and final, and the magisterial control collapsed. He launched himself across the few feet of wet sand.

The stranger hit him, one straight jab to the centre of the charging, incoherent face. He hit the Admiral with the weeks of anger behind him, and the faces of all the dead souls in front of him, and the Admiral dropped like a shattered mast.

He floundered on his knees, hands splashing in the chuckling water. 'Roscarrock!' he called out, but the stranger had turned and was striding into the waves. The voice rose, desperate, afraid and alone. 'Roscarrock – please!' Building to a scream: 'Roscarrock!'

But there was no one to answer to that name now. As the sea surged up against the land, wiping clean everything in its path, the man who had been Tom Roscarrock began to kick with long steady strokes towards the shore.